A
DISTANT CRY

for Sally

Stories from East Anglia

Chosen by
Peter Tolhurst

Introduced by
Louis de Bernières

Black Dog Books

First published in England 2002
by Black Dog Books
104 Trinity Street, Norwich, Norfolk, NR2 2BJ.

Foreword © 2002 Louis de Bernières.
Stories © Individual Authors/Authors' estates.

A CIP record of this book is available from the British Library.

ISBN 0 - 9528839 - 5 - 3

Typeset in 11 point Berkeley Bold.

Printed in Great Britain
by Biddles Ltd., *www.biddles.co.uk*

Contents

Acknowledgements

I would like to thank the following for permission to reproduce copyright material:

For *Seascape - Small Birds and Boat* by John Morley, the artist & David Messum Fine Art; For *The Mildenhall Treasure* from *The Wonderful Story Of Henry Sugar* (1977) by Roald Dahl published by Jonathan Cape, David Higham Associates on behalf of the author's estate; for *Taking An Interest* from *After Bathing At Baxters* (1999) and for *Passage Migrants*, D J Taylor; for *The Maze* from *The Salutation* (1932) and for *On Living For Others* from *A Spirit Rises* (1962), both by Sylvia Townsend Warner and both published by Chatto & Windus, Susanna Pinney & The Random House Group Limited; for *No Other Answer*, Edward Storey; for *An Extravagant Fondness For The Love Of Women* from *Who Do You Think You Are* (1976) by Malcolm Bradbury published by Picador, Lady Bradbury & Curtis Brown; for *First Love, Last Rites* from *First Love, Last Rites* (1973) by Ian McEwan published by Jonathan Cape, Rogers, Coleridge & White; for *And The Green Grass Grew All Around* from *The Stories Of Ronald Blythe* (1985) and for *The Catch* from *Immediate Possession* (1961), both published by Chatto & Windus, Ronald Blythe; for *The Mermaid* from *The Leper's Companions* (1999) published by Vintage, Julia Blackburn; for *Missing* from *New Writing 10* (2001) published by Picador and for *Carborundum*, Elspeth Barker; for *Front Seat* from *The Fever Tree* (1983) and for *The Orchard Walls* from *The New Girl Friend* (1982) published by Arrow, Ruth Rendell; for *The Visit*, Esther Freud; for *Corruption* from *Pack Of Cards* (1986) published by Heinemann, Penelope Lively; for *Mr Proudham And Mr Sleight* from *A Bit Of Singing And Dancing* (1972) by Susan Hill, published by Penguin, Sheil Land Associates; for *A Warning To The Curious* from *Collected Ghost Stories* (1931) by M R James, Nick James; for *Jeeves And The Impending Doom* from *Very Good Jeeves* (1930) by P G Wodehouse published by Hutchinson, The Random House Group Limited; for *A Shooting Season* from *The Colonel's Daughter And Other Stories* (1984) and for *Wildtrack* from *The Garden Of The Villa Mollini* (1986), both by Rose Tremain and published by Vintage, Sheil Land Associates; for *Acky And Justice* from *Acky* (1973) by George Ewart Evans published by Faber & Faber, Martin Evans on behalf of the author's estate; for *The Vendor*, Terence Blacker.

Peter Tolhurst
Black Dog Books

Foreword

LOUIS DE BERNIÈRES

I find myself in the difficult position of wanting to praise East Anglia, but without encouraging any more people to move here. I grew up in southern Surrey, which I still miss and love, but my family has had connections with Norfolk for a century and a half. My mother came to Wroxham as a little girl to recover from a life-threatening illness, and my father had two relatives in the Norfolk regiment, whose barracks he used to visit in Norwich. I spent three years in Ipswich, which were, admittedly, just about the worst three years of my life, but I came here finally as a refugee from London. Dr Johnson famously said that 'When a man is tired of London he is tired of life; for there is in London all that life can afford.' The truth is, however, that when a man is tired of London, it really is because he is tired of London, and wants something more than London life affords. Johnson's statement may be witty and famous, but it is fatuous and false. London life affords noise, stink, hassle, jostle, danger, ill-health, frustration, and the hope of pleasures that never materialise, and I would guess that it always has. London is the great puce-faced mewling baby with muck-filled nappies, howling for its disproportionate share of attention down at the far end of the country. I spent ten years there, and ended up kicking the furniture and fleeing to East Anglia in search of a better quality of life. I found it instantly, and now cannot imagine ever living in the metropolis again. It can, as far as I am concerned, stay where it is, at the other end of an inconvenient journey, and the only thing I miss is seeing all the pretty foreign girls on the tube. Certainly, I have seen more of my London friends since I have been here than I ever did when I was still in London, simply because they are all desperate to get out and enjoy a couple of days in Arcadia.

If Londoners suffer from the delusion of being at the centre of the world, East Anglians suffer from the opposite delusion, which perhaps explains the otherwise curious title of this anthology. We are rather like Canadians and New Zealanders, who have such a fear of being abandoned out on the edge of things that we make a special effort to know what is going on, with the paradoxical consequence that we are usually more in the swim than those who do actually live in the 'happening' places.

East Anglians are egalitarian, tolerant, friendly without being nosey, modest, determined, creative, and self-sufficient. In my village there are frequent entertainments, and even a club that makes cider. The area abounds with drama societies, small galleries, potteries, artisan windmills, and amateur orchestras. Everything is done without hysterics, and even when the Jehovah's Witnesses come round, we usually end up talking about old cars, having dealt with the forthcoming apocalypse somewhat cursorily.

Inevitably, there are entertaining but false East Anglian stereotypes. One of my London friends was horrified when I told him I was moving here, saying 'They're narrowminded, they have pointy heads, and they marry their sisters.' He'd never been here of course. 'Oh, it's so flat,' people say; but any cyclist will tell you that it's simply that our slopes are extremely long rather than extremely steep. Having said that, the first time I ever saw both ends of a rainbow was across the Waveney valley, when the marshes had flooded, and it was a sight so beautiful and wondrous that I had to stop the car. Moonlight on the floods is similarly magical, and so are the hares that box each other there in spring when the floods recede.

To begin with I regretted the cosy wooded villages of the place where I grew up, but very soon found that in fact there are thousands of them hidden away in our infinitely complicated labyrinth of tiny minor roads. These villages conceal most of the variety of English life. You will find your retired brigadiers living alongside violin makers, thespian homosexuals, solid peasantry, good Christians, vegan pagans, dentists, motor mechanics, and information technologists. In every market town you will find a tandoori, a Chinese takeaway, a Thai restaurant if you are lucky, and a kebab shop. The only extreme rarity is a policeman. To see one is infinitely more surprising than to see a black person, and if you need the police you will have to wait for them to come from up to thirty miles away. If your wife is horribly killed in suspicious circumstances, they will tell you on the phone to let them know if anything like that happens again, and then they'll see what they can do. Traffic police, of course are very common indeed, but otherwise our chocolate fireguard has altogether melted away.

One of the oddest things about East Anglia is that no-one knows where it starts or finishes. Norfolk and Suffolk are definitely in it, but many East Anglians would like to exclude southern Essex on the grounds that it is insufficiently interesting. Cambridge is always included, but one suspects that the rest of Cambridgeshire is not, as if it has a guilty secret that excludes it from the club, but which we are all too discreet to disclose. It seems to me that Lincolnshire must be in it, but no-one every says so, and perhaps we ought to include Bedfordshire and Holland on the grounds that they epitomise East Anglian flatness rather better than East Anglia does.

People are fond of saying that East Anglia is not on the way to anywhere else, and that is why it remains relatively unpopulated and unexploited. We have no motorways, the A roads are always clogged with tractors, and there isn't even a decent railway link between Norwich and Cambridge. The railway system was destroyed by Beeching. What this means is that you only live here if you really want to. They say that Norfolk is the graveyard of ambition, but the truth is that Norfolk is where you come if your ambition is to live in Norfolk. You don't go there to get within easy commuting distance of some other place. People live there because that is where they are happy. The village where I grew up in Surrey is on the Portsmouth line to London, and the house that my parents once bought for eight thousand is now worth a million. Poorer people have had to move into rented accommodation in towns, and old-fashioned organic village life has disappeared. I love my old village with a fierce, loyal, nostalgic ache, but I love where I am now because it has given me back the kind of life that I could no longer have in the place that I was raised. I am nearer the source here than I would be at the source itself.

The arts are alive and thriving in East Anglia, not least because we are not given them on a plate. We make and remake them continuously for ourselves, in a time when official funding comes and goes inexplicably and is parcelled out capriciously. There seems to be a general consensus these days that television is inexorably getting worse, and perhaps this is why there is such a burgeoning of DIY culture, not just here, but all over the country. Those of us East Anglians who are involved in 'cultural production' may be part of an East Anglian tradition, but I would think that most of us are probably unaware of it, the important thing being to work fruitfully, rather than to look for something to fit into. I would say that a reading of this book reveals that really there is no such thing as an identifiable East Anglian literature. This area is non-conformist, after all, and even Malcolm Bradbury's famous writing course at East Anglia University turned out writers who are quite different from each other. What we do have is plenty of East Anglian writers, and plenty of writers who have drawn sustenance and inspiration from East Anglia, writers as incompatibly diverse as John Skelton, Rider Haggard and Esther Freud. In this volume you will find a small selection from a vast literature, much of it incontestably brilliant. It should not be thought of as a commemoration of brilliance that has passed, but as a celebration of a brilliance that continues to be alive and well, and will undoubtedly become even greater in the future.

Badlands

Roald Dahl: Long before the success of *Charlie and the Chocolate Factory* (1963) established him as one of the great children's authors, Dahl was still living with his mother in Oxfordshire where he managed to scrape a living as a short story writer. In April 1946 he read about the fabulous hoard of Roman silver that had been unearthed in the fens. The richness of the hoard and the mysterious nature of its discovery excited the young writer and he set off immediately for Suffolk in search of Gordon Butcher, the ploughman who had found the treasure four years earlier. Dahl overcame Butcher's initial reluctance to talk by promising to write an honest account of what had happened and to give Butcher half the proceeds from the story which he sold soon after to an American newspaper. It was another thirty years before *The Mildenhall Treasure* first appeared in this country in *The Wonderful Story of Henry Sugar* (1977).

The Mildenhall Treasure

ROALD DAHL

Around seven o'clock in the morning, Gordon Butcher got out of bed and switched on the light. He walked barefoot to the window and drew back the curtains and looked out.

This was January and it was still dark, but he could tell there hadn't been any snow in the night.

'That wind,' he said aloud to his wife. 'Just listen to that wind.'

His wife was out of bed now, standing beside him near the window, and the two of them were silent, listening to the swish of the icy wind as it came sweeping in over the fens.

'It's a nor'-easter,' he said.

'There'll be snow for certain before nightfall,' she told him. 'And plenty of it.'

She was dressed before him, and she went into the next room and leaned over the cot of her six-year-old daughter and gave her a kiss. She called out a good morning to the two other older children in the third room, then she went downstairs to make breakfast.

At a quarter to eight, Gordon Butcher put on his coat, his cap and his leather gloves, and walked out of the back door into the bitter early-morning winter weather. As he moved through the half-daylight over the yard to the shed where his bicycle stood, the wind was like a knife on his cheek. He wheeled out the bike and mounted and began to ride down the middle of the narrow road, right into the face of the gale.

Gordon Butcher was thirty-eight. He was not an ordinary farm labourer. He took orders from no man unless he wished. He owned his own tractor, and with this he ploughed other men's fields and gathered other men's harvests under contract. His thoughts were only for his wife, his son, his two daughters. His wealth was in his small brick house, his two cows, his tractor, his skill as a ploughman.

Gordon Butcher's head was very curiously shaped, the back of it protruding like the sharp end of an enormous egg, and his ears stuck out, and a front tooth was missing on the left side. But none of this seemed to matter very much when you met him face to face in the open air. He looked at you with steady blue eyes that were without any malice or cunning or greed. And the mouth didn't have those thin lines of bitterness around the edges which one so often sees on men who work the land and spend their days fighting the weather.

His only eccentricity, to which he would cheerfully admit if you asked him, was in talking aloud to himself when he was alone. This habit, he said, grew from the fact that the kind of work he did left him entirely by himself for ten hours a day, six days a week. 'It keeps me company,' he said, 'hearing me own voice now and again.'

He biked on down the road, pedalling hard against the brutal wind.

'All right,' he said, 'all right, why don't you blow a bit? Is that the best you can do? My goodness me, I hardly know you're there this morning!' The wind howled around him and snapped at his coat and squeezed its way through the pores of the heavy wool, through his jacket underneath, through his shirt and vest, and it touched his bare skin with an icy finger-tip.

'Why,' he said, 'it's lukewarm you are today. You'll have to do a sight better than that if you're going to make me shiver.

And now the darkness was diluting into a pale grey morning light, and Gordon Butcher could see the cloudy roof of the sky very low above his head and flying with the wind. Grey-blue the clouds were, flecked here and there with black, a solid mass from horizon to horizon, the whole thing moving with the wind, sliding past above his head like a great grey sheet of metal unrolling. All around him lay the bleak and lonely fen-country of Suffolk, mile upon mile of it that went on for ever.

He pedalled on. He rode through the outskirts of the little town of Mildenhall and headed for the village of West Row where the man called Ford had his place.

He had left his tractor at Ford's the day before because his next job was to plough up four and a half acres on Thistley Green for Ford. It was not Ford's land. It is important to remember this, but Ford was the one who had asked him to do the work.

Actually, a farmer called Rolfe owned the four and a half acres.

Rolfe had asked Ford to get it ploughed because Ford, like Gordon

4

Butcher, did ploughing jobs for other men. The difference between Ford and Gordon Butcher was that Ford was somewhat grander. He was a fairly prosperous small-time agricultural engineer who had a nice house and a large yard full of sheds filled with farm implements and machinery. Gordon Butcher had only his one tractor.

On this occasion, however, when Rolfe had asked Ford to plough up his four and a half acres on Thistley Green, Ford was too busy to do the work so he hired Gordon Butcher to do it for him.

There was no one about in Ford's yard when Butcher rode in. He parked his bike, filled up his tractor with paraffin and petrol, warmed the engine, hitched the plough behind, mounted the high seat and drove out to Thistley Green.

The field was not half a mile away, and around eight-thirty Butcher drove the tractor in through the gate on to the field itself. Thistley Green was maybe a hundred acres all told, with a low hedge running round it. And although it was actually one large field, different parts of it were owned by different men. These separate parts were easy to define because each was cultivated in its own way. Rolfe's plot of four and a half acres was over to one side near the southern boundary fence. Butcher knew where it was and he drove his tractor round the edge of the field, then inward until he was on the plot.

The plot was barley stubble now, covered with the short and rotting yellow stalks of barley harvested last autumn, and only recently it had been broad-sheared so that now it was ready for the plough.

'Deep-plough it,' Ford had said to Butcher the day before. 'It's for sugar-beet. Rolfe's putting sugar-beet in there.'

They only plough about four inches down for barley, but for sugar-beet they plough deep, to ten or twelve inches. A horse-drawn plough can't plough as deep as that. It was only since motor-tractors came along that the farmers had been able to deep-plough properly. Rolfe's land had been deep-ploughed for sugar-beet some years before this, but it wasn't Butcher who had done the ploughing and no doubt the job had been skimped a bit and the ploughman had not gone quite as deep as he should. Had he done so, what was about to happen today would have happened then, and that would have been a different story.

Gordon Butcher began to plough. Up and down the field he went, lowering the plough deeper and deeper each trip until at last it was cutting twelve inches into the ground and turning up a smooth even wave of black earth as it went.

The wind was coming faster now, rushing in from the killer sea, sweeping over the flat Norfolk fields, past Saxthorpe and Reepham and Honingham and Swaffham and Larling and over the border to Suffolk, to Mildenhall and to Thistley Green where Gordon Butcher sat upright high on the seat of his tractor, driving back and forth over the plot of yellow barley stubble that belonged to Rolfe. Gordon Butcher could smell the sharp crisp smell of snow not far away, he could see the low roof of the sky – no longer flecked with black, but pale and whitish grey – sliding by overhead like a solid sheet of metal unrolling.

'Well,' he said, raising his voice above the clatter of the tractor, 'you are surely fashed at somebody today. What an almighty fuss it is now of blowin' and whistlin' and freezin'. Like a woman.' he added. 'Just like a woman does sometimes in the evening,' and he kept his eye upon the line of the furrow, and he smiled.

At noon he stopped the tractor, dismounted and fished in his pocket for his lunch. He found it and sat on the ground in the lee of one of the huge tractor-wheels. He ate large pieces of bread and very small pieces of cheese. He had nothing to drink, for his only Thermos had got smashed by the jolting of the tractor two weeks before, and in wartime, for this was in January 1942, you could not buy another anywhere. For about fifteen minutes he sat on the ground in the shelter of the wheel and ate his lunch. Then he got up and examined his peg.

Unlike many ploughmen, Butcher always hitched his plough to the tractor with a wooden peg so that if the plough fouled a root or a large stone, the peg would simply break at once, leaving the plough behind and saving the shares from serious damage. All over the black fen country, just below the surface, lie enormous trunks of ancient oak trees, and a wooden peg will save a ploughshare many times a week out there. Although Thistley Green was well-cultivated land, field-land, not fen-land, Butcher was taking no chances with his plough.

He examined the wooden peg, found it sound, mounted the tractor again, and went on with his ploughing.

The tractor nosed back and forth over the ground, leaving a smooth black wave of soil behind it. And still the wind blew colder but it did not snow.

Around three o'clock the thing happened.

There was a slight jolt, the wooden peg broke, and the tractor left the plough behind. Butcher stopped, dismounted and walked back to the plough to see what it had struck. It was surprising for this to have happened here, on field-land. There should be no oak trees underneath the soil in this place.

He knelt down beside the plough and began to scoop the soil away around the point of the ploughshare. The lower tip of the share was twelve inches down. There was a lot of soil to be scooped up. He dug his gloved fingers into the earth and scooped it out with both hands. Six inches down ... eight inches ... ten inches ... twelve. He slid his fingers along the blade of the ploughshare until they reached the forward point of it. The soil was loose and crumbly, and it kept falling back into the hole he was digging. He could not therefore see the twelve-inch-deep point of the share. He could only feel it. And now he could feel that the point was indeed lodged against something solid. He scooped away more earth. He enlarged the hole. It was necessary to see clearly what sort of an obstacle he had struck. If it was fairly small, then perhaps he could dig it out with his hands and get on with the job. If it was a tree-trunk he would have to go back to Ford's and fetch a spade.

'Come on,' he said aloud. 'I'll have you out of there, you hidden demon, you rotten old thing.' And suddenly, as the gloved fingers scraped away a final handful of black earth, he caught sight of the curved rim of something flat, like the rim of a huge thick plate sticking up out of the soil. He rubbed the rim with his fingers and he rubbed again. Then all at once, the rim gave off a greenish glint, and Gordon Butcher bent his head closer and closer still, peering down into the little hole he had dug with his hands. For one last time, he rubbed the rim clean with his fingers, and in a flash of light, he saw clearly the unmistakable blue-green crust of ancient buried metal, and his heart stood still.

It should be explained here that farmers in this part of Suffolk, and particularly in the Mildenhall area, have for years been turning up ancient objects from the soil. Flint arrowheads from very long ago have been found in considerable numbers, but more interesting than that, Roman pottery and Roman implements have also been found. It is known that the Romans favoured this part of the country during their occupation of Britain, and all local farmers are therefore well aware of the possibility of finding something interesting during a day's work. And so there was a kind of permanent awareness among Mildenhall people of the presence of treasure underneath the earth of their land.

Gordon Butcher's reaction, as soon as he saw the rim of that enormous plate, was a curious one. He immediately drew away. Then he got to his feet and turned his back on what he had just seen. He paused only long enough to switch off the engine of his tractor before he walked off fast in the direction of the road.

He did not know precisely what impulse caused him to stop digging and walk away. He will tell you that the only thing he can remember about those first few seconds was the whiff of danger that came to him from that little patch of greenish blue. The moment he touched it with his fingers, something electric went through his body, and there came to him a powerful premonition that this was a thing that could destroy the peace and happiness of many people.

In the beginning, all he had wished was to be away from it, and to leave it behind him and be done with it for ever. But after he had gone a few hundred yards or so, he began to slow his pace. At the gate leading out from Thistley Green, he stopped.

'What in the world is the matter with you, Mr Gordon Butcher?' he said aloud to the howling wind. 'Are you frightened or something? No, I'm not frightened. But I'll tell you straight, I'm not keen to handle this alone.'

That was when he thought of Ford.

He thought of Ford at first because it was for him that he was working. He thought of him second because he knew that Ford was a kind of collector of old stuff, of all the old stones and arrowheads which people kept digging up from time to time in the district, which they brought to Ford and which Ford placed upon the mantel in his parlour. It was believed that Ford sold these things, but no one knew or cared how he did it.

Gordon Butcher turned towards Ford's place and walked fast out of the gate on to the narrow road, down the road around the sharp left-hand corner and so to the house. He found Ford in his large shed, bending over a damaged harrow, mending it. Butcher stood by the door and said, 'Mr Ford!'

Ford looked around without straightening his body.

'Well, Gordon,' he said, 'what is it?'

Ford was middle-aged or a little older, bald-headed, long-nosed, with a clever foxy look about his face. His mouth was thin and sour, and when he looked at you, and when you saw the tightness of his mouth and the thin, sour line of his lips, you knew that this was a mouth that never smiled. His chin receded, his nose was long and sharp and he had the air about him of a sour old crafty fox from the woods.

'What is it?' he said looking up from the harrow.

Gordon Butcher stood by the door, blue-cheeked with cold, a little out of breath, rubbing his hands slowly one against the other.

'The tractor left the plough behind,' he said quietly. 'There's metal down there. I saw it.'

Ford's head gave a jerk. 'What kind of metal?' he said sharply.

'Flat. Quite flat like a sort of huge plate.'

'You didn't dig it out?' Ford had straightened up now and there was a glint of eagles in his eyes.

Butcher said, 'No, I left it alone and came straight on here.'

Ford walked quickly over to the corner and took his coat off the nail. He found a cap and gloves, then he found a spade and went towards the door. There was something odd, he noticed, in Butcher's manner.

'You're sure it was metal?'

'Crusted up,' Butcher said. 'But it was metal all right.'

'How deep?'

'Twelve inches down. At least the top of it was twelve inches down. The rest is deeper.'

'How d'you know it was a plate?'

'I don't,' Butcher said. 'I only saw a little bit of the rim, but it looked like a plate to me. An enormous plate.'

Ford's foxy face went quite white with excitement. 'Come on,' he said. 'We'll go back and see.'

The two men walked out of the shed into the fierce, ever-mounting fury of the wind. Ford shivered.

'Curse this filthy weather,' he said. 'Curse and blast this filthy freezing weather,' and he sank his pointed foxy face deep into the collar of his coat and began to ponder upon the possibilities of Butcher's find.

One thing Ford knew which Butcher did not know. He knew that back in 1932 a man called Lethbridge, a lecturer in Anglo-Saxon Antiquities at Cambridge University, had been excavating in the district and that he had actually unearthed the foundations of a Roman villa on Thistley Green itself. Ford was not forgetting that, and he quickened his pace. Butcher walked beside him without speaking and soon they were there. They went through the gate and over the field to the plough which lay about ten yards behind the tractor.

9

Ford knelt down beside the front of the plough and peered into the small hole Gordon Butcher had dug with his hands. He touched the rim of green-blue metal with a gloved finger. He scraped away a bit more earth. He leaned further forward so that his pointed nose was right down the hole. He ran fingers over the rough green surface. Then he stood up and said, 'Let's get the plough out of the way and do some digging.' Although there were fireworks exploding in his head and shivers running all over his body, Ford kept his voice very soft and casual.

Between them they pulled the plough back a couple of yards.

'Give me the spade,' Ford said, and he began cautiously to dig the soil away in a circle about three feet in diameter around the exposed patch of metal. When the hole was two feet deep, he threw away the spade and used his hands. He knelt down and scraped the soil away, and gradually the little patch of metal grew and grew until at last there lay exposed before them the great round disc of an enormous plate. It was fully twenty-four inches in diameter. The lower point of the plough had just caught the raised centre rim of the plate, for one could see the dent.

Carefully Ford lifted it out of the hole. He got to his feet, and stood wiping the soil away from it, turning it over and over in his hands. There was nothing much to see, for the whole surface was crusted over with a thick layer of a hard greenish-blue substance. But he knew that it was an enormous plate or dish of great weight and thickness. It weighed about eighteen pounds!

Ford stood in the field of yellow barley stubble and gazed at the huge plate. His hands began to shake. A tremendous and almost unbearable excitement started boiling up inside him and it was not easy for him to hide it. But he did his best.

'Some sort of a dish,' he said.

Butcher was kneeling on the ground beside the hole. 'Must be pretty old,' he said.

'Could be old,' Ford said. 'But it's all rusted up and eaten away.'

'That don't look like rust to me,' Butcher said. 'That greenish stuff isn't rust. It's something else ...'

'It's green rust,' Ford said rather superbly, and that ended the discussion.

Butcher, still on his knees, was poking about casually in the now three-feet-wide hole with his gloved hands. 'There's another one down here,' he said.

10

Instantly, Ford laid the great dish on the ground. He knelt beside Butcher, and within minutes they had unearthed a second large green-encrusted plate. This one was a shade smaller than the first, and deeper. More of a bowl than a dish.

Ford stood up and held the new find in his hands. Another heavy one. And now he knew for certain they were on to something absolutely tremendous. They were on to Roman Treasure, and almost without question it was pure silver. Two things pointed to its being pure silver. First the weight, and second, the particular type of green crust caused by oxidation.

How often is a piece of Roman silver discovered in the world?

Almost never any more. And had pieces as large as this ever been unearthed before?

Ford wasn't sure, but he very much doubted it.

Worth millions it must be.

Worth literally millions of pounds.

His breath, coming fast, was making little white clouds in the freezing atmosphere.

'There's still more down here, Mr Ford,' Butcher was saying, 'I can feel bits of it all over the place. You'll need the spade again.'

The third piece they got out was another large plate, somewhat similar to the first. Ford placed it in the barley stubble with the other two.

When Butcher felt the first flake of snow upon his cheek he looked up and saw over to the north-east a great white curtain drawn across the sky, a solid wall of snow flying forward on the wings of the wind.

'Here she comes!' he said, and Ford looked round and saw the snow moving upon them and he said. 'It's a blizzard. It's a filthy stinking blizzard!'

The two men stared at the blizzard as it raced across the fens towards them. Then it was on them, and all around was snow and snowflakes in the eyes and ears and mouth and down the neck and all around. And when Butcher glanced down at the ground a few seconds later it was already white.

'That's all we want,' Ford said. 'A filthy rotten stinking blizzard,' and he shivered and sunk his sharp and foxy face deeper into the collar of his coat. 'Come on,' he said. 'See if there's any more.'

Butcher knelt down again and poked around in the soil, then in the slow and casual manner of a man having a lucky dip in a barrel of sawdust, he pulled out another plate and held it out to Ford. Ford took it and placed it with the other three. Now Ford knelt down beside Butcher and began to dip into the soil with him.

For a whole hour the two men stayed out there digging and scratching in that little three-foot patch of soil. And during that hour they found and laid upon the ground beside them *no less than thirty-four separate pieces!* There were dishes, bowls, goblets, spoons, ladles and several other things, all of them crusted over but each one recognizable for what it was. And all the while the blizzard swirled around them and the snow gathered in little mounds upon their caps and on their shoulders and the flakes melted on their faces so that rivers of icy water trickled down their necks. A large globule of half-frozen liquid dangled continually, like a snow drop, from the end of Ford's pointed nose.

They worked in silence. It was too cold to speak. And as one precious article after the other was unearthed, Ford laid them carefully on the ground in rows, pausing every now and then to wipe the snow away from a dish or a spoon which was in danger of being completely covered.

At last Ford said, 'That's the lot, I think.'

'Yes.'

Ford stood up and stamped his feet on the ground. 'Got a sack in the tractor?' he said, and while Butcher walked over to fetch the sack, he turned and gazed upon the four-and-thirty pieces lying in the snow at his feet. He counted them again. If they were silver, which they surely must be, and if they were Roman, which they undoubtedly were, then this was a discovery that would rock the world.

Butcher called to him from the tractor, 'It's only a dirty old sack.'

'It'll do.'

Butcher brought the sack over and held it open while Ford carefully put the articles into it. They all went in except one. The massive two-foot plate was too large for the neck of the sack.

The two men were really cold now. For over an hour they had knelt and scratched about out there in the open field with the blizzard swirling around them. Already, nearly six inches of snow had fallen. Butcher was half-frozen. His cheeks were dead-white, blotched with blue, his feet were numb like wood, and when he moved his legs he could not feel the ground beneath his feet. He was much colder than Ford. His coat and clothes were not so thick, and ever since early morning he had been sitting high up on the seat of the tractor, exposed to the bitter wind. His blue-white face was tight and unmoving. All he wanted was to get home to his family and to the fire that he knew would be burning in the grate.

Ford, on the other hand, was not thinking about the cold. His mind was concentrated solely upon one thing – how to get possession for himself of this fabulous treasure. His position, as he knew very well, was not a strong one.

In England there is a very curious law about finding any kind of gold or silver treasure. This law goes back hundreds of years, and is still strictly enforced today. The law states that if a person digs up out of the ground, even out of his own garden, a piece of metal that is either *gold* or *silver*, it automatically becomes what is known as Treasure Trove and is the property of the Crown. The Crown doesn't in these days mean the actual King or Queen. It means the country or the government. The law also states that it is a criminal offence to conceal such a find. You are simply not allowed to hide the stuff and keep it for yourself. You must report it at once, preferably to the police. And if you do report it at once, you as the finder will be entitled to receive from the government in money the full amount of the market value of the article. You are not required to report the digging up of other metals. You are allowed to find as much valuable pewter, bronze, copper or even platinum as you wish, and you can keep it all, but not gold or silver.

The other curious part of this curious law is this: it is the person who *discovers* the treasure in the first place who gets the reward from the government. The owner of the land gets nothing – unless of course the finder is trespassing on the land when he makes the discovery. But if the finder of the treasure has been hired by the owner to do a job on his land, then he, the finder, gets all the reward.

In this case, the finder was Gordon Butcher. Furthermore, he was not trespassing. He was performing a job which he had been hired to do. This treasure therefore belonged to Butcher and to no one else. All he had to do was to take it and show it to an expert who would immediately identify it as silver, then turn it in to the police. In time, he would receive from the government one hundred per cent of its value – perhaps a million pounds.

All this left Ford out in the cold and Ford knew it. He had no rights whatsoever to the treasure by law. Thus, as he must have told himself at the time, his only chance of getting hold of the stuff for himself lay in the fact that Butcher was an ignorant man who didn't know the law and who did not anyway have the faintest idea of the value of the find. The

13

probability was that in a few days Butcher would forget all about it. He was too simple-minded a fellow, too artless, too trusting, too unselfish to give the matter much thought.

Now, out there in the desolate snowswept field, Ford bent down and took hold of the huge dish with one hand. He raised it but he did not lift it. The lower rim remained resting on the snow. With his other hand, he grasped the top of the sack. He didn't lift that either. And there he stooped amid the swirling snowflakes, both hands embracing, as it were, the treasure, but not actually taking it. It was a subtle and a canny gesture. It managed somehow to signify ownership before ownership had been discussed. A child plays the same game when he reaches out and closes his fingers over the biggest chocolate éclair on the plate and then says, 'Can I have this one, Mummy?' He's already got it.

'Well, Gordon,' Ford said, stooping over, holding the sack and the great dish in his gloved fingers. 'I don't suppose you want any of this old stuff.'

It was not a question. It was a statement of fact framed as a question.

The blizzard was still raging. The snow was falling so densely the two men could hardly see one another.

'You ought to get along home and warm yourself up,' Ford went on. 'You look frozen to death.'

'I feel frozen to death,' Butcher said.

'Then you get on that tractor quick and hurry home,' said the thoughtful, kind-hearted Ford. 'Leave the plough here and leave your bike at my place. The important thing is to get back and warm yourself up before you catch pneumonia.'

'I think that's just what I will do, Mr Ford,' Butcher said. 'Can you manage all right with that sack? It's mighty heavy.'

'I might not even bother about it today,' Ford said casually. 'I just might leave it here and come back for it another time. Rusty old stuff.'

'So long then, Mr Ford.'

'Bye, Gordon.'

Gordon Butcher mounted the tractor and drove away into the blizzard.

Ford hoisted the sack on to his shoulder, and then, not without difficulty, he lifted the massive dish with his other hand and tucked it under his arm.

'I am carrying,' he told himself, as he trudged through the snow, 'I am now carrying what is probably the biggest treasure ever dug up in the whole history of England.'

When Gordon Butcher came stamping and blowing through the back door of his small brick house late that afternoon, his wife was ironing by the fire. She looked up and saw his blue-white face and snow-encrusted clothes.

'My goodness, Gordon, you look froze to death!' she cried.

'I am,' he said. 'Help me off with these clothes, love. My fingers aren't hardly working at all.'

She took off his gloves, his coat, his jacket, his wet shirt. She pulled off his boots and socks. She fetched a towel and rubbed his chest and shoulders vigorously all over to restore the circulation. She rubbed his feet.

'Sit down there by the fire,' she said, 'and I'll get you a hot cup of tea.'

Later, when he was settled comfortably in the warmth with dry clothes on his back and the mug of tea in his hand, he told her what had happened that afternoon.

'He's a foxy one, that Mr Ford,' she said, not looking up from her ironing. 'I never did like him.'

'He got pretty excited about it all, I can tell you that,' Gordon Butcher said. 'Jumpy as a jack-rabbit he was.'

'That may be,' she said. 'But you ought to have had more sense than to go crawling about on your hands and knees in a freezing blizzard just because Mr Ford said to do it.'

And that, believe it or not, was about the last time the subject of the treasure was discussed in the Butcher household for some years.

The reader should be reminded that this was wartime, 1942. Britain was totally absorbed in the desperate war against Hitler and Mussolini. Germany was bombing England, and England was bombing Germany, and nearly every night Gordon Butcher heard the roar of motors from the big aerodrome at nearby Mildenhall as the bombers took off for Hamburg, Berlin, Kiel, Wilhelmshaven or Frankfurt. Sometimes he would wake in the early hours and hear them coming home, and sometimes the Germans flew over to bomb the aerodrome, and the Butcher house would shake with the crumph and crash of bombs not far away.

Butcher himself was exempt from military service. He was a farmer, a skilled ploughman, and they had told him when he volunteered for the army in 1939 that he was not wanted. The island's food supplies must be kept going, they told him, and it was vital that men like him stay on their jobs and cultivate the land.

Ford, being in the same business, was also exempt. He was a bachelor, living alone, and he was thus able to live a secret life and to do secret things within the walls of his home.

And so, on that terrible snowy afternoon when they dug up the treasure, Ford carried it home and laid everything out on a table in the back room.

Thirty-four separate pieces! They covered the entire table. And by the look of it, they were in marvellous condition. Silver does not rust. The green crust of oxidation can even be protection for the surface of the metal underneath. And with care, it could all be removed.

Ford decided to use an ordinary domestic silver polish known as Silvo, and he bought a large stock of it from the ironmonger's shop in Mildenhall. Then he took first the great two-foot plate which weighed more than eighteen pounds. He worked on it in the evenings. He soaked it all over with Silvo. He rubbed and rubbed. He worked patiently on this single dish every night for more than sixteen weeks.

At last, one memorable evening, there showed beneath his rubbing a small area of shining silver, and on the silver, raised up and beautifully worked, there was a part of a man's head.

He kept at it, and gradually the little patch of shining metal spread and spread, the blue-green crust crept outward to the edges of the plate until finally the top surface of the great dish lay before him in its full glory, covered all over with a wondrous pattern of animals and men and many odd legendary things.

Ford was astounded by the beauty of the great plate. It was filled with life and movement. There was a fierce face with tangled hair, a dancing goat with a human head, there were men and women and animals of many kinds cavorting around the rim, and no doubt all of them told a story.

Next, he set about cleaning the reverse side of the plate. Weeks and weeks it took. And when the work was completed and the whole plate on both sides was shining like a star, he placed it safely in the lower cupboard of his big oak sideboard and locked the cupboard door.

One by one, he tackled the remaining thirty-three pieces. A mania had taken hold of him now, a fierce compulsion to make every item shine in all its silver brilliance. He wanted to see all thirty-four pieces laid out on the big table in a dazzling array of silver. He wanted that more than anything else, and he worked desperately hard to achieve his wish.

He cleaned the two smaller dishes next, then the large fluted bowl, then the five long-handled ladles, the goblets, the wine-cups, the spoons. Every single piece was cleaned with equal care and made to shine with equal brilliance, and when they were all done, two years had passed and it was 1944.

But no strangers were allowed to look. Ford discussed the matter with no man or woman, and Rolfe, the owner of the plot on Thistley Green where the treasure had been found, knew nothing except that Ford, or someone Ford had hired, had ploughed his land extremely well and very deep.

One can guess why Ford hid the treasure instead of reporting it to the police as Treasure Trove. Had he reported it, it would have been taken away and Gordon Butcher would have been rewarded as the finder. Rewarded with a fortune. So the only thing Ford could do was to hang on to it and hide it in the hope, presumably, of selling it quietly to some dealer or collector at a later date.

It is possible, of course, to take a more charitable view and assume that Ford kept the treasure solely because he loved beautiful things and wanted to have them around him. No one will ever know the true answer.

Another year went by.

The war against Hitler was won.

And then, in 1946, just after Easter, there was a knock on the door of Ford's house. Ford opened it.

'Why hello, Mr Ford. How are you after all these years?'

'Hello, Dr Fawcett,' Ford said. 'You been keeping all right?'

'I'm fine, thank you,' Dr Fawcett said. 'It's been a long time, hasn't it?'

'Yes,' Ford said. 'that old war kept us all pretty busy.'

'May I come in?' Dr Fawcett asked.

'Of course,' Ford said, 'Come on in.'

Dr Hugh Alderson Fawcett was a keen and learned archaeologist who before the war had made a point of visiting Ford once a year in search of old stones or arrowheads. Ford had usually collected a batch of such items during the twelve months and he was always willing to sell them to Fawcett. They were seldom of great value, but now and again something quite good had turned up.

'Well,' said Fawcett, taking off his coat in the little hall. 'Well, well, well. It's been nearly seven years since I was here last.'

'Yes, it's been a long time,' Ford said.

Ford led him into the front room and showed him a box of flint arrowheads which had been picked up in the district. Some were good, others not so good. Fawcett picked through them, sorted them, and a deal was done.

'Nothing else?'

'No, I don't think so.'

Ford wished fervently that Dr Fawcett had never come. He wished even more fervently that he would go away.

It was at this point that Ford noticed something that made him sweat. He saw suddenly that he had left lying on the mantel over the fireplace the two most beautiful of the Roman spoons from the treasure hoard. These spoons had fascinated him because each was inscribed with the name of a Roman girl child to whom it had been given, presumably as a christening present, by Roman parents who had been converted to Christianity. One name was Pascentia, the other was Papittedo. Rather lovely names.

Ford, sweating with fear, tried to place himself between Dr Fawcett and the mantelpiece. He might even, he thought, be able to slip the spoons into his pocket if he got the chance.

He didn't get the chance.

Perhaps Ford had polished them so well that a little flash of reflected light from the silver caught the doctor's eye. Who knows? The fact remains that Fawcett saw them. The moment he saw them, he pounced like a tiger.

'Great heavens alive!' he cried. 'What are these?'

'Pewter,' Ford said, sweating more than ever. 'Just a couple of old pewter spoons.'

'Pewter?' cried Fawcett, turning one of the spoons over in his fingers. 'Pewter! You call this *pewter*?'

'That's right,' Ford said. 'It's pewter.'

'You know what this is?' Fawcett said, his voice going high with excitement. 'Shall I tell you what this *really* is?'

'You don't have to tell me,' Ford said, truculent. 'I know what it is. It's old pewter. And quite nice, too.'

Fawcett was reading the inscription in Roman letters on the scoop of the spoon. 'Papittedo!' he cried.

'What's that mean?' Ford asked him.

Fawcett picked up the other spoon. 'Pascentia,' he said. 'Beautiful!

These are the names of Roman children! And these spoons, my friend, are made of solid silver! Solid Roman silver!'

'Not possible,' Ford said.

'They're magnificent!' Fawcett cried out, going into raptures. 'They're perfect! They're unbelievable! Where on earth did you find them? It's most important to know where you found them! Was there anything else?' Fawcett was hopping about all over the room.

'Well ...' Ford said, licking dry lips.

'You must report them at once!' Fawcett cried. They're Treasure Trove! The British Museum is going to want these and that's for certain! How long have you had them?'

'Just a little while,' Ford told him.

'And *who* found them?' Fawcett asked, looking straight at him. 'Did you find them yourself or did you get them from somebody else? This is vital! The finder will be able to tell us all about it!'

Ford felt the walls of the room closing in on him and he didn't quite know what to do.

'Come on, man! Surely you know where you got them! Every detail will have to come out when you hand them in. Promise me you'll go to the police with them at once?'

'Well ...' Ford said.

'If you don't, then I'm afraid I shall be forced to report it myself,' Fawcett told him. 'It's my duty.'

The game was up now and Ford knew it. A thousand questions would be asked. How did you find it? When did you find it? What were you doing? Where was the exact spot? Whose land were you ploughing? And sooner or later, inevitably, the name of Gordon Butcher would have to come into it. It was unavoidable. And then, when Butcher was questioned, he would remember the size of the hoard and tell them all about it.

So the game was up. And the only thing to do at this point was to unlock the doors of the big sideboard and show the entire hoard to Dr Fawcett.

Ford's excuse for keeping it all and not turning it in would have to be that he thought it was pewter. So long as he stuck to that, he told himself, they couldn't do anything to him.

Dr Fawcett would probably have a heart-attack when he saw what there was in that cupboard.

'There is actually quite a bit more of it,' Ford said.

19

'Where?' cried Fawcett, spinning round. 'Where, man, where? Lead me to it!'

'I really thought it was pewter,' Ford said, moving slowly and very reluctantly forward to the oak sideboard. 'Otherwise I would naturally have reported it at once.'

He bent down and unlocked the lower doors of the sideboard. He opened the doors.

And then Dr Hugh Alderson Fawcett very nearly did have a heart-attack. He flung himself on his knees. He gasped. He choked. He began spluttering like an old kettle. He reached out for the great silver dish. He took it. He held it in shaking hands and his face went as white as snow. He didn't speak. He couldn't. He was literally and physically and mentally struck absolutely dumb by the sight of the treasure.

The interesting part of the story ends here. The rest is routine. Ford went to Mildenhall Police Station and made a report. The police came at once and collected all thirty-four pieces, and they were sent under guard to the British Museum for examination.

Then an urgent message from the Museum to the Mildenhall Police. It was far and away the finest Roman silver ever found in the British Isles. It was of enormous value. The Museum (which is really a public governmental institution) wished to acquire it. In fact, they insisted upon acquiring it.

The wheels of the law began to turn. An official inquest and hearing was arranged at the nearest large town, Bury St Edmunds. The silver was moved there under special police guard. Ford was summoned to appear before the Coroner and a jury of fourteen, while Gordon Butcher, that good and quiet man, was ordered also to present himself to give evidence.

On Monday, July the first, 1946, the hearing took place, and the Coroner cross-questioned Ford closely.

'You thought it was pewter?'

'Yes.'

'Even after you had cleaned it?'

'Yes.'

'You took no steps to inform any experts of the find?'

'No.'

'What did you intend to do with the articles?'

'Nothing. Just keep them.'

And when he had concluded his evidence, Ford asked permission to go outside into the fresh air because he said he felt faint. Nobody was surprised.

Then Butcher was called, and in a few simple words he told of his part in the affair.

Dr Fawcett gave his evidence, so did several other learned archaeologists, all of whom testified to the extreme rarity of the treasure. They said that it was of the fourth century after Christ; that it was the table silver of a wealthy Roman family; that it had probably been buried by the owner's bailiff to save it from the Picts and Scots who swept down from the north in about A.D.365-7 and laid waste many Roman settlements. The man who buried it had probably been liquidated either by a Pict or a Scot, and the treasure had remained concealed a foot below the soil ever since. The workmanship, said the experts, was magnificent. Some of it may have been executed in England, but more probably the articles were made in Italy or in Egypt. The great plate was of course the finest piece. The head in the centre was that of Neptune, the sea-god, with dolphins in his hair and seaweed in his beard. All around him, sea-nymphs and sea-monsters gambolled. On the broad rim of the plate stood Bacchus and his attendants. There was wine and revelry. Hercules was there, quite drunk, supported by two satyrs, his lion's skin fallen from his shoulders. Pan was there, too, dancing upon his goat-legs with his pipes in his hand. And everywhere there were maenads, female devotees of Bacchus, rather tipsy women.

The court was told also that several of the spoons bore the monogram of Christ (Chi-Rho), and that the two which were inscribed with the names Pascentia and Papittedo were undoubtedly christening presents.

The experts concluded their evidence and the court adjourned. Soon the jury returned, and their verdict was astonishing. No blame was attached to anyone for anything, although the finder of the treasure was no longer entitled to receive full compensation from the Crown because the find had not been declared at once. Nevertheless, there would probably be a measure of compensation paid, and with this in view, the finders were declared to be jointly Ford and Butcher.

Not Butcher. Ford and Butcher.

There is no more to tell other than that the treasure was acquired by the British Museum, where it now stands proudly displayed in a large glass case for all to see. And already people have travelled great distances to go and look upon those lovely things which Gordon Butcher found beneath

21

his plough on that cold and windy winter afternoon. One day, a book or two will be compiled about them, full of suppositions and abstruse conclusions, and men who move in archaeological circles will talk for ever about the Treasure of Mildenhall.

As a gesture, the Museum rewarded the co-finders with one thousand pounds each. Butcher, the true finder, was happy and surprised to receive so much money. He did not realise that had he been allowed to take the treasure home originally, he would almost certainly have revealed its existence and would thus have become eligible to receive one hundred per cent of its value, which could have been anything between half and a million pounds.

Nobody knows what Ford thought about it all. He must have been relieved and perhaps somewhat surprised when he heard that the court had believed his story about the pewter. But above all he must have been shattered by the loss of his great treasure. For the rest of his life he would be kicking himself for leaving those two spoons on the mantel above the fireplace for Dr Fawcett to see.

* * * * *

D J Taylor was born and educated firstly in Norwich to which he and his family have recently returned. His first, partly autobiographical, novel *English Settlement* (1996) won the Grinzane Cavour Award. He has also written several studies of modern British fiction and a biography of Thackeray. His most recent novel *The Comedy Man* (2001) is set partly in Great Yarmouth. Several short stories with an East Anglian setting, including *Taking An Interest*, appeared in his collection *After Bathing At Baxter's* (1997) while *Passage Migrants* (page 87) was one of the series 'Tales from East Anglia' broadcast last year on BBC Radio 3. Taylor's centenary biography of George Orwell will be published in 2003.

Taking An Interest

D J TAYLOR

My mother lived in the Breckland for thirty years: at Brandon, Feltwell, Northwold; always in the same rackety houses looking out over the heath. During that time she devised theories about her neighbours: theories of closeness, obduracy, idiosyncrasy. Trammelled by poverty, inertia and isolation, she suggested, the Brecklanders reverted to an inbred primordial oddity. My mother told stories of elderly men bicycling twenty miles to Norwich on a whim, middle-aged sisters found together in a bed that also contained their father's corpse, lawless children running unchecked through a landscape of virid sedge.

Few of these legends survived. Returning to the western seam of Norfolk a decade after her death, I found a world grown matter-of-fact. The tied cottages, refurbished and extended, housed Cambridge dons and their families; the farm workers had migrated to the soft fruit factories near the coast; shiny new estates edged out the pre-war warrens. A handful of the bicycling old men endured, but they did so with extreme self-consciousness, as vain and dignified as artists' models. Even then, though, I was not discouraged. I knew how slowly time passes out there on the windblown heaths, in the lee of the fens, and sure enough, only a month had passed before I turned up Thetford Jim.

'Always take an interest,' my mother had said of her dealings with the Breckland people, 'never interfere.' To this end she had patronised village charities, exhibited cakes in draughty barns and church halls, and very occasionally – for my mother was a liberal-minded woman – circulated leaflets on contraception. Thetford Jim loomed into view late one Saturday night at a pub talent evening in Brandon, in the slipstream of two stand-up comedians and a xylophonist, when a deedy-looking ancient clambered on to the makeshift stage to announce 'Here's something for you old-timers to enjoy'. There was a smattering of applause and a short, spare man in middle age began to sing in a reedy tenor, accompanying himself with a limping acoustic guitar. The first half-minute of the performance escaped me, so absorbed was I with the singer's appearance: knobby forehead, horn-rimmed glasses, disappearing hair; an ageless peasant's face, toothy, preoccupied, innocent and conniving by turns. To begin with he played a couple of country and western numbers, but there was a song called 'The Squire's Walk', about harvesting in the 1930s, so far as I could deduce, another called 'We Got Married in Church', with a chorus of *a register office wouldn't suit her ma*. He had a clipped west-of-the-county accent which pronounced 'do' as *du*, and the songs were clearly self-penned as I noticed he had a handwritten lyric sheet unravelled on the sidetable next to his half-pint of Adnams.

Who to ask for information? The vicar had been there for four years, a grain in the hourglass of this remote, rural life. The local lore accumulated by the handful of solicitors and bureaucrats with whom I was on nodding terms rarely exceeded the London timetable. Fortunately Mrs Nokes, who cleaned for me two mornings a week, had the story. 'It was a shame really, that Jim – and his name's not really Jim, it's Trevor, Trevor Bell. His dad used to work over at Watton in the painting and decorating line. His mother, she was a Fisher, big local family they was sixty or seventy years back, all gone now. But Jim's dad, he died young, and Jim's mum, she took on over Jim. Never would leave him be. He joined the Navy once, but he came back in three months on account of she said she missed him. And then when she died, five years back, people thought Jim wouldn't stand it. Rode that motorbike of his round the place at all hours. Calmed down a bit now, Jim has. Still lives in the old house, but I hear he does carpentering work out Garboldisham way.' I saw it all, or I thought I did: the slow, intent life, the long-burning fuse suddenly exploding. I remembered, too, a few subdued remarks heard in the pub. 'Did they? I mean . . . ' Mrs Nokes shrugged tolerantly, in the way that I recalled my mother shrugging when confronted with a broken gate, a badger killed on the swarming roads. 'You don't want to believe talk,' she pronounced. 'Jim was struck on his mum, and they was close as peas in a pod, but that's as far as it went and don't let anyone tell you different.' I had the feeling that Mrs Nokes was holding something in reserve about Jim, some prized nugget of data not to be vouchsafed to writers in four-bedroomed houses with city minds.

Take an interest; never interfere. It was difficult to establish where these injunctions broke apart from one another. Once a bundle of my mother's leaflets from the Brook Advisory Clinic had been pushed back through her letter box, doused in petrol and set aflame. After that I began to notice Jim, a small element in a wider tableau suddenly foregrounded by ulterior knowledge. I saw him astride his elderly Triumph motorcycle, labouring along the country backroads, buying groceries in Northwold. He had that vague, dreamy countryman's look, the kind that does not so much see through one as round one, a nod that might have been an acknowledgement or a dismissal. On the pretext of wanting some shelves, I even drove over to the cottage, a mile out of Feltwell, halfway along a lane that went nowhere, crowded out by osiers and long-dead elms. He was cagey but affable, admitting that he did 'carpenteering', that shelves 'wouldn't be no trouble'. At close hand, I saw, his face had even more that rapt, simpleton's stare. The cottage was small, dark, meekly furnished. From mantels, tables and wall-brackets, parched Norfolk faces stared out of their frames: old men in caps flanking dray horses, a labourer with pitchfork flung over his shoulder like a gun. Mrs Bell hung above the fireplace: bolster figure, the same vague eyes, set in brick-red nutcracker features. Jim's guitar lay propped against the table edge.

Putting up the shelves took a couple of visits. He came early in the morning, tapping on the hall door at half-seven, quarter-to-eight. I imagined him caught in the old fieldhand routine mandated by his mother forty years before: rise at dawn, main meal at midday, bed at sunset. While he worked he smoked tiny, pungent cheroots: the inside of his right index finger was a long, mahogany smear. He was friendly enough, but I fancied that he half-despised me, wondered at the cossetted, idler's life that could contract out the putting up of shelves. On the second visit I asked him about the songs. As I suspected, they were his own compositions, or at any rate familial. 'My old dad now, he was a singer. Sung in the pubs, Watton way. Lot of them I got from him. Others are my own. "Sheringham train takes a fine long time", now, I did that years ago, back when they were thinking on cutting the service.' He pronounced it *sarvice*, in a way I hadn't heard for twenty years.

By degrees I discovered a context in which Jim's songs lived and grew. The county radio station sometimes featured what it called 'local entertainers'. They had stage names like Dandelion Joe or the Buttercup Boy, dressed up in smocks and other yokel appurtenances, sang irksome songs about shovelling muck and cows' udders, and conducted beauty pageants at the village fêtes. Set against this tide of bucolic idiocy, Jim looked like a folk poet, a gentle elegist of bygone rural decencies. In amongst the book reviews and the grinning 'middles', I was writing a column for a Sunday newspaper called 'Country Retreats'. I put Jim in it, talked about a few of the songs, mentioned some contemporary folk singers with whom I thought he could stand some sort of comparison. The piece was headed 'Norfolk Voices'. Later, there was a clutch of letters, from people who wanted to buy records or claimed to have heard him singing in pubs. On the Monday morning I put a copy of the article through Jim's rusting letterbox. Passing me on the road a day or two later he made a definite salutation, arm raised stiffly in greeting like a flipper.

Mrs Nokes approved of my interest. 'There were folks used to reckon Jim was simple,' she explained cautiously. 'Kids mostly. They used to stand in the lanes and shout at him when he went past. But you have to make allowances. Jim's dad now, he could hardly write. And the old mawther, well, she'd die sooner than have to fill in a form. Come election time you couldn't get her to vote for love nor money.'

Another piece in the jigsaw of Jim's early life clicked into place. Even now, I realised, beneath the surface old patterns of existence ran on, like black hounds under the moon. An old woman died in Watton that summer, aged eighty-seven, carrying a tumour on her abdomen that weighed eleven pounds. 'We didn't want to go bothering the doctor,' her daughter was reported as saying.

The shelves had been up a fortnight now. The topmost one was slightly askew. I put it down to a craftsman's disdain of perfection, a humility before the absolutes of wood and metal. But something still irritated me about Thetford Jim: a talent not recognised, an ingenuousness not rewarded. A producer I knew on Radio Norfolk was non-committal, but he agreed to investigate. There was another talent night a week later at the pub in Brandon. As the teenaged impressionist gave way to a staggeringly inept magician, I saw the producer's eye list desperately in boredom. But he cheered up at 'The Squire's Walk' and a song I'd not heard before, a plaintive and sentimental number about a village cemetery. 'It's authentic,' he said. When I looked inquisitive, he went on: "You wouldn't believe the kind of thing that passes for Norfolk these days. Had a character in my office last week called Sid the Ratcatcher. You know how they get themselves up – smock, shepherd's crook – Christ knows what that's got to do with ratcatching. Sang a song about sheep dips. It turns out he's an accountant, lives near Lynn. Does the Rotary Club and the after-dinner circuit. But this one reminds me of the Singing Postman – you remember, the little chap with the glasses who used to sing about ha' you got a light boy? Do you suppose he's ever played to more than twenty people?'

Two days later I met Jim in Northwold high street with a large black labrador loping resignedly at his heel. 'This here dog is my cousin's dog,' he explained. 'I'm seeing to him on account of she's away.' I explained about the producer. 'Uh ho. The radio and that. They wouldn't want me to dress up funny or nothing?' he asked tolerantly. 'I shouldn't think so.' 'OK,' he said, and he articulated it *ooh-kay*, with a satirical glint of the eye. 'I reckon I'll sit myself down and do some practising.' I watched him amble away down the street, the dog dragging at his ankles, fearful of the gulf that separated us. My mother would have known how to deal with Thetford Jim; she would have drawn him out, conquered his reserve. I was simply a fantastic alien who wrote about him in newspapers and wanted to put him on the radio.

There was a Sunday afternoon show on Radio Norfolk, squeezed up between *Memories of my Golden Years* and the religious slot, called *Bandstand*. It was supposed to be live, although in fact the majority of the show went out on tape and only the announcer's feed-ins and the 'star guest' admitted a margin of error. They had him booked in for the Sunday before Christmas – 'Thetford Jim: the sound of Norfolk' – and a photographer came over from Diss to take his picture for the *Eastern Daily Press*: myopic, mild-eyed, gazing out from under a peaked cap he sometimes wore. I was in London, as it happened, seeing an editor or chasing a profile, but the story kept warm. On the Friday before the show someone peppered the downstairs windows of the cottage with buckshot. Puttering down the lane the next morning, Jim ran into a trip wire stretched at shoulder-height between two dead elms and broke his collar bone. Of various local informants only Mrs Nokes offered an explanation. 'All on account of that Tracy Sutton. Just after his mother died.' The name meant nothing. 'Only fourteen, she was. One of those ones that look seventeen. And act like it, too. Who do you blame? In the end they only gave him a suspended sentence, but Tracy's dad always swore he'd get even.'

They discharged him from hospital two days later, and I called round. The door was locked and stayed unanswered, though light burned from the upstairs shuttering. Then in the New Year, out on the bike again coming back from a job at Northwold, he careered across the road and into a file of schoolchildren. No one was badly hurt, but they kept him in Brandon police station overnight 'for his own protection' as the desk sergeant I spoke to put it. After that he disappeared: off to the far side of the county, people said, working at Channings jam factory near King's Lynn. Mrs Nokes, who had access to this kind of information, reported that he was living in a Salvation Army hostel. The look in her eye hinted that I shouldn't visit. An elm smashed against the side of the cottage in the March gales and knocked half a wall away: no one came to repair it. And then, idling in a newsagent's queue with Mrs Nokes, I saw a vast, sandbag-shaped girl with gappy teeth and witless eyes chewing her underlip at the counter. 'Tracy Sutton,' Mrs Nokes whispered pityingly, and I turned away, finally aware of having taken a step too far, like some startled explorer descending into that lost world beyond the mountain who glimpses a pterodactyl taking wing into the gloomy sky.

* * * * *

Sylvia Townsend Warner: In 1922 Warner travelled to East Chaldon in Dorset to meet the writer T F Powys whose allegorical tales she much admired. As a result she decided to rent a cottage in the village and a highly influential friendship grew out of that first meeting. Through her contact with David Garnett at Chatto and Windus Warner arranged for Powys' stories to be published. Four years later, following the appearance of her own first novel *Lolly Willows*, Warner went to stay with Garnett at Hilton Hall on the edge of the fens. There she was much taken with the pillar on the green erected to the memory of William Sparrow in the centre of a turf maze cut by him to celebrate the Restoration of 1660. *The Maze*, in which Mr Slumber is, by her own admission, an affectionate portrait of Garnett, appeared in *The Salutation* (1932), Warner's collection of decidedly Powysian short stories.

The Maze

SYLVIA TOWNSEND WARNER

The village of Wootton was introspective, as most villages are, but it had noticed one thing about the outside world: that whatever was transplanted thence into the local soil might be expected to do something surprising.

Wootton is in the Fen country, and the local soil is a dark, rich and heavy loam, so retentive of moisture that if a pit be dug in it the pit in a few hours' time has become a puddle. Knowing this the inhabitants do not dig pits, and build their houses without basements. But when Sir Alfred Marsala bought Wootton Court he insisted on undermining it with a cellar, though he was advised not to. A great many ingenious drains and damp-courses were arranged by his London architect, but for all that, Sir Alfred's cellar was soon filled to the brim with water, which was far from what he had intended.

This to-do about the cellar and the way he danced for rage amid his marble statuary made Sir Alfred quite as surprising as the village could wish. But such human examples were rare, for few strangers settled in Wootton, and as a rule the metagrobolising properties of the local soil were demonstrated in vegetables.

An everlasting pea given to the washerwoman produced one sky-blue blossom and died within the week. Some sunflowers out of a penny packet shot up to a height of eighteen feet, and when their seeds were thrown to the hens the next brood that hatched out were all cockerels. When the postman hoped for horseradish he got nothing but dock; on the other hand, the vegetable marrows grown by Mr Slumber's gardener were the pride of the district – as large, of as glowing a yellow and as savagely striped as man-eating tigers.

With this continual raree-show coming up before their eyes the villagers led a happy life, while summer-long their geese roamed over the

29

village green, growing fatter and more confident day by day.

Beside the green and reflecting itself in the village pond was a grove of elms; it was said that there had once been a rookery in it, but that the rooks had been frightened away by a jackass. If you followed the path through the grove where the young women took their sweethearts it brought you out by the sexton's cottage, and before you was another expanse of the green, more geese, and the Trott Monument; but this was very old, an octagonal pillar of stone with a knob on top, that had never been known to alter, so no one paid it the slightest attention.

No one – till Mr Lubin came to the village, renting the small white house with the cucumber frames, and engaging a housekeeper; then the Trott Monument was compromised by Mr Lubin's behaviour and thus shared in the attention naturally paid to a newcomer.

Mr Lubin took his house from Midsummer, and on the first Thursday in July he arrived. He did not come with his furniture, which preceded him in a van from Cambridge; he did not come flourishing in a motor car; he did not even bowl up in a gig. Mr Lubin came on foot, about tea-time, and walked into his house as calmly as though he had lived there for years, and was just returning from a stroll through the fields.

That day the village saw no more of him. His housekeeper slipped down to the Floral Knot just before closing time and reported that he seemed a quiet enough gentleman so far, although he took his tea without milk.

About ten o'clock on the morrow Mr Lubin walked out. Would he go to the post office, would he examine the church, would he call on Mr Slumber? He did none of these things.

Mr Lubin disappeared into the grove.

Would he? . . . Was he? . . . Mrs Welkin hurried out to call up her fowls and feed them with Indian corn, for that was the first pretext that occurred to her. The fowls were delighted; they said to themselves: The world's great age begins anew.

But Mr Lubin stayed no longer in the grove than was required to walk through it at a moderate pace. He came out by the sexton's cottage and saw before him the Trott Monument. He had met his destiny and he hastened forward to greet it, for he loved antiquities, Latin inscriptions, all mouldering keepsakes and remembrancers of stone. Sure enough, there was a Latin inscription by which Mr Lubin learnt from one Ludowick Trott how he had left his native village of Wootton in the year 1639 and gone forth as a wanderer for many years and into many countries, and in the end had made a prosperous return to his own place, setting up this memorial of his travels, of his steadfast mind and of his homecoming.

That was what the inscription said. The lettering was worn and shadowy, and some of the contractions posed him, but Mr Lubin was able to make out the sense of it. He moved round to see whether there was any more . . . to the west there were two words: *Ad Hoc*; and to the north two more: *Ab Hoc*; and to the east two more again: *Per Hoc. Ad Hoc; Ab Hoc; Per Hoc*. What did it mean? Mr Lubin stood in thought. He cast down his eyes to the ground, he noticed something odd about it, he looked more carefully.

In approaching the Monument he had received a vague impression that the grass round about it was curiously broken, trenched and tussocky, as though marked with old wheel-tracks. Now he saw that he was surrounded by a network of shallow trenches extending to a distance of twenty to thirty paces, and that these trenches, albeit crumbled and blurred with grass and weeds, were no wheel-tracks but had been shaped by the spade; and as he looked more attentively he saw too that they followed some sort of design and expressed some calculated intention.

A few minutes after this, Mr Powley, a labourer, and Mr Codd, a farrier whose wife made sausages, walked by together. They saw the newcomer – indeed they had come out to see him; but he surpassed their expectations, for there he was, not merely taking the air like anyone else, but shuffling up and down, turning, doubling, and, with an intent face and looks cast down to the ground, circling round and round the Trott Monument.

What was he doing? Mr Lubin answered their unspoken question; for now he exclaimed in the loud voice of one who congratulates himself upon a discovery,

'I'm in a maze!'

Mr Powley and Mr Codd both heard the exclamation. They glanced at each other as if to say, 'Well, that's quick work!' – but with the discretion of true scientific observers they did not venture to express an opinion yet, but went on their business after exchanging a few words about the look of the sky.

Each, however, had formed his hypothesis.

Mr Powley understood Mr Lubin's exclamation not in its literal sense but as a metaphor. That is to say, he supposed him to be stricken with madness, or at least loss of memory, and considering his behaviour the supposition seemed not unreasonable.

31

Mr Codd, who was a little hard of hearing, had not caught the words so exactly. He believed Mr Lubin to have cried out, 'I am amazed!' Mr Codd could put two and two together as well as any man in the village; obviously what had amazed Mr Lubin was the Trott Monument.

The afternoon was spent by Mr Lubin threading the maze, and in the evening at the Floral Knot his conduct was discussed by a full house. But Powley and Codd, who alone had been privileged to hear his exclamation, lorded it over the tumult like Plato and Aristotle, and soon the company was ranged into two schools of thought.

Was Mr Lubin overtaken with madness, or was he overcome by surprise?

The Powleian hypothesis had the merit of simplicity and of probability; for what was more likely than that the stranger should have lost his wits? Thus had Sir Alfred Marsala, dancing among his statuary, reacted to the local soil; thus too the sunflowers and the everlasting pea. The Powleian hypothesis was in accordance with Wootton traditions, it was supported by parallel cases in the past. Moreover, everyone knew that Mr Codd was deaf, so it was inherently more likely than that the Powleian hypothesis preserved the exact form of Mr Lubin's words.

Mr Codd's theory involved a much greater stretch of the imagination, two stretches in fact: first, that Mr Lubin was in his senses, and second, that there was anything amazing about the Trott Monument. With daring constructiveness, Mr Codd overcame these two difficulties by going one stretch further. Mr Lubin (he advanced) had been more than amazed: he had been shocked, shocked into righteous horror at the sight of the Monument; which well he might be, for it was a shameful object for any village green. Mr Codd had more than suspected this himself, but he had locked his suspicions within his own bosom as being too lofty and improper to be shared with other men. Now, borne out by the independent indignation of Mr Lubin, he would let them know his opinion of the Trott Monument; which was, that it was nothing more or less than a heathen idol. Had it not, Mr Codd enquired, a Roman inscription on it? We all know what those Romans were like. And then, lowering his voice, Mr Codd asked whether the Trott Monument was not close to the grove? And they all knew what doings went on there. Well might Mr Lubin cry out in horror at discovering an altar to Ashtoreth on a Christian village green.

The assembly was silent, for this view of things was too startling to be lightly pronounced on.

Mrs Welkin was the first to speak. Her enquiry was a pertinent one.

If Mr Lubin was such a pious man and found the Monument so shocking, what she wanted to know was, why did he spend the whole afternoon walking round the abomination as though he were in love with it?

Mrs Welkin's question produced a temporary schism in the Codd party, for some intemperate enthusiasts for Ashtoreth rushed into the conclusion that Mr Lubin wasn't as good as he was painted, in fact that he might have come to Wootton for no better purpose than to gloat over an improper object. But really this wouldn't hold water – Mr Lubin was so obviously branded with every sign of goodness that the badness of his character couldn't bear a moment's scrutiny. And so they fell back to discussing whether he was mazed or amazed.

As for the truth of the matter, no one gave it a glance. Why should they? The maze had always been there, it was even cleaned out by the Vicar's gardener every now and then.

The gardener acted under orders; he didn't trouble himself. There had always been those old ruts round the Monument: why shouldn't there be? If they were anything, they were a phenomenon of nature, manifestations of some activity of the soil in times long past.

Meanwhile the taproom grew hotter and hotter, and a bunch of flowers which the landlady had picked that afternoon and put in a jam-pot drooped limp and discoloured. When closing time came and the company quitted the inn the air outside was only one degree less stifling. A few of the controversialists tried to keep up the discussion, standing in a group under the elm; but the utter silence and darkness of the night daunted them. There was thunder in the air, it seemed to be close above their heads as though it were nested in the dark unmoving bulk of the tree.

That was Friday. On Saturday it was as sultry as ever, and some clouds the colour of charred paper appeared on the western horizon. Mr Lubin spent the afternoon in the maze; he did not walk about in it, however, he sat on a camp stool making a watercolour sketch of the Monument, with a burdock leaf under his hat. The sketch was not a success. The Monument he washed in neatly enough, but there was a queer light on the landscape which did not lend itself to watercolours.

On his way home he passed a knot of villagers looking at a gander. He stopped and asked them about the ruts, for he avoided using the term maze, thinking that it would not be understood. They told him that it was all said to be very old and that, except in very dry summers such as this,

33

the ruts soon filled up with water. When they had given this information and finished it off with a few grunts they were silent, looking at him as though he were a great deal harder to account for.

Mr Lubin felt abashed. They must think me a fool, he said to himself as he turned away. And perhaps I am. But I have always liked anything old, and I should be pleased if I could solve the maze. And then he began wondering whether he could make a plan of it, and what would be the best way to set about it. It would be almost a surveyor's job to do it properly, he would need measuring tapes and a number of little pegs. Yes, that would be the way, with tapes raying out from the centre to the circumference, dividing it into slices like a cake. Then by measuring and drawing each slice he could put the drawings together, and the secret of the maze would be his. That was one way. Another way would be to walk about in it until his feet stumbled on the solution. It was hard to remember which way he had come, which turnings he had taken . . . A clue, a silken thread such as Ariadne gave to Theseus, that was what he needed. He could hold the ball in his hand and pay out the thread after him. A rose-coloured thread would show well on the grass . . .

That night Mr Lubin dreamed he had unravelled the maze by turning to the right when he came to a large plantain. He woke eager to put his dream to the test; as he passed the Monument on his way to Morning Prayer he gave it several longing glances, and not even the serious and important sensations of attending a new church could keep his thoughts from wandering round it.

In spite of the heat (for now it was hotter than ever, and the clouds covered the western heavens almost to the zenith, no longer like charred paper but swollen and reddish-purple as ripe figs), Mr Lubin set out for the maze immediately after lunch. Rather to his surprise he saw a number of people gathered there, looking at the Monument. But he was not to be turned aside by a little attention, and he went boldly forward, whereon they retired a short way and feigned to be admiring the paeonies in the sexton's garden.

But though they might retire, the villagers of Wootton had no intention of quitting the field, and when they saw that Mr Lubin was well into the maze they crept softly back again and stood round about, watching him. And more and more people came, some through the grove, some noiselessly over the green, some even along the road from Mindon and Cowley, for the news of the Wootton wonder had spread far and wide; all dressed seriously in their Sunday clothes, all with their faces arranged into

34

looks of impassivity. Thus one by one or in little groups they came, and scarcely greeting each other they ranged themselves round Mr Lubin and the Monument, waiting to see what they should see.

On Mr Lubin they looked with dispassionate curiosity, but when they looked at the Monument they frowned. For now there was scarcely one among them still holding to the Powleian hypothesis, the darker doctrine overshadowed their minds. Mr Codd's eloquence had done much to persuade them, and what is terrible and fanatic has a natural empire over the thoughts of these Fen-dwellers, whose forefathers were ruthless alike to persecute and to endure persecution; but it was the weather that had settled it: with a thunderstorm brewing for three days above their heads, with a sky like painted brass and the scorched landscape looking haggard with fear, the villagers of Wootton were compelled very naturally into the opinion that there was an abomination in their midst. Nothing could have been more exciting, but it was also a little painful, for no one could hold himself securely blameless in the matter; even the most austere chapel-goer had, as it were, countenanced the abomination by never suspecting how abominable it was, and as for those who had had dealings in the grove – well, it was being brought home to them how wicked such dealings are. But now, as the minutes passed by and still Mr Lubin continued to pace round and round the Monument, and still the clouds mounted above the trees, and still the watchers stood motionless and silent, waiting to see what they should see, all individual fears and speculations were fused into one enormous communal anxiety, a kind of delighted dread.

At a quarter to four, just after the church clock had struck, a low peel of thunder was heard. The villagers glanced upward: the storm was imminent now, for the cloud was right overhead, as dark as a dragon, and a cold air came from under its wings. Again the thunder sounded, much louder this time, and before it had ceased there was heard a great hooting and resounding as three charabancs containing an excursion from Bedford passed through the village. The charabancs stopped. The excursionists had noticed the crowd on the green, and whether it were a fight, an accident, or a cricket match, they were not going to miss the fun. Laughing and talking in loud gay voices, the excursionists streamed across the grass and joined in the circle of watchers. By nudging and jostling they soon made their way in, and saw Mr Lubin walking in the maze.

'What is it?' 'What's he doing? 'Is it a bet?'

No one answered them, no one even looked at them, and as for Mr

Lubin, though they called to him with many remarks, most of which were insulting, he did not even turn his head.

For Mr Lubin was past speech now, almost past thought. His situation was horrible to him, and yet he could conceive no possibility of escape, for his body was cowed with fatigue and his mind was all in a confusion. He felt like the beast that, wearied out, sinks trembling down to death in the ring of its tormentors, flogged to death by their pitiless glances.

But still the excursionists continued to call out,

'What's up?' 'Damn it, what's up?' 'What's the old blighter doing?' 'Is it a bet?'

And suddenly the sky, the air, the earth itself, was rent open by a blinding flash, a flame that scorched on their faces and buried itself in the ground. And noiselessly before their eyes, for no sound could be heard above the clang of the thunder, the Trott Monument split in two and fell ruining down into a shapeless heap of stones.

God had spoken. He had sent fire from Heaven and the Wootton abomination was no more.

Mr Codd shouted out, 'It's dead! It's dead! Glory Hallelujah! Hurrah!'

And all the villagers, kindled by his example, began to cheer and cheer again and again, and the excursionists cheered too, and made catcalls, the whole green rang with the sound of cheering; and though the storm raged over them, and though a drenching rain hammered them from the cloud, every one continued to stand round the ruins of the Trott Monument, cheering and shouting as though they would never leave off.

The uproar was heard by Mr Slumber, sitting quietly in his study. Mr Slumber prided himself on being a rational creature, he had not gone to the window to look at the storm, but continued to read Herodotus, frowning a little because the room had grown so dark. But the cheering did what the voice of the thunder could not do: it made him lay down his book and return from Egypt to Wootton.

'I pretend to be a historian,' he said to his cat; 'and yet I care nothing for what is going on in my own village.'

Having thus justified himself in his own eyes, and perhaps in the cat's eyes too, he found his umbrella and walked out into the storm.

The cheering continued, though with less conviction, for the rain was watering it down. Three empty charabancs stood on the road; they were open charabancs, and pools of water were collecting on their seats. Mr Slumber walked past the charabancs and came in sight of the Monument, or rather of the crowd which surrounded the place where it had stood.

36

They were all talking and waving their arms, and Mr Slumber surveyed them with the smile of a rational creature, for there was not an umbrella among them.

He came closer, he recognised Powley. 'What is it?' he asked.

'Oh, sir, what a sight you've missed!'

There was a strong smell of burning; Mr Slumber saw the heap of blackened stones and guessed what had happened. But he could not account for the high spirits that all those very wet people were in. On every face he saw looks of excitement and ravenous joy. He questioned Powley, but could get nothing from him but exclamations, and thinking to himself, the mob is always the same. Whether Rome burns or a village monument they will warm their senses at the blaze, he was about to turn away, when he noticed a small dejected figure sitting on the ground quite close to the Monument and seeming to take no part in the general hubbub.

Mr Slumber elbowed his way through the crowd. He approached the seated figure, and bending over it said gently, 'I hope you are not hurt.'

Mr Lubin started and turned his face towards the voice that spoke him friendly.

'My eyes,' he said. 'Something has happened to them. I am blind.'

Mr Slumber helped him to rise. Holding him closely, indeed almost carrying him, he guided Mr Lubin away. Immediately the crowd came about them, asking questions and offering to help. Mr Slumber gave them a look or two, and they drew back ashamed.

'It often happens so,' said Mr Slumber, speaking comfortably to the trembling Mr Lubin; 'but the loss of sight is only temporary, perhaps only for a day or two.'

'I hope so. I'm sure you are very kind,' answered Mr Lubin, stumbling over the maze. 'But I feel as though I were blinded for life.'

Mr Lubin was right. He was blinded for life; but that was not for long, since on the following morning he died.

There was an inquest, at which Mr Slumber was highly commended for his humanity; and after the inquest there was a magnificent funeral, attended by all the villagers, three representative excursionists, and Sir Alfred Marsala's confidential man, who brought a broken column made of grey moss and white carnations.

Mr Slumber also attended the funeral. He did not go to church as a rule, but in the short time allowed him for making Mr Lubin's acquaintance he had grown extremely fond of him, and he did not like the idea of him

37

being put into the ground without a single friend to stand by and see fair play. Being unused to Christian rites, Mr Slumber listened attentively to the funeral service. One sentence from it made a great impression upon him; it rang in his mind as he walked homeward alone, and as he sat drinking tea in his garden (for the air was exquisitely fresh after the storm), and eating white currants in the shade of the mulberry tree.

'We therefore commit his body to the ground; earth to earth, ashes to ashes, dust to dust; in sure and certain hope of the Resurrection to eternal life, through our Lord Jesus Christ.'

A strange thing, thought he, that Mr Lubin thus firmly and deeply planted in the local soil should rise again, no longer a small, subdued middle-aged gentleman, but a blessed and immortal spirit. More strange (if true) than any other of the Wootton rarities – the sunflowers even, or the everlasting pea, the horseradish or the vegetable marrows.

* * * * *

Edward Storey was born at Whittlesey near Peterborough in 1930. Several generations of his family have lived and worked in the fens and since the appearance of his first volume of poetry in 1969 Storey has become a solitary chronicler of this unique landscape in over twenty volumes of essays, poetry, autobiography and short stories. He is vice president of the John Clare Society and wrote *A Right To Song* in 1982, a long awaited biography of the poet. Having lived in East Anglia most of his life, Storey and his wife recently moved to the Welsh border where distance from his homeland has brought the flat landscape into sharper focus.

No Other Word For It

EDWARD STOREY

When I was a boy my mother often said things that I did not understand. Sometimes she used words which I'm sure she did not fully comprehend herself – words like 'fornicating' and 'lascivious', which I'm certain she would not have known how to spell. But when she spoke those words they rang through our small house with an authority that made me realise that we were on the threshold of something momentous, even evil. The memory of them came back to me recently when one of the words was the answer to a crossword puzzle clue, causing me some distraction.

Mother was not a loquacious person but she did have this extraordinary vocabulary for someone whose formal education was basic and brief. Another word which she used frequently was 'pontificating' and she often described people of definite views to be 'pontificators'. To be guilty of 'fornicating', 'lasciviousness' or 'pontificating' was close to treachery, murder, or being Anglican. My family had long been non-conformists with no time for the Church of England, which they saw as the Conservative Party in robes.

For centuries people in the Fens created their own dramas. Living on that vast landscape, where nothing appeared to happen, any scandal or crisis caused great excitement and kept conversations going for weeks. Nature occasionally provided its own theatrical events like floods, fires, or gale-force winds but we still needed human frailty to spice up the plot. We had the stage on which to act out our lives. All we needed in our town of Ewesley were the leading players to give us the heroes and villains who would add colour to our place in history.

There were three people in particular who regularly provoked mother into her priceless moments of eloquence. One was Sandy Chapple, who had never been inside a place of worship since his mother had him baptised – 'if she ever did.' Another was Rita Luke – 'that brazen little hussy' who was know to have several lovers in town, and a few beyond. The third was Gladstone Patterson who was, in mother's opinion, the world's greatest pontificator. How the three came to be linked together in the folklore of our town could not have been predicted.

Sandy had been sixty-years old since he left school and would remain sixty for the rest of his life. Mischievous, rebellious, but not unliked, he had been a merry widower for several years. He was fond both of drink and women. Intoxication made him merry, not violent. His flirtations made him adventurous, not offensive. As far as I know he never harmed anyone and most of the townsfolk were prepared to laugh-off any misdemeanour with – 'that's Sandy for you. 'E's drunk like a fish all 'is life and allus bin a ladies' man, just like his father.' But mother only had to hear one rumour about him and would say – 'What d'you expect of a fornicating old devil like him! His poor wife was a saint.'

I can remember Sandy waking me from my schoolboy sleep on many occasions as he staggered down our street, trying to wheel his bike when he was incapable of riding it after a convivial evening at 'The Black Swan'. He had a fairly good singing voice and, between his laughter and cursing, would entertain us with 'When the roll is called up yonder, I'll be there,' heretic though he was.

Gladstone Patterson could never have been accused of any of Sandy's sins. He was a strict teetotaller, a bachelor, town-councillor, and local preacher. He also owned the local chemist shop and liked to give one-off lectures to the small W.E.A. group that met once a week in the parish hall during the winter. He had an opinion about everything and considered himself a world authority on anything from bee-keeping and botany to zoology and Zen Buddhism. His knowledge and interpretation of the bible was intimidating and tempted some to believe he had written it.

Rita Luke was in a class of her own when it came to gossip. With her extravagant sexuality she courted scandal if only to earn what she saw as popularity. 'It doesn't matter what you're popular for, duckie, so long as you're popular. Who wants to be a nobody?' As schoolboys we considered her as provocative as the pin-ups we saw but could not reach on the top shelf of the newsagent's. When she passed the school playground at break-time she would give us a saucy wink and we'd wolf-whistle. She'd then pull her blouse or sweater more tightly over her breasts so that we could whistle again, even louder. She had already borne two illegitimate children, whose fathers were believed to be living respectable lives in the town, but she never openly named them as long as they dropped a five-pound note through her letter-box every month. Her customers knew her well enough to know that beneath her favours was a heart of stone.

Next to her lasciviousness, her greatest sin in mother's eyes was that she dyed her hair, though mother would not have used the word dye, it was peroxide. 'She's no more blonde than my Aunt Fanny,' she'd say contemptuously. As we had no aunt of that name I was not sure what mother was referring to, or why the colour of Rita's hair provoked such scorn. Perhaps all Jezebels were meant to be blonde.

Despite her uncompromising views my mother was not an unkind, or unreasonable person. On the contrary. Beneath the fire and brimstone she was compassionate and practical, always ready to help a neighbour, or even a beggar who might call at the house, provided he had clean shoes. She'd not had an easy life herself. Her father was killed in a farming accident when she was only three years old and, when her mother married again, she was brought up by her grand-parents. At the age of fourteen she was put into service as a scullery-maid to Major-General Coverley and his family who were then powerful farmers in the Fens. At nineteen she secretly married one of the house-keepers and, consequently, they were both dismissed.

It was whilst she was there that I think she must have acquired her unusual vocabulary. The Major-General's wife was the daughter of a tea-planter and regularly gave dinner-parties for guests from far beyond the local gentry. When mother progressed from scullery-maid to the pantry, and eventually to serving at table, she would have heard good conversation. She was also allowed to read what she could of the previous day's newspapers but was forbidden to borrow any books from her master's library. But was it there, I wonder, where she picked up words like 'fornicating', 'lascivious' and 'pontificating?' Or were they more likely to have come from the Baptist Chapel which she was permitted to attend every Sunday evening as part of her half-day off? Whichever way she came by them, she put them to good use for the rest of her life.

I was away at college when a new scandal, or rather tragedy, suddenly thrust our town into the national newspapers. I felt shocked because it all seemed so personal and humiliating. I knew things like it happened in other places but not in Ewesley. Rita Luke had been found murdered in a disused mill near the railway station, her throat cut, her face bruised. I knew the place well. It was one of our secret hideouts as boys when playing games, the place where we tried our first breath-choking cigarettes. Now it was no longer secret. The whole world knew about it.

41

My mother soon started sending me news-cuttings from the local papers, adding her own thoughts on the crime. The last person who was seen talking to Rita was Sandy who'd bought her a drink at 'The White Horse' that evening before he left, looking uncommonly preoccupied. Rita had followed a few minutes later, without saying goodnight. One or two customers who gave evidence at the trial said that from the snatches of conversation they'd overheard, something serious was being discussed but they couldn't say exactly what. When Rita's body was discovered next day by some boys using the mill as their hideout, Sandy was immediately seen as the prime suspect and, by six o'clock, had been arrested. Ginger hairs found on Rita's dress gave the police the only other proof they thought was needed.

But several people in town were not happy and argued that Sandy would not have cut her throat. He was not a brutal man. Even if they'd had differences about something he would not have punched her, or threatened her with a knife. Such a premeditated act was out of character. But Councillor Patterson said that when he saw Sandy in Station Road he was drunk and apparently still in a bad mood. The court then heard that a note from Rita has been found in the pocket of the jacket that Sandy was wearing on the night of the murder. In her bold handwriting she was begging him to lend her £100. But, as Sandy's lawyer said, it was not a demand note, simply a desperate plea from the deceased for help, an appeal to a man who was known to have a soft spot for her and had helped her before. The prosecution counsel suggested this was supposition, not fact. The accused had a long history of heavy drinking and instability, a bit of a wheeler-dealer and poacher, a man not to be trusted. Why was he seen walking down Station Road when his home was in the opposite direction?

When cross-examined, Sandy admitted that he was in a bad mood that night, that he was in Station Road, but never went anywhere near the mill. He may have seen Mr Patterson but he wasn't sure. They had nothing in common and so seldom spoke to each other. The only reason why he was in Station Road was to get a drink at 'The Carpenters' Arms' because the landlord there was kind enough to let him have a few on the slate when he was short of cash: 'He knew he'd allus get paid,' said Sandy. 'My income was, as you might say, slightly irregular.'

The trial lasted for six weeks and the press began to lose interest. It had become tedious rather than sensational. There were no other dark confessions from murky waters, no one else involved. Sandy had no alibi and Rita's demand for cash at a time when Sandy himself was broke was motive enough for him to bring the matter to an end.

For some reason my mother did not believe it was as straightforward as that. 'There's never been a truer saying than "the law's an ass" and this appears to me to be too easily sewn up. I know a bad egg when I see one and, with all his faults, Sandy Chapple's not that rotten. This crime has a different smell from a bit of poaching, or being drunk and disorderly. There's more to it than that.'

Before the judge's final summing-up Sandy surprised everyone by asking if he could make a statement. He was not an eloquent man when sober and usually found it difficult to construct coherent sentences, but now the words came quietly and with ease – 'I beg to ask that the character of Rita Luke is not made worse by the decision of this court, whatever happens to me. She was not blackmailing me, and I swear I did not kill her. Her note was simply asking me for a loan, to help her with an operation. But I couldn't do anything this time and felt disappointed with myself for letting her down. I wanted a few more drinks to enable me to think things out. We were two of a kind, and both of us innocent. She at least should be forgiven.'

Forgiveness is never easy in the Fens. Grudges are often borne for a lifetime, from generation to generation. Most of the town had already sentenced Sandy to life imprisonment and more than a few were not sorry to know that Rita Luke could hold no further threat over them. There was even some disappointment when the judge's verdict was one of manslaughter and sentenced Sandy to only fifteen years in jail.

When I next came home from college I found the town strangely subdued, even changed. It was no longer the place I used to know. No one wanted to talk about the trial or Sandy, and I was puzzled by their silence. It was as if they wanted to erase the episode from their minds. Any hope of that was shattered though when, two months later, another body was found in the mill. But this time it was not murder. Gladstone Patterson had shot himself. The question then was why? After all, he owned the chemist shop. He could have chosen poison. Was that not violent enough? Did he see an execution as more appropriate?

A sealed letter which the police found when they searched his home, gave the answers. For several years he'd had a relationship with Rita, who had borne his first child and was expecting his second. It was he she had been blackmailing and, when he refused to give her any more money, she threatened him with a letter she was going to send to every local paper,

43

exposing him as the hypocrite he was. He invited her to meet him at the mill, to renew, he said, their old relationship and talk things over. And there he murdered her, killing not only the mother of his child but also condemning an innocent man to fifteen years in jail. He could not live with that guilt, or shame, for the rest of his life.

If the town had been shocked by Rita's death, it was rocked to its foundations by Gladstone Patterson's confession of a double life. The proud pontificator was now spoken of in the pubs as 'a rotten bastard' and in the chapels as 'a wicked Pharisee.' Mother summed it up in her own way. 'You should never put your trust in a man who thinks he is perfect. Besides, he never came from these parts anyway,' which put fen people on a pedestal that not even I had recognised before. Perhaps that was why it took them a long time to come to terms with their collective shame. I then began to see it as a guilt that cast a shadow, not only over the town, but over the surrounding fens already heavy with past silences. They also take a long time to forgive.

It might have taken longer for the memory of those gruesome days to return had it not been for that crossword puzzle clue: 'To let off steam a short pope and I went catering without the queen. (13).'

Would mother have worked that out any quicker than I had done? With her intuition, or simply guesswork, maybe so. She was no fool.

* * * * *

Sir Malcolm Bradbury was Emeritus Professor of English and American Studies at the University of East Anglia where he will always be most closely associated with the creative writing course he founded with Angus Wilson in 1970. As a writer of fiction Bradbury gave us the 'Campus Novel' in the shape of *The History Man*, but *An Extravagant Fondness For The Love Of Women*, published the following year in the collection *Who Do You Think You Are*, is more in the nature of the 'Collegiate Short Story'. In this parody, as Bradbury calls it, he provides us with the record of a meeting between, what were then, two of modern fiction's most familiar characters, C P Snow's Lewis Eliot and Kingsley Amis's Jim Dixon. Bradbury refrains from disclosing which novelist recorded the meeting beyond stating that 'it comes from a forty-volume *roman-fleuve* called "Staircases of Disputation." '

An Extravagant Fondness For The Love Of Women
MALCOLM BRADBURY

A warm fire burned in my grate, its flicker illuminating the book-lined walls, as I sat in my Cambridge room that evening in the early Sixties – I am usually either sitting or eating when I begin a chapter. My fire, my leather-bound volumes, my warm body in the armchair formed a little pool of civilization, though through the medieval wainscoting the draught from outside struck cold. Below, in the wintry courtyard, tourists with plastic cameras walked clumsily on the lawns, or kicked against buckets in the narrow Tudor passageways; being, however, from a lowly background, I felt this quite excusable. I could hear their murmurs of veneration for the ancient college, and realised how they would envy me my traditional rights and comforts, could they see me sitting there with the tray the gyp had left me, on it a decanter of nuts and a bowl of sherry. The rain rattled my windows. The leather-bound tome on my lap struck cold, or warm, I hardly remember which; after all, this is fifteen years ago. The book was a study of the Martyrdom of Polycarp, an old and well-loved interest of mine; and I was so deeply engrossed that I did not notice the step on my staircase, until someone knocked several times, with heavy knuckles, on my oak door.

'Come,' I called; and I looked up to see Dixon enter. The fire was, as I said, warm, the books radiant in its glow; but Dixon's entrance brought in the draught and wet of the weather outside, which struck cold into the room, and I hastily bade him shut the door.

'Well, wotcha, old sock,' he said, taking his place before my fire (not his fire) and warming his youthful, fleshless buttocks impetuously, 'I suppose this is what you call studying then. Do a lot of that, do you?' As he spoke, his eyes flickered enviously over my ample chairs, my seventeenth-century tapestries, the rows of diaries, the volumes of briefs, the scientific notes, the political memoirs that betokened my eclectic interests; and his features assumed an expression which bore, I noticed, an extraordinary physical similarity to that of Dame Edith Sitwell.

'Do be seated Dixon,' I said, and Dixon sat down. He was a young man of thirty-five, though from his youthful manner many thought him younger; however, I happen to be remarkably good about knowing the right age of people. He had been elected to a college fellowship only a week or so previous, and in somewhat mysterious circumstances. One of the Fellows, a man with a taste for the untoward, had proposed the name of L S Caton, an eminent medieval historian, who was, however, we were warned, travelling abroad. Though none of the Fellows had met him, his name had, after the necessary disputation and colloguing, the familiar backstairs struggles and flagrant sexual innuendos always invoked in a college election, been selected; but at the start of term, on Caton's expected day of arrival, Dixon had appeared instead. His claim that Caton was the pseudonym under which he published his many bulky monographs had not convinced some of the older Fellows, struck by his utter want of accurate historical knowledge; but naturally they had said nothing to him directly, preferring to bicker and calumniate in small groups on the bends of staircases, where the air struck cold. Other fellows had taken the view that his tendency to confuse the events of the twelfth with those of the fifteenth century had a simpler explanation: Dixon had confessed that he had taught once in a provincial university. I myself had not taken sides, as is my custom, and had already talked to Dixon occasionally in hall. Within days, though he was in character and spirits my direct opposite, we had formed a relationship. He clearly liked and respected me, while I regarded him with that amiable, rather contemptuous distance it is always pleasant to adopt towards a willing protégé.

So it had gone on, though from the start Dixon had mystified me. He struck me oddly, as a man curiously uninterested in power. Jago had told me that he had seen in him an extravagant fondness for the love of women, and it was probably this propensity that corrupted his natural instincts. He had avoided our cabals, remained unspeaking during our gossip, and had taken a negligible part in our recent poisoning attempt upon the Provost. On the other hand, my gyp told me one morning, when he drew my curtains and cut me my first cigar of the day, that Dixon was in the habit of scraping acquaintance with working-class barmaids from the suburbs who served beer and other brews in the local hostelries, and of escorting them along the tree-lined walks beside the Cam, where the air struck very cold indeed, and whence their faint giggles and occasional cries could be heard even in the Provost's Lodge. He was, I supposed, a man who suffered from the frets of sensual love, who 'let the heart lead the head', and who dangerously lacked the subtlety to conceal his tastes, for I had heard discussions of his conduct on several evenings over dessert in the combination room. It was, however, hardly my business to warn or criticize; and, in any case, if a man is not prepared to accept and take on his own terms every Fellow of the college, he is hardly likely to acquire enough material for a *roman-fleuve*.

'Sherry,' I said, looking up at Dixon.

'I'm all right.' He produced, with a lithe movement, a small can of beer from the pocket of his turd-brown anorak and, from another of his many pockets, drew out a metal bottle-opener of the kind then recently introduced to facilitate this new fashion of drinking. With this, he succeeded in penetrating the circular container, and put it to his lips. It was not one of the more expensive or better reputed kinds of beer and he gulped it inattentively.

'I'm not disturbing you, am I?' he then went on, 'I see you're only reading. The kind of bloody boring stuff us chaps have to do to pretend we're up to something, eh, Lew?'

'One tries to keep up,' I said.

'Actually,' said Dixon, 'I hoped I'd catch you in. I wanted you to know that last evening I was accorded one of those there signal honours. In the election after dinner I emerged victor. I'm now captain of the darts team down the Feathers.'

'You know how delighted I am. Perhaps you'll allow me to present a bottle this evening, and record the occasion in the wine-book.'

Dixon sometimes gave the appearance of brashness, but I could see that he was taken right aback. He gave a shy, somewhat diffident smile. Down below in the court someone walked towards the chapel, whistling a passage of *Carmen*. Dixon seemed affected by this, and, as if to draw attention away from his embarrassed gratitude, he snatched up a small eighteenth-century alabaster figurine from my mantleshelf and crossed to the window. After a moment's pause, he opened the window, so that a draught of air struck cold to my chair, and hurled out the precious object. The throw was evidently accurate; outside the music ceased, and a sailor's oath reminded me that Crystal had promised the Duke of Edinburgh as his guest at the feast that evening. Dixon pulled down the window, giving the rain something to rattle against (it had had to stop for a second or two) and came back to the fire (which had kept going throughout).

'With increasing years has come wisdom, Lew,' he said smiling down at me, and twanging his braces inconsequentially, 'One learns the art of not getting caught. Or even of getting others caught. Bloody Beethoven.'

'Bizet,' I said.

'Oh, so-so,' he replied. Then, collecting himself, he said: 'But I haven't come just for that small triumph. I've come, Lew, for your support. You see, I'm a fresh eye here, and I probably notice a number of things about this place you older blokes would miss. I've never been a straight academic. I've always detested books, something of a barrier in this racket. I can't do research, and libraries give me dandruff. As for this sherry bum, and gyp bum and Martyrdom of Polycarp bum, it gets on my, you know, wick. Then I've spent some time outside the academic world. In fact I worked as a personal secretary in London until I was fi . . . until I resigned. I know you've spent some time sodding about in the corridors of power too. You see now why I've come to you.'

'Men do,' I said, inhaling, unobtrusively, the bouquet of my glass of Montrachet. I wondered what it was, apart from my natural gift for eliciting the most profound of confidences, that made Dixon speak so to me. All men seek for power, I thought, and those in universities do little other. But what was Dixon seeking? His appearance suggested that he had no aims, which made me, of course, suspicious; for me, that meant he had every aim. His guileless face, the absence of any air of deception, made me conscious of all the possible deceptions such a pose could conceal. Was he after the Provostship already? Or was it rather my work on the double helix, a part-time preoccupation of mine, later taken further by others? I answered him non-committally; after all, you never get anything out of me until the twelfth chapter, and then not a lot.

'Port?' I said.

Dixon replied comically, claiming that port always sent him running for the lavatories, clutching at his bowels. He was, I saw, a man unfinished, a man unpretentious because he had not realized his pretensions; I admired him for it. But then, with a decisive gesture of his feet, he came suddenly to the point.

'Look, I don't know whether you've spotted this yet, Lew, but there's one thing gravely lacking in this college. Something I think I could give a little assistance with. It's something that every sound society requires, and I think we should act decisively and together, old sock.'

He stood there gravely, dressed with subfusc taste in anorak and jeans, waiting for me to encourage him to go on.

'Go on,' I said.

'It's tail, Lew. Women. I've looked around carefully, and all the Fellows here are men.'

We are a small college, and it took me only a moment to hurry mentally through the thirteen Fellows, calling each vividly to mind. They were – you're sure you don't mind when I hold the action up to tell you things like this? – from a mixture of subjects, and they revealed that mixture of natures one finds in any sodality. There were the grave and the gay, the deceitful, the likeable, the noble, the weak. Four of them lay dying, in unutterably painful circumstances; two were now held in prison, bearing treason charges with stoic endurance; at least one was an adulterer, another a blackmailer, a third an arrant political opportunist. They made a varied group, like any other group of people drawn together by profession or interest. Yet I quickly saw Dixon's point; various they were, but one thing was theirs in common. All were men.

'Claret?' I said. I felt, with my deep experience of people, I understood Dixon now. Like so many men, he had fallen in love with the college, and wanted to give himself to it entirely. It had won his dedication, his faith. He came from a lower middle-class background, and he had expressed radical sympathies to me in secret, sympathies that I recognised from the struggles of my own one-time youth. There was nothing in his heritage or history that could have prepared him for anything like this; none the less, faced with its medieval grandeur, with the feudalism and simplicity of its life, with the possibility of escape from the overweening century we live in, with the opportunity of stimulating company from men like myself, he had yielded himself heart and soul. The college offered a draught of certainty in the lonely anguish of mortal personal life.

'It's not just that,' he said, 'It's the lavatories. Not enough to go round. Something nasty's going to happen one of these days. Of course, the place really wants pulling down.'

'Nuts?' I said.

'And you,' he said. 'And now we're speaking frankly, well, it's a case, Lew, of under which king, Bezonian, if you catch my meaning.'

'I think I know four people we could get on our side,' I said to him, 'Then come dreary weeks of bargaining and colloguing . . .'

'I don't see why we shouldn't put a match to it now.'

I have always been excited by young rebels, and found them often quite as natural company as merchant-bankers, statesmen, international scientists, judges. It was hard not to yield to his young enthusiasm, his appeal to the future, but the spirit of intelligent compromise which has made me all things to all men asserted itself.

'May I propose to *part* of it?' I said.

Dixon smiled. 'Beer?' he asked, offering me a can. Then, allowing his lower lip to droop forward and raising his arm loosely in the air, as if depending on some imaginary branch, he did a gibbering ape imitation around the room.

The air struck cold as, some little time later, Dixon and I went out into the court. In the further corner stood one of the latest additions to the college, a wing built during an access of wealth in the middle nineteenth century, and now given over almost entirely to freshmen, though the Bursar's rooms were there too. It had little architectural merit, and was evidently rather jerry-built, for the flames spread through it from end to end as soon as we tossed our matches into the petrol. The fire flickered brightly on the Tudor stone of the old quadrangle, forming a bright pool of warmth, though further away, of course, the cold struck colder than ever. After the last ember had died and the last scream faded, I returned to my rooms to wash off some of the dirt deposited by the evening's adventure.

I felt uneasy and a thought depressed. Perhaps I had let my hot-cold imagery take me a mite too far. Further, I felt that I had fallen under Dixon's spell, been taken further than by nature I would wish to go. My gyp had left me a pitcher of water, laced with rose petals, and as I slopped it in the bowl I caught sight of my features in the mirror. An idea struck me. If I loosened up my clauses, let my dialogue dangle a bit, and twisted my plot into a grimace, I could make my style exactly like Kingsley Amis's. I put it to the test. 'Filthy grass-eating codpiece,' I said to my features. 'Toad-faced hanger about ladies' lavatories,' I continued. The image stared stiffly back and then suddenly yielded; and a moment later, when my gyp came in, I was doing a gibbering ape imitation about the room.

* * * * *

Ian McEwan is one of the country's most distinguished writers, the author of eight novels including *The Cement Garden, The Child in Time, Amsterdam* which won the 1998 Booker Prize, *Enduring Love* and his most recent work, the critically acclaimed *Atonement*. The title story of his first collection of short stories *First Love, Last Rites* (1973) is set in Kings Lynn. This disturbing tale of adolescence grew out of his time at the University of East Anglia where he became the first graduate of Malcolm Bradbury's creative writing course.

First Love, Last Rites

IAN McEWAN

From the beginning of summer until it seemed pointless, we lifted the thin mattress on to the heavy oak table and made love in front of the large open window. We always had a breeze blowing into the room and smells of the quayside four floors down. I was drawn into fantasies against my will, fantasies of the creature, and afterwards when we lay on our backs on the huge table, in those deep silences I heard it faintly running and clawing. It was new to me, all this, and I worried, I tried to talk to Sissel about it for reassurance. She had nothing to say, she did not make abstractions or discuss situations, she lived inside them. We watched the seagulls wheeling about in our square of sky and wondered if they had been watching us up there, that was the kind of thing we talked about, mildly entertaining hypotheses of the present moment. Sissel did things as they came to her, stirred her coffee, made love, listened to her records, looked out the window. She did not say things like I'm happy, or confused, or I want to make love, or I don't, or I'm tired of the fights in my family, she had no language to split herself in two, so I suffered alone what seemed like crimes in my head while we fucked, and afterwards listened alone to it scrabbling in the silence. Then one afternoon Sissel woke from a doze, raised her head from the mattress and said, 'What's that scratching noise behind the wall?'

My friends were far away in London, they sent me anguished and reflective letters, what would they do now? Who were they, and what was the point of it all? They were my age, seventeen and eighteen, but I pretended not to understand them. I sent back postcards, find a big table and an open window, I told them. I was happy and it seemed easy, I was making eel traps, it was so easy to have a purpose. The summer went on and I no longer heard from them. Only Adrian came to see us, he was Sissel's ten-year-old brother and he came to escape the misery of his

51

disintegrating home, the quick reversals of his mother's moods, the endless competitive piano playing of his sisters, the occasional bitter visits of his father. Adrian and Sissel's parents after twenty-seven years of marriage and six children hated each other with sour resignation, they could no longer bear to live in the same house. The father moved out to a hostel a few streets away to be near his children. He was a businessman who was out of work and looked like Gregory Peck, he was an optimist and had a hundred schemes to make money in an interesting way. I used to meet him in the pub. He did not want to talk about his redundancy or his marriage, he did not mind me living in a room over the quayside with his daughter. Instead he told me about his time in the Korean war, and when he was an international salesman, and of the legal fraudery of his friends who were now at the top and knighted, and then one day of the eels in the River Ouse, how the river bed swarmed with eels, how there was money to be made catching them and taking them live to London. I told him how I had eighty pounds in the bank, and the next morning we bought netting, twine, wire hoops and an old cistern tank to keep eels in. I spent the next two months making eel traps.

On fine days I took my net, hoops and twine outside and worked on the quay, sitting on a bollard. An eel trap is cylinder-shaped, sealed at one end, and at the other is a long tapering funnel entrance. It lies on the river bed, the eels swim in to eat the bait and in their blindness cannot find their way out. The fishermen were friendly and amused. There's eels down there, they said, and you'll catch a few but you won't make no living on it. The tide'll lose your nets fast as you make them. We're using iron weights, I told them, and they shrugged in a good-natured way and showed me a better way to lash the net to the hoops, they believed it was my right to try it for myself. When the fishermen were out in their boats and I did not feel like working I sat about and watched the tidal water slip across the mud, I felt no urgency about the eel traps but I was certain we would be rich.

I tried to interest Sissel in the eel adventure, I told her about the rowing-boat someone was lending to us for the summer, but she had nothing to say. So instead we lifted the mattress on to the table and lay down with our clothes on. Then she began to talk. We pressed our palms together, she made a careful examination of the size and shape of our hands and gave a running commentary. Exactly the same size, your fingers are thicker, you've got this extra bit here. She measured my eyelashes with the end of her thumb and wished hers were as long, she told me about the dog she had when she was small, it had long white eye-lashes. She looked at the sunburn on my nose and talked about that, which of her brothers and sisters went red in the sun, who went brown, what her youngest sister said once. We slowly undressed. She kicked off her plimsolls and talked about her foot rot. I listened with my eyes closed, I could smell mud and seaweed and dust through the open window. Wittering on, she called it, this kind of talk. Then once I was inside her I was moved, I was inside my fantasy, there could be no separation now of my mushrooming sensations from my knowledge that we could make a creature grow in Sissel's belly. I had no wish to be a father, that was not in it at all. It was eggs, sperms, chromosomes, feathers, gills, claws, inches from my cock's end the unstoppable chemistry of a creature growing out of a dark red slime, my fantasy was of being helpless before the age and strength of this process and the thought alone could make me come before I wanted. When I told Sissel she laughed. Oh, Gawd, she said. To me Sissel was right inside the process, she *was* the process and the power of its fascination grew. She was meant to be on the pill and every month she forgot it at least two or three times. Without discussion we came to the arrangement that I was to come outside her, but it rarely worked. As we were swept down the long slopes to our orgasms, in those last desperate seconds I struggled to find my way out but I was caught like an eel in my fantasy of the creature in the dark, waiting, hungry, and I fed it great white gobs. In those careless fractions of a second I abandoned my life to feeding the creature, whatever it was, in or out of the womb, to fucking only Sissel, to feeding more creatures, my whole life given over to this in a moment's weakness. I watched out for Sissel's periods, everything about women was new to me and I could take nothing for granted. We made love in Sissel's copious, effortless periods, got good and sticky and brown with the blood and I thought we were the creatures now in the slime, we were inside fed by gobs of cloud coming through the window, by gases drawn from the mudflats by the sun. I worried about my fantasies, I knew I could not come without them. I asked Sissel what she thought about and she giggled. Not feathers and gills, anyway. What *do* you think about, then? Nothing much, nothing really. I pressed my question and she withdrew into silence.

I knew it was my own creature I heard scrabbling, and when Sissel heard it one afternoon and began to worry, I realised her fantasies were involved too, it was a sound which grew out of our lovemaking. We heard it when we were finished and lying quite still on our backs, when we were empty and clear, perfectly quiet. It was the impression of small claws

53

scratching blindly against a wall, such a distant sound it needed two people to hear it. We thought it came from one part of the wall. When I knelt down and put my ear to the skirting-board it stopped, I sensed it on the other side of the wall, frozen in its action, waiting in the dark. As the weeks passed we heard it at other times in the day, and now and then at night. I wanted to ask Adrian what he thought it was. Listen, there it is, Adrian, shut up a moment, what do you think that noise is, Adrian? He strained impatiently to hear what we could hear but he would not be still long enough. There's nothing there, he shouted. Nothing, nothing, nothing. He became very excited, jumped on his sister's back, yelling and yodelling. He did not want whatever it was to be heard, he did not want to be left out. I pulled him off Sissel's back and we rolled about on the bed. Listen again, I said, pinning him down, there it was again. He struggled free and ran out of the room shouting his two-tone police car siren. We listened to it fade down the stairs and when I could hear him no more I said, Perhaps Adrian is really afraid of mice. Rats, you mean, said his sister, and put her hands between my legs.

By mid-July we were not so happy in our room, there was a growing dishevelment and unease, and it did not seem possible to discuss it with Sissel. Adrian was coming to us every day now because it was the summer holidays and he could not bear to be at home. We could hear him four floors down, shouting and stamping on the stairs on his way up to us. He came in noisily, doing handstands and showing off to us. Frequently he jumped on Sissel's back to impress me, he was anxious, he was worried we might not find him good company and send him away, send him back home. He was worried too because he could no longer understand his sister. At one time she was always ready for a fight, and she was a good fighter, I heard him boast that to his friends, he was proud of her. Now changes had come over his sister, she pushed him off sulkily, she wanted to be left alone to do nothing, she wanted to listen to records. She was angry when he got his shoes on her skirt, and she had breasts now like his mother, she talked to him now like his mother. Get down off there, Adrian. Please, Adrian, please, not now, later. He could not quite believe it all the same, it was a mood of his sister's, a phase, and he went on taunting and attacking her hopefully, he badly wanted things to stay as they were before his father left home. When he locked his forearms round Sissel's neck and pulled her backwards on to the bed his eyes were on me for encouragement, he thought the real bond was between us, the two men against the girl. He did not see there was no encouragement, he wanted it so badly. Sissel never sent Adrian away, she understood why he was here, but it was hard for her. One long afternoon of torment she left the room almost crying with frustration. Adrian turned to me and raised his eyebrows in mock horror. I tried to talk to him then but he was already making his yodelling sound and squaring up for a fight with me. Nor did Sissel have anything to say to me about her brother, she never made general remarks about people because she never made general remarks. Sometimes when we heard Adrian on his way up the stairs she glanced across at me and seemed to betray herself by a slight pursing of her beautiful lips.

There was only one way of persuading Adrian to leave us in peace. He could not bear to see us touch, it pained him, it genuinely disgusted him. When he saw one of us move across the room to the other he pleaded with us silently, he ran between us, pretending playfulness, wanted to decoy us into another game. He imitated us frantically in a desperate last attempt to show us how fatuous we appeared. Then he could stand it no more, he ran out of the room machine-gunning German soldiers and young lovers on the stairs.

But Sissel and I were touching less and less now, in our quiet ways we could not bring ourselves to it. It was not that we were in decline, nor that we did not delight in each other, but that our opportunities were faded. It was the room itself. It was no longer four floors up and detached, there was no breeze through the window, only a mushy heat rising off the quayside and dead jellyfish and clouds of flies, fiery grey flies who found our armpits and bit fiercely, houseflies who hung in clouds over our food. Our hair was too long and dank and hung in our eyes. The food we bought melted and tasted like the river. We no longer lifted the mattress on to the table, the coolest place now was the floor and the floor was covered with greasy sand which would not go away. Sissel grew tired of her records, and her foot rot spread from one foot to the other and added to the smell. Our room stank. We did not talk about leaving because we did not talk about anything. Every night now we were woken by the scrabbling behind the wall, louder now and more insistent. When we made love it listened to us behind the wall. We made love less and our rubbish gathered around us, milk bottles we could not bring ourselves to carry away, grey sweating cheese, butter wrappers, yoghurt cartons, over-ripe salami. And among it all Adrian cart-wheeling, yodelling, machine-gunning and attacking Sissel. I tried to write poems about my fantasies, about the creature, but I could see no way in and I wrote nothing down, not even a first line. Instead I took long walks along the river dyke into the Norfolk hinterland of dull beet fields, telegraph poles, uniform grey skies. I had two more eel nets to make, I was forcing myself to sit down to them each day. But in my heart I was sick of them, I could not really believe that eels would ever go inside them and I wondered if I wanted them to, if it was not better that the eels should remain undisturbed in the cool mud at the bottom of the river. But I went on with it because Sissel's father was ready to begin, because I had to expiate all the money and hours I had spent so far, because the idea had its own tired, fragile momentum now and I could no more stop it than carry the milk bottles from our room.

Then Sissel found a job and it made me see we were different from no one, they all had rooms, houses, jobs, careers, that's what they all did, they had cleaner rooms, better jobs, we were anywhere's striving couple. It was one of the windowless factories across the river where they canned vegetables and fruit. For ten hours a day she was to sit in the roar of machines by a moving conveyor belt, talk to no one and pick out the rotten carrots before they were canned. At the end of her first day Sissel came home in a pink-and-white nylon raincoat and pink cap. I said, Why don't you take it off? Sissel shrugged. It was all the same to her, sitting around in the room, sitting around in a factory where they relayed Radio One through speakers strung along the steel girders, where four hundred women half listened, half dreamed, while their hands spun backwards and forwards like powered shuttles. On Sissel's second day I took the ferry across the river and waited for her at the factory gates. A few women stepped through a small tin door in a great windowless wall and a wailing siren sounded all across the factory complex. Other small doors opened and they streamed out, converging on the gates, scores of women in pink-and-white nylon coats and pink caps. I stood on a low wall and tried to see Sissel, it was suddenly very important. I thought that if I could not pick her out from this rustling stream of pink nylon then she was lost, we were both lost and our time was worthless. As it approached the factory gates the main body was moving fast. Some were half running in the splayed, hopeless way that women have been taught to run, the others walked as fast as they could. I found out later they were hurrying home to cook suppers for their families, to make an early start on the housework. Latecomers on the next shift tried to push their way through in the opposite direction. I could not see Sissel and I felt on the edge of panic, I shouted her name and my words were trampled underfoot. Two older women who stopped by the wall to light cigarettes grinned up at me. Sizzle yerself. I walked home by the long way, over the bridge, and decided not to tell Sissel I had been to wait for her because I would have to explain my panic and I did not know how. She was sitting on the bed when I came in, she was still wearing her nylon coat. The cap was on the floor. Why don't you take that thing off? I said. She said, Was that you outside the factory? I nodded. Why didn't you speak to me if you saw me standing there? Sissel turned and lay face downwards on the bed. Her coat was stained and smelt of machine oil and earth. I dunno, she said into the pillow. I didn't think. I didn't think of anything after my shift. Her words had a deadening finality, I glanced around our room and fell silent.

Two days later, on Saturday afternoon, I bought pounds of rubbery cows' lungs sodden with blood (lights, they were called) for bait. That same afternoon we filled the traps and rowed out into mid-channel at low tide to lay them on the river bed. Each of the seven traps was marked by a buoy. Four o'clock Sunday morning Sissel's father called for me and we set out in his van to where we kept the borrowed boat. We were rowing out now to find the marker buoys and pull the traps in, it was the testing time, would there be eels in the nets, would it be profitable to make more nets, catch more eels and drive them once a week to Billingsgate market, would we be rich? It was a dull windy morning, I felt no anticipation, only tiredness and a continuous erection. I half dozed in the warmth of the van's heater. I had spent many hours of the night awake listening to the scrabbling noises behind the wall. Once I got out of bed and banged the skirting-board with a spoon. There was a pause, then the digging continued. It seemed certain now that it was digging its way into the room. While Sissel's father rowed I watched over the side for markers. It was not as easy as I thought to find them, they did not show up white against the water but as dark low silhouettes. It was twenty minutes before we found the first. As we pulled it up I was amazed at how soon the clean white rope from the chandlers had become like all other rope near the river, brown and hung about with fine strands of green weed. The net too was old-looking and alien, I could not believe that one of us had made it. Inside were two crabs and a large eel. He untied the closed end of the trap, let the two crabs drop into the water and put the eel in the plastic bucket we had brought with us. We put fresh lights in the trap and dropped it over the side. It took another fifteen minutes to find the next trap and that one had nothing inside. We rowed up and down the channel for half an hour after that without finding another trap, and by this time the tide was coming up and covering the markers. It was then that I took the oars and made for the shore.

We went back to the hostel where Sissel's father was staying and he cooked breakfast. We did not want to discuss the lost traps, we pretended to ourselves and to each other that we would find them when we went out at the next low tide. But we knew they were lost, swept up or downstream by the powerful tides, and I knew I could never make another eel trap in my life. I knew also that my partner was taking Adrian with him on a short holiday, they were leaving that afternoon. They were going to visit military airfields, and hoped to end up at the Imperial War Museum. We ate eggs, bacon and mushrooms and drank coffee. Sissel's father told me of an idea he had, a simple but lucrative idea. Shrimps cost very little on the quayside here and they were very expensive in Brussels. We could drive two vanloads across there each week, he was optimistic in his relaxed, friendly way and for a moment I was sure his scheme would work. I drank the last of my coffee. Well, I said, I suppose that needs some thinking about. I picked up the bucket with the eel in, Sissel and I could eat that one. My partner told me as we shook hands that the surest way of killing an eel was to cover it with salt. I wished him a good holiday and we parted, still maintaining the silent pretence that one of us would be rowing out at the next low tide to search for the traps.

After a week at the factory I did not expect Sissel to be awake when I got home, but she was sitting up in bed, pale and clasping her knees. She was staring into one corner of the room. It's in here, she said. It's behind those books on the floor. I sat down on the bed and took off my wet shoes and socks. The mouse? You mean you heard the mouse? Sissel spoke quietly. It's a rat. I saw it run across the room, and it's a rat. I went over to the books and kicked them, and instantly it was out, I heard its claws on the floorboards and then I saw it run along the wall, the size of a small dog it seemed to me then, a rat, a squat, powerful grey rat dragging its belly along the floor. It ran the whole length of the wall and crept behind a chest of drawers. We've got to get it out of here, Sissel wailed, in a voice which was strange to me. I nodded, but I could not move for the moment, or speak, it was so big, the rat, and it had been with us all summer, scrabbling at the wall in the deep, clear silences after our fucking, and in our sleep, it was our familiar. I was terrified, more afraid than Sissel, I was certain the rat knew us as well as we knew it, it was aware of us in the room now just as we were aware of it behind the chest of drawers. Sissel was about to speak again when we heard a noise outside on the stairs, a familiar stamping, machine-gunning noise. I was relieved to hear it. Adrian came in the way he usually did, he kicked the door and leapt in, crouching low, a machine-gun ready at his hip. He sprayed us with raw noises from the back of his throat, we crossed our lips with our fingers and tried to hush him. You're dead, both of you, he said, and got ready to cartwheel across the room. Sissel shushed him again, she tried to wave him towards the bed. Why sshh? What's wrong with you? We pointed to the chest of drawers. It's a rat, we told him. He was down on his knees at once, peering. A rat? he gasped. Fantastic, it's a big one, look at it. Fantastic. What are you going to do? Let's catch it. I crossed the room quickly and picked up a poker from the fireplace, I could lose my fear in Adrian's excitement, pretend it was just a fat rat in our room, an adventure to catch it. From the bed Sissel wailed again. What are you going to do with that? For a moment I felt my grip loosen on the poker, it was not just a rat, it was not an adventure, we both knew that. Meanwhile Adrian danced his dance, Yes, that, use that. Adrian helped me carry the books across the room, we built a wall right round the chest of drawers with only one gap in the middle where the rat could get through. Sissel went on asking, What are you doing? What are you going to do with that? but she did not dare leave the bed. We had finished the wall and I was giving Adrian a coat-hanger to drive the rat out with when Sissel jumped across the room and tried to snatch the poker from my hand. Give me that, she cried, and hung on to my lifted arm. At that moment the rat ran out through the gap in the books, it ran straight at us and I thought I saw its teeth bared and ready. We scattered, Adrian jumped on the table, Sissel and I were on the bed. Now we all had time to see the rat as it paused in the centre of the room and then ran forward again, we had time to see how powerful and fat and fast it was, how its whole body quivered, how its tail slid behind it like an attendant parasite. It knows us, I thought, it wants us. I could not bring myself to look at Sissel. As I stood up on the bed, raised the poker and aimed it, she screamed. I threw it as hard as I could, it struck the floor point first several inches from the rat's narrow head. It turned instantly and ran back between the gap in the books. We heard the scratch of its claws on the floor as it settled itself behind the chest of drawers to wait.

I unwound the wire coat-hanger, straightened it and doubled it over and gave it to Adrian. He was quieter now, slightly more fearful. His sister sat on the bed with her knees drawn up again. I stood several feet from the gap in the books with the poker held tight in both hands. I glanced down and saw my pale bare feet and saw a ghost rat's teeth bared and tearing nail from flesh. I called out, Wait, I want to get my shoes. But it was too late, Adrian was jabbing the wire behind the chest of drawers and now I dared not move. I crouched a little lower over the poker, like a batsman. Adrian climbed on to the chest and thrust the wire right down into the corner. He was in the middle of shouting something to me, I did not hear what it was. The frenzied rat was running through the gap, it was running at my feet to take its revenge. Like the ghost rat its teeth were bared. With both hands I swung the poker down, caught it clean and whole smack under its belly, and it lifted clear off the ground, sailed across the room, borne up by Sissel's long scream through her hand in her mouth, it dashed against the wall and I thought in an instant, It must have broken its back. It dropped to the ground, legs in the air, split from end to end like a ripe fruit. Sissel did not take her hand from her mouth, Adrian did not move from the chest, I did not shift my weight from where I had struck, and no one breathed out. A faint smell crept across the room, musty and intimate, like the smell of Sissel's monthly blood. Then Adrian farted and giggled from his held-back fear, his human smell mingled with the wide-open rat smell. I stood over the rat and prodded it gently with the poker. It rolled on its side, and from the mighty gash which ran its belly's length there obtruded and slid partially free from the lower abdomen a translucent purple bag, and inside five pale crouching shapes, their knees drawn up around their chins. As the bag touched the floor I saw a movement, the leg of one unborn rat quivered as if in hope, but the mother was hopelessly dead and there was no more for it.

Sissel knelt by the rat, Adrian and I stood behind her like guards, it was as if she had some special right, kneeling there with her long red skirt spilling round her. She parted the gash in the mother rat with her forefinger and thumb, pushed the bag back inside and closed the blood-spiked fur over it. She remained kneeling a little while and we still stood behind her. Then she cleared some dishes from the sink to wash her hands. We all wanted to get outside now, so Sissel wrapped the rat in newspaper and we carried it downstairs. Sissel lifted the lid of the dustbin and I placed it carefully inside. Then I remembered something, I told the other two to wait for me and I ran back up the stairs. It was the eel I came back for, it lay quite still in its few inches of water and for a moment I thought that it too was dead till I saw it stir when I picked up the bucket. The wind had dropped now and the cloud was breaking up, we walked to the quay in alternate light and shade. The tide was coming in fast. We walked down the stone steps to the water's edge and there I tipped the eel back in the river and we watched him flick out of sight, a flash of white underside in the brown water. Adrian said goodbye to us, and I thought he was going to hug his sister. He hesitated and then ran off, calling out something over his shoulder. We shouted after him to have a good holiday. On the way back Sissel and I stopped to look at the factories on the other side of the river. She told me she was going to give up her job there.

We lifted the mattress on to the table and lay down in front of the open window, face to face, the way we did at the beginning of summer. We had a light breeze blowing in, a distant smoky smell of autumn, and I felt calm, very clear. Sissel said, This afternoon let's clean the room up and then go for a long walk, a walk along the river dyke. I pressed the flat of my palm against her warm belly and said, Yes.

* * * * *

And The Green Grass Grew All Around

RONALD BLYTHE

Seventeen is the age of longing, if there is ever such a thing, and when I was seventeen I longed to be accepted by Mrs Carron-Wilson more than anything else in the world. By being 'accepted' I mean to have gone to all her little, glittering, impromptu parties and not to have to endure the particular brand of flawless reservation which blunted her conversation when she remembered to speak to me.

'Stephen!' she would exclaim in the voice she saved up for me, and I hated her unimpeded view of my innocence. Her small, well-shaped eyes would crinkle with what I learned later was real affection, only then I could hardly bear to look at them and found myself studying instead the bumpy paint on her laughing mouth. She never used this voice for her own sons, although Euen and Godfrey were younger than myself. If anything she became even more adult when speaking to them, as if they and herself existed in a more magnificent intellectual sphere than the rest of us, which I realise now they did.

Euen was fifteen and Godfrey was sixteen. They were like a pair of precocious Tudor youths, small, dark and with some iridescent quality about them which cut them off, not only from my comprehension but from my epoch. They smiled very freely and with, to me, still in my last year at my public school, an almost scandalous lack of inhibition, showing their very clean but rather crammed teeth and setting their faces into masks of classical enjoyment. Neither had been to school in the ordinary way. Euen had entered himself for a term here and a term there as the fancy took him, including six months at the Anchors Away School near Loch Duirinish, where all the character-building antics, plus the cold, had left him weak with laughter and a tendency for pneumonia. Godfrey was eventually going up to Trinity. He had a way of standing near me as I got deeper and deeper into some argument or other, his hand stroking his narrow body through a gap in his grubby shirt, his head twisted whimsically away from me, and then saying when I had faltered to a stop, 'So *that* is what you believe!' And immediately my carefully erected ideas would collapse like a heap of badly balanced junk.

Yet I liked Godfrey and Euen, though even if I had not I would have endured far more than their unique brand of mockery to be near Mrs Carron-Wilson. She was in her mid-forties then. Considering everything – considering chiefly the state of her house, the threadbare carpets mapped all over with paraffin-stain islands, the custard-coloured walls burdened to the wainscoting with Ginners, Bevans, Steers, Tonks's and Brangwyns; the meandering archipelagos of little tables, each with its distinctive afforestation of bottles, handcraft equipment and used plates; the grotesquely elegant looking-glasses which pitted one's image with a silvery eczema, and whose frames writhed with their rococo stalks through a dusty harvest of curling 'At Home' cards, and the preponderance of divans which crowded the rooms, some of them heaped with runs of magazines, one of them usually revealing Euen or Godfrey sound asleep in the middle of the day – Mrs Carron-Wilson maintained an astonishing chic.

Her figure had a restrained opulence. She seemed to be remembering the fact that she wasn't very tall all the time because she moved with a rather exciting erectness which tilted her full breasts and caused tremulous shadows to flicker over the planes of her thickening flanks. Her head, with its triumphant plume of dyed creamy-ivory hair making a dramatic contrast to her careful sun-tan, was held back as though in constant expectation of interesting news or an embrace. 'Rather *avid*,' my father once described it. 'No, no, Gilbert!' my mother had protested. 'Not darling C-W!'

And that is how she was known, by my family and everyone else in the village. By rights the Carron-Wilsons should have been both anathema and an enigma to us; instead, by some hidden power which they surprisingly possessed, they dominated our moral as well as our cultural climate. She had been – was still – the wife of J L Wilson the novelist. All his early books were dedicated to her, although when I hunted these old novels out and read their inscriptions – 'For Blanche, who made it possible' etc – they didn't seem to connect with C-W, Euen, Godfrey and Mallards Point, the ramshackle house which was for me the entrance to the fuller life. None of us had ever seen J L Wilson and it had never been explained why he had left C-W or why she had left him.

Mallards Point was a nice house, even beautiful in its way, but the Carron-Wilsons treated it as they treated everything else, with just a hint of disdain. It was cottagey Queen Anne, chunky where it should have shown elegance and strength and stiff where it should have been symmetrical. It was in the most fearful disorder. The doors didn't fit and none of them would lock, the warped shutters in the drawing-room were permanently half-closed and they swung across the tall windows like crippled fans. There was a bath with a furry green bottom and a rubber ball for a plug, and a bookcase in the lavatory. The garden, a long thin one, ran down to our little river and was private in a way I knew no other garden to be. It was, needless to say, a wilderness of unkempt grass, scarcely traceable paths and shapeless shrubs. It had a distinction of the utmost charm. When Euen and Godrey were small C-W had attended a local sale and bought the horses and cocks from an ancient roundabout. The carnival *elan* of these creeper-bound creatures, weathered of all paint, their combs or nostrils flaring above the tangled beds, lent the garden a magic almost indescribable.

What strikes me now, looking back on those days, was the marvellous availability of it all. We came and went as we chose. We were always welcome it seemed. Why? 'We' included my parents, my father always a trifle drunk, my mother skilfully persuading others as well as herself that he was not; the rector, old Doctor Gould and his receptionist Miss Follet ('Receptionist! – the Greeks couldn't have done better,' my father had remarked coarsely); the Misses Nightingale who wrote detective stories under the name of Ben Carver, Sir John and Lady Tinnington, and a dozen other faces from the neighbourhood. There was no deliberate effort to entertain us. When their own lifeless cottages became too much for them, people strolled to Mallards Point as they might have strolled along to a club had they been in town.

It never occurred to me then, as it frequently does now, how Mrs Carron-Wilson could put up with us. There was every indication that she had known the real thing – indeed, was the real thing. Yet she listened to our gabble about books and plays with apparent interest. It was only when we talked 'county' or chattered about ordinary country things that a distinct look of weariness, and sometimes an undisguised and unrepentant sourness would cloud her normally too-forgiving face. It occurred to me that she hated the country, actually loathed it, and it took me some little time to recover my feelings for her as being anti-country was just a trifle worse than being anti-God in our set. It was odd that she should prefer our half-baked views on Dorothy Richardson or Stanley Spencer to our lively informed comment on what was going on around us. Yet she did and I loved her because of it, though it took me some practice to acquire her heresy.

This made a subtle change in our relationship. Now that I was committed, as it were, to her intellectual freedom, now that I had rejected all the rules and regulations, I wanted some acknowledgement from her to prove to myself that I was different from the rest. When it never came I was bewildered. Mrs Carron-Wilson merely went on being kind to me. 'Euen's in the garden,' she would say, and, 'Godfrey's just gone to the Post Office on his bicycle. He won't be long. Is your father coming this evening?' And so, in about half a dozen sentences rattled off in her breathy, kindly voice, she refused my allegiance.

'I should like to know what C-W really thinks of me,' I said to Euen one day.

'Fishing?' he suggested, his small, Renaissance head tilted mockingly to one side. 'Well, I'll tell you. She thinks you're a clean-limbed-young-Englishman and getting more so every day. Pure Henty.'

'She didn't say that.'

'The last bit? No, she didn't. But you are, aren't you? Well *look* at you!'

'I don't happen to spend my time looking at myself,' I said.

'It wouldn't alter my opinion of you if you did. I am reading the memoirs of Cellini and I wouldn't be able to do that if Cellini hadn't taken a very long look at himself.'

'I'm not Cellini,' I said oafishly. Euen could reduce me to feeling big and stupid in a matter of minutes.

'True. "My glass shall not persuade me I am old . . ." '

'Oh shut up!'

'That, presumably, is the conclusion to all enlightened argument in your jolly decent school.'

'I think you're mad – you're all mad.'

'And you want to be, but you can't quite manage it?' said Euen with cruel percipience. Then he jumped up from the dusty, book-strewn sofa with that sudden switch to a demonstrative affection I found even more petrifying than his malice, and with a contrite look on his face. 'I didn't

65

mean that, Stephen.'

'Oh yes you did!'

The unnatural roar of my voice and the slam of the rickety door fell like a safety curtain between us, and I picked my way through the muddled rooms of Mallards Point with the detachment of one who has seen a good drama and who now has to face the facts of ordinary life outside the theatre. Mrs Carron-Wilson was scratching mud off her shoes with a twig in the porch, her brightly painted mouth screwed up with distaste. I edged past her as she sat on the top step. There were pale orange freckles on the back of her neck and a crescent of astonishingly white and naked flesh was visible between the sun-tanned skin and the collar of her frock.

'Goodbye,' I said. My voice, I thought, held the right note of valedictory regret mixed with icy purpose. I was leaving Mallards Point for good. But Mrs Carron-Wilson did not appear to notice. The mud came out of the welt of her shoe like a black worm.

'Don't forget about tonight, Stephen. And *make* your father come.'

'I can't . . . he can't . . . '

'Oh, not *again*! You tell him when he's "better" that he's a bore. He won't like that but that is what he is. Tell him I don't love him. What was it Willie Maugham used to tell me about drunks . . . I can't remember. Never mind. It'll come to me when I'm not trying to think. Isn't Fen mud quite the most foul mud there is! There's something about it in one of Mary Butt's stories, something about Ely being hidden in it like a jewel in a toad's head. Except Ely isn't hidden, is it? It sticks up for miles, thank goodness. Let's go over and listen to them singing Taverner next week. It will be good for us and good for them.'

I felt myself choking. 'Goodbye,' I repeated unsteadily. There suddenly seemed so much more to say goodbye to.

She then looked up at me for the first time. 'Goodbye,' she said. Her small eyes were vivid with a mixture of resignation, bravura and courage, and I realised that people had said goodbye to her before.

'For three whole hours!' I laughed jerkily and bent down and touched the top of her head with my lips. Her hair smelt of rain-water and vinegar. When I reached the gate she called out:

'Never mind about telling your father what I said.'

And forgiveness stretched between us in the still afternoon air like a garland.

When I got back to Mallards Point at a little after six Euen and Godfrey had left for Cambridge in the local bus. I recalled now that something had been mentioned about their going to see a film and I felt relieved that they weren't to be present. Lady Tinnington was in the drawing-room. She'd emptied all the flowers from the vases on to pages from *The Times* and was busy re-arranging them. Her birdy legs in their knitted stockings twinkled as she trotted in and out of the kitchen trailing bits of chicken-wire and jugs of clean water. The only other people present were the Nightingale sisters. They sat together on the sofa, beaming and happy. They had brought their latest joint effort detective story for Mrs Carron-Wilson and it nestled in their heap of discarded voile scarfs on the table before them. It was bright yellow and was lettered *This is Death, Ducky*, another great suspense story by Ben Carver. They giggled when they saw me looking at it and then C-W came in and we all began to laugh our congratulations. The Misses Nightingale flushed with genuine modesty. Neither of them had ever quite recovered from the miracle of being able to make close on a thousand pounds a year from such an activity. They pushed up their spectacles and dabbed away at their good-natured, colourless eyes with scratchy handkerchiefs. They were twins and spent all the time when they weren't being Ben Carver bottling fruit for the W I shop in Ely.

Lady Tinnington finished the flowers and we sat there, the five of us, drinking sherry and talking about Cambridge, and I remember C-W saying, as though it was a kind of social duty on her part, 'I *must* get Gwen Raverat over. She's such good value.' I had noticed that none of the celebrities with whom Mrs Carron-Wilson spiced her conversation had ever arrived at Mallards Point, so I just smiled when the others cried, 'Lovely!' and 'Oh, *do* . . . '

She bent forward to pick up the detective story and when she settled back again there was a white flash near the hem of her skirt. I thought it was her slip but when the whiteness persisted in burning against the edge of my vision I stole another rapid glance. Blood pounded in my temples and my fingers seemed to terminate in little islands of delicious, feathery pain. The accidently exposed inside flesh of her thigh faded away into a rich darkness, like the the flesh on the legs of Rembrandt's 'Woman bathing'. Then she moved to pass the novel on to Lady Tinnington and her clothes fell into place. I brought my eyes up to her face, convinced that she must know, only to see that she was unusually relaxed and easy. A ghostly air of girlishness hung about her, defying the comfortable proportions of her somewhat elaborate dress – it had occurred to me before how rarely she wore country clothes. She gave me the slightly roguish look one might give a child and I was mildly affronted. It did not belong to the new role she was about to play in my life. I stretched until my feet made an untidy masculine muddle in front of the half circle of chairs. I was glad I was sprawling, big, ungainly, fair. Euen's repeated remark now seemed a great compliment. I was at the gate of the marvellous adult world and it should be no idiot pick-up who would guide me through, but Mrs Carron-Wilson. In the *Decameron* and in the *Romance of the Rose* generous matrons were always rewarded with the love of gallant striplings.

I felt I had to convey the approaching change in our relationship at once.

'But it's a gorgeous title, darling!' she was exclaiming.

'No it's not. It's terrible. You know it is,' Miss Connie Nightingale was protesting. 'But of course we don't choose them ourselves. *They* do.'

'They have a young man who does nothing else,' said Miss Nancy Nightingale.

'Well, you're still very clever anyway – both of you. Gloriously clever – don't you think so, Stephen?'

I nodded and entangled her in a challenging stare. She returned this with a silently enquiring interest, then, when it made no sense to her, she dropped her eyes and gave the faintest of faint shrugs. I realised that she thought I was hoping to include her in some unspoken mockery of the Nightingales. I blushed and at that moment she looked at me again, as though wanting me to understand that she hadn't meant to snub me. Her small, slightly discoloured teeth were set in the phantom of a smile and for the first time I was struck by the curious amount of gold in her eyes, and that it was this which gave her her touch of animality. I tried to pass through this controlled blaze into the wild awareness behind it. She wrinkled her nose at me and immediately we were both back in our hateful schoolboy-sensible woman positions.

'I don't know why you are all so wonderfully sweet to me,' she said, holding out her stout little arms to include Lady Tinnington, who, unable to sit still for more than five minutes at a time, was busily turning out a revolving bookcase. 'The awful thing about it is, I never read your thrillers – it's no good pretending. But I know they're good. Jimmy Agate and everybody says so. It's just that I've got a blind spot where whodunits are concerned. I'm missing somewhere.'

'Don't explain. We all love you just the same – don't we, Stephen?' Miss Connie's cosy Wind-in-the-Willows face beamed at me.

I hesitated, then I said, '*A sine qua non.*'

Mrs Carron-Wilson gave a rushing, breathless laugh. 'Oh, I hope not. Love should never "go without saying", as it were, or be without its qualifications. Really, Stephen!'

I felt I had made some headway, though goodness knows why. I was plunged into a dream in which her hard little hands were on my body and was dragged back by a friendly, despairing squeezing of my arm and her voice crying:

'Look at him – he hasn't heard a word I've been saying. Now I shall have to start all over again. Molly' (this was Lady Tinnington) 'has let her lodge to a genius. He'll be our *douanier*. They'll be here directly, I've asked them up for drinks.'

'Them?' I said.

'There's a Mrs Douanier. She's going to take standard one in the village school. She'll be worthy, I'm afraid, but we must all be nice to her because of *him.*'

'They just arrived at my house one morning,' explained Lady Tinnington from the carpet, 'and asked was the lodge empty? I said yes it was and had been for heaven knows how long, but that it had light and water and things, and he thought it would do but she couldn't make up her mind. Anyway, they've taken it – they moved in last Thursday. He hasn't got a job, I've just learnt.'

'But he's a poet, Molly, a kind of Clare figure.'

'Oh, I hope not!'

'Well W H Davies then.'

'That's almost as bad. I'm not worrying about the rent, if that is what you're thinking, C-W, I'm worried about *her.*'

'I know she's having a baby. He told me when I met him in the lodge garden. But later on she's going to provide the bread and butter so that he can devote himself to writing. I think it's wonderful, considering the – well – kind of people they are.'

Lady Tinnington banged the dust from a few more books and then she said, 'There's a good bit of ground there. At least they won't want for fruit and vegetables.'

'But he's not fit to garden, Molly! His back hurts when it bends. He told me it did.'

And then she jumped up, ran to the french window and began to wave. 'Hoorah! they have found the right house.' She smoothed her dress over her plump hips and went outside to meet them. No sooner had she disappeared than Lady Tinnington said hurriedly, 'This is going to be awkward. She doesn't understand, bless her. He's a layabout – you've only got to look at him. Oh dear, how horrible I am to say these things. I ought to let you make your own judgement . . .'

When Mrs Carron-Wilson returned she was leading by the hand a prim, quiet-looking woman of about thirty whose advanced pregnancy was clumsily exaggerated by the lumpy folds of a ginger tweed overcoat. She wore a tammy and big, round, silver-rimmed spectacles. Behind the spectacles her eyes strained forward in a mixture of watery perplexity and myopia. There was so great a degree of dullness about her that it drew from one the same kind of dutiful consideration as if she had been physically afflicted, blind or something. We all began to stretch out our hands to her and, like a figure in an Indian temple dance, she turned her hands away from us and locked them loosely above her great belly. She smiled insipidly and blinked. She didn't speak. Behind her was a tall, thin youngish man whose slender legs seemed fixed in a malachite base until he began to shuffle forward, when the dark shine became an enormous pair of well-polished workman's boots, obviously too large for him and uncomfortable. In spite of the mild summery evening he was wrapped up in a melton overcoat, its neck opening showing a neat V of white silk. He was grinning broadly, his lips turned back over a full set of strong brown teeth. It was a grin of foolhardy self-confidence. It stated, blandly and bravely, that he was going to brazen it out in our little community. Here comes the poet, his staring eyes declared. He had too much hair, thick hanks of dark brown hair rolling back from his brow in oily convolutions and a frizzy scrub of yellowish-red hair whose slightly indecent quality puzzled me at first, until all at once I realised that his beard had a pubic texture, as did his little matted eyebrows. I could see that he thought our flutter of concern was for him.

'Don't get up! Don't get up!' he insisted, flapping his hand. Then, seeing Lady Tinnington, 'Hullo-hullo-hullo! Who have we here?'

'Now whom haven't you met? said C-W, and then began to laugh off the introductions in her infectious way. 'This is Miss Nancy Nightingale and this is Miss Constance Nightingale – oh, and this is Stephen. Mr Turp, Mrs Turp,' she finished.

The inevitable catechism followed. Where had they lived, would they like this village did they think? And a hundred other questions. The greatest care was taken not to let them see what we were all wondering, which was what they would live on. Mrs Turp sat near the bookcase and the fat swollen egg of her stomach fascinated me. It was the first time I had really noticed a pregnant woman and now I was able to look at one with an inquisitive detachment and without pity, for I found Mrs Turp herself stupid and despicable. She never uttered a word. She blinked and smiled and shook her head at the sherry. There were ragged patches of brown pigmentation here and there under the flaccid white skin of her face, making it look rather grubby. This, and her Eton-cropped hair, and the square shoulders of her ginger coat, made her slightly monstrous, a travestied youth above the breast-line and a fertility goddess below it. Her bare legs above her ankle socks were polished by the sun.

It was absurd to hear the Nightingales, when they spoke to Mr Turp, going out of their way not to wound a sensitivity which did not exist.

'Then you think that society's obligation towards the artist is a thousand times greater than the artist's obligation towards society?' Miss Nancy was saying. 'I see' she added.

'I certainly think that,' said Mr Turp in his flat Midlands voice. 'I'm an artist and I'm a victim of the system. If society doesn't help me it closes my mouth, and if you close a poet's mouth you murder him.'

'How "help"?' asked Molly Tinnington from the carpet.

Mr Turp hesitated. Two long sherry-flushed ribs of flesh shone below his cheek-bones and the rest of his face was hot and sticky. His eyes were gaudily blue and danced about in their moist sockets.

'Mr Turp means patronage perhaps?' said Miss Connie Nightingale.

'Does he? Is it patronage that you mean, Mr Turp?' Lady Tinnington asked. She was suddenly tortured about their rent for the lodge. Was twelve and six a week beyond them? Had she asked too much? Was poetry going to suffer because of it – or that poor baby?

It was C-W who finally had to discover what everybody in the room wanted to know.

'What *do* you live on actually, Michael?' she asked.

The reverberation set up by the blunt question and the Christian name was still tingling in our ears when Mrs Turp spoke for the first time.

'On me,' she said simply.

I looked at Mr Turp, expecting to see the indignant reaction of a puppet, or to watch him turn pale with fear or redder than he already was with anger, only to see him looking amused – even pleased. Then the Cambridge bus squealed to a standstill outside and Euen and Godfrey raced into the room. In the confusion C-W's *savoir-faire* collapsed completely. She was seized with a violent fit of *rire-étouffé* and as Euen and Godfrey succumbed in languorous sprawls on the sofa cushions she fled from the room.

'It's the coffee!' I said, running after her. 'I'll give a hand. It must be boiled away.'

She was standing with her back to the Welsh dresser and shaking with the laughter which still had not managed to force its way out of her and as I passed, grinning a good deal myself, she put out her hand and clung to me for support. We rocked together in a sweet conspiracy of mockery. The peculiar tension of the evening vanished and the curious feeling that our standards had been debased and made to look pretentious disappeared.

'Do you know what?' I murmured in her ear, which was just beneath my chin.

'No. What?'

'I think he's the end.'

She stopped the gentle cosy rocking and said, 'No, no. You mustn't say that. Anyway, it's not just them I'm laughing at but all of us. I suddenly saw all our faces. So solemn! Well, at least he's nice to look at.'

'*Nice*?'

'Uh-huh. A nice red fox with his head in the hen-run.'

She brushed the crook of her little finger up under her lashes to brush the tears from her mascara, a little feminine movement of hers which I always found overwhelmingly endearing. Her other hand still rested lightly on my arm just above the wrist. From her hair rose the fresh rain-water and vinegar smell, its innocence in flagrant conflict with the scent she was wearing. Stooping quickly, I kissed her but my mouth slipped on her soft powdery skin and my determined second kiss landed harmlessly near her eye. The rest of my kisses were a confusion as her head twisted and turned and the gold flickered in her half-closed eyes. It was a muddle of faces and breathing and my disappointment was intense. Then an almost paralysing degree of consciousness returned as the hand she had against my waist ran between my jacket and my shirt. She gave a little gasp and hugged me and for a second her firm round body touched mine all the way down. There was a scalding sensation as the lively, scratchy fingers trailed across my buttocks and raced along my thigh, and then we were each yards away from one another, driven apart by some hateful sanity. The place where her breasts had crushed against my shirt-front felt cold and neglected, and I knew that I desired C-W as much as I had once wanted her to desire me. None of this took much more than a minute.

When she said, 'We'll use those pink cups Euen won at the fair last year', her voice was steady and normal – not even tinged with that post-*contretemps* note of wistful regret. Yet I knew that what had happened was hurting her and would continue to hurt her for as long as she believed she had hurt me.

'And let's have that tray we got from the Omega Workshop,' she said.

We returned to the confused babble of the drawing room. The Misses Nightingale had seized hold of each other's wrists and were staring at the time. Lady Tinnington was fiddling with the wireless, and gaudy bellows of Walton's *Belshazzar's Feast* broke in upon the talk. Euen and Godfrey were squashed up on the window seat and chattering softly in mutually amused voices, though what about it was impossible to tell. They had turned themselves into an island – a favourite trick of theirs. Mrs Turp, her spectacles shimmering in the lamplight, sat and stared into a void. I could hear Mr Turp talking loudly and indistinctly above the general hubbub. He had taken off the melton overcoat at last, though not the scarf, which hung with ecclesiastic nicety in two snowy parallels over his frowsty jacket. C-W pressed into this uproar, vaguely and dreamily, and I followed with the coffee tray. Her speckled golden shoulders and arms, and her languorous movements reflected a cat-like repose and *douceur*, each a strange repudiation of her normal vivacity. I felt half-suffocated with lust, desire and love, as well as elated that I constituted for her at least one of these things. It didn't seem to matter which. I edged in front to hand round the cups. When it came to her cup I steadied myself to meet her gaze. To my astonishment her eyes were fixed on Michael Turp as he half sat, half squatted in the tub chair, his long, straight legs rushing out of it in two shiny serge peninsulas.

'Christianity has failed. Do *you* know why it has failed?' he shouted at Lady Tinnington. 'Well, I'll tell you. It has failed because it has substituted the cup of blood for the pillar of blood.'

He lurched back, immensely pleased with himself.

'That sounds very much like the kind of remark D H Lawrence told me,' said Lady Tinnington. 'Only he put those kind of remarks into his books, not into his conversation.' Her tone was crushing. She wasn't certain that what she had said was true but she felt she had to beat her way out of the vulgarity of the evening somehow.

'Bravo!' said C-W, though not at Lady Tinnington's statement, which she affected not to have heard, but at Mr Turp's epigram. And from that moment, and during the weeks that followed, we each had to fight for our friendship with C-W. Even my father fought. I had not reckoned on his affection for the evenings at Mallards Point. 'Damn' layabout!' he snuffled. 'Only time when you can get C-W alone these days is when he's in Ely drawin' the dole. Too good-hearted, that's what she is. Feller takes advantage y'know.'

As for myself, I sincerely believed that I was heartbroken and acted accordingly. I mooned around her and carefully worked out little ways in which we might come into seemingly accidental physical contact. But the old free and easy intimacy had vanished for myself as well as for the others. Meanwhile, C-W concentrated on the great task of launching her protégé. She was deliberately mysterious about his work. 'We would see,' she said. Eventually, under Lady Tinnington's blunt insistence, a sheaf of grubby ruled paper pinned together by one of J L Wilson's bulldog clips was handed to us. Silently, amazedly, we passed them round the room. The poems were scrawled in large uneven pencilled letters. They were formless, badly spelt and frequently indecent. They left one a trifle frightened and speechless.

'They're only the roughs of course,' C-W told us. There was no hint of apology or explanation in her voice. She folded them carefully and replaced them in her bureau. As we walked down the lane – she was on her way to the Turps' lodge – she drew me aside and said:

'Stephen dear, there's something I've been meaning to tell you. The boys are off to Cornwall tomorrow as you know. So – well, what I mean is, don't feel that you have to waste your summer holiday by entertaining us old fogies at Mallards Point. It's nice for us, of course, but it must often be ghastly dull for you.'

'When will they be back?' I asked, not really caring but unable to think of anything else to say. I felt ashamed and humiliated.

'The twenty-eighth, as usual.'

We came to the lodge and through the open window I could see Mrs Turp, static and motionless. She didn't even look up when C-W called, 'Coo-ee!'

For more than a fortnight I kicked my heels round the village, playing tennis at the rectory, rowing with my father and bicycling along the tedious black Fenland roads in the August heat. Two days before Euen and Godfrey returned from their holidays I went for a long walk and came back along the road which led past Mallards Point, and rather than risk being seen I strolled along the field path which ran parallel with the garden wall, and led to the river. I thought I would climb the wall, at the bottom, cross the tangled garden and make my way home across the park. The sun was brassy and nothing moved except the heat mist on the distant water-meadows. When I was within a few yards of the river I climbed the orange brick wall. Espaliered pears and apricots had run riot and made a dense fringe above the parapet. I sat among the pear leaves with my feet dangling in the brown cool branches and looking down into the dear, familiar garden, noting the creeper-bound fair horses and cockerels, the peeling white greenhouse and the uncut lawns. I wondered if C-W's battered punt was still moored to its willow. To see the water I had to stand up on the wall and keep my balance by clinging to the twigs.

Swaying unsteadily, I peered through the ripening fruit into the still and mysterious depths of a Giorgione. The river was a hard metallic aquamarine and the punt was soldered to it by the intense blackish gold sunlight. Rushes were stacked at its fringe like green weapons. They cast long stabbing shadows on the bank. Two figures lying on the bank had their heads in the darkest of these shadows and their white, nerveless nakedness sprawling on the grass had a tragic quality, like the torsos of lovers who had been discovered and decapitated. The man had a delicate marbled refinement, his limbs were long and slender and very white. A watch glittered on his wrist. He was smoking and one pale arm rose and fell. The woman had wandered into the Giorgione mystery by mistake. She was one of Rubens' crushed-raspberry-and-milk Sabines. Her rich shapeless flesh was heaped on the ground and in the ruthless sunlight demanded pity.

Suddenly the youth propped himself up on his elbow. The effect of Mr Turp's mottled bearded head on the pure classical shoulders was grotesque. He was angry and his flat voice reverberated in the motionless afternoon. I slipped from the wall into the neighbouring field, my heart beating wildly.

'What do you mean, "it can't go on"?'

C-W's voice hovered between common sense and sentiment in the way

75

I had always found enchanting.

'You know exactly what I mean, Michael. I don't have to go over everything again. The boys are coming home on Thursday, and well, the holidays are over. Let's leave it like that.'

'Let's leave it like that, eh!' He imitated her speech. 'Let's leave it that you've had your bit of fun and I can go to hell!'

There was a defensive argument by C-W which I couldn't catch and then I heard her cry out, 'Michael, oh, Michael!'

But although I knew she was alone and weeping by the water I didn't go to her because her tears had no relevance for me. Though I did go to Mallards Point the following week-end. We were all present except the poet, his wife and my father, who was poorly.

'I must get Rose Macaulay to come down,' said C-W. 'She's *such* good value . . .'

* * * * *

Shorelines

Julia Blackburn lives with her family in Suffolk and is the author of nine books, most of them a mixture of biography, travel and what Blackburn calls 'thinking aloud'. They include *The Emperor's Last Island, Daisy Bates In The Desert, The Book Of Colour* and her most recent work *Old Man Goya*, published earlier this year. *The Mermaid*, set on the Norfolk coast in the area around Holkham and Stiffkey during the middle ages, is taken from her novel *The Leper's Companions* (1999) in which the leper and a group of villagers set out from their remote fishing community on a long and arduous pilgrimage to the Holy Land. A similar piece first appeared in *Granta: The Sea* (1998).

The Mermaid

JULIA BLACKBURN

There was a village not far from where she lived. It was close to the sea and when the tide was out the shallow water was pulled back to reveal a huge expanse of rippling sand. The place had such a quality of silence and emptiness to it that sometimes, especially at night, she could find quiet just by imagining herself there. She would walk in her mind across the sand, feeling its ridges under her bare feet and she would look at the sea and be comforted.

At one end of the village was a very old church; a yew tree stood close to the entrance gate, wild flowers bloomed among the grass, the gravestones were pockmarked by lichen and the weather. A mermaid with sharp teeth and a lascivious smile was carved above the east door and a man with leaves in his hair leered down from a corner of the roof and vomited a stream of water from his open mouth when it was raining.

The air inside the church was damp and cold even on a summer's day and the light had a dim underwater quality to it. A fragment of the original stained glass had survived in one of the windows. It showed an angel with narrow seagull wings sprouting from his back and pointed feathers covering the nakedness of his body. His feet were bare with long toes and he was marooned on a little patch of black and white tiled floor with an expanse of plain glass all around him. The expression on his face was gentle and compassionate, and sometimes she would sit beside him in her thoughts until their eyes met across the infinite space that divided them and she was comforted.

And then one night in the month of February when the east wind was bitterly cold and she felt so sad she didn't know what to do, she found herself going down the main street of the village. The ground beneath her feet was as hard as rock and deeply rutted by the wheels of carts. The houses on either side of her were small and battered; they reminded her of the nests of birds, as if something like a swallow could have made them from river silt and twigs. The church was newly built, the stones yellow and clean. Everything was different to how she had known it and yet she was shocked by the sense of intense familiarity that surrounded her, the sense of coming home.

Following a path that led to the sea, she reached a rickety wooden hut and a few fishing boats. She accidentally trod on a pile of empty oyster shells and felt them splintering under her feet.

A dog with pale eyes watched as she approached and that surprised her because she had somehow presumed there would be no life here, nothing apart from the shifting of wind and sunlight and the movement of the waves.

She sat with her back to the hut and looked out across the shimmering expanse of sand and sea. 'I have left one place and come to another,' she thought to herself. 'I have stepped out of the time I was in and now I will be here for a while, until things change and pass.'

I was sitting with my back propped against a wooden hut and I was lost in thought, although if anyone had asked me what I was thinking about I would not have had an answer. I was drifting in the dark while all around me the sun was bright and the sky was blue and the air was filled with that yearning cry of seabirds which can so easily bring me close to tears.

Far away on the glistening sand I saw the silhouetted figure of a man bending over something that lay heaped at his feet. It could have been part of a wrecked ship, the trunk of a tree, a bundle of sail. It could have been a fish or a seal or even a person drowned and washed ashore by the tide.

I knew I could pull the whole image nearer to me just by concentrating on it and then I would understand what was happening, but for the moment I chose to leave it undisturbed. Even from this distance I could sense that the man was fascinated by the thing he had found, but afraid of it as well.

I became aware of someone sitting next to me, his back also leaning against the hut. It was an old man busy mending the broken mesh of a fishing net and singing to himself in a soft monotone as he struggled with the task. His fingers were bunched together like the feet of dead birds and I could feel the tiredness in them, and the ache. I knew that in a few days he would be setting out alone in a boat and he would never return to this place, but for now he was here in the sunshine with the sound of his own voice echoing around his head.

I got up and followed the path that led to the village. Mud as hard as stone and grass burnt yellow by the last frost. Nervous chickens scratching for food, a goat tethered to a post, a pig in a pen and a dog with pale eyes watching me. There were people here as well and I could recognise each one of their restless faces, although I could not necessarily put a name to them. Even the smiling mermaid carved above the church door and the man with a wide mouth through which the rainwater streamed were as familiar to me as the details of my own life.

The first to move close was a young woman called Sally, the fisherman's daughter. She had gap teeth, rough awkward hands, and a round moon face in which the shadows of her own uncertainty were clearly visible. She blushed easily and I could feel how the sudden heat swept across the surface of her skin, making her tremble with confusion.

The shoemaker's wife was next, with big breasts and softly curling hair, her body heavy with the weight of the baby she was carrying: an elbow pushing sharp against the inside of her womb, a head poised above the bone cup of the pelvis, ready for the slow fall. Only a few more days and the process of birth would begin. This was to be her last child.

Her husband the shoemaker was there working at his bench, his shoulders hunched forward. He looked tired and the blindness which would make him feel cut off from the world was already closing in, tightening its grip. The priest was standing silently beside him, staring towards me but not seeing me. I recognised him as the angel from the church window, but then again as someone I had once known long ago.

Which was when I saw the leper, or to be more precise, I heard him, since it was the beating of the wooden clapper that warned me of his approach. He was just passing the boundary stone close to the last house and was walking straight towards me. His body was draped in a long brown cloak and his face was shielded by a hood.

The leper was the only one here who was a complete stranger to me. I knew nothing about where he had come from or where he was going. I had no idea of what he had looked like before he became ill or how badly he had been disfigured by the sickness. He walked past me without saying a word and was gone.

I went back along the path that led to the wooden hut and the fishing boats. I had decided to see what it was that the man had found washed up by the tide.

The man was poised in indecision, staring at the thing which lay heaped at his feet. I saw then that it was not a human corpse, or the trunk of a

81

tree, or a bundle of sail that he had found, but a mermaid. She was lying face down, her body twisted into a loose curl, her hair matted with scraps of seaweed.

The year was fourteen hundred and ten, and it was very early in the morning, with the sun pushing its way gently through a covering of mist that floated aimlessly over the land and the water.

The man had never seen a mermaid before except for the one carved in stone above the east door of the church. She had very pointed teeth and a double tail like two soft and tapering legs, while this one had a single tail which could have belonged to a large halibut or a cod.

The man stepped forward and squatted down beside her. The pattern of her interlinking scales glinted with an oily light. He stroked them along the direction in which they lay and they were wet and slippery, leaving a coating of slime on his palm. But when his hand moved over the pale skin of her back it was dry and cold and rough as a cat's tongue.

He lifted a hank of dark hair, feeling its weight. Little translucent shrimps were tangled within its mesh and struggling to free themselves. A yellow crab scuttled around the curve of the waist and dropped out of sight.

He hesitated for a moment, but then he took hold of the mermaid's shoulders and rolled her over. The sand clung in patches on her body like a map of some forgotten country. Her nipples were as red as sea anemones. Her navel was deep and round. Her eyes were wide open and as blue as the sky could ever be. As he gazed at her, a lopsided smile drifted over her face.

He had presumed that she was dead and with the shock of finding her alive he let out a cry and jumped to his feet. He turned and began to run as fast as he could over the ridges of muddy sand and towards the village.

I watched as he trampled on the grey scrub of sea lavender and the low samphire bushes, their thin skins so easily broken. But he trod more carefully once he had reached the strip of pale stones littered with the sharp empty shells of clams and oysters, and with his heart thumping in his throat he was beside the fishing boats and the wooden hut battered out of shape by the north wind.

The old fisherman was sitting there just as before, his legs stretched out stiffly in front of him and his bones aching. He made no response when the young man tried to explain what the sea had thrown on to the land; he didn't even raise his head to look at the speaker.

The young man ran on again until he arrived at the first house of the village. The shoemaker's wife was standing by the door, her arms cradling her huge belly.

'There is a mermaid!' he said to her, but she was lost in thought and hardly heard him, although her baby lurched violently inside her womb as if shocked by the news. She remembered that later.

The man went into the house and from a back room he fetched one of those narrow wooden spades that are used for digging lugworms. Then he returned by the way he had come. He meant to bury the mermaid even if she was still alive and his task made him walk slowly now, with the solemnity of an executioner.

He looked out across the expanse of sand shimmering like an ocean of calm water. He saw how a flock of gulls had settled into a noisy mass on the place where the mermaid was lying, and as he drew closer they lifted, screaming and turning into the air.

But the mermaid had gone. Nothing remained of her except for a single lock of dark hair which resembled a ribbon of torn seaweed.

Nevertheless the man dug a hole as deep as a grave: the salty water seeping into it, the sides crumbling away and seeming to melt like snow. And as he dug the surface brightness of the sand was replaced by greasy layers of black and grey mud smelling of age and decay.

When the hole was ready he picked up the hair and dropped it in, covering it over quickly and stamping it down. He marked the place with a big black stone.

That evening he sat with the old fisherman, drinking from a jug of beer and going over the story of what he had seen and what he had done. During the night his wife Sally shook him awake because she could hear the sound of a woman crying, desperate and inconsolable. On the following morning a cow died for no good reason and the shoemaker's wife gave birth to a baby with the head of a monstrous fish which only lived for a few hours.

Everyone agreed that this must be the mermaid's fault and they told the priest to do something. So the priest went with the man to where the hair was buried. He took a holy candle with him which kept on going out in the wind and he had a bottle of holy water to sprinkle over the sand. In his spidery handwriting he had copied three paternosters on to a scrap of vellum and he tucked these under the black stone while reciting a prayer to protect them all from harm.

After that things were quiet again for a while, but it was as if a lid had been clamped down on a pot that was bound to boil over sooner or later. The mermaid had disturbed the pattern of life in the village and people waited with growing apprehension for what might follow.

The man who had stroked her rough skin had a dream in which she slithered over his body like a huge eel and wrapped her tail tight around his legs. He was crying when he woke up. He kept on stumbling against her image in a corner of his mind. Whenever he went out with his boat he would hope to find her glistening among the fish he had caught in his nets. He began to travel farther and farther from the shore, searching for her.

The old fisherman stopped mending his nets. His hands were stiff and painful and he laid them side by side on his lap, the fingers bunched together like the feet of dead birds.

For as long as he kept singing he was cocooned in images: he was out at sea among the rolling waves of a storm, the backs of whales and silver fishes breaking through the surface of the water all around him. A catch of living things was thrashing at his feet in the boat, struggling for breath. But then as soon as his voice was silent, he was only here, frail in the sunshine and thinking about his daughter Sally.

She was not yet fifteen but already pregnant with her first child. The old fisherman was afraid that the birth might kill her and with that thought he realized he could not bear to lose her. She was what connected him to the village and to the land itself and if she was gone he would be homeless.

Every night he dreamed of his fear. He saw her as a child giving birth to a child much bigger than she was. He saw her body split open like a ripe seedpod and a mass of maggot babies crawling over her, eating her flesh until there was nothing left but clean white bones. He told no one of these dreams because that would only make them more solid and more dangerous.

Sometimes in the morning he would wake to imagine finding her beside his bed, a tiny moonfaced child who had just learned to walk, staring at him with all the tenderness and seriousness of the very young.

He rarely went out to sea these days, but when he did, Sally was the one who waited for his return. She would stand on the beach pulling at the thread which connected them as if he were a fish on a line.

Her husband was also uneasy about what was happening to her; the skin of her swollen belly luminous and blue, so that you could see every detail of the vast creature inhabiting her.

He gave her oily herrings to eat, saying the oil would help the baby slip out. He lay awake at night, watching her in the moonlight, her face flickering with shifting emotions, now peaceful, now in despair.

The straw of the mattress rustled as she moved and turned. She often talked in her sleep, although he could never understand what she was saying. He stroked her damp skin and as he did so she sometimes became the mermaid lying next to him, rough and cold and smiling, with hair that wrapped itself around his fingers.

On the morning when the waters broke and soaked into the straw they fetched the woman who knew how to deliver babies. She brought a flask of water that had been used to wash the hands of a murderer, ground pepper to help with the contractions, and a greasy salve smelling of rancid butter to rub over the tight belly.

The yellow sunlight flickered on the walls of the room and the bed creaked when the girl was thrown sideways with the first spasm of pain.

'You have to let go,' the midwife said. 'It will be easier once you have let go.'

She unplaited Sally's flat hair and spread it loose across her shoulders. She opened the lid of a wooden chest and took out the few clothes and the sheepskin rug it contained, scattering them over the floor. She opened the door of a cupboard and removed a bundle of knotted ropes that had been left there, carefully undoing the knots and laying the pieces in straight lines. The spasms continued and became more violent than ever.

Sally's husband was sitting in the room next door, close to the smoking fire, gutting herrings and rubbing them with salt. When he heard his wife screaming he sharpened his blade and continued with his work.

Her father was down by the shore but he heard the screams as well. They echoed in his head like the cries of the seabirds.

He rose slowly to his feet and walked to the church. Pushing the door open, he went to stand in front of the painting of Margaret of Antioch, the saint who is able to help women in labour.

The painting was done on wood in rich dark colours. It was divided into six squares, and each square showed a stage of the saint's life. In the first square Margaret was cast out of her house by her cruel father and you could see her walking into the hills with her head bowed. In the second square the Roman Patriarch, whose name the fisherman could not remember, tried to rape her, but she resisted him. In the third square she was hung on a rack that was similar to the racks used in the village for drying fish. Two soldiers were scraping at her body with an iron hook so that the bones were revealed, and the blood fell from her like red water. Next she was put into prison and the bars of her cage were all around her.

While she was in prison the Devil appeared in the form of a green dragon and with its hot breath it sucked the saint into its mouth. You could see her standing with bare feet on the soft red tongue, the row of teeth hanging down above her like icicles around the eaves of a house. But now that she was inside the body of the dragon she held up an iron cross and spoke the name of God. The dragon exploded and she was delivered safely back into the world and out of danger.

The old fisherman stood there in the dim light of the church, gazing at the white face of the saint, at her gold halo like the sun at harvest time, at the dragon's scaly skin, the teeth, the blood. And he began to sing the story of what was happening. He sang the saint out of the sorrow of leaving home, out of the fear of rape. He gave her courage when the metal hook bit into her flesh. He comforted her in the loneliness of the prison and he prayed for her when she was trapped inside the dragon's body until he could feel her breaking through and escaping.

When the story was completed he told the saint that if his daughter survived he would show his thanks by setting out as a pilgrim to Jerusalem. He would go in a boat across the North Sea and then he would walk to Venice, where a ship could take him to the port of Jaffa. From there he knew it was not far to the Holy City. If he died on the way he would accept that the saint was exchanging his life for his daughter's.

He returned to the house and went to sit by the fire next to his son-in-law. The noise had subsided and everything was poised in the quiet of anticipation. The midwife appeared with blood on her clothes and said the two men could enter the bedroom. There they found Sally as limp as a fish with a little baby suckling at her breast.

Her father fulfilled the vow he had made to Saint Margaret. He left early one morning and his boat faded from sight as it approached the horizon.

Before he went he explained to Sally what it was that he had to do. She did not disagree with him or try to make him stay, but as soon as he had gone she was as desolate as a child for whom the present moment has no end.

Her husband spent more and more time out at sea searching for the mermaid, coming back with his nets empty. Finally he did not come back at all for several days. Sally found him washed up by the tide, naked and cold, not far from the black stone under which the lock of hair was buried.

* * * * *

86

Passage Migrants

D J TAYLOR

Come mid-August the light in Sheringham began to change. In the past it had hung in duck-egg blues and greys over the warm summer sand. Now it had turned gun-metal: cloudy even when there was no cloud. Morris watched it again that morning as he stood in the big, untidy room that looked out on to the beach, pulling a hand uncertainly over the three days of stubble on his chin. On the couch, a yard or two distant from the high windows, snug under blankets and Morris's old parka jacket, the girl from the Marine Ballroom slept soundly on, orange hair thrown back over a makeshift pillow of supermarket bags.

It was about half-past eight. Outside there were terns massed on the sandbar: two hundred of them at least, Morris calculated. Further out, beyond the upturned boats and the wreck of a giant sandcastle built three days before, gulls skirmished over the breakers. Once, at dusk on a day such as this, Morris had seen what he assumed was a purple heron rooting through driftwood in the shallows, but for some reason the hastily-palmed camera had realised only vague shapes of grey and cobalt, the bird itself gathered up and lost in shadow. Thinking of the heron made him remember the figure on the couch. Morris hadn't meant to come home with the girl from the Marine ballroom. To find her there eight hours later, pinched face white against the black cushions, was to register a troubling shift in routine, like setting out along the coast path on the cliff to find it strewn with granite blocks from the sea defences.

Traipsing along the sea front on his way to get a paper – the door slammed sharply behind him by way of a hint – Morris watched the tern armies huddled against the breeze. In an hour or so they would head north to the flats at Cley or Brancaster. He walked back the way he had come, noting other routines that were undisturbed: fishermen hauling

87

crab boats over the shale; an ice-cream van being restocked from a delivery truck; dog-walkers silhouetted against the shore line. Back at the flat he found the girl from the Marine Ballroom sitting at the big deal table wearing one of his old tee-shirts and eating slices of unbuttered toast.

'This bread must be a week old,' she said. 'Look, it's got green bits growing out of it.'

Her hair was redder then he'd thought, Morris realised: a kind of scarlet orange with magenta tints. Seeing it bobbing above the table-top nonplussed him. It was outside his range. There was a rucksack he hadn't noticed yet, half-open on the floor and spilling books and tissues out over the sandy hardboard.

'Nice place you've got here,' the girl went on. 'Apart from the cafeteria.'

Morris reckoned she must be a year or two younger than himself: twenty-two maybe, or twenty-three. He lingered for a moment by the window, gently lashing the sill with the furled copy of the *Cromer Mercury*, meditating another hint.

'Where are you staying?'

'The Beeches. Out on the Holt Road. I don't suppose you know how to get there?'

Morris nodded. Everyone in Sheringham knew about The Beeches. On Friday nights Range Rovers drove out from Norwich, Cambridge – even as far as London – dropping off gangs of moneyed teenagers at the gate. Two years ago there had been a scandal when a girl drowned in the swimming pool. Still rapping the sill with the newspaper, he gave directions. Beyond the window the sky threatened rain.

'I've to go to work,' he said, casting out the final hint.

'That's OK. I'll let myself out.'

Morris left her there among the mouldy bread-crusts, the stacked crockery and the copies of *Norfolk Bird Club Bulletin*. Looking up at the window a moment or two later, as the flock of terns swept northward over his head, he could see her moving beyond the glass: a ball of orange flame bleeding into the nondescript greys and fawns behind.

Down at the marina they were gearing up for the late-summer rush. Mr Silverton thought the season would last another fortnight. Then the schools would go back and the trippers start to disappear. Morris sold ice-cream, mended a catch that had come off one of the fun-pool cubicles and retrieved a walkman that someone had dropped into the deep end. At the mid-morning break he and Doug, the other assistant, sat and smoked cigarettes on upturned crates in the yard, hunched against the tubs of chlorine and the rusty generator spares, while Mr Silverton came down from the upstairs office and took a turn at the front desk. Outside fine rain fell against the Perspex dividing wall and they could see the shapes of the holidaymakers clustered against the big overhanging sign that said SHERINGHAM'S NEWEST INDOOR AQUATIC EXPERIENCE.

Curiously, the girl – her name was Alice, he now remembered – was there again at lunchtime. From his eyrie above the soft drinks dispenser, where the wiring had begun to come away from the wall, he noticed her turning over the rubbish in the bargain swimwear trays that Mr Silverton bought in job lots on the back of Norwich market: nonchalantly, but with an undisguised sense of purpose. When she saw him she came over and stood by the dispenser, waiting for him to descend.

'Does it always rain like this? In this part of the world, I mean.'

Out of the corner of his eye he could see Doug regarding him sardonically from the desk. 'Pretty much.'

'Do you get a lunch break?'

'It's another half an hour.'

Waiting in the foyer while he sold tickets to a cub pack superintended by two mountainous Akelas, she looked oddly out of place, Morris thought, like one of the birds you saw at the big reserves further up the coast: blown off course, not sure what the food was like or whether the natives were friendly. They had a ploughman's in one of the pubs along the front, in a small room hemmed in by fishing nets and ancient lobster shells. Alice was a student, taking a year out between degrees. Mostly she lived at her parents' house in London, but there was talk of Edinburgh, Exeter, places even further flung. There were other people from The Beeches in the pub: two girls in striped men's shirts and sunglasses and a boy carrying a copy of *A History of Western Philosophy*. At intervals their mobile phones went off, and they fished unselfconsciously in bags and pockets to answer them. Bored with the conversation, Morris stared out over the beach and its flotsam: marauding bands of children, an old man in an antique bathing dress tottering gamely towards the sea. 'There's a party on Wednesday at the house,' Alice said, when he got up to go. 'Why don't you come along?' 'I'll do that,' Morris said. Wednesday was the day he worked late.

Back at the marina he found Mr Silverton cross-legged on the floor beside the ice-cream cabinet, surrounded by a pile of melting choc-ices and sky-ray lollies, trying to mend an electrical fault. He was a plumpish, middle-aged man with thick, brindled hair like a badger, whom Morris and Doug had christened "The Fatman". 'There's a bloke in the foyer wants to know about a party booking for the Bank Holiday,' he said, without looking up. 'You'd better go and talk to him.' Heading off to reception, Morris found that Alice's pale parched face, the flock of terns on the beach, had mysteriously coalesced in his head, so much so as to displace the other things that burned there.

The afternoon wore on. Mr Silverton finished repairing the ice-cream cabinet and went off to do errands in town.

'What happens here in winter?' Morris wondered over their tea-break.

Doug, who lived down the coast at Cromer, nodded at the imputation of local expertise. 'You ever been here in November Morrie boy? Half the shops shut down. Fatman takes six weeks in Torremolinos. Day a week maintenance for the likes of us, if we're lucky.'

Though we would never dream of interfering, Morris's sister Julie had written a couple of days before from her house in Slough, *Gary and I feel it is time you faced up to your responsibilities*. It all depended on what your responsibilities were, Morris thought. He had a memory of walking through the front door in Slough a year before and Gary instantly asking him to wipe his feet. There was a fifty pence piece lying on the scuffed lino beneath the reception desk, and he picked it up and put it in the till.

'Soft bugger, you are,' Doug said, without malice. Outside an ice-cream van's klaxon rose like an air-raid warning over the silent streets.

Late summer came. Waking up in the flat, Morris could feel the time slipping away, like sand from the high dunes falling out of his hands, down to the distant beach. Alice had left a paperback novel behind her on the couch: puzzling, unrecognisable spoor, about a group of girls sharing a flat in Bayswater. Morris examined it a couple of times before he handed it back. There was nothing in it that he could fasten on, still less any clue to Alice. In the evenings they went exploring the empty Norfolk back-lanes to Holt, Happisburgh and Burnham Market. Here there were unexpected surprises: two blind men playing chess in a café near Wells; an artist in a graveyard near Gresham busily transforming the church into a terrifying surrealist skyscraper; an older world, turned in on itself, inviolate. Julie wrote again, gossip and warnings jumbled together. The children were doing well at school. His mother was ill. There was a bed for him whenever he wanted it. On the Bank Holiday it rained for seven hours. Mr Silverton sat at the reception desk ostentatiously leafing his way through travel agents' brochures. Doug had disappeared, gone off to Norwich or working at Yarmouth funfair: nobody quite knew. Julie's letters lay face-up on the deal table, covered with beer can ring-pulls and postcards of Sheringham seafront. 'Do you ever write back?' Alice wondered, putting a pack of groceries down on the floor. She had taken to buying him things, Morris registered: bags of sugar; men's magazines; Mars bars. There was a soft, proprietorial air to the way she moved round the flat. 'What are you doing at the weekend?' he asked, on a whim. 'Nothing.' 'There's somewhere we could go,' he explained. 'Somewhere I haven't shown you.' 'OK,' Alice said. 'I like surprises.' Morris could see that she was intrigued, that it was the right thing to have done.

'Next week,' Alice said, as they sped out on the coast road that Sunday, 'I shall have to be getting back. Really and truly.' Morris nodded, hoping that this would absolve him from speech. There were teal flying alongside the car, a long line of them heading north to the Wash. The sanctuary at Titchwell was just as he remembered it: a pinewood shop selling bird books and pairs of binoculars, elderly men in waders and soft felt hats drinking coffee out of thermos flasks in the yard. On the sheet of card tacked to the wall there were details of the passage migrants: stone curlews, avocets, an osprey that had flown in that morning with a Swedish ring tag round one of its claws. Later they wandered off along the path to the sea, past the twitchers' hides and the observation points. The light had gone grey again, Morris saw, turning the sky the colour of the filing cabinets in Mr Silverton's office.

'What was that?' Alice wondered, tugging suddenly at his sleeve. Morris felt rather than saw the blur of movement at his feet – like a brightly-coloured paper bag, he thought later, lofted skywards by the wind. Watching it come to rest, a dozen yards down the path, orange crest bobbing above the dark wings, he felt a surge of exhilaration. 'It's a hoopoe,' he said. 'Look! I never saw one before.' There was a file of middle-aged women in mackintoshes coming along the path towards them. Boxed in, the hoopoe took flight again, westward over the salt marshes. Morris watched it go. Not long after it began to rain again and they retired to the car. 'That festival I was telling you about in Devon,' Alice said briskly. 'Once I've parked my stuff in town I'm off down there.

You ought to come.' Morris stared through the streaming window as the bird-watchers' cars manoeuvred through the mud. The hoopoe would be somewhere over the north sea now, far away from the cam-corders and the binocular arcs, out where he couldn't follow. 'Sorry,' he said, seeing the beach in winter, snow on the breakers, blanketing the rock pools in soft white fur. 'Things to do.'

* * * * *

Elspeth Barker was married to the poet George Barker and has lived for many years in north Norfolk on the Blickling estate. Her first novel *O Caledonia*, published to great acclaim in 1991, was shortlisted for the Whitbread First Novel award and won the David Higham Prize. *Carborundum* was prompted some years ago by a report in *The Guardian* on the death, in similar circumstances, of an elderly Yarmouth resident. The progression of saints and huntsmen in *Missing*, (page 198) which was published last year in *New Writing 10*, first emerged during repairs to two ancient houses near Norwich.

Carborundum

ELSPETH BARKER

She was perfecting her wintry smile in a hand mirror tarnished with verdigris. The face that looked back at her was white as snow, or chalk rather, powdery. When she ran her hands down her cheeks, smoothing away the excess, it settled in a fine dust over her shoulders. The wind whisked long hanks of grizzled hair across her eyes and a cold sun dazzled her. She reached beneath the tarpaulin and withdrew her mother's old magenta jumper. It was shrunken now and felted with the years of damp and dews, but it provided just enough protection for this November afternoon. Carefully she lowered her legs over the edge of the platform and began the slow descent, breathing a little heavily now as the soles of her boots tested, then found purchase on the slippery ladder rungs. As always, she felt a flicker of relief when she reached the carpet of beech nut husks and sodden leaves.

She dragged the high old pram out of the shed and set forth along the cliff track, gripping the handle tightly, bent against the wind. Beneath, the sea prowled back and forth, complaining.

When she trudged along like this, she was able to think, or, more importantly, remember. Up in her trees she was too busy; life hung on a concatenation of infinitely laborious small tasks, and as she grew older, everything took longer. This was how she wanted it to be. She was eking out existence, waiting to go. For others all things might be passing, but for her all things long since had passed. And the fact that she generally remembered the same things did not trouble her. For so long things had been the same, two separate samenesses, one more detailed than the other. Thirty years rotting away with mother, thirty years in the trees. Was there a story at all, a shape? Is there ever?

The lofty rocking motion of the ancient perambulator had perhaps been a foreshadow of the swaying beech tree branches, systole and diastole of wind and weather, the rhythms of her world; for as an infant she had occupied this very vehicle, propped on lace edged pillows of cambric, propelled back and forth by adoring relatives. Who had all died. Except, of course, for mother, who had died later, far too late and had certainly not adored her. Even now, the thought of her mother made her knuckles strain white under their carapace of rough red skin, brown blotches, veins serpentine and glaucous. 'Won't you ever take pride in your appearance, Marjory?' demanded a ghostly voice. 'Look at your hands. Anyone would think you were a skivvy.' Her heart then had cried out in silence that she was indeed a skivvy, enslaved by a cold and cruel despot who had tricked her into servitude and would not ever release her.

The summer when she had finished boarding school and was about to go to university she had found herself consumed by a great weariness, headaches and shooting pains, so that she could scarcely get out of bed, could not eat, could not speak. The doctor said she had brain fever and she must rest for a long time or it would not go away. How mother's eyes shone; she was sharpening her knives. 'Just you stay in bed, darling, and I'll look after you. It will be fun to have you properly at home after all these years I've been on my own. While *you've* been off being *educated*' she added with a tinkly laugh. 'And what an expense that was' she said a few weeks later. 'Really, I have to say I'm quite glad that university is out of the question now.' 'Only for this year, surely?' mumbled an alarmed Marjory, capable now of speech, less capable of enduring interminable afternoons by the unlit drawing room fire, gazing out at the merge of pale sea and pale sky. 'Time will tell' said mother, her eyes no longer bright but dull and critical. 'Certainly you won't be going anywhere at all unless you put on some weight'. How could anyone gain weight on a diet of calves' foot jelly and tripe, borne grudgingly on trays to her room? She was forbidden to eat downstairs; she realised that this was because mother was eating normal food and would find her company and the sight of her not eating her invalid food unbearably irritating.

So began the sequestration, the erosion of possibility and aspiration, stretching into years, into forever. For when at last Marjory was well again, mother chose to retire to her bed, suffering from some unidentifiable malaise. 'Perhaps I've caught that nasty disease off you, after all that time nursing you. Dr Fox is baffled of course. So lucky for me that you're here, darling.' This was the second time in two years that she had called Marjory darling.

As she reached the outskirts of the village, a shower of pebbles skittered against the pram wheels and ricocheted off, stinging into her ankles. She stopped stock still and turned her chalky face towards the jeering children; slowly, deliberately, she smiled her frozen smile, her eyes expressionless. The children melted into the dunes and marram grass. The village shop smelt of paraffin and apples as it always had done, and no one flinched at her appearance. They packed her box up as usual and it was only after she had laboured out with it to the pram, refusing offers of help, and had moved into her return journey that one rolled eyes at another, heads were shaken, voices lowered. Just for a moment; there were more interesting topics with novelty value, winter holiday tenants, the tideline of wreckage left by the half term break, the occupants of the bus shelter. Marjory plodded on, up to the cliff top path and the stir of the wind. Already the light was fading and the bleached grasses shivered; the sea was ruffled, metallic grey in the chill of evening. An occasional poppy still trembled on the dunes' edge and as the path climbed she could distinguish the small pale stars of camomile, but colour was leaching from the landscape, into a dying winter world. She looked back at the lit windows of the village and was unmoved. Once she would have envied the lives she imagined in those lamp-lit rooms, familial meals, exchange of the day's events, a loving kindness reserved for those within, implicit in the shrug and glide of curtains drawn against the outsider. Exclusion was now her natural state; no doubt it always had been, but then she had not recognised it, then when she still had small hopes of a normal life and believed what people said.

The summer mother had gone there had been a song blaring endlessly from the wireless in the shop and from people's cars; most of the words were unintelligible to her, but there was a single line refrain, 'The day the music died.' That was the summer when one life had ended and another begun, the day Alan's letter had come and the wedding was off, the dining room full of presents which she would never use, the accoutrements of a real house, an undiscovered place waiting to be realised. The wedding dress in its shrouds of tissue swayed and twisted in the draught from her bedroom window; it watched her, the faceless ghost of her trusting self; and she thought it mocked her. 'How could you think you could ever be a bride?' it whispered. 'Be loved and cherished and make golden perfect toast in the toaster, wake to the welcome of the Goblin Teasmaid, iron crisp, fragrant linen on that pristine padded ironing board. Share your life in the warmth while the sea wind batters the windows.' There might have been a dog, and cat, even a child. All gone that day, the day the music died, the day she took to the trees.

She stood on the cliff edge, where you could see nothing but sea and sky and the curved rim of the horizon, and heard the hushed roar of water ceaselessly shifting stones. All things were temporal and passing; the cliff itself, perilously layered, would slither some day soon into the heave of ocean, and the white birds floating beneath her now, untroubled, would find themselves new sanctuaries on the raw exposed rock face. Turning away, she was aware of sharp pain in her hips and in her knees where her old bones scraped and ground each other into rough jagging surfaces. The stones were better served by the sea; it left them smooth and shining. Cliff and sea, hip and knee; a cheerless little grindstone song. Near to shore on a post, a cormorant was drying his outspread wings densely black and cruciform against the swelling tide.

At the back gate she glanced into the letterbox. Nothing but snails. Beyond the parched winter grasses and shrivelled stands of dock leaves the house loomed, blinded by shutters. Sometimes she played with the notion of going in there; sometimes she crept around it like a thief, peering through cracks in the shutters and cobwebs at vistas and sepia rooms lined with bookcases, heavy mahogany tables, grimly upholstered armchairs. But when she saw the wedding presents still there in the dining room, and when she thought of the dress performing its twirling dance upstairs, her heart would thump and she would begin to shake.

That night, in the tree house, her eagle home, she could not sleep for the pain in her hips. Each morning she would wake colder and stiffer. In the light of day she knew the rooks were watching her. It was too late now for it to matter where or whether she lived or died. This pain and cold would also pass. All those years of falling leaves and rooks nesting and spring's return, distant foghorns, drownings and foundering ships, wind and weather, had purged her, bleached her like driftwood. She was memory now, nothing more nor less. One day, maybe this day, in a flurry of shining leaves and eyes and beaks she would have gone and then the rooks would have her. So let it be; her story was over.

* * * * *

Front Seat

RUTH RENDELL

Along the sea front, between the pier and the old town, was a row of wooden seats. There were six of them, regularly spaced on the grass, and they faced the dunes, the sea wall, and the sea. To some people, including Mrs Jones, they were known by name as Fisher, Jackson, Teague, Prendergast, Lubbock and Rupert Moore. It was on this last, the one that was curiously known by the Christian as well as the family name of the man it commemorated, that Mrs Jones invariably chose to sit.

She sat there every day, enjoying the peace and quiet, looking at the sea and thinking about the past. It was most pleasant on mild winter days or on those days of summer when the sky was overcast, for then the holiday visitors stayed in their cars or went off to buy prawns and crabs and expensive knick-knacks. Mrs Jones thought how glad she was that last year, when Mr Jones had been taken from her, she had bought the house in the old town, even though this had meant separating herself from her daughter. She thought about her son in London and her daughter in Ipswich, good loving children that they were, and about her grandchildren, and sometimes about her good fortune in having a comfortable annuity as well as her pension.

But mostly, sitting on Rupert Moore, between Fisher and Teague, she thought about the first man in her life to whom even now, after so long, she always referred to as her darling. She had so accustomed herself to calling him this that to her the endearment had become his name. My darling, thought Mrs Jones, as some other old woman might have thought of John or Charlie or Tom.

She felt closer to him here than anywhere, which was why she chose to rest on this seat and not on one of the others.

On 15 July, St Swithin's Day, Hugh and Cecily Branksome sat in their car which was was parked on the promenade, and looked at the grey choppy sea. Or, rather, Hugh looked at the sea while Cecily looked at Mrs Jones. The temperature was around ten degrees, according to Cecily who moved with the times, or fifty, according to Hugh who did not. It was not yet raining, though the indications were that it soon would be. Hugh was wishing they had gone to the Costa Brava where there would have been high-rise blocks and fish and chips and bull fights, but at least the sun would have shone. Cecily had got it into her head that it was bourgeois and unpatriotic to go abroad for one's holidays.

'I wonder why she always sits there,' said Cecily.

'Who sits where?'

'That old woman. She always sits on that particular seat. She was there yesterday and the day before.'

'Didn't notice,' said Hugh.

'You never notice anything. While you were in the pub yesterday,' said Cecily with emphasis, 'I waited till she'd gone and then I read the inscription on that seat. On the metal plate on the back. D'you know what it says?'

'Of course I don't,' said Hugh, opening the window to let out cigarette smoke. An icy breeze hit him in the face.

'Do close that window. It says: "Rupert Moore gave this seat to Northwold in thanks for his deliverance. I was in prison and ye came unto me, Matthew, chapter twenty-five, verse thirty-five." How about that?'

'Remarkable.' Hugh thought he knew all about being in prison. He looked at his watch. 'Opening time,' he said. 'We can go and get a drink, thank God.'

On the following morning he went out fishing without her. They met in their room before dinner, Hugh bracing himself to face certain sarcastic questions, not without precedent, as to whether he had had a nice day. Forestalling them by telling her they had caught only one small mackerel, for the censure would be greater if he had enjoyed himself, he was soon interrupted.

'I've got the whole story about the seat out of that nice man with the beard.'

Hugh's memory was poor and for a moment he didn't know which seat she was talking about, but he recognised the nice man from her description. A busybody know-all who lived in Northwold and hung about the hotel bar.

'He insisted on buying me a drink. Well, two, as a matter of fact.' She smiled archly, and patted her hair as if the bearded know-all had, at the very least, invited her to Aldeburgh for the weekend. 'He's called Arnold Cottle and he said this Rupert Moore put that seat there because he'd murdered his wife. He was put on trial and he was acquitted and that's what it means about "deliverance" and being in prison.'

'You can't say he murdered his wife if he was acquitted.'

'You know what I mean.' said Cecily. 'It was ages ago, in 1930. I mean, I was only a baby.' Hugh thought it was wiser not to point out that at ten one is hardly a baby. 'They acquitted him, or he got off on appeal, something like that, and he came back here to live and had that seat put there. Only the local people didn't want a murderer and they broke his windows and called after him in the street and he had to go.'

'Poor devil,' said Hugh.

'Well, I don't know about that, Hugh. From what Arnold said, the case was very unsavoury. Moore was quite young and very good looking and he was a painter, though he had a private income. His poor wife was much older and an invalid. He gave her cyanide they'd got for killing wasps. He gave it to her in a cup of coffee.'

'I thought you said he didn't do it.'

'Everyone *knew* he'd done it. He only got off because the judge misdirected the jury. You can't imagine how anyone would have the nerve to put up a sort of monument, can you, after a thing like that?'

Hugh started to run his bath. Resignedly, he accepted the fact, from past experience, that part of the evening would be spent in the company of Arnold Cottle. Cecily was not, and never had been, particularly flirtatious except in her own imagination. It was not that. Rather it was that she liked to get hold of causes or what she called examples of injustices or outrage and worry at them, roping in to assist her any helper that might be on hand. There had been the banning of the proposed motorway, the petition against the children's playground, the eviction of the squatters down the road. She was not always reactionary, for she worshipped free speech and racial equality and health foods and clean air. She was a woman of principle who threw herself whole-heartedly into upheaval and change and battles that right might be done, and sometimes into cults for the improvement of her soul. The unfortunate part of all this, or one of the unfortunate parts, was that it brought her so often into the company of bores or rogues. Hugh wondered what she was up to now, and why, and hoped it might be, though it seldom was, a flash in the pan.

Two hours later he found himself with his wife and Arnold Cottle, standing on the wet grass and examining the inscription on the Rupert Moore seat. It wasn't yet dark and wouldn't be for an hour. The sky was heavily overcast and the sea the colour of a recently scoured aluminium pot. No one would have supposed, thought Hugh, that somewhere up there in the west was the sun which, contrary to all present evidence, science told him was throwing off light at the rate of two hundred and fifty million tons a minute.

The others were too rapt to be distracted. He had a look at Fisher ('In memory of Colonel Marius Fisher, V.C., D.S.O., 1874–1951') and at Teague ('William James Teague, of this Town, lost at the Battle of Jutland') and then he prodded Rupert Moore and announced, for something to say, 'That's oak.'

'It is indeed, my dear old chap.' Arnold Cottle spoke to Hugh very warmly and kindly, as if he had decided a priori that he was a harmless lunatic. 'You could get oak in those days. This one was made by a chap called Sarafin, Arthur Sarafin. Curious name, eh? Corruption of Seraphim, I daresay. Fine craftsman, lived up the coast at Lowestoft, but he died quite young, more's the pity. My father knew him, had some of the furniture he made. You can see his initials up there where the crossbar at the top joins the post. A.S. in a little circle, see?'

Hugh thought this most interesting. He had done a bit of carpentry himself until Cecily had stopped it on the ground that she needed his workshop for her groups. That was in the days when she was into Gestalt. Hugh preferred not to think about them. He had a look at Prendergast ('This seat was placed here by the Hon. Clara Prendergast that the weary might find rest') and was about to ask Cottle if this one was oak or teak, when Cecily said: 'Where did he get the cyanide?'

'Moore?' said Cottle. 'It was never actually proved that he did it. He said they kept some in their garden shed for killing wasps and his wife had taken it herself. In point of fact, Mrs Moore had written to her sister, saying her life wasn't worth living and she wanted to put an end to it. But this gardener chappie said he'd thrown the wasp killing stuff away a year before.'

'It must have come from somewhere,' said Cecily in such a hectoring tone and looking so belligerent that Hugh felt even more sympathy for Rupert Moore.

Cottle didn't seem to mind the tone or the look. 'Moore had been to

100

several chemists' shops in the area, though not actually in Northwold, and tried to buy cyanide, ostensibly for killing wasps. No chemist admitted to having let him have it. There was one in Tarrington, up the coast there, who sold him another kind of vespicide that contained no cyanide and got him to sign the poison book. Dear Cecily, since you're so interested, why don't you read up the case in the library? Perhaps I might have the pleasure of taking you there tomorrow?'

The offer was accepted with enthusiasm. They all went into the Cross Keys where Hugh bought three rounds of drinks and Arnold Cottle brought none, having failed to bring his wallet with him. Cecily fastened on to the barman and elicited from him that the old woman who always sat on the Rupert Moore seat was called Mrs Jones, that she had come to Northwold the year before from Ipswich and was of Suffolk, though not Northwold, origins.

'Why does she always sit there?'

'Ask me another,' said the barman, presumably meaning this rejoinder rhetorically, which was not the way Cecily took it.

'What's so fascinating about that seat?'

'It seems to fascinate you,' said Hugh. 'Can't you give it a rest? The whole thing's been over and done with for going on fifty years.'

Cecily said, 'There's nothing else to do in this damned place,' which displeased the barman so much that he moved off in a huff. 'I've got a very active brain, Hugh. You ought to know that by now. I'm afraid I'm not content to fuddle it with drink or spend ten hours pulling one poor fish out of the sea.'

The library visit, from which Hugh was excused, took place. But books having been secured, a journey had to be made to the house in which Rupert Moore had lived with his wife and painted his pictures and where the crime had been committed. Arnold Cottle seemed delighted at the prospect, especially as the excursion, at Cecily's suggestion, was to include lunch. Hugh had to go because Cecily couldn't drive and he wasn't going to lend his car to Cottle.

The house was a dull and ugly mansion, now used as a children's home. The superintendent (quite reasonably, Hugh thought) refused to let them tour the interior, but he had no objection to them walking round the grounds. It was bitterly cold for the time of year, but not cold enough to keep the children indoors. They tagged around behind Arnold Cottle and the Branksomes, making unfriendly or impertinent remarks. One of them, a boy with red curly hair and a cast in his eye, threw an apple core at Cecily and when reproved, used a word which, though familiar, is still unexpected on the lips of a five-year-old.

They had lunch, and throughout the meal Cecily read aloud extracts from the trial of Rupert Moore. The medical evidence was so unpleasant that Hugh was unable to finish his steak *au poivre*. Cottle drank nearly a whole bottle of Nuits St Georges and had a double brandy with his coffee. Hugh thought about men who murdered their wives, and how much easier it must have been when you could get wasp killer made out of cyanide and weed killer made of arsenic. But even if he could have got those things, or have pushed Cecily downstairs, or fixed it for the electric wall heater to fall into the bath while she was in it, he knew he never would. Even if he got away with it, as poor Rupert Moore had done, he would have the shame and the fear and the guilt for the rest of his life, again as had been the case with Rupert Moore.

Not that he lived for long. 'He died of some kidney disease just twelve months after they let him out,' said Cecily, 'and by then he'd been hounded out of the place. He had Sarafin make that seat and that was about the last thing he ever did in Northwold.' She scanned through the last chapter of her book. 'There doesn't seem to have been any real motive for the murder, Arnold.'

'I suppose he wanted to marry someone else,' said Cottle, swigging brandy. 'I remember my father saying there were rumours he'd had a girlfriend but nobody seemed to know her name and she wasn't mentioned at the trial.'

'She certainly wasn't,' said Cecily, flicking back in her book so rapidly that she nearly knocked Hugh's coffee cup over. 'You mean there was no clue as to who she was?' How did the rumours start, then?'

'Dear Cecily, how do rumours ever start? In point of fact, Moore was known often to have been absent from home in the evenings. There was gossip he'd been seen in Clacton with a girl.'

'Fascinating,' said Cecily. 'I shall spend the rest of the day thoroughly studying all this literature. You and Hugh must amuse yourselves on your own.'

After a dreadful afternoon spent listening to Cottle's troubles, how enemies had prevented him making a success at any career, how his two attempts at getting married had been scotched by his mother, and how his neighbours had a vendetta against him, Hugh finally escaped. Though not before he had lent Cottle ten pounds, this being the lowest of the sums his guest had suggested as appropriate. Cecily had a wonderful time, making herself conversant with the Moore case and now she was in the bath. Hugh wondered if a mighty thump on the bedroom side of the bathroom wall would dislodge the heater and make it fall into the water, but this was merely academic speculation.

After dinner he went for a walk on his own in the rain while Cecily made notes – but for what purpose Hugh neither knew nor cared. He poked about in the ruins of the castle; he bought two tickets for the repertory theatre on the following night, hoping that the play, though it was called *Murder-on-Sea*, might distract Cecily; he wandered about the streets of the old town and he had a drink in the Oyster Catcher's Arms. On the whole, he didn't have a bad time.

The morning being better – a pale, sickly sun was shining and making quite attractive tints on the undersides of black clouds – he thought they might go to the beach. But Cecily had other plans. She got him to take her to Tarrington, and in the little shopping centre she left him to his own devices which included buying two pairs of thicker socks. After that, because it was raining again, there was nothing to do but sit in the car park. She kept him waiting two hours.

'What d'you think?' she said. 'I found that chemist, the one that sold Rupert Moore the wasp killer that hadn't got cyanide in it. And, would you believe it, it's still the same firm. The original pharmacist's grandson is the manager.'

'I suppose,' said Hugh, 'that he told you his grandfather had made a deathbed confession he did give Moore the cyanide after all.'

'Do try not to be so silly. I already knew they had cyanide wasp killer in the shop. It said so in the library book. This young man, the grandson, couldn't tell me much, but he did say his grandfather had had a very pretty young girl assistant. How about that?'

'I've noticed that very pretty young girls often do work in chemists' shops.'

'I'm glad you notice something at any rate. However, she is not the one. The grandson knows her present whereabouts, and she is a Mrs Lewis. So I shall have to look elsewhere.'

'What d'you mean, the one?' said Hugh dismally.

'My next task,' said Cecily, taking no notice, 'will be to hunt for persons in this case of the name of Jones. Young women, that is. I know where to begin now. Sooner or later I shall root out a girl who was an assistant in a chemist's shop at the time and who married a Jones.'

'What for?'

'That right may be done,' said Cecily solemnly. 'That the truth may at last come out. I see it as my mission, Hugh. It was the merest chance we happened to come to Northwold because Diana Richards recommended it. You wanted to go to Lloret del Mar. I feel it was meant we should come here because there was work for me to do. I am convinced Moore was guilty of this crime, but not alone in his guilt. He had a helper who, I believe, is alive at this moment. I'd like you to drive me to Clacton now. I shall begin by interviewing some of the oldest inhabitants.'

So Hugh drove to Clacton where he lost a pound on the fruit machines. Indefatigably, Cecily pursued her investigations.

Mrs Jones came back from morning service at St Mary's and although she was a good walker and not at all tired, for she had slept well ever since she came to Northwold, she sat down for half an hour on her favourite seat. Two other elderly people who had also been in church were sitting on Jackson ('In memory of Bertrand Jackson, 1859–1924, Philanthropist and Lover of the Arts'). Mrs Jones nodded pleasantly at them; but she didn't speak. It wasn't her way to waste in chat time that was more satisfactorily spent in reminiscence.

A pale grey mackerel sky, a fitful sun. Perhaps it would brighten up later. She thought about her daughter who was coming to lunch. Brenda would be tired after the drive, for the children, dears though they were, would no doubt be troublesome in the car. They would all enjoy that nice piece of sirloin and the Yorkshire pudding and the fresh peas and the chocolate ice cream. She had got in a bottle of sherry so that she and Brenda and Brenda's husband could have a glass each before the meal.

Her son and daughter had been very good to her. They knew she had been a devoted wife to their father, and they didn't resent the place in her love she kept for her darling. Not that she had ever spoken of him in front of their father or of them when they were small. That would have been unkind and in bad taste. But later she had told them about him and told Brenda, in expansive moments, about the long-past happiness and the tragedy of her darling's death, he so young and handsome and gifted. Perhaps, this afternoon when the rest of them were on the beach, she might allow herself the luxury of mentioning him again. Discreetly, of course, because she had always respected Mr Jones and loved him after a fashion, even though he had taken her away to Ipswich and never attained those heights of talent and success her darling would have enjoyed had he lived. Tranquilly, not unhappily, she recalled to her mind his face, his voice, and some of their conversations.

Mrs Jones was disturbed in her reverie by the presence of that tiresome woman. She had seen her before, hanging about on the promenade and once examining the seat Mrs Jones thought of as her own. An ugly, thin, neurotic-looking woman who was sometimes in the company of a sensible elderly man and sometimes with that shameless scrounger, old Cottle's boy, whom Mrs Jones in her old-fashioned way called a barfly. Today, however, she was alone and to Mrs Jones's dismay was approaching her with intent to speak.

'Do excuse me for speaking to you but I've seen you here so often.'

'Oh, yes?' said Mrs Jones. 'I've seen you too. I'm afraid I have to go now. I've guests for lunch.'

'Please don't go. I won't keep you more than a moment. But I must tell you I'm terribly interested in the Moore case. I can't help wondering if you knew him, you're here so much.'

'I knew him,' said Mrs Moore distantly.

'That's terribly exciting.' And the woman did look very excited. 'I expect you first met him when he came into the shop?'

'That's right,' said Mrs Jones and she got up. 'But I don't care to talk about it. It's a very long time ago and it's best forgotten. Good morning.'

'Oh, but please. . . !'

Mrs Jones ignored her. She walked far more rapidly than usual, breathing heavily, along the path towards the old town. She was flustered and upset and very put out. To rake up all that now just when she was thinking of the lovely events of that time! For that day, though not, she hoped, for the future, the encounter had spoiled the seat for her.

'Had a good day with Cottle?' said Hugh.

'Don't speak to me about that man. Can you imagine it, I gave him a ring and a woman answered! She turned out to be some creature on holiday like us who was taking him to Lowestoft in her car. I could come too if I liked. No, thank you very much, I said. And he was pleased to tell me I was getting *obsessional*. So I gave him a piece of my mind, and that's the last of Arnold Cottle.'

And the last of his ten pounds, thought Hugh. 'So you went on the beach instead?'

'I did not. While you were out in that boat I researched on my own. And most successfully, I may add. You remember that old man in Clacton, the one in the old folks' home? Well, he was quite fit enough to see me today, and I questioned him exhaustively.'

Hugh said nothing. He could guess which of them had been exhausted.

'Ultimately,' said Cecily, 'I was able to prod him into remembering. I asked him to try and recall everyone he had ever known called Jones. And at last he remembered a local policeman, Constable Jones, who got married in or around 1930. And the girl he married worked in *a local chemist's shop*. How about that?'

'You mean she was Moore's girlfriend?'

'Isn't it obvious? Her name was Gladys Palmer. She is now Mrs Jones. Moore was seen about with a girl in Clacton. This girl lived in Clacton and worked in a Clacton chemist's shop. Now it's quite evident that Moore was having a love affair with Gladys Palmer and that he persuaded her to give him the cyanide from the shop where she worked. The *real* evidence is that, according to all the books, that was one of the few chemist's shops from which Moore *never tried to obtain cyanide*!'

'That's real evidence?' said Hugh.

'Of course it is, to anyone with any deductive powers. Gladys Palmer took fright when Moore was found guilty, so she married a policeman for protection, and the policeman's name was Jones. Isn't that proof?'

'Proof of what?'

'Don't you remember anything? The barman in that Cross Keys place told us the old woman who sits on the Rupert Moore seat was a Mrs Jones.' Cecily smiled triumphantly. 'They are one and the same.'

'But it's a very common name.'

'Maybe. But Mrs Jones had admitted it. I spoke to her this morning before I went to Clacton. She has admitted knowing Moore and that she first met him when he came into the shop. How about that? And she was very nervous and upset, I can tell you, as well she might be.'

Hugh stared at his wife. He didn't at all like the turn things were taking. 'Cecily, it may be so. It looks like it, but it's no business of ours. I wish you'd leave it.'

'Leave it!' For nearly fifty years this woman has got off scot-free when she was as much guilty of the murder of Mrs Moore as Moore was, and you say leave it! It's her guilt brings her to that seat day after day, isn't it? Any psychologist would tell you that.'

'She must be at least seventy. Surely she can be left in peace now?'

'I'm afraid it's much too late for that, Hugh. There must be an inquiry, all the facts must come out. I have written three letters, one to the Home Secretary, one to the Chief Commissioner at Scotland Yard, and a third to the author of this very incomplete book. There they are on the dressing table. Perhaps you'd like to look at them while I have my bath.'

Hugh looked at them. If he were to tear them up she would only write them again. If he walked into the bathroom now and dislodged the heater from the wall and it fell into the water, and she died and it was called an accident . . . The letters would never be sent, and he could have his workshop back, he could chat up pretty girls who worked in chemist's shops and go on holiday to the Costa Brava and be free. He sighed heavily and went down to the bar to get a drink.

Thank goodness, thought Mrs Jones, that woman wasn't anywhere to be seen this morning. The intrusion of yesterday had upset her for hours, even after Brenda arrived, but she was getting over it now. Unfortunately in a way, the weather had taken a turn for the better, and several of the seats were occupied. But not Rupert Moore. Mrs Jones sat down on it and put her shopping bag on the ground at her feet.

She was aware of the proximity of the barfly who was sitting on Lubbock ('Elizabeth Anne Lubbock, for many years Headmistress of Northwold Girls' High School') and with him was a different woman, much younger than the other and very well dressed. With an effort, Mrs Jones expelled them from her mind. She looked at the calm blue sea and felt the warm and firm pressure of the oak against her back and thought about her darling. How sweet their love and companionship had been! It had endured for such a short time, and then separation and the unbearable loneliness. But she had been right to marry Mr Jones, for he had been a good husband and she the wife he wanted, and without him there would have been no Brian and no Brenda and no money to buy the house and come here every day to remember. If her darling had lived, though, and the children had been his, and if she had had him to sit beside her on his seat and be the joy of her old age . . .

'Do forgive me,' said a voice, 'but I'm a local man myself, and I happened to be in Lowestoft yesterday and someone told me they'd heard you'd come back to this part of the world to live.'

Mrs Jones looked at the barfly. Was there to be no end to this kind of thing?

'I've seen you on this seat and I did wonder, and when this friend in Lowestoft told me your present name, all was made plain.'

'I see,' said Mrs Jones, gathering up her shopping bag.

'I want you to know how greatly I admire his work. My father had some charming examples of it – all sold now, alas – and anyone can see that this seat was made by a craftsman compared with the others.' Her stony face, her hostility, made him hesitate. 'You are,' he said, 'who I think you are, aren't you?'

'Of course I am,' said Mrs Jones crossly, another morning spoilt. 'Arthur Sarafin was my first husband. And now I really must be on my way.'

* * * * *

Esther Freud's first novel *Hideous Kinky* was published in 1992 and made into a film starring Kate Winslet. The following year she was chosen by Granta as one of the Best of Young British Novelists. She has gone on to write *Peerless Flats*, *Gaglow* and most recently *The Wild*, published last year. Freud lives with her family in London and Suffolk and is currently working on her fifth novel. In it Lily rents a cottage in Steerborough hoping to find out more about the subject of her thesis, a German architect who spent time in the village in the 1950s. She comes armed with a bundle of letters from the architect to his wife and as she translates them she becomes fascinated by their lives and what led them to this remote village on the Suffolk coast. Freud's short story *The Visit* has evolved out of this work in progress.

The Visit

ESTHER FREUD

Everywhere Lily looked now she saw Grae. Without the car, she supposed, he was bringing his work home. The back garden had turned into a workshop. A work bench was permanently set up and lengths of wood and half finished constructions were propped against the shed. He wore the same checked jacket and the same hat through sun and rain, and one evening when she went out to fill the coal scuttle he offered her a box of kindling for the fire. Soft white ends of wood that needed to be burned. The rain was falling, it was starting to get dark, but he carried on sawing and measuring, never breaking his stride even when Em and Arri called to him, hungry, from the back door.

It was May bank holiday and Nick was driving up. 'Right,' he said, 'I've got a pen. How do I get out of London.' Lily stood in the phone box and weighed a small brown pebble in her palm. 'Christ,' she heard Nick sigh, 'I can't believe you're doing this to me . . .'

'Well . . .' Lily said. 'You head for the M25 . . . and go East . . . you know . . . the opposite direction from Heathrow?'

'East . . . not . . . to . . . Heathrow.' Nick murmured as he copied her instructions down.

'And Nick . . .' she warned him as gently as she could, 'bring some warm clothes . . . and no . . . no white trousers.'

'No white trousers.' He paused to make a note of it and they both began to laugh. The year before they'd spent a week in Cornwall during which Nick had almost immediately run out of clothes. He'd packed two T-shirts, no jumper, and one pair of oatmeal-coloured jeans. 'How was I to know?' Nick had protested. 'I'm a city boy. I've lived my whole life in Shepherd's Bush.'

'So . . .' Lily could hardly believe that he was really coming.

'I'll see you tonight then. About nine?'

'Yes, I'll ring you from the car . . . oh bollocks . . . I forgot, you don't have a phone.'

'Sorry to deprive you of that call to say you're nearly there.'

'Bitch.'

'See you later then, drive carefully.' Her money was running out.

'Lily . . .'

'Yes?' But the last coin made a hollow echo as it dropped into the box.

Lily stood in Stoffers wondering what she could possibly give Nick to eat. Everything that had seemed tempting to her before, now seemed inedible. Crumpets, bacon, vacuum-pressed salami and ham. There was shortcake and treacle tart in silver foil cases, one over-ripe tomato, a cluster of cauliflowers, a sack of onions and three leeks. Instead she hired a bike from the rack outside the shop and set off for Eastonknoll, taking the back lane that cut across the river. It ran through fields of cows penned in by ditches and was edged in places by huge flowering bushes of bright yellow gorse. Lily rattled over the bailey bridge and set off across the corner of the golf course, glancing up at the shadow of the water tower, careful to avoid being hit by flying balls. She came out on the common and swooped down towards the sea. The wind was fierce on the promenade, rippling the beige macs of the pensioners, ruffling their dogs, forcing them to clasp each other hard against the rails. Lily wheeled her bike along the sea front and bought tea at the kiosk, where the chairs were stacked three deep to buoy them down. She sat, as if in a high chair, her legs dangling inches from the ground, and watched the woman shutter up the hut. Above her, at the top of a steep flight of steps she could see a ship's figurehead arching out from the wall of a large house. 'I might as well close up,' the woman stood before her, her apron flying, her sleeves flapping as she rolled the tables in.

Lilly carried her bike up the steps towards the figurehead. It was not, as she'd imagined it, a mermaid or a queen, but a neat girl with a hat on, an umbrella at her side. Was she the captain's daughter, or the ship owner's young wife? and Lily saw that she had lost one of her arms, leaving a clean white plaster stump. Beside the building a mast was planted in the ground. Arrows fluttered from it, pointing the way towards Denmark and Holland, out over the open sea. 'The Sailors Reading

Room.' The words were moulded onto a plaque and Lily realised the house was a museum, open to the public, with arched white doors, and a well worn copper catch. There was no one inside the Reading Room, and nothing very much to read. Just three copies of the *East Anglian Times* and two brown chairs. Around the walls in high glass cases were models of ships. Punts and schooners, battleships and yawls. Each plank of wood, each tiny rope and sail, minutely replicated, washed down, painted and oiled. All around the walls were photographs of fishermen and sailors, notebooks held open at the records of each voyage. There were lists of names, Harper, Seal, Child. Harry, Bertie, Kitner. And beside each name the dates which spanned their lives. There was another door at the back of the room, marked private, covered in green baize. There was a round window half way up, not much bigger than an orange and Lily pressed her face against it. To her surprise she saw two men playing billiards, a third reading a newspaper, a fourth doing nothing at all. She squeezed closer, peering to the side, catching sight of a ship's wheel, balanced on a bench, and then someone tapped her on the arm. 'We're closing up now.' The man had a peaked hat, braided with blue cord, and he was wearing rubber Wellingtons turned over at the knee. The clock behind him chimed as it reached five, a rich warm gong that warmed the room. 'Thank you.' Lily glanced around her at the photographs of men, the tools and scrolls and telescopes, the doomed faces of Seal, Harry, Child, all drowned in 1951. 'I'll come back when there's more time.' The man watched her until she was out of the room and then she heard him locking himself in.

There was a delicatessen in the market square that sold fresh parmesan, black pasta, Greek yoghurt and organic crisps. Lily filled two bags and topped them up with lambs lettuce and fruit. Slowly she cycled home, her shopping hanging from each handle like the saddlebags of a mule. The wind had dipped, the sun hung low and warm, and in each hollow hovered the thick, sweet coconut smell of gorse. Lily meandering up and over a tiny ridge of hills, stretching her legs as she reached the top and letting the bike coast down. She was a child again. Warm and safe and happy, skittering and playing, bathed in breeze and birdsong and the Ambre Solair smell of a beach. And then a man stepped out of the hedge. Lily's heart jolted so violently it strained against her ribs. Her blood spiralled, and as if it were a horse, shying, her bike lurched over to one side. The man stood in the narrow path, so squarely that she couldn't pass. She was caught, halfway down a slope, too weighted to peddle backwards, too frightened to go on. A tin of tomato puree rolled into the hedge and she heard the crunch of the spaghetti as the strands began to snap. The man took two steps towards her. He was wrapped in strips of plastic bag; his feet, his body, the top half of his head wound round with black. There was a sound, like hissing, rising from his legs, and his face was grizzled, camouflaged by beard. Lily glanced behind her. There was no one, nothing, as far as she could see. The scream that had been rising in her died. Keep calm, she told herself, keep calm. The man had picked up speed. He was lumbering towards her, his body squat, his eyes rimmed round with red, and then just as he was almost upon her, he keeled away through a thicket of tall grass. Lily gasped. It was possible he hadn't even seen her. His eyes, as he passed, were fixed on something else. Lily hauled up her bike and watched him go. He was walking through a field of heffers, following a path ridged up out of the ground. Ahead of him on the horizon was a small clump of trees, a white wooden signpost where the path split into three, and beyond that, just visible, a cottage, the roof of which was bare.

Lily scrabbled the lost shopping back into her bag. Her legs felt weak, her arms still and painful, but as she cycled on she found that she was shaking her head and laughing with relief.

At eight o'clock Lily moved her car. She hadn't used it for almost two weeks and it took her hands and feet a moment to find their way around the gears. She backed it out and then parked it again, right over by the wall, so that when Nick arrived he'd be able to glide in beside her, and wouldn't block the lane. She made a fire, and found an old checked blanket to throw over the sofa and soften at least some of the brown. From time to time she went to the door and looked out, in case, just in case Nick might be planning to surprise her. She could, she thought, go to the phone box and find out how far he was on his way, but she had an image of him racing over the Orwell bridge, the wind tugging at his car, forcing him to swerve into a line of trucks as he reached out for the phone.

'My sweet L,' she read instead. She had become an expert on Lehman's handwriting, the curls of it, the widened lines of his pen as it swept up and down. It amused her to think of the agonies of her school German, the endless repetitions of the grammar, the feminine, the masculine, the

112

neuter, and how finally they had proved to be of use. 'Today,' Lehman wrote, 'your first letter to arrive here was brought to me as I ate breakfast and all the tears that would have rolled down my cheeks because of your being alone were swiftly dried up by the sun. It sounds like you have been working very hard my El, and you've told me about it all so beautifully, apart from the meals, which hopefully you haven't forgotten to have? Last night I couldn't sleep and I thought of all the things I wanted to tell you. Are you shopping properly for yourself? And when the doorbell rings, do you always look through the spyhole before you fling open the door and welcome whoever is there? Won't you get a chain put on? Write it down now so that you don't forget. And please don't get up too early, and don't race around after any trains. I could fill up this whole pad writing to you with cautions and good pieces of advice. Don't forget My L love, my sweet body L, I want this child as much as you.

P.S. You've forgotten to tell me about your evenings. AND what you had to eat.'

Lily was woken by a pounding on the door. The fire had died down, and when she jolted up, letters and deep purple flashes of the undersides of envelopes scattered to the floor. 'I'm coming,' she called, and then remembering where she was, 'Come in, come in. It's open.' She turned, running her fingers through her hair, straightening her clothes. 'How was it?' she called out and then she gave a little yelp. Grae was standing in the hall. 'Oh.' She caught sight of the kitchen clock, and her face in the mirror below it, creased and red on one side where she'd been lying on a seam. It was ten-thirty. 'I'm sorry. I was expecting somebody else.'

Grae looked uncomfortable, his shoulders hunched a little in the narrow hall. 'I'm sorry to disturb you, so late . . . it's just . . . your car . . it's parked too close to the gate and I've got to bring some wood through, not now, but first thing in the morning. I saw your light on . . . and . . . well . . . I though it would be better than waking you at six.'

Lily stared at him. She was only now starting to wake up. Pins and needles were tingling in one leg and her pulse was racketing. Where's Nick? she thought. He can't still be on the road. 'Of course. I'll move it now.' Like a sleepwalker she backed the car away from the side gate. 'Is that enough, it's just I'm expecting some one.' Lily peered at the black mass of the Green. 'I'd better call.' But she felt terrified of stepping into darkness, of being inside the phone box, sealed into its tower of light, the only object visible while all around was night.

'Excuse me . . . would it, could I use your phone?'

The back door of Grae's cottage opened straight into the house. A tiny kitchen, neat and tidy and a sitting room with a patterned bedspread thrown over a chair.

It's on the windowsill.' Grae said, and she sat on the arm of the sofa and dialled. What if no one answered? She imagined Nick's phone flung away from him, his car a shattered wreck, the ringing, the only sound on the black road. 'Yup.' Nick's voice was gruff and confident. Lily felt so angry tears sprung into her eyes. 'Where are you?'

'In London.' Nick sounded as if he was entirely in the right. 'Sitting here, waiting for you to ring.'

'You said that you'd be here by nine.'

'Listen, five minutes after I spoke to you something came up.' He lowered his voice as if to lure her. 'An unbelievably exciting project. I even tried ringing you back in that bloody phone box, but . . . well, I . . . with the exception of sending a carrier pigeon . . . Lily, I'm sorry. You've got to get a mobile phone.'

Lily sat in silence in Grae's sitting room. In the corner was an orange-crate full of the girls' toys. Teddies and stripped naked dolls, and a thread of cotton reels strung in a long line. 'So, when are you coming?'

There was a pause at the other end, and the unmistakable buzz and chatter of a bar. 'I don't see how I'm going to make it now. It's a huge project. If we start straight away, work on it all weekend and every second of next week, maybe there's a chance of winning the account.'

'Right . . .'

'And you'll be back next week anyway. Won't you? Lily? Come on, don't be like that.'

Lily felt Grae watching her, leaning into the frame of the door. He was waiting for her. Waiting for her to finish so that he could go to bed.

'Let's talk about it tomorrow.' She tried to sound breezy, as if she didn't care. 'It's just I'm . . . using someone's phone.' 'Oh.' Nick's voice was deflated as if he'd been looking forward to a row. 'Right then, speak to you then.'

'Goodnight,' she said cheerfully, and she turned into the room. 'Thanks so much. Can I give you something towards . . .'

'No, no, it's fine.' Grae went to the back door, and without another word, held if open for her as she slipped out. She stood in the still dark, the stars clustered above her, hard and glinting, crackling with light. 'Bastard,' she let herself say it out loud, and warm tears of disappointment sprung into her throat.

There followed three days of unseasonably hot weather. Lily took her towel and a bag of books and straight after breakfast she walked down to the beach. She lay there, soaking in the sun, leafing through photographic studies of the buildings that had been thrown up in Europe between the First and Second wars. Long low houses, great sheets of glass, and she looked at these structures and thought that despite their modernist predictions most people still lived in tall narrow terraces, row after row of them, stretching interminably through city streets. She read the short biographies of each of Lehman's colleagues, Austrian and German, for the most part Jews. She traced their migration to Britain or America, the influence they had had there, or the inevitable dates of their deaths if they stayed on. But hard as she tried to concentrate she soon became distracted by the beach. She had to sit up to watch the old lady who lived across the lane, her shoulders sloped and freckled, her dressing gown, a warm white puddle on the sand. There was something magisterial about the way she strode into the sea and the moment when the orange flowers of her costume disappeared from view. Shortly afterwards a man came to exercise his horse. He thundered it along the sand, pulling it back time and again from its natural desire to swim. The horse was wild, its head bent like the waves and its front legs bucked and charged as it tried to escape the harness of its reins. Shortly before eleven women with small children arrived, dragging pushchairs, windbreaks, bags packed with bottles, blankets and spare clothes. Sometimes Lily got up to help them. She could see the women, caught between laughter and despair, as one child dashed towards the sea while another, wailing, lay face down on the ground. They stood there paralysed, unable to move back or forward with the packhorse of a pushchair stranded wheel deep in sand. By mid morning Em and Arri would arrive. Lily watched them as they scouted round the beach. They liked to surprise her, to jump out at her from behind a dune, and they'd wait until she least expected it before creeping up and digging a moat around her towel.

'What do they say at school?' she asked eventually when the day-trippers had receded, and they had the beach back to themselves. 'Don't they mind, about you never going in?' She was stretched out, still and patient, while they buried her with sand. The sand was damp below the surface and the dry grains on top tickled as they layered it on. 'It's half term.' They shook their heads, staggered by her ignorance. 'And anyway,' Em said, 'we saw you sunbathing. You said you were only renting Fern Cottage so that you could do your work?' She picked up one of Lily's books. 'Which house would you like best?' And the girls hovered over it, gasping, sighing, muttering, as they flicked through for their dream home.

Penelope Lively is the author of many prize-winning novels and collections of short stories for both adults and children. She was shortlisted for the Booker Prize in 1977 for her first novel *The Road To Lichfield* and again in 1984 for *According To Mark* before winning it three years later with *Moon Tiger*. This widely acclaimed novel, like her autobiographical memoir *Oleander, Jacaranda*, draws on her childhood days in Egypt during the second war. Penelope Lively has also written radio and television scripts, is a popular children's author and has won both the Carnegie Medal and the Whitbread Award. *Corruption*, which first appeared in *Encounter* in 1984, is based on an anecdote told to the author by the wife of a judge. It became the title story of a selection published later that year and is included in the author's collected stories *Pack Of Cards* (1986).

Corruption

PENELOPE LIVELY

The judge and his wife, driving to Aldeburgh for the weekend, carried with them in the back of the car a Wine Society carton filled with pornographic magazines. The judge, closing the hatchback, stared for a moment through the window; he reopened the door and put a copy of *The Times* on top of the pile, extinguishing the garish covers. He then got into the driving seat and picked up the road atlas. 'The usual route, dear?'

'The usual route, I think. Unless we spot anything enticing on the way.'

'We have plenty of time to be enticed, if we feel so inclined.'

The judge, Richard Braine, was sixty-two; his wife Marjorie, a magistrate, was two years younger. The weekend ahead was their annual and cherished early summer break at the Music Festival; the pornographic magazines were the impounded consignment of an importer currently on trial and formed the contents of the judge's weekend briefcase, so to speak. 'Chores?' his wife had said, and he had replied, 'Chores, I'm afraid.'

At lunchtime, they pulled off the main road into a carefully selected lane and found a gate-way in which to park the car. They carried the rug and picnic basket into a nearby field and ate their lunch under the spacious East Anglian sky, in a state of almost flamboyant contentment. Both had noted how the satisfactions of life have a tendency to gain intensity with advancing years. 'The world gets more beautiful,' Marjorie had once said, 'not less so. Fun is even more fun. Music is more musical, if you see what I mean. One hadn't reckoned with that.' Now, consuming the thoughtfully constructed sandwiches and the coffee from the thermos, they glowed at one another amid the long thick grass that teemed with buttercup and clover; before them, the landscape retreated into blue distances satisfactorily broken here and there by a line of trees, the tower of a church or a rising contour. From time to time they exchanged remarks of pleasure or anticipation: about the surroundings, the weather, the meal

117

they would eat tonight at the little restaurant along the coast road, tomorrow evening's concert. Richard Braine, who was a man responsive to the moment, took his wife's hand; they sat in the sun, shirt-sleeved, and agreed conspiratorially and without too much guilt that they were glad that the eldest married daughter who sometimes accompanied them on this trip had not this year been able to. The daughter was loved, but would just now have been superfluous.

When they arrived at the small hotel it was early evening. The judge carried their suitcase and the Wine Society carton in and set them down by the reception desk. The proprietor, bearing the carton, showed them to their usual room. As she was unpacking, Marjorie said, 'I think you should have left that stuff in the car. Chambermaids, you know . . .' The judge frowned. 'That's a point.' He tipped the contents of the box into an emptied suitcase and locked it. 'I think I'll have a bath before we go out.'

He lay in the steamy cubicle, a sponge resting upon his stomach. Marjorie, stripped to a pair of pants, came in to wash. 'The dear old avocado suite again. One day we must have an avocado bathroom suite at home.' The judge, contemplating the rise of his belly, nodded; he was making a resolution about reduction of the flesh, a resolution which he sadly knew would be broken. He was a man who enjoyed food. His wife's flesh, in the process now of being briskly soaped and scrubbed, was firmer and less copious, as he was fully prepared to concede. He turned his head to watch her and thought for a while in a vague and melancholy way about bodies, about how we inhabit them and are dragged to the grave by them and are conditioned by them. In the course of his professional life he had frequently had occasion to reflect upon the last point: it had seemed to him, observing the faces that passed before him in courtrooms, that confronted him from docks and witness boxes, that not many of us are able to rise above physical appearance. The life of an ugly woman is different from that of a beautiful one; you cannot infer character from appearance, but you can suspect a good deal about the circumstances to which it will have given rise. Abandoning this interesting but sombre theme, he observed his wife's breasts and muscular but not unshapely thighs and the folds of skin upon her neck and remembered the first time he had seen her with no clothes on. She turned to look at him; 'If you're jeering at my knickers, they're a pair of Alison's I grabbed out of the laundry basket by mistake.' Alison was their youngest, unmarried daughter. 'I hadn't really noticed them,' said the judge politely. 'I was thinking about something quite different'. He smiled. 'And don't leer,' said his wife, flicking him with her flannel. 'It's unbecoming in a man of your age.' 'It's a tribute to your charms, my dear,' said the judge. He sat up and began to wash his neck, thinking still about the first time; they had both been embarrassed. Embarrassment had been a part of the pleasure, he reflected. How odd, and interesting.

It was still daylight when they drove to the restaurant, a violet summer twilight in which birds sang with jungle stridency. Marjorie, getting out of the car, said, 'That veal and mushroom in cream sauce thing for me, I think. A small salad for you, without dressing.'

'No way,' said the judge.

'I admire your command of contemporary speech.' She went ahead into the restaurant, inspecting the room with bright, observant eyes. When they were sitting at the table she whispered, 'There's that same woman we met last year. Remember? The classy type who kept putting you right about Britten.'

The judge, cautiously, turned his head. 'So it is. Keep a low profile.'

'Will do, squire,' said Marjorie applying herself to the menu. 'Fifteen all?' she added. 'Right?'

'Right,' said her husband.

Their acquaintance, leaving before them, stopped to exchange greetings. The judge, mildly resenting the interruption to his meal, left the work to Marjorie. The woman, turning to go, said, 'So nice to see you again. And have a lovely break from juries and things.' She gleamed upon the judge.

He watched her retreating silk-clad back. 'Rather a gushing creature. How the hell does she know what I do?'

'Chatting up the hotel people, I don't doubt. It gives you cachet, you note, your job. Me, on the other hand, she considers a drab little woman. I could see her wondering how I came by you.'

'Shall we enlighten her? Sheer unbridled lust . . .'

'Talking of which,' said Marjorie. 'Just how unprincipled would it be to finish off with some of that cheese-cake?'

Back at the hotel, they climbed into bed in a state of enjoyable repletion. The judge put on his spectacles and reached out for the suitcase. 'You're not going to start going through that stuff *now* . . . ' said Marjorie. 'At least have one whole day off work.'

'You're right,' he said. 'Tomorrow will do. I'll have that Barbara Pym novel instead.'

The judge, waking early the next morning, lay thinking about the current trial. He thought, in fact, not about obscenity or pornography but about the profit motive. He did not, he realised, understand the profit motive; he did not understand it in the same way in which he did not understand what induced people to be cruel. He had never coveted the possessions of others or wished himself richer than he was. He held no stocks or shares; Marjorie, once, had been left a small capital sum by an aunt; neither he nor she had ever been able to take the slightest interest in the financial health of her investments. Indeed, both had now forgotten what exactly the money was in. All this, he realised, was the position of a man with a substantial earned income; were he not paid what he was he might well feel otherwise. But he had not, in fact, felt very much otherwise as an impecunious young barrister. And importers of pornography tend, he understood, to be in an upper income bracket. No – the obstacle, the barrier requiring that leap of the imagination, was this extra dimension of need in some men that sought to turn money into yet more money, that required wealth for wealth's sake, the spawning of figures. The judge himself enjoyed growing vegetables; he considered, now, the satisfaction he got from harvesting a good crop of french beans and tried to translate this into a manifestation of the profit motive. The analogy did not quite seem to work.

The profit motive in itself, of course, is innocuous enough. Indeed, without it societies would founder. This was not the point that was bothering the judge; he was interested in those gulfs of inclination that divide person from person. As a young man he had wondered if this restriction makes us incapable of passing judgement on our fellows, but had come to realise at last that it does not. He remembered being involved in an impassioned argument about apartheid with another law student, an Afrikaner; 'You cannot make pronouncement about our policies,' the man had said, 'when you have never been to our country. You cannot understand the situation.' Richard Braine had known, with the accuracy of a physical response, that the man was wrong. Not misguided; simply wrong. A murderer is doing wrong, whatever the circumstances that drive him to his crime.

The profit motive is not wrong; the circumstances of its application may well be. The judge – with a certain irritation – found himself recalling the features of the importer of pornography: a nondescript, bespectacled man memorable only for a pair of rather bushy eyebrows and a habit of pulling an ear-lobe when under cross-examination. He pushed the fellow from his mind, determinedly, and got out of bed. Outside the window, strands of neatly corrugated cloud coasted in a milky-blue sky; it looked as though it would be a nice day.

The Braines spent the morning at Minsmere bird sanctuary; in the afternoon they went for a walk. The evening found them, scoured by fresh air and slightly somnolent, listening to Mozart, Bartok and Mendelssohn. The judge, who had never played an instrument and regarded himself as relatively unmusical, nevertheless responded to music with considerable intensity. It aroused him in various ways; in such different ways, indeed, that, being a thorough and methodical man, he often felt bemused, caught up by the onward rush of events before he had time to sort them out. Stop, he wanted to say to the surging orchestra, just let me have a think about that bit . . . But already he would have been swept onwards, into other moods, other themes, other passions. Marjorie, who played the piano in an unspectacular but competent way, had often suggested that the problem might be solved at least in part if he learned to read music.

She was no doubt right, he thought, wrestling now with a tortuous passage. When I retire; just the thing for a man reduced to inactivity. The judge did not look forward to retirement. But a few moments of inattention had been fatal – now the music had got away from him entirely, as though he had turned over two pages of a book. Frowning, he concentrated on the conductor.

Standing at the bar in the interval, he found himself beside their acquaintance from the restaurant, also waiting to order a drink. Gallantry or even basic good manners required that he intervene. 'Oh,' she said. 'How terribly sweet of you. A gin and tonic would be gorgeous.' With resignation, he led her back to where Marjorie awaited him.

'Your husband was so sweet and insistent – I'm all on my own this evening, my sister had a splitting headache and decided not to come.' She was a tall woman in her early fifties, too youthfully packaged in a flounced skirt and high-heeled boots, her manner towards the judge both sycophantic and faintly roguish. 'I was reading about you in *The Times* last month, some case about people had up for embezzling, of course I didn't understand most of it, all terribly technical, but I said to Laura, I *know* him, we had such a lovely talk about Britten at the Festival.'

'Ah,' said the judge, studying his programme: the Tippett next.

'I'm Moira Lukes, by the way – if you're anything like me names just *evaporate,* but of course I remembered yours from seeing it in the paper.' She turned to Marjorie. 'Aren't you loving the concert?'; patronage discreetly flowed, the patronage of a woman with a sexual history towards one who probably had none, of a lavishly clad woman towards a dowdy one. The judge's antennae slightly quivered, though he was not himself sure why. Marjorie blandly agreed that the concert was superb. 'Excuse me,' she said. 'I'm going to make a dash to the loo while there's time.'

The judge and Moira Lukes, left alone, made private adjustments to each other's company: the judge cleared his throat and commented on the architecture of the concert hall; Moira moved a fraction closer to him and altered the pitch of her voice, probably without being aware that she did either. 'You must lead such a satisfying life,' she said. 'I mean, you must come across such extraordinary people. Dickensian types. I don't think I've ever set eyes on a criminal.'

The judge thought again of the importer of pornography. 'Most of them are rather mundane, when it comes to the point.'

'But you must get to know so much about people.' She was looking very directly at him, with large eyes; a handsome woman, the judge conceded, rather a knock-out as a girl, no doubt. He agreed that yes, one did get a few insights into the ways in which people carry on.

'Fascinating,' said Moira Lukes again. 'I expect you have the most marvellous stories to tell. I envy your wife no end.' The large eyes creased humorously at the corners; a practised device, though the judge did not recognise this. 'In fact I think she's a lucky woman – I still remember that interesting chat you and I had last year.' And she laid on his arm a hand, which was almost instantly removed – come and gone as briefly as though a bird had alighted for a fleeting second. The judge, startled in several ways, tried to recall this chat: something about when *Peter Grimes* was first performed, or was it *The Turn of the Screw?* The interest of it, now, escaped him. He cast a quick glance across the foyer in search of Marjorie, who seemed to be taking an awfully long time. Moira Lukes was talking now about the area of Sussex in which she lived. Do, she was saying, look in and have lunch, both of you, if you're ever in that part of the world. The judge murmured that yes, of course if they were . . . He noticed the rings on her hand and wondered vaguely what had become of Mr Lukes; somehow one knew that he was no longer around, one way or the other.

'The only time,' she said, 'I've ever personally had anything to do with the law was over my rather wretched divorce.' The judge took a swig of his drink. 'And then actually the lawyer was most awfully sweet, in fact he kept my head above water through it all.' She sighed, a whiff of a sigh, almost imperceptible; thereby, she implied most delicately, hung a tale. 'So I've got rather a soft spot for legal people.'

'Good,' said the judge heartily. 'I'm glad to hear you've been well treated by the profession.'

'Oh, *very* well treated.'

No sign of Marjorie, still. Actually, the judge was thinking, this Moira Whatshername wasn't perhaps quite so bad after all, behind that rather tiresome manner; appearances, inevitably, deceive. One got the impression, too, of someone who'd maybe had a bit of a rough time. 'Well, it's a world that includes all sorts, like most. And it brings you up against life, I suppose, with all that that implies.'

The respect with which these banalities were received made him feel a little cheap. In compensation, he told her an anecdote about a case in which he had once been involved; a *crime passionnel* involving an apparently wronged husband who had turned out in fact to be the villain of the piece. 'A mealy-mouthed fellow, and as plausible as you like, but apparently he'd been systematically persecuting her for years.' Moira Lukes nodded sagely. 'People absolutely are not what they seem to be.'

'Well,' said the judge. 'Yes and no. On the other hand, plenty of people give themselves away as soon as they open their mouths.'

'Oh, goodness,' said Moira Lukes. 'Now I'll feel I daren't utter a word ever again.'

'I had in mind those I come across professionally rather than in private life.'

'Ah, then you think I'm safe?'

'Now, whatever could you have to conceal?' said the judge amiably. A bell went. 'I wonder where Marjorie's got to.' I suppose we'd better start going back in.'

Moira Lukes sighed. She turned those large eyes upon him and creased them once again at the corners. 'Well, this has been so nice. I'm sure we'll run into each other again over the weekend. But do bear in mind that I'm in the East Sussex phone book. I remember that case I read about was in Brighton – if you're ever judging there again and want a few hours' retreat on your own, do pop over and have a drink.' She smiled once more, and walked quickly away into the crowd.

The judge stood for a moment, looking after her. He realised with surprise that he had been on the receiving end of what is generally known as a pass. He realised also that he was finding it difficult to sort out exactly what he felt about this; a rational response and his natural judgement of people (he didn't in fact all that much care for the woman) fought with more reprehensible feelings and a certain complacency (so one wasn't a total old buffer just yet). In this state of internal conflict he made his way back into the concert hall, where he found Marjorie already in her seat.

'What on earth happened to you?'

'Sorry,' she said cheerfully. 'There was an awful queue in the ladies' and by the time I got out it wasn't worth coming to find you. How did you make out with our friend?'

The judge grunted, and applied himself to the programme. The lights went down, the conductor reappeared, the audience sank into silence . . . But the music, somehow, had lost its compulsion; he was aware now of too much that was external – that he could achieve no satisfactory position for his legs, that he had slight indigestion, that the chap in front of him kept moving his head. Beside him, he could see Marjorie's face, rapt. The evening, somehow, had been corrupted.

The next morning was even more seraphic than the one before. 'Today,' said Marjorie, 'we are going to sit on the beach and bask. We may even venture into the sea.'

'That sounds like a nice idea.' The judge had thought during the night of the little episode with that woman and, in the process, a normal balance of mind had returned; he felt irritated – though more with himself than with her – that it had interfered with his enjoyment of the concert. It was with some annoyance, therefore, that he spotted her now across the hotel dining-room, with the sister, lifting her hand in a little finger-waggling wave of greeting.

'What's the matter?' said Marjorie, with marital insight. 'Oh . . . Her. Well, I'll leave you to hide behind the paper. I'm going upstairs to get sorted out for the beach.'

He was half-way through the Home News page when he felt her standing over him. Alone. The sister, evidently, had been disposed of.

'Another heavenly day. Aren't we lucky! All on your own? I saw your wife bustling off . . . ' She continued to stand, her glance drifting now towards the coffee pot at the judge's elbow.

I am supposed, he thought, to say sit down and join me – have a cup of coffee. And he felt again that quiver of the antennae and knew now the reason. Marjorie does indeed bustle, her walk is rather inelegant, but it is not for you to say so, or to subtly denigrate a person I happen to love. He rattled, slightly, his newspaper. 'We're off to the beach shortly.'

'Oh, lovely. I daresay we'll go down there later. I wonder . . . Goodness, I don't know if I ought to ask you this or not . . . ' She hesitated, prettily, seized, it seemed, with sudden diffidence. 'Oh, I'll be brave. The thing is,

I have this tiresome problem about a flat in London I'm buying, something to do with the leasehold that I simply do not follow, and I just do not have absolute faith in the man who's dealing with it for me – the solicitor, you know – *could* I pick your brains about it at some point?'

The judge, impassive, gazed up at her.

'I don't mean *now* – not in the middle of your holiday weekend. My sister was noticing your address in the hotel register and believe it or not my present flat is only a few minutes away. What would be lovely would be if you could spare an hour or so to look in for a drink on your way home one evening – and your wife too of course, only it might be awfully boring for her if you're going to brief me. Is that the right word? Would it be an imposition? When you're on your own like I am you are so very much at the mercy of . . . ' she sighed – 'people, the system, I don't know what . . . Sometimes I get quite panic-stricken.'

I doubt that, thought the judge. He put the newspaper down. ' Mrs Lukes . . .'

'Oh, Moira . . . please.'

He cleared his throat. 'Conveyancing, as it happens, is not my field. Anything I said might quite possibly be misleading. The only sensible advice I can give is to change your solicitor if you feel lack of confidence in him.'

Her eyes flickered; that look of honest appeal dimmed suddenly. 'Oh . . . I see. Well, I daresay you're right. I must do that, then. I shouldn't have asked. But of course the invitation stands, whenever you're free.'

'How kind,' said the judge coolly. He picked up his paper again and looked at her over the top of it; their eyes met in understanding. And he flinched a little at her expression; it was the look of hatred he had seen from time to time, over the years, across a courtroom, on the face in the dock.

'Have a *lovely* day,' said Moira Lukes. Composure had returned; she gleamed, and wrinkled her eyes, and was gone. Well, thought the judge, there's no love lost there, now. But it had to be done, once and for all. He folded the paper and went in search of Marjorie.

She was packing a beach-bag with costumes and towels. The judge, unlocking the suitcase, took out a stack of the pornographic magazines and pushed them into the bottom of the bag. 'Oh, lor,' said Marjorie, 'I'd forgotten about them. Must you?'

"Fraid so. The case resumes tomorrow. It's the usual business of going through them for degrees of obscenity. There are some books too.'

'I'll help you,' said Marjorie. 'There – greater love hath no woman . . .'

The beach was agreeably uncrowded. Family parties were dotted in clumps about the sand; children and dogs skittered in and out of the surf; gulls floated above the water and a party of small wading birds scurried back and forth before the advancing waves like blown leaves. The judge, who enjoyed a bit of unstrenuous bird-watching, sat observing them with affection. The weather, this particularly delectable manifestation of the physical world and the uncomplicated relish of the people and animals around him had induced a state of general benignity. Marjorie, organising the rug and wind-screen, said, 'All right?' 'All right,' he replied. They smiled at each other, appreciating the understatement.

Marjorie, after a while, resolutely swam. The judge, more craven, followed her to the water's edge and observed. As they walked back up the beach together he saw suddenly that Moira Lukes and her sister were encamped not far off. She glanced at him and then immediately away. Now, at midday, the beach was becoming more occupied, though not disturbingly so. A family had established itself close to the Braines' pitch: young parents with a baby in a pram and a couple of older children now deeply engaged in the initial stages of sandcastle construction. The judge, who had also made a sandcastle or two in his time, felt an absurd urge to lend a hand; the basic design, he could see was awry and would give trouble before long. The mother, a fresh-faced young woman, came padding across the sand to ask Marjorie for the loan of a tin-opener. They chatted for a moment; the young woman carried the baby on her hip. 'That sort of thing,' said Marjorie, sitting down again, 'can still make me broody, even at my time of life.' She too watched the sandcastle-building; presently she rummaged in the picnic basket and withdrew a plastic beaker. 'Turretts,' she explained to the judge, a little guiltily. 'You can never do a good job with a bucket . . .' The children received her offering with rewarding glee; the parents gratefully smiling; the sandcastle rose, more stylish.

The judge sighed, and delved in the beach-bag. 'To work, I suppose,' he said. Around them, the life of the beach had settled into a frieze, as though the day were eternal: little sprawled groups of people, the great arc of the horizon against which stood the grey shapes of two far-away ships, like cut-outs, the surface animation of running dogs and children and someone's straw hat, tossed hither and thither by the breeze that had sprung up.

The judge and his wife sat with a pile of magazines each. Marjorie said,

126

'This is a pretty gruesome collection. Can I borrow your hankie, my glasses keep getting salted over.'

The judge turned over pages, and occasionally made some notes. Nothing he saw surprised him; from time to time he found himself examining the faces that belonged to the bodies displayed, as though in search of explanations. But they seemed much like any other faces; so presumably were the bodies.

Marjorie said, 'Cup of tea? Tell me, why are words capable of so much greater obscenity than the pictures?' She was glancing through a book, or something that passed as such.

'That, I imagine, is why people have always gone in for burning them, though usually for quite other reasons.'

It was as the judge was reaching out to take the mug of tea from her that the wind came. It came in a great wholesome gust, flinging itself along the beach with a cloud of brown sand and flying plastic bags. It sent newspapers into the air like great flapping birds and spun a spotted football along the water's edge as though it were a top. It lifted rugs and pushed over deckchairs. It snatched the magazines from the judge's lap and from Marjorie's and bore them away across the sand in a helter-skelter whirl of colourful pages, dropping them down only to grab them again and fling them here and there: at the feet of a stout lady snoozing in a deckchair, into the pram of the neighbouring family's baby, on to people's towels and Sunday papers.

Marjorie said, 'Oh *lor* . . .'

They got up. They began, separately, to tour the beach in pursuit of what the wind had taken. The judge found himself, absurdly, feeling foolish because he had left his jacket on his chair and was plodding along the sand in shirt-sleeves (no tie, either) and tweed trousers. The lady in the deckchair woke and put out a hand to quell the magazine that was wrapping itself round her leg. 'Yours?' she said amiably, looking up at the judge, and as she handed him the thing it fell open and for a moment her eyes rested on the central spread, the *pièce de resistance*; her expression changed, rubbed out as it were by amazement, and she looked again at the judge for an instant, and became busy with the knitting on her lap.

Marjorie, stumping methodically along, picked up one magazine and then another, tucking them under her arm. She turned and saw that the children had observed the crisis, abandoned their sandcastle and were scurrying here and there, collecting as though involved in a treasure hunt. The mother, too, had risen and was shaking the sand from a magazine that

127

had come to rest against the wheels of a pram. As Marjorie reached her the little girl ran up with an armful. 'Good girl, Sharon,' said her mother, and the child – six, perhaps, or seven – virtuously beamed and held out to Marjorie the opened pages of the magazine she held. She looked at it and the mother looked at it and Marjorie looked and the child said, 'Are those flowers?' 'No, my dear,' said Marjorie sadly. 'They aren't flowers,' and she turned away before she could meet the eyes of the young mother.

The judge collected a couple from a man who handed them over with a wink, and another from a boy who stared at him expressionless, and then he could not find any more. He walked back to their pitch. Marjorie was shoving things into the beach-bag. 'Shall we go?' she said, and the judge nodded.

It was as they were folding the rug that Moira Lukes came up. She wore neatly creased cotton trousers and walked with a spring. 'Yours, apparently,' she said; she held the magazine between a finger and thumb, as though with tongs, and dropped it on the sand. She looked straight at the judge. 'How awfully true,' she said, 'that people are not what they seem to be.' Satisfaction flowed from her; she glanced for an instant at Marjorie, as though checking that she had heard, and walked away.

The Braines, in silence, completed the assembly of their possessions. Marjorie carried the rug and the picnic basket and the judge bore the beach-bag and the wind-screen. They trudged the long expanse of the beach, watched, now, with furtive interest by various eyes.

* * * * *

Susan Hill: Aldeburgh, with its echoes of Crabbe and more recently its music festival, has acted as a magnet to writers over the years. Brought up on the Suffolk coast, Susan Hill was drawn back to the place by Britten's *Sea Interludes* and each winter throughout the 1970s she rented a cottage on the sea front. These were productive years for Hill. The clear, vibrant air seemed charged with an intensity and the stories began to flow as she tramped for miles along the shore. The result is a series of moving tales set on this bleak stretch of coast, notably her novella *The Albatross* and several short stories including *Mr Proudham And Mr Sleight* in the collection *A Bit Of Singing And Dancing* (1973).

Mr Proudham And Mr Sleight

SUSAN HILL

That evening, I saw Mr Proudham and Mr Sleight for the first time. I had set out to walk all the way along the sea front but the sleet and a north-easterly wind soon drove me back to the tall, Edwardian house in which I rented a flat. I had chosen to come here at the bleakest time of year, partly because I gained an obscure satisfaction from physical endurance. But mainly because nobody would trouble me. The flat had no telephone.

The sky was gunmetal grey. Only two or three other people had ventured out, women briskly walking their dogs. They wore long tweed coats padded out with cardigans underneath and sensible, sheepskin-lined boots and scarves wound round their heads for the protection of mouths and ears. Nobody looked at me.

But when I opened the front gate of the house Mr Proudham and Mr Sleight were looking. It was almost dark and they had not put the light on in their ground floor window. They stood side by side, shadowy, improbable figures. I was to see them like that so often during the weeks to come – Mr Proudham, immensely tall and etiolated, with a thin head and unhealthy yellowish skin: and Mr Sleight, perhaps five feet one or two, with a benevolent, rather stupid moon of a face. He was bald: Mr Proudham had dingy-white hair, worn rather long.

I hesitated, fiddling with the latch. They stood, watching. They made no secret of their curiosity, they had no net curtain behind which they might hide. But their faces were curiously expressionless. The sleet had turned to hail. I went quickly inside. Mr Proudham and Mr Sleight continued to watch me until I had passed out of sight, under the shadow of the porch.

It was a full week before they introduced themselves – or rather, before Mr Proudham introduced them, for little Mr Sleight nodded and beamed and clicked his false teeth but rarely spoke. When he did, it was to murmur with his friend.

Each time I left the house they were watching me. And I began, a little more surreptitiously, to watch them. They had a dog, an overgrown sooty poodle which was clipped in not quite the usual fashion, but in horizontal bands going round its body and up the tail, so that from a distance it appeared to be striped in two-tone grey. Mr Proudham always held the lead and Mr Sleight trotted alongside keeping time with the dog.

They went out three times a day, at ten, at two and at six. In addition, Mr Proudham went out at eleven each morning carrying a shopping bag of a drab olive cloth. And it was in a shop, Cox's Mini-Market, that I first came face to face with him. He was buying parsnips and because I was standing at the back of the queue I had a chance to study him. He was considerably older than I had at first thought, with heavy-lidded eyes that drooped at the corners and a mouth very full of teeth. On top of the off-white hair he wore a curious woollen beret, rather like that of a French onion-seller but with a pompom on the top. As he turned to leave the shop he saw me. He stopped. Then, as though he had considered the situation carefully, he bowed, and lifted his hand. For a moment I wondered if he were going to raise the little woollen hat. But he only gave a half-salute.

'Good morning.'

But that time he did not reply.

Later, I was working at my desk in the window when I saw the two of them go off down the path for their two o'clock walk. It was one of those lowering, east coast days which had never come fully light. Both men wore long knitted scarves in bright multi-colours, which hung down their backs like those of children or students. But only Mr Proudham had a hat – the woolly beret. As they reached the gate they turned and looked up at my window. They did not seem in the least disconcerted that I was sitting there, looking back at them. For what can only have been ten seconds but felt considerably longer they stood, so that I almost waved, to prevent embarrassment. But I did not, and eventually they moved off on their walk.

That evening, Mr Proudham spoke. I had been out to post a letter. The temperature had dropped again, so that my breath smoked on the air and the sea was glistening with reflected frost. It was quite dark. As I came up the alleyway between two houses, which led from the High Street on to the sea front, I saw them a few yards away. The dog was sniffing busily around the concrete bollard. Some decision must have been reached by them earlier for, as though they had been waiting for this moment, Mr Proudham stepped forward to meet me.

'I am Mr Proudham, this is Mr Sleight. How do you do?'

It was a formal little speech. He had a rather high-pitched voice, and I saw that there were even more teeth than I had first noticed, long and crowded together. We shook hands and the dog turned its attention from the bollard and began to sniff me.

'We do hope you are comfortable at number forty-three? We do hope you have everything you require?'

Yes, I said, I was very comfortable. And I looked at Mr Sleight, who at once blushed and glanced at Mr Proudham, and then away, and then down at the dog. He did not speak, though I thought that the movement of his mouth indicated that he might wish to.

'We do hope you were not expecting better weather. Alas, it is never better than this in late November.'

I told him it was what I had been prepared for.

'Yes. I see, I see, I see.'

Then abruptly he pulled at the dog's lead and touched the arm of Mr Sleight. Mr Sleight jumped and his eyes began to swivel about again. He was smiling into space.

'I'm afraid there is not much entertainment here,' Mr Proudham said. They were already moving off, so that when he repeated the sentence, his words were carried away down the sea front on the wind.

'No entertainment . . . '

'Goodbye.' But they were already out of earshot. I looked back at them, the tall, thin figure and the short round one with the brightly coloured scarves hanging like pigtails down behind. The striped dog was pulling at the end of the lead, so that Mr Proudham had to bend forward. I smiled. But there was something about them that was not altogether funny.

At the front door I looked for their names above the bell. "Proudham and Sleight" were written like a firm of solicitors. No initials. Proudham and Sleight.

I drew my curtains and switched on the electric fire. I would work for another couple of hours before supper. A little later, I heard them come in, heard doors open and close gently. They were very quiet, Mr Proudham and Mr Sleight, they did not seem to have a television or wireless set, or to shout to one another from room to room, as is sometimes the habit of those who live together. Most of the time, there might have been no one at all in the flat below.

I had gone there to work undisturbed, but I also spent a good time walking, either along the beach itself for several miles or on the

131

promenade which followed the shore from the south side, where I was living, right up to the breakwater at the most northerly point of the town. It was here that a few amusements were situated. Most of them were closed at this time of year but I liked to wander past the canvas-shrouded dodgem cars and the shuttered gift stalls, I enjoyed the tawdriness of it all, the blank lights and peeling paint. There was an open air swimming pool, drained for the winter, and sand and silt had been washed over the rim by the storm tides. Near to this was a café and one amusement centre, called Gala Land, both of which remained open.

I could not keep away from Gala land. It had a particular smell which drew me down the steep flight of concrete steps to the pay desk below. It was built underground in a sort of valley between two outcrops of rock, over which was a ribbed glass roof, like those of Victorian railway stations and conservatories. The walls were covered in greenish moss and the whole place had a close, damp, musty smell and although it was lit from end to end with neon and fluorescent lights, everything looked somehow dark, furtive and gone to seed. Some of the booths were closed down here, too, and those which kept open must have lost money, except perhaps on the few days when parties of trippers came from inland, in the teeth of the weather, and dived down for shelter to the underground fun palace. Then, for a few hours, the fruit and try-your-strength and fortune card machines whirred, loud cracks echoed from the rifle ranges, hurdy-gurdy music sounded out, there was a show of gaiety. For the rest of the time the place was mainly patronized by a few unemployed men and teenage boys, who chewed gum and fired endless rounds of blank ammunition at the bobbing rows of duck targets, and by older schoolchildren after four o'clock. At the far end was a roller skating rink which drew a good crowd on Saturday afternoons.

I liked that sad, shabby place, I liked its atmosphere. Occasionally I put a coin into a fruit machine or watched What the Butler Saw. There was a more gruesome peepshow, too, in which one could watch a condemned man being led on to a platform, hooded and noosed and then dropped snap, down through a trapdoor to death. I watched this so often that, long after I had left the town, this scene featured in my nightmares, I smelled the brackish, underground smell.

It was in Gala Land, early one Thursday afternoon, that I saw Mr Proudham. He was alone, and operating one of the football machines. A dropped coin set a small ball rolling among a set of figures which could be swivelled from side to side by means of a lever. The aim was to make one of them bang the ball into the goal before it rolled out of sight down a slot in the side. Mr Proudham was concentrating hard, bending over the machine and manipulating the handles with great energy. He wore, as usual, the woolly pompom hat and a grey mackintosh. I watched him as he had three tries and then succeeded in knocking the ball into a goal with the fourth. He stood upright and retrieved his coin from the metal dish.

'Well done!' I said.

He turned, and for a moment I thought he was going to scuttle away, pretending that he had not recognised me. Instead he smiled, showing all those teeth. I would have asked if he came here often, but at once, he said, 'Today is Mr Sleight's day at the clinic. I always come down here to pass the time you know, until he is due to return. I have somehow to pass the time.'

I hoped that Mr Sleight was not seriously ill. Mr Proudham leaned forward a little, lowering his voice. 'It's the massage, you see. He goes for the massage.'

I did not like to inquire further and I would have made some excuse to leave quickly then, in case Mr Proudham felt embarrassed at being caught in Gala Land. But he asked, with a rather strange, cat-like expression on his face, if I would care for some tea.

'There is quite a *clean* cafe, just beside the pool, they do make a very reasonable cup of tea. I generally go there on Mr Sleight's day at the clinic. It passes the time. I like to give myself something to do. Yes.'

And so he escorted me out of the damp-smelling, half-empty funfair and up to ground level, where Timpson's Seagull Cafe was also half-empty, and smelled of china tiles and urn-tea.

I did not know what I might talk to Mr Proudham about, over our pot of tea, but I need not have worried because, as though he wanted to deflect any attention from himself, he began to ask me questions, about my work, my life in London, London itself. They were not personal, probing questions – I could answer them in detail and yet not give much away. Mr Proudham listened, smiling every now and again with all those teeth. He was the one who poured out the tea. I noticed that his eyes were bloodshot and that the yellowish cheeks were shot through here and there with broken veins. How old was he? Seventy? Perhaps not quite, or perhaps a year or two more, it was hard to tell.

Suddenly he said, 'Behind you is a photograph of my mother.' I looked round.

The picture was an old one, in an oak frame, of the grandstand which had been demolished during the last war. There were flowers, mostly

133

hydrangeas, banked around the base and awnings draped above, hung with tassels. Sitting in the bandstand was a Ladies' Orchestra. They were all dressed in white, Grecian style garments, hanging in folds to the floor, with floral headbands. They looked wide-eyed, vacant and curiously depressed.

'My mother,' said Mr Proudham, 'is the Lady Conductor.'

And there she was, a large-bosomed woman with wildly curling hair, who clutched her baton like a fairy's wand.

I said, how interesting.

'She died in 1937,' Mr Proudham said. 'I myself was never musical. It was her great sadness.'

'So you have always lived here?'

Mr Proudham inclined his head. Then, as if he were afraid of having given too much away, he looked up brightly, clapping his hands together.

'Now – I hope you are not a believer in blood sports.'

We stayed in Timpson's Seagull Café until just before five o'clock, when he jumped up and began to pull on gloves and wind his scarf anxiously, for Mr Sleight would be home from the clinic.

'And I make a point of being in,' Mr Proudham said, 'I think that is so important, don't you? To be in. I am always waiting.'

He shook hands with me, across the green formica table, as though one of us were departing on a journey, and rushed away.

After that I saw them together most days, and Mr Proudham always spoke and Mr Sleight smiled and looked nervous, and once or twice I bumped into Mr Proudham alone. But Mr Sleight was never alone. I wondered if he might be a little simple, unable to cope with the outside world by himself. On Thursday afternoons a taxi drew up and he went off in it to the clinic. Mr Proudham left the house shortly after, to walk in the direction of the funfair and the Seagull Café.

The week before Christmas they issued an invitation. I had been for a walk along the beach, in the snow, and when I returned there was an envelope pushed underneath my door.

Would you care to take tea with us on Saturday next? Unless we hear to the contrary, we greatly look forward to seeing you at 4.30 pm.

The note was written in a neat, rather childish hand on cream paper. I replied to it, putting my own card underneath the door while they were out on their six o'clock walk. For I wanted to satisfy my curiosity about them, I wanted to see inside their flat. And I felt rather sorry for them, a pair of elderly men who never had a visitor.

On that Saturday morning, Mr Proudham went out alone not once but twice and returned each time with a full shopping bag. I put on a red dress, and wished I had some gift I could take with me.

Mr Proudham opened the door. He was wearing a canary yellow waistcoat, over a boldly checked shirt and matching cravat. In the sitting room I found Mr Sleight with his bald head almost invisible over the polo neck of a bright orange jumper. We made a highly-coloured trio standing uncertainly together in the centre of the room, which was stiflingly hot, with a log fire and three radiators turned on to full. 'Now please sit down, please sit down.' I picked a chair well away from the hearth and, for a moment, Mr Proudham and Mr Sleight both stood over me, their faces beaming proudly. Perhaps no one had been here to tea before.

When Mr Proudham did speak, it was a little 'Ah!' like a sigh of satisfaction, as though he were a photographer who had arranged a perfect tableau. 'Ah!' and he glanced at Mr Sleight and nodded and smiled and held out a hand in my direction. Mr Sleight smiled. I smiled. The hot room was full of bonhomie.

They might have been expecting a party of schoolboys for tea. There was white and brown bread and butter, muffins, toast, gentleman's relish, honey, crab apple jelly, fruit loaf, fruit cake, chocolate gâteau, éclairs, meringues, shortbread fingers. I ate as much as I could, but Mr Proudham and Mr Sleight ate a good deal more, cake after cake, and drank cups of sugary tea. Conversation lapsed. The poodle dog watched from the other side of the room. I wondered how we would get through the time after tea, and whether Mr Sleight were dumb.

They had bought or inherited some beautiful furniture – a set of Chippendale chairs, a Jacobean oak table, a dresser hung with Crown Derby china. The carpet was Persian, there were Cotman and Birkett Foster watercolours on the walls. And in an alcove near the window stood an enormous tropical fish tank. In another corner, a parrot in a cage sat so perfectly still and silent I thought it might be a dummy.

Eventually, Mr Proudham wiped crumbs of meringue from around his mouth with a purple handkerchief. He said, 'I think that Mr Sleight has something to *show* you.' It was the tone a mother would use about her child which has some drawing or piece of handiwork to proffer. Mr Sleight gave a little nervous cough.

I could not have been in the least prepared for what I was to see. Mr Sleight led me, with a slightly flustered air, out of the room and down a short passage, and through a heavily beaded curtain which he held aside for me, and which rattled softly as he let it go. Mr Proudham stood well back.

'Now this is Mr Sleight's territory. I never interfere. This is *all* his own.'

It was rather dark, apart from two spotlights attached to a wall above a long workbench. Shelves had been fitted all round the room, and displayed on the shelves, as well as on the window-ledge and several small tables, were rows of wax-work models. They were a little larger than children's puppets, and similarly grotesque, but a good deal more carefully made.

Mr Sleight stood back, his eyes flicking here and there about the room, occasionally resting on me for a second, as he tried to judge what I was thinking. I stepped closer to the bench and looked down at the two models which were in progress, at enamel bowls of wax, rubber moulds and papier-mache bases, and small chisels and blades and neat little piles of hair. And, looking round, I saw the faces of Mr Proudham and Mr Sleight, smiling and motionless like two, larger wax-works, dressed in those startling colours.

'Well? Well?' Mr Proudham said, and lifted a hand to finger his cravat.

'Does he . . .' I corrected myself. 'Do you make all these yourself, by hand?' Mr Sleight blushed and nodded, and at once glanced for confirmation at Mr Proudham.

'Oh yes, yes, nothing to do with *me*. I was never at all a handyman, I wouldn't be the slightest help, oh no! Everything is done by Mr Sleight, all by himself.'

The waxworks were very bizarre characters from Japanese No plays and from Grimm, African warriors in war paint, animal masks attached to human bodies, hideous Punch and Judy figures: and then, familiar, ordinary-looking men in ordinary clothes who were, I realised with a shock, tiny replicas of the figures in the Chamber of Horrors – Crippen and Haigh and Christie. The clothes, down to the last button and shoelace and cufflink, were perfect.

'They're superb.'

'We don't *sell* then, you know,' Mr Proudham said. 'We don't do this for money, it's a craft, what you might call a pastime. Mr Sleight works away in here day after day. But we are not a *commercial* enterprise.'

The room smelled of old, spent matches and cooling wax, like a church after candles have been snuffed out. I wondered whether Mr Sleight would gradually fill the whole, already crowded flat with his shelves of models. They were disturbing, curiously life-like, utterly dead. I wanted to leave.

Later, as I was thanking them for the tea, Mr Sleight disappeared, and came scurrying back with one of the puppets in his hand, his face very pink.

'Well!' Mr Proudham clasped his hands together. 'Well, you *are* honoured!'

Mr Sleight was pressing the model into my hands. It was a Chinese Court Lady, with exquisitely small hands, and feet covered in beaded slippers. She wore a gold brocade kimono and a sash embroidered with flights of tiny butterflies and bumble bees.

'All for you!'

I was touched by Mr Sleight's gesture, and by the silent, beaming face. But oddly repelled by the small figure which felt so stiff and cold in my hands. I knew it was generous of him to give it. I wished very much that he had not.

I had reached the door of my own flat when Mr Proudham caught up with me. He was out of breath and his face was suddenly very old and anxious. 'I had to say – you see Mr Sleight takes to people so very rarely, he knows no one here, he . . . You will keep it, won't you? You do appreciate . . . He never gives them away, he has never done it before. You will *treasure* it, won't you?'

I reassured him. Inside my flat I examined the doll more closely. The workmanship was astonishing. I imagined Mr Sleight's pale, plump hands moulding, embroidering. I did not think I had heard him speak at all, there were only the nods and smiles, the shifting glances. I put the wax doll on the mantlepiece.

On Christmas Eve it snowed. The tide was running high and there was the hardest frost of the year. In the middle of the night I was awakened by the sound of raised voices. I had worked late and not been very long in bed. It was perhaps one o'clock. Mr Proudham and Mr Sleight were quarrelling. Ever since I was a young child in the home of unhappy, incompatible parents I had been used to hearing the sound of bitter argument in another room, so that now I felt the old misery and apprehension, wanting it to stop, wanting a reconciliation. The voices went on. A door banged, then another.

It was after two before I went to sleep. When I woke again it was past five. The shouting had ceased. My room was bitterly cold. I got up and went to the window. There was a full moon and the pebbles of the beach gleamed pale, the sea was very still. A light shone out of the flat below on to the small front garden. I stood looking down for a long time, until I began to shiver and had to go in search of another blanket. There might have been no one else awake in the whole world. It was a quiet house in any case, the top floor flat was closed up for the winter. I thought of Mr Sleight's workroom behind the beaded curtain, of the rows of black figures. It was a long time before I went back uneasily to sleep.

On Christmas morning, I went out early to spend the day with friends inland, and it was gone midnight when I returned. The ground floor flat was in darkness, all the curtains were drawn. I was not woken up that night.

The next day, a thaw set in. I spent most of it working, and beyond the window I could see sky and sea merged together in the rain, everything was leaden grey. At eleven o'clock and at two Mr Proudham went out alone with the dog, at six it was Mr Sleight, draped in a mackintosh that reached to his ankles. Neither of them glanced up at my window. I was puzzled by the small changes in routine.

The rain continued all night, rolling down the gutters and lashing against the glass. For the first time, I felt lonely here, I missed London where there was always someone to call on, something to do, the streets always lighted and full of people. I began to be sick of the endlessly rolling grey sea and the cawing of gulls. So I was glad of any company when, the following evening, Mr Proudham came to my door. I asked him to go back and fetch his friend, we would all have a festive drink.

Mr Proudham stood half in and half out of the hallway, his hands moving about nervously inside the pockets of his long, beige cardigan. He looked ill, the skin was markedly more yellow than usual and there were dark smears like thumb-prints beneath his eyes. His hair was uncombed, his shirt, open at the neck, was not particularly clean. He had always struck me as a fastidious man.

'Is everything all right, Mr Proudham?'

'No. Oh no, I'm afraid it is not – I'm afraid . . . I'm sorry, but it is not possible for me to fetch Mr Sleight – you are very kind but Mr Sleight has gone.' He was biting the side of his mouth anxiously.

'Really, I should not have come up, it has nothing to do with you – why should you have any idea what has happened?'

'Where has Mr Sleight gone to?'

'If I knew that . . .' He jumped suddenly, as though there were somebody behind him. I persuaded him to come inside, and in the light of the sitting room he looked even more ill and distressed.

'It isn't the first time, you see, it has happened before.'

Outside the sea roared up and hit the shingle and hissed back again into the darkness.

'He is not well, that is the point, he cannot manage alone, wherever he may have gone. He is not at all well.'

I wondered whether it were physically or mentally, but did not like to ask.

'We had – there were *words*, you see, I was impatient. Oh, it is a long story, it was nothing . . . But then everything seemed to blow over again, we had settled down. But he is not an easy man, I can never tell, you see, never be quite sure . . . he says so little. Well, you will have noticed. But now, today, he has disappeared again, and how can he manage, in this weather? I did wonder if perhaps you had heard something, seen something? I have been searching all over the town, asked everyone. I wondered if you . . .'

I had not, of course, and had to tell him so.

'No. No, you would not know. You could not be expected.'

'Does he have friends to go to? Have you tried telephoning relatives?'

'He has none. There is no one.'

'Has he taken anything with him? Clothes? A suitcase?

'Nothing. But he is not *well* – he has, fits, he cannot manage alone.' His face crumpled, the mouth sagged suddenly, until I thought that he would cry.

'I shall go out again. There is nothing else for it. I shall go out looking for him. I shall find him in the end.'

At the door he turned and gave a little, formal bow, like that with which he first greeted me.

'Perhaps I can help? Would you like me to come with you?'

'It is better for me to go alone.'

I watched him go down the stairs.

The next five days were extremely distressing for Mr Proudham, who paced the beaches and the streets of that bleak little town, and telephoned ceaselessly to hospitals and police stations, and for me, too, who watched him and could not help, could not even inquire too closely. The rain did not cease, twice the tide spilled over the sea wall and flooded part of the front garden. Mr Proudham went out in Wellington boots, carrying the poodle dog. I tried to work and could not. Every so often my eye fell on the tiny wax doll.

And then, just before six o'clock one evening, when I had drawn my curtains against the cold, wet night, I heard footsteps coming quickly up the stairs, the doorbell rang urgently.

'He is found!' Mr Proudham's eyes were full of excited tears, he clasped and unclasped his hands. 'He is found! Oh, he has been very ill, *is* very ill, he wandered away for miles, got on to a bus . . . he is in hospital. But he is not drowned, not dead, I felt sure that he would be dead. But he is alive!'

I was delighted, and said so, and he stood on the doorstep for several minutes, chattering with relief.

'But I must go to see him, I thought I would just tell you, but now I must get everything ready, I am sure they will let him come home soon.'

As it happened they did not, not for another three weeks. He was perhaps more seriously ill than was at first thought. Every afternoon, Mr Proudham went off to visit him, every evening he came upstairs to report on his friend's progress – though I thought that there was something he was keeping back. Once or twice I gave him a meal or a drink for he was not accustomed to managing on his own.

'It is Mr Sleight who cooks and keeps us tidy, you know. It has always been Mr Sleight who has managed things.' I was surprised, the partnership seemed to have been based upon the quickness and efficiency of the talkative Mr Proudham.

I did not really come to know him, though we talked a good deal, he told me stories about the past, about his childhood, in theatrical boarding houses with his mother, of the ladies' orchestra. But although I knew selected facts I felt that he was holding anything of himself, of his own emotions or beliefs, back from me. He framed his formal, old-fashioned sentences, but that was all. Of his life with Mr Sleight he told me nothing, except that they had been together for more than twenty years.

The day before Mr Sleight was to come home, I offered to go downstairs and help with any cleaning there might be to do. Mr Proudham seemed offended and rather shocked, he would not hear of such a thing, and I was embarrassed. I had not intended to seem curious or interfering.

'I shall take pleasure in it,' he said stiffly. 'It is the least I can do, after all, the proper way for me to welcome him home.'

I understood, and listened all that day to the sounds of cleaning, saw Mr Proudham shake rugs and mops out of the window, wearing a mauve plastic apron. The poodle dog had been freshly clipped, so that brownish-pink skin showed through the shaven, horizontal bands and a red bow was tied around the top knot between its ears.

An ambulance brought Mr Sleight home. And as soon as I saw him, wrapped in a blanket and wheeled up the path in a chair, I knew that something was very wrong. He was much smaller, he seemed to have shrunk into himself, the skin was creased and folded, and his eyes darted wildly in the bony face. His hands, resting on the padded arms of the wheelchair, were white as claws. Mr Proudham, wearing the canary yellow waistcoat, fluttered around in attendance, smiling, smiling.

I had intended to wait a day or so until Mr Sleight had settled in, and then to take down some magazines and fruit, for he seemed unlikely to have any other visitors. But the morning after his return, Mr Proudham met me by the front door. He looked tired.

'In case you were wondering . . . in case you thought of paying Mr Sleight a visit.'

I told him what I planned.

'Oh no. No, really you had far better not. You are very kind, but you see . . . things are not quite as they were, Mr Sleight has . . . is a little changed, not up to seeing visitors, he may not know you, or rather . . . Well, he is disturbed just at the moment. He has had a shock. They found him wandering, you know, he had had nothing to eat, his clothes . . . I really do think . . .'

I interrupted to save his obvious embarrassment, told him that of course I understood and would not dream of causing either of them any distress. Mr Proudham's face relaxed, but there was still something, an anxiety, a fear in his bloodshot eyes, he fidgeted more than ever. 'Thank you, thank you, thank you,' he said, and went into the flat, closing the door behind him very quickly.

Every day after that he went out with the dog, and to do the shopping, always alone. He grew paler and more worn-looking, he took on a dishevelled, even grubby appearance. I worried about him from time to time, about both of them, so isolated and dependent. The winter weather was the worst for several years, snow and frost set in and showed no signs of thawing by early March.

My work was coming to an end, and I began to think I had had enough of the place. Once or twice, during those last weeks, I felt strongly that all was not as it should be with Mr Proudham and Mr Sleight. Several times I heard raised voices and now and then a loud banging on the floor, as though with a stick.

I came home as it was getting dark one evening, and as I turned from the gate, I caught sight of a pale, still face in the ground floor window. Mr Sleight was propped up on a sofa and he was staring intently at me. The beam, and the rather amusing self-consciousness had quite gone. His face was thin. He did not take his eyes off me and I saw that they had the intense yet oddly blank look of the very mad. He held in his hands one of the wax models: it was unfinished, without clothes and without any features moulded in its smooth, oval face. He held it up a little and, as I stared, began to twist one of the legs. If I had stayed there I should have seen it come away in his hands. I did not, I ran up the path and Mr Sleight watched me, unblinking, unsmiling. That night, the quarrelling began again, one of the voices rose to a scream. In the morning I saw Mr Proudham go out with the dog, and his face was grey.

A week later, I left. When I met Mr Proudham in the path, he seemed alarmed, we shook hands, and he ducked back at once into the flat. I heard the key turn in the lock. When I shut the gate behind me for the last time, I saw the two figures, so changed, watching me as they had watched when I arrived, Mr Proudham standing a little bent at the shoulders behind the chair of Mr Sleight. I hesitated, half-raised a hand to them. There was no response. I moved quickly away.

It was on Good Friday that the name of the town happened to catch my eye in the daily paper. There was a small paragraph. Police were investigating the deaths of Mr Albert Proudham and Mr Victor Sleight, whose bodies were found in a gas-filled room. A poodle dog and a parrot were also dead. I would have thought it an accident on the part of poor, harassed Mr Proudham, if it had not also been reported that the flat was in considerable disorder, a large number of 'dolls and puppets' having been found, broken and mutilated, and strewn about the floor.

* * * * *

M R James: This son of a Suffolk clergyman established a brilliant reputation as a medievalist at King's Cambridge. He eventually became University Chancellor but is best remembered for the ghost stories he wrote to amuse fellow students. *A Warning To The Curious* (1925) is set in Aldeburgh, a place James knew well from visits to his grandparents. As an antiquarian he was also familiar with the barrow-digging exploits of Victorian archaeologists and the local legend of the three crowns which gave him the idea for this cautionary tale.

A Warning To The Curious

M R JAMES

The place on the east coast the reader is asked to consider is Seaburgh. It is not very different now from what I remember it to have been when I was a child. Marshes intersected by dykes to the south, recalling the early chapters of *Great Expectations*; flat fields to the north, merging into heath; heath, fir woods, and, above all, gorse, inland. A long sea-front and a street: behind that a spacious church of flint, with a broad, solid western tower and a peal of six bells. How well I remember their sound on a hot Sunday in August, as our party went slowly up the white, dusty slope of road towards them, for the church stands at the top of a short, steep incline. They rang with a flat clacking sort of sound on those hot days, but when the air was softer they were mellower too. The railway ran down to its little terminus farther along the same road. There was a gay white windmill just before you came to the station, and another down near the shingle at the south end of the town, and yet others on higher ground to the north. There were cottages of bright red brick with slate roofs . . . but why do I encumber you with these commonplace details? The fact is that they come crowding to the point of the pencil when it begins to write of Seaburgh.

Walk away from the sea and the town, pass the station, and turn up the road on the right. It is a sandy road, parallel with the railway, and if you follow it, it climbs to somewhat higher ground. On your left is heath, on your right is a belt of old firs, wind-beaten, thick at the top, with the slope that old seaside trees have; seen on the skyline from the train they would tell you in an instant, if you did not know it, that you were approaching a windy coast. Well, at the top of my little hill, a line of these firs strikes out and runs towards the sea, for there is a ridge that goes that way; and the ridge ends in a rather well-defined mound commanding the level fields of rough grass, and a little knot of fir trees crowns it. And here you may sit on a hot spring day, very well content to look at blue sea, white windmills, red cottages, bright green grass, church tower, and distant martello tower on the south.

As I have said, I began to know Seaburgh as a child; but a gap of a good many years separates my early knowledge from that which is more recent. Still it keeps its place in my affections, and any tales of it that I pick up have an interest for me. One such tale is this: it came to me in a place very remote from Seaburgh, and quite accidentally, from a man whom I had been able to oblige – enough in his opinion to justify his making me his confidant to this extent.

I know all that country more or less (he said). I used to go to Seaburgh pretty regularly for golf in the spring. I generally put up at the 'Bear', with a friend – Henry Long it was, you knew him perhaps – ('Slightly,' I said) and we used to take a sitting-room and be very happy there. Since he died I haven't cared to go there. And I don't know that I should anyhow after the particular thing that happened on our last visit.

It was April, 19—, we were there, and by some chance we were almost the only people in the hotel. So the ordinary public rooms were practically empty, and we were the more surprised when, after dinner, our sitting-room door opened, and a young man put his head in. We were aware of this young man. He was rather a rabbity anaemic subject – light hair and light eyes – but not unpleasing. So when he said: 'I beg your pardon, is this a private room?' we did not growl and say: 'Yes, it is,' but Long said, or I did – no matter which: 'Please come in.'

'Oh may I?' he said, and seemed relieved. Of course it was obvious that he wanted company; and as he was a reasonable kind of person – not the sort to bestow his whole family history on you – we urged him to make himself at home. 'I daresay you find the other rooms rather bleak,' I said. Yes, he did: but it was really too good of us, and so on. That being got over, he made some pretence of reading a book. Long was playing Patience, I was writing. It became plain to me after a few minutes that this visitor of ours was in rather a state of fidgets or nerves, which communicated itself to me, and so I put away my writing and turned to at engaging him in talk.

After some remarks, which I forget, he became rather confidential. 'You'll think it very odd of me,' (this was the sort of way he began) 'but the fact is I've had something of a shock.' Well, I recommended a drink of some cheering kind, and we had it. The waiter coming in made an interruption (and I thought our young man seemed very jumpy when the door opened), but after a while he got back to his woes again. There was nobody he knew in the place, and he did happen to know who we both were (it turned out there was some common acquaintance in town), and really he did want a word of advice, if we didn't mind. Of course we both said: 'By all means,' or 'Not at all,' and Long put away his cards. And we settled down to hear what his difficulty was.

'It began,' he said, 'more than a week ago, when I bicycled over to Froston, only about five or six miles, to see the church; I'm very much interested in architecture, and it's got one of those pretty porches with niches and shields. I took a photograph of it, and then an old man who was tidying up in the churchyard came and asked if I'd care to look into the church. I said yes, and he produced a key and let me in. There wasn't much inside, but I told him it was a nice little church, and he kept it very clean, "but," I said, "the porch is the best part of it." We were just outside the porch then, and he said, "Ah, yes, that is a nice porch; and do you know, sir, what's the meanin' of that coat of arms there?"

'It was the one with the three crowns, and though I'm not much of a herald, I was able to say yes, I thought it was the old arms of the kingdom of East Anglia.

' "That's right, sir," he said, "and do you know the meanin' of them three crowns that's on it?"

'I said I'd no doubt it was known, but I couldn't recollect to have heard it myself.

' "Well, then," he said, "for all you're a scholard, I can tell you something you don't know. Them's the three 'oly crowns what was buried in the ground near by the coast to keep the Germans from landing —ah, I can see you don't believe that. But I tell you, if it hadn't have been for one of them 'oly crowns bein' there still, them Germans would a landed here time and again, they would. Landed with their ships, and killed man, woman and child in their beds. Now then, that's the truth what I'm telling you, that is; and if you don't believe me, you ast the rector. There he comes: you ast him, I says."

'I looked round, and there was the rector, a nice-looking old man, coming up the path; and before I could begin assuring my old man, who was getting quite excited, that I didn't disbelieve him, the rector struck in, and said: "What's all this about, John? Good day to you, sir. Have you been looking at our little church?"

'So then there was a little talk which allowed the old man to calm down, and then the rector asked him again what was the matter.

' "Oh," he said, "it warn't nothink, only I was telling this gentleman he'd ought to ast you about them 'oly crowns."

' "Ah, yes, to be sure," said the rector, "that's a very curious matter, isn't it? But I don't know whether the gentleman is interested in our old stories, eh?"

' "Oh, he'll be interested fast enough," says the old man, "he'll put his confidence in what you tells him, sir; why, you known William Ager yourself, father and son too."

'Then I put in a word to say how much I should like to hear all about it, and before many minutes I was walking up the village street with the rector, who had one or two words to say to parishioners, and then to the rectory, where he took me into his study. He had made out, on the way, that I really was capable of taking an intelligent interest in a piece of folk-lore, and not quite the ordinary tripper. So he was very willing to talk, and it is rather surprising to me that the particular legend he told me has not made its way into print before. His account of it was this: "There has always been a belief in these parts in the three holy crowns. The old people say they were buried in different places near the coast to keep off the Danes or the French or the Germans. And they say that one of the three was dug up a long time ago, and another has disappeared by the encroaching of the sea, and one's still left doing its work, keeping off invaders. Well, now, if you have read the ordinary guides and histories of this county, you will remember perhaps that in 1687 a crown, which was said to be the crown of Redwald, King of the East Angles, was dug up at Rendlesham, and alas! alas! melted down before it was even properly described or drawn. Well, Rendlesham isn't on the coast, but it isn't so very far inland, and it's on a very important line of access. And I believe that is the crown which the people mean when they say that one has been dug up. Then on the south you don't want me to tell you where there was a Saxon royal palace which is now under the sea, eh? Well, there was the second crown, I take it. And up beyond these two, they say, lies the third."

' "Do they say where it is?" of course I asked. 'He said, "Yes, indeed, they do, but they don't tell," and his manner did not encourage me to put the obvious question. Instead of that I waited a moment, and said: "What did the old man mean when he said you knew William Ager, as if that had something to do with the crowns?"

' "To be sure," he said, "now that's another curious story. These Agers – it's a very old name in these parts, but I can't find that they were ever people of quality or big owners – these Agers say, or said, that their branch of the family were the guardians of the last crown. A certain old Nathaniel Ager was the first one I knew – I was born and brought up quite near here

– and he, I believe, camped out at the place during the whole of the war of 1870. William, his son, did the same, I know, during the South African War. And young William, *his* son, who has only died fairly recently, took lodgings at the cottage nearest the spot, and I've no doubt hastened his end, for he was a consumptive, by exposure and night watching. And he was the last of that branch. It was a dreadful grief to him to think that he was the last, but he could do nothing, the only relations at all near to him were in the colonies. I wrote letters for him to them imploring them to come over on business very important to the family, but there has been no answer. So the last of the holy crowns, if it's there, has no guardian now.'

'That was what the rector told me, and you can fancy how interesting I found it. The only thing I could think of when I left him was how to hit upon the spot where the crown was supposed to be. I wish I'd left it alone.

'But there was a sort of fate in it, for as I bicycled back past the churchyard wall my eye caught a fairly new gravestone, and on it was the name of William Ager. Of course I got off and read it. It said 'of this parish, died at Seaburgh, 19–, aged 28.' There it was you see. A little judicious questioning in the right place, and I should at least find the cottage nearest the spot. Only I didn't quite know what was the right place to begin my questioning at. Again there was fate: it took me to the curiosity shop down that way – you know – and I turned over some old books, and, if you please, one was a prayer book of 1740 odd, in a rather handsome binding – I'll just go and get it, it's in my room.'

He left us in a state of some surprise, but we had hardly time to exchange any remarks when he was back, panting, and handed us the book opened at the fly-leaf, on which was, in a straggly hand:

> *Nathaniel Ager is my name and England is my nation,*
> *Seaburgh is my dwelling place and Christ is my Salvation,*
> *When I am dead and in my Grave, and all my bones are rotton,*
> *I hope the Lord will think of me when I am quite forgotton.'*

This poem was dated 1754, and there were many more entries of Agers, Nathaniel, Frederick, William, and so on, ending with William, 19—.

'You see,' he said, 'anybody would call it the greatest bit of luck. *I* did, but I don't now. Of course I asked the shopman about William Ager, and of course he happened to remember that he lodged in a cottage in the North Field and died there. This was just chalking the road for me. I knew which the cottage must be: there is only one sizable one about there. The next thing was to scrape some sort of acquaintance with the people, and

I took a walk that way at once. A dog did the business for me: he made at me so fiercely that they had to run out and beat him off, and then naturally begged my pardon, and we got into talk. I had only to bring up Ager's name, and pretend I knew, or thought I knew something of him, and then the woman said how sad it was him dying so young, and she was sure it came of him spending the night out of doors in cold weather. Then I had to say: "Did he go out on the sea at night?" and she said: "Oh, no; it was on the hillock yonder with the trees on it." And there I was.

'I know something about digging in these barrows: I've opened many of them in the down country. But that was with owner's leave, and in broad daylight and with men to help. I had to prospect very carefully here before I put a spade in: I couldn't trench across the mound, and with those old firs growing there I knew there would be awkward tree roots. Still the soil was very light and sandy and easy, and there was a rabbit hole or so that might be developed into a sort of tunnel. The going out and coming back at odd hours was going to be the awkward part. When I made up my mind about the way to excavate I told the people that I was called away for a night, and I spent it out there. I made my tunnel: I won't bore you with the details of how I supported it and filled it in when I'd done, but the main thing is that I got the crown.'

Naturally we both broke out into exclamations of surprise and interest. I for one had long known about the finding of the crown at Rendlesham and had often lamented its fate. No one has ever seen an Anglo-Saxon crown – at least no one had. But our man gazed at us with a rueful eye. 'Yes,' he said, 'and the worst of it is I don't know how to put it back.'

'Put it back?' we cried out. 'Why, my dear sir, you've made one of the most exciting finds ever heard of in this country. Of course it ought to go to the Jewel House at the Tower. What's your difficulty? If you're thinking about the owner of the land, and treasure trove, and all that, we can certainly help you through. Nobody's going to make a fuss about technicalities in a case of this kind.'

Probably more was said, but all he did was to put his face in his hands, and mutter: 'I don't know how to put it back.'

At last Long said: 'You'll forgive me, I hope, if I seem impertinent, but are you *quite* sure you've got it?' I was wanting to ask much the same question myself, for of course the story did seem a lunatic's dream when one thought over it. But I hadn't quite dared to say what might hurt the poor young man's feelings. However, he took it quite calmly – really, with the calm of despair, you might say. He sat up and said: 'Oh, yes, there's no doubt of that: I have it here, in my room, locked up in my bag. You can come and look at it if you like: I won't offer to bring it here.'

We were not likely to let the chance slip. We went with him; his room was only a few doors off. The boots was just collecting shoes in the passage: or so we thought: afterwards we were not sure. Our visitor – his name was Paxton – was in a worse state of shivers than before, and went hurriedly into the room, and beckoned us after him, turned on the light, and shut the door carefully. Then he unlocked his kit-bag, and produced a bundle of clean pocket handkerchiefs in which something was wrapped, laid it on the bed, and undid it. I can now say I *have* seen an actual Anglo-Saxon crown. It was of silver – as the Rendlesham one is always said to have been – it was set with some gems, mostly antique intaglios and cameos, and was of rather plain, almost rough workmanship. In fact, it was like those you see on the coins and in the manuscripts. I found no reason to think it was later than the ninth century. I was intensely interested, of course, and I wanted to turn it over in my hands, but Paxton prevented me. 'Don't *you* touch it,' he said, 'I'll do that.' And with a sigh that was, I declare to you, dreadful to hear, he took it up and turned it about so that we could see every part of it. 'Seen enough?' he said at last, and we nodded. He wrapped it up and locked it in his bag, and stood looking at us dumbly. 'Come back to our room,' Long said, 'and tell us what the trouble is.' He thanked us, and said: 'Will you go first and see if – if the coast is clear?' That wasn't very intelligible, for our proceedings hadn't been, after all, very suspicious, and the hotel, as I said, was practically empty. However, we were beginning to have inklings of – we didn't know what, and anyhow nerves are infectious. So we did go, first peering out as we opened the door, and fancying (I found we both had the fancy) that a shadow, or more than a shadow – but it made no sound – passed from before us to one side as we came out into the passage. 'It's all right,' we whispered to Paxton – whispering seemed the proper tone – and we went, with him between us, back to our sitting-room. I was preparing, when we got there, to be ecstatic about the unique interest of what we had seen, but when I looked at Paxton I saw that would be terribly out of place, and I left it to him to begin.

'What *is* to be done?' was his opening. Long thought it right (as he explained to me afterwards) to be obtuse, and said: 'Why not find out who the owner of the land is and inform . . . ' 'Oh, no, no!' Paxton broke in impatiently, 'I beg your pardon: you've been very kind, but don't you see it's *got* to go back, and I daren't be there at night, and daytime's impossible.

Perhaps, though, you don't see: well, then, the truth is that I've never been alone since I touched it.' I was beginning some fairly stupid comment, but Long caught my eye, and I stopped. Long said: 'I think I do see, perhaps: but wouldn't it be . . . a relief . . . to tell us a little more clearly what the situation is?'

Then it all came out: Paxton looked over his shoulder and beckoned to us to come nearer to him, and began speaking in a low voice: we listened most intently, of course, and compared notes afterwards, and I wrote down our version, so I am confident I have what he told us almost word for word. He said: 'It began when I was first prospecting, and put me off again and again. There was always somebody . . . a man . . . standing by one of the firs. This was in daylight, you know. He was never in front of me. I always saw him with the tail of my eye on the left or the right, and he was never there when I looked straight for him. I would lie down for quite a long time and take careful observations, and make sure there was no one, and then when I got up and began prospecting again, there he was. And he began to give me hints, besides; for wherever I put that prayer book . . . short of locking it up, which I did at last – when I came back to my room it was always out on my table open at the fly-leaf where the names are, and one of my razors across it to keep it open. I'm sure he just can't open my bag, or something more would have happened. You see, he's light and weak, but all the same I daren't face him. Well, then, when I was making the tunnel, of course it was worse, and if I hadn't been so keen I should have dropped the whole thing and run. It was like someone scraping at my back all the time: I thought for a long time it was only soil dropping on me, but as I got nearer the . . . the crown, it was unmistakable. And when I actually laid it bare and got my fingers into the ring of it and pulled it out, there came a sort of cry behind me . . . oh, I can't tell you how desolate it was! And horribly threatening too. It spoilt all my pleasure in my find – cut it off that moment. And if I hadn't been the wretched fool I am, I should have put the thing back and left it. But I didn't. The rest of the time was just awful. I had hours to get through before I could decently come back to the hotel. First I spent time filling up my tunnel and covering my tracks, and all the while he was there trying to thwart me. Sometimes, you know, you see him, and sometimes you don't, just as he pleases, I think: he's there, but he has some power over your eyes. Well, I wasn't off the spot very long before sunrise, and then I had to get to the junction for Seaburgh, and take a train back. And though it was daylight fairly soon, I don't know if that made it much better. There were always hedges, or gorse bushes, or park fences along the road – some sort of cover,

I mean – and I was never easy for a second. And then when I began to meet people going to work, they always looked behind me very strangely: it might have been that they were surprised at seeing anyone so early; but I didn't think it was only that, and I don't now: they didn't look exactly at *me*. And the porter at the train was like that too. And the guard held open the door after I'd got into the carriage – just as he would if there was somebody else coming, you know. Oh, you may be sure it isn't my fancy,' he said with a dull sort of laugh. Then he went on: 'And even if I do get it put back, he won't forgive me: I can tell that. And I was so happy a fortnight ago.' He dropped into a chair, and I believe he began to cry.

We didn't know what to say, but we felt we must come to the rescue somehow, and so – it really seemed the only thing – we said if he was so set on putting the crown back in its place, we would help him. And I must say that after what we had heard it did seem the right thing. If these horrid consequences had come on this poor man, might there not really be something in the original idea of the crown having some curious power bound up with it, to guard the coast? At least, that was my feeling, and I think it was Long's too. Our offer was very welcome to Paxton, anyhow. When could we do it? It was nearing half-past ten. Could we contrive to make a late walk plausible to the hotel people that very night? We looked out of the window: there was a brilliant full moon – the Paschal moon. Long undertook to tackle the boots and propitiate him. He was to say that we should not be much over the hour, and if we did find it so pleasant that we stopped out a bit longer we would see that he didn't lose by sitting up. Well, we were pretty regular customers of the hotel, and did not give much trouble, and were considered by the servants to be not under the mark in the way of tips; and so the boots *was* propitiated, and let us out on to the sea-front, and remained, as we heard later, looking after us. Paxton had a large coat over his arm, under which was the wrapped-up crown.

So we were off on this strange errand before we had time to think how very much out of the way it was. I have told this part quite shortly on purpose, for it really does not represent the haste with which we settled our plan and took action. 'The shortest way is up the hill and through the churchyard,' Paxton said, as we stood a moment before the hotel looking up and down the front. There was nobody about – nobody at all. Seaburgh out of the season is an early, quiet place. 'We can't go along the dyke by the cottage, because of the dog,' Paxton also said, when I pointed to what I thought was a shorter way along the front and across two fields. The reason he gave was good enough. We went up the road to the church, and turned in at the churchyard gate. I confess to having thought that there might be someone lying there who might be conscious of our business: but if it was so, they were also conscious that one who was on their side, so to say, had us under surveillance, and we saw no sign of them. But under observation we felt we were, as I have never felt it at another time. Specially was it so when we passed out of the churchyard into a narrow path with close high hedges, through which we hurried as Christian did through that Valley; and so got out into open fields. Then along hedges, though I would sooner have been in the open, where I could see if anyone was visible behind me; over a gate or two, and then a swerve to the left, taking us up on to the ridge which ended in that mound.

As we neared it, Henry Long felt, and I felt too, that there were what I can only call dim presences waiting for us, as well as a far more actual one attending us. Of Paxton's agitation all this time I can give you no adequate picture: he breathed like a hunted beast, and we could not either of us look at his face. How he would manage when we got to the very place we had not troubled to think: he had seemed so sure that that would not be difficult. Nor was it. I never saw anything like the dash with which he flung himself at a particular spot in the side of the mound, and tore at it, so that in a very few minutes the greater part of his body was out of sight. We stood holding the coat and that bundle of handkerchiefs, and looking, very fearfully, I must admit, about us. There was nothing to be seen: a line of dark firs behind us made one skyline, more trees and the church tower half a mile off on the right, cottages and a windmill on the horizon on the left, calm sea dead in front, faint barking of a dog at a cottage on a gleaming dyke between us and it; full moon making that path we know across the sea; the eternal whisper of the Scotch firs just above us, and of the sea in front. Yet, in all this quiet, an acute, an acrid consciousness of a restrained hostility very near us, like a dog on a leash that might be let go at any moment.

Paxton pulled himself out of the hole, and stretched a hand back to us. 'Give it to me,' he whispered, 'unwrapped.' We pulled off the handkerchiefs, and he took the crown. The moonlight just fell on it as he snatched it. We had not ourselves touched that bit of metal, and I have thought since that it was just as well. In another moment Paxton was out of the hole again and busy shovelling back the soil with hands that were already bleeding. He would have none of our help, though. It was much the longest part of the job to get the place to look undisturbed: yet – I don't know how – he made a wonderful success of it. At last he was satisfied, and we turned back.

We were a couple of hundred yards from the hill when Long suddenly said to him: 'I say, you've left your coat there. That won't do. See?' And I certainly did see it – the long dark overcoat lying where the tunnel had been. Paxton had not stopped, however: he only shook his head, and held up the coat on his arm. And when we joined him, he said, without any excitement, but as if nothing mattered any more: 'That wasn't my coat.' And, indeed, when we looked back again, the dark thing was not to be seen.

Well, we got out on to the road, and came rapidly back that way. It was well before twelve when we got in, trying to put a good face on it, and saying – Long and I – what a lovely night it was for a walk. The boots was on the look-out for us, and we made remarks like that for his edification as we entered the hotel. He gave another look up and down the sea-front before he locked the front door, and said: 'You didn't meet many people about, I s'pose, sir?' 'No, indeed, not a soul,' I said; at which I remember Paxton looked oddly at me. 'Only I thought I see someone turn up the station road after you gentlemen,' said the boots. 'Still, you was three together, and I don't suppose he meant mischief.' I didn't know what to say; Long merely said 'Good night,' and we went off upstairs, promising to turn out all lights, and to go to bed in a few minutes.

Back in our room, we did our very best to make Paxton take a cheerful view. 'There's the crown safe back,' we said; 'very likely you'd have done better not to touch it' (and he heavily assented to that), 'but no real harm has been done, and we shall never give this away to anyone who would be so mad as to go near it. Besides, don't you feel better yourself? I don't mind confessing,' I said, 'that on the way there I was very much inclined to take your view about – well, about being followed; but going back, it wasn't at all the same thing, was it?' No, it wouldn't do: '*You've* nothing to trouble yourselves about,' he said, 'but I'm not forgiven. I've got to pay for that miserable sacrilege still. I know what you are going to say. The Church might help. Yes, but it's the body that has to suffer. It's true I'm not feeling that he's waiting outside for me just now. But . . .' Then he stopped. Then he turned to thanking us, and we put him off as soon as we could. And naturally we pressed him to use our sitting-room next day, and said we should be glad to go out with him. Or did he play golf, perhaps? Yes, he did, but he didn't think he should care about that tomorrow. Well, we recommended him to get up late and sit in our room in the morning while we were playing, and we should have a walk later in the day. He was very submissive and *piano* about it all: ready to do just what we thought best, but clearly quite certain in his own mind that what was coming could not be averted or palliated. You'll wonder why we didn't insist on accompanying him to his home and seeing him safe into the care of brothers or someone. The fact was he had nobody. He had had a flat in town, but lately he had made up his mind to settle for a time in Sweden, and he had dismantled his flat and shipped off his belongings, and was whiling away a fortnight or three weeks before he made a start. Anyhow, we didn't see what we could do better than sleep on it – or not sleep very much, as was my case – and see what we felt like tomorrow morning.

We felt very different, Long and I, on as beautiful an April morning as you could desire; and Paxton also looked very different when we saw him at breakfast. 'The first approach to a decent night I seem ever to have had,' was what he said. But he was going to do as we had settled: stay in probably all the morning, and come out with us later. We went to the links; we met some other men and played with them in the morning, and had lunch there rather early, so as not to be late back. All the same, the snares of death overtook him.

Whether it could have been prevented, I don't know. I think he would have been got at somehow, do what we might. Anyhow, this is what happened.

We went straight up to our room. Paxton was there, reading quite peaceably. 'Ready to come out shortly?' said Long, 'say in half an hour's time?' 'Certainly,' he said, and I said we would change first, and perhaps have baths, and call for him in half an hour. I had my bath first, and went and lay down on my bed, and slept for about ten minutes. We came out of our rooms at the same time, and went together to the sitting-room. Paxton wasn't there . . . only his book. Nor was he in his room, nor in the downstairs rooms. We shouted for him. A servant came out and said: 'Why, I thought you gentlemen was gone out already, and so did the other gentleman. He heard you a-calling from the path there, and run out in a hurry, and I looked out of the coffee-room window, but I didn't see you. 'Owever, he run off down the beach that way.'

Without a word we ran that way too – it was the opposite direction to that of last night's expedition. It wasn't quite four o'clock, and the day was fair, though not so fair as it had been, so there was really no reason, you'd say, for anxiety: with people about, surely a man couldn't come to much harm.

But something in our look as we ran out must have struck the servant, for she came out on the steps and pointed, and said, 'Yes, that's the way he went.' We ran on as far as the top of the shingle bank, and there pulled up. There was a choice of ways: past the houses on the sea-front, or along the sand at the bottom of the beach, which, the tide being now out, was fairly broad. Or of course we might keep along the shingle between these two tracks and have some view of both of them; only that was heavy going. We chose the sand, for that was the loneliest, and someone *might* come to harm there without being seen from the public path.

Long said he saw Paxton some distance ahead, running and waving his stick, as if he wanted to signal to people who were on ahead of him. I couldn't be sure: one of those sea mists was coming up very quickly from the south. There was someone, that's all I could say. And there were tracks on the sand as of someone running who wore shoes; and there were other tracks made before those – for the shoes sometimes trod in them and interfered with them – of someone not in shoes. Oh, of course, it's only my word you've got to take for all this: Long's dead, we'd no time or means to make sketches or take casts, and the next tide washed everything away. All we could do was to notice these marks as we hurried on. But there they were over and over again, and we had no doubt whatever that what we saw was the track of a bare foot, and one that showed more bones than flesh.

The notion of Paxton running after – after anything like this, and supposing it to be the friends he was looking for, was very dreadful to us. You can guess what we fancied: how the thing he was following might stop suddenly and turn round on him, and what sort of face it would show, half-seen at first in the mist – which all the while was getting thicker and thicker. And as I ran on wondering how the poor wretch could have been lured into mistaking that other thing for us, I remembered his saying, 'He has some power over your eyes.' And then I wondered what the end would be, for I had no hope now that the end could be averted, and . . . well, there is no need to tell all the dismal and horrid thoughts that flitted through my head as we ran on into the mist. It was uncanny, too, that the sun should still be bright in the sky and we could see nothing. We could only tell that we were now past the houses and had reached that gap there is between them and the old martello tower. When you are past the tower, you know, there is nothing but shingle for a long way – not a house, not a human creature, just that spit of land, or rather shingle, with the river on your right and the sea on your left.

But just before that, just by the martello tower, you remember there is the old battery, close to the sea. I believe there are only a few blocks of concrete left now: the rest has all been washed away, but at this time there was a lot more, though the place was a ruin. Well, when we got there, we clambered to the top as quick as we could to take breath and look over the shingle in front if by chance the mist would let us see anything. But a moment's rest we must have. We had run a mile at least. Nothing whatever was visible ahead of us, and we were just turning by common consent to get down and run hopelessly on, when we heard what I can only call a laugh; and if you can understand what I mean by a breathless, a lungless laugh, you have it. It came from below, and swerved away into the mist. That was enough. We bent over the wall. Paxton was there at the bottom.

You don't need to be told that he was dead. His tracks showed that he had run along the side of the battery, had turned sharp round the corner of it, and, small doubt of it, must have dashed straight into the open arms of someone who was waiting there. His mouth was full of sand and stones, and his teeth and jaws were broken to bits. I only glanced once at his face.

At the same moment, just as we were scrambling down from the battery to get to the body, we heard a shout, and saw a man running down the bank of the martello tower. He was the caretaker stationed there, and his keen old eyes had managed to descry through the mist that something was wrong. He had seen Paxton fall, and had seen us a moment after, running up – fortunate this, for otherwise we could hardly have escaped suspicion of being concerned in the dreadful business. Had he, we asked, caught sight of anybody attacking our friend? He could not be sure.

We sent him off for help, and stayed by the dead man till they came with the stretcher. It was then that we traced out how he had come, on the narrow fringe of sand under the battery wall. The rest was shingle, and it was hopelessly impossible to tell whither the other had gone.

What were we to say at the inquest? It was a duty, we felt, not to give up, there and then, the secret of the crown, to be published in every paper. I don't know how much you would have told; but what we did agree upon was this: to say that we had only made acquaintance with Paxton the day before, and that he told us he he was under some apprehension of danger at the hands of a man called William Ager. Also that we had seen some other tracks besides Paxton's when we followed him along the beach. But of course by that time everything was gone from the sands.

No one had any knowledge, fortunately, of any William Ager living in the district. The evidence of the man at the martello tower freed us from all suspicion. All that could be done was to return a verdict of wilful murder by some person or persons unknown.

Paxton was so totally without connections that all the inquiries that were subsequently made ended in a No Thoroughfare. And I have never been at Seaburgh, or even near it, since.

* * * * *

Heartland

P G Wodehouse: Norfolk has good reason to be regarded as 'official' Wodehouse country. The author was descended from one of the county's old established families whose ancestral home had been Kimberley Hall near Wymondham. In the late 1920s Wodehouse had been a frequent visitor at Hunstanton Hall as the guest of Sir Hamon Le Strange and although he chose to relocate the country seat of Bertie Wooster's fearsome Aunt Agatha in the Home Counties, the Le Strange family home is a more likely candidate for Woollam Chersey. The octagonal folly that features so prominently in *Jeeves And The Impending Doom* (1930) is still clearly visible in the park at Old Hunstanton. It was apparently built in 1655 as a music room where Sir Hamon Le Strange could practice his violin out of earshot, a fanciful story that Wodehouse could not resist repeating.

Jeeves And The Impending Doom
P G WODEHOUSE

It was the morning of the day on which I was slated to pop down to my Aunt Agatha's place at Woollam Chersey in the county of Herts for a visit of three solid weeks; and, as I seated myself at the breakfast table, I don't mind confessing that the heart was singularly heavy. We Woosters are men of iron, but beneath my intrepid exterior at the moment there lurked a nameless dread.

'Jeeves,' I said, 'I am not the old merry self this morning.'

'Indeed, sir?'

'No, Jeeves. Far from the old merry self.'

'I am sorry to hear that, sir.'

He uncovered the fragrant eggs and b., and I pronged a moody forkful.

'Why – this is what I keep asking myself, Jeeves – why has my Aunt Agatha invited me to her country seat?'

'I could not say, sir.'

'Not because she is fond of me.'

'No, sir.'

'It is a well-established fact that I give her a pain in the neck. How it happens I cannot say, but every time our paths cross, so to speak, it seems to be a mere matter of time before I perpetrate some ghastly floater and have her hopping after me with her hatchet. The result being that she regards me as a worm and an outcast. Am I right or wrong, Jeeves?'

'Perfectly correct, sir.'

'And yet now she has absolutely insisted on my scratching all previous engagements and buzzing down to Woollam Chersey. She must have some sinister reason of which we know nothing. Can you blame me, Jeeves, if the heart is heavy?'

'No, sir. Excuse me, sir, I fancy I heard the front-door bell.'

He shimmered out, and I took another listless stab at the e. and bacon.

159

'A telegram, sir,' said Jeeves, re-entering the presence.

'Open it, Jeeves, and read contents. Who is it from?'

'It is unsigned, sir.'

'You mean there's no name at the end of it?'

'That is precisely what I was endeavouring to convey, sir.'

'Let's have a look.'

I scanned the thing. It was a rummy communication. Rummy. No other word.

As follows:

Remember when you come here absolutely vital meet perfect strangers.

We Woosters are not very strong in the head, particularly at breakfast-time; and I was conscious of a dull ache between the eyebrows.

'What does it mean, Jeeves?'

'I could not say, sir.'

'It says "come here". Where's here?'

'You will notice the message was handed in at Woollam Chersey, sir.'

'You're absolutely right. At Woollam, as you very cleverly spotted, Chersey. This tells us something, Jeeves.'

'What, sir?'

'I don't know. It couldn't be from my Aunt Agatha, do you think?'

'Hardly, sir.'

'No; you're right again. Then all we can say is that some person unknown, resident at Woollam Chersey, considers it absolutely vital for me to meet perfect strangers. But why should I meet perfect strangers, Jeeves?'

'I could not say, sir.'

'And yet, looking at it from another angle, why shouldn't I?'

'Precisely, sir.'

'Then what it comes to is that the thing is a mystery which time alone can solve. We must wait and see, Jeeves.'

'The very expression I was about to employ, sir.'

I hit Woollam Chersey at about four o'clock, and found Aunt Agatha in her lair, writing letters. And, from what I know of her, probably offensive letters, with nasty postscripts. She regarded me with not a fearful lot of joy.

'Oh, there you are, Bertie.'

'Yes, here I am.'

'There's a smut on your nose.'

I plied the handkerchief.

'I am glad you have arrived so early. I want to have a word with you before you meet Mr Filmer.'

'Who?'

'Mr Filmer, the Cabinet Minister. He is staying in the house. Surely even you must have heard of Mr Filmer?'

'Oh, rather,' I said, though as a matter of fact the bird was completely unknown to me. What with one thing and another, I'm not frightfully up in the personnel of the political world.

'I particularly wish you to make a good impression on Mr Filmer.'

'Right-ho.'

'Don't speak in that casual way, as if you supposed that it was perfectly natural that you would make a good impression upon him. Mr Filmer is a serious-minded man of high character and purpose, and you are just the type of vapid and frivolous wastrel against which he is most likely to be prejudiced.'

Hard words, of course, from one's own flesh and blood, but well in keeping with past form.

'You will endeavour, therefore, while you are here not to display yourself in the *rôle* of a vapid and frivolous wastrel. In the first place, you will give up smoking during your visit.'

'Oh, I say!'

'Mr Filmer is president of the Anti-Tobacco League. Nor will you drink alcoholic stimulants.'

'Oh, dash it!'

'And you will kindly exclude from your conversation all that is suggestive of the bar, the billiard room, and the stage door. Mr Filmer will judge you largely by your conversation.'

I rose to a point of order.

'Yes, but why have I got to make an impression on this – on Mr Filmer?'

'Because,' said the old relative, giving me the eye, 'I particularly wish it.'

Not, perhaps, a notably snappy come-back as come-backs go; but it was enough to show me that that was more or less that; and I beetled out with an aching heart.

I headed for the garden, and I'm dashed if the first person I saw wasn't young Bingo Little.

Bingo Little and I have been pals practically from birth. Born in the same village within a couple of days of one another, we went through

161

kindergarten, Eton, and Oxford together; and, grown to riper years, we have enjoyed in the old metrop. full many a first-class binge in each other's society. If there was one fellow in the world, I felt, who could alleviate the horrors of this blighted visit of mine, that bloke was young Bingo Little.

But how he came to be there was more that I could understand. Some time before, you see, he had married the celebrated authoress, Rosie M. Banks; and the last I had seen of him he had been on the point of accompanying her to America on a lecture tour. I distinctly remembered him cursing rather freely because the trip would mean his missing Ascot.

Still, rummy as it might seem, here he was. And aching for the sight of a friendly face, I gave tongue like a bloodhound.

'Bingo!'

He spun round; and, by Jove, his face wasn't friendly after all. It was what they call contorted. He waved his arms at me like a semaphore.

'Sh!' he hissed. 'Would you ruin me?'

'Eh?'

'Didn't you get my telegram?'

'Was that *your* telegram?'

'Of course it was my telegram.'

'Then why didn't you sign it?'

'I did sign it.'

'No, you didn't. I couldn't make out what it was all about.'

'Well, you got my letter.'

'What letter?'

'My letter.'

'I didn't get any letter.'

'Then I must have forgotten to post it. It was to tell you that I was down here tutoring your Cousin Thomas, and that it was essential that, when we met, you should treat me as a perfect stranger.'

'But why?'

'Because, if your aunt supposed that I was a pal of yours, she would naturally sack me on the spot.'

'Why?'

Bingo raised his eyebrows.

'Why? Be reasonable, Bertie. If you were your aunt, and you knew the sort of chap you were, would you let a fellow you knew to be your best pal, tutor your son?'

162

This made the old head swim a bit, but I got his meaning after a while, and I had to admit that there was much rugged good sense in what he said. Still, he hadn't explained what you might call the nub or gist of the mystery.

'I thought you were in America,' I said.

'Well, I'm not.'

'Why not?'

'Never mind why not, I'm not.'

'But why have you taken a tutoring job?'

'Never mind why, I have my reasons. And I want you to get it into your head, Bertie — to get it right through the concrete — that you and I must not be seen hobnobbing. Your foul cousin was caught smoking in the shrubbery the day before yesterday, and that has made my position pretty tottery, because your aunt said that, if I had exercised an adequate surveillance over him, it couldn't have happened. If, after that, she finds out I'm a friend of yours, nothing can save me from being shot out. And it is vital that I am not shot out.'

'Why?'

'Never mind why.'

At this point he seemed to think he heard somebody coming, for he suddenly leaped with incredible agility into a laurel bush. And I toddled along to consult Jeeves about these rummy happenings.

'Jeeves,' I said, repairing to the bedroom, where he was unpacking my things, 'you remember that telegram?'

'Yes, sir.'

'It was from Mr Little. He's here, tutoring my young Cousin Thomas.'

'Indeed, sir?'

'I can't understand it. He appears to be a free agent, if you know what I mean; and yet would any man who was a free agent wantonly come to a house which contained my Aunt Agatha?'

'It seems peculiar, sir.'

'Moreover, would anybody of his own free will and as a mere pleasure-seeker tutor my Cousin Thomas, who is notoriously a tough egg and a fiend in human shape?'

'Most improbable, sir.'

'These are deep waters, Jeeves.'

'Precisely, sir.'

'And the ghastly part of it all is that he seems to consider it necessary, in order to keep his job, to treat me like a long-lost leper. Thus killing my only chance of having anything approaching a decent time in this abode of desolation. For do you realise, Jeeves, that my aunt says I mustn't smoke while I'm here?'

'Indeed, sir?'

'Nor drink.'

'Why is this, sir?'

'Because she wants me – for some dark and furtive reason which she will not explain – to impress a fellow named Filmer.'

'Too bad, sir. However, many doctors, I understand, advocate such abstinence as the secret of health. They say it promotes a freer circulation of the blood and insures the arteries against premature hardening.'

'Oh, do they?' Well, you can tell them next time you see them that they are silly asses.'

'Very good, sir.'

And so began what, looking back along a fairly eventful career, I think I can confidently say was the scaliest visit I have ever experienced in the course of my life. What with the agony of missing the lifegiving cocktail before dinner; the painful necessity of being obliged, every time I wanted a quiet cigarette, to lie on the floor in my bedroom and puff the smoke up the chimney; the constant discomfort of meeting Aunt Agatha round unexpected corners; and the fearful strain on the morale of having to chum with the Right Hon. A. B. Filmer, it was not long before Bertram was up against it to an extent hitherto undreamed of.

I played golf with the Right Hon. every day, and it was only by biting the Wooster lip and clenching the fists till the knuckles stood out white under the strain that I managed to pull through. The Right Hon. punctuated some of the ghastliest golf I have ever seen with a flow of conversation which, as far as I was concerned, went completely over the top; and, all in all, I was beginning to feel pretty sorry for myself when, one night as I was in my room listlessly donning the soup-and-fish in preparation for the evening meal, in trickled young Bingo and took my mind off my own troubles.

For when it is a question of a pal being in the soup, we Woosters no longer think of self; and that poor old Bingo was knee-deep in the bisque was made plain by his mere appearance – which was that of a cat which has just been struck by a half-brick and is expecting another shortly.

'Bertie,' said Bingo, having sat down on the bed and diffused silent gloom for a moment, 'how is Jeeves's brain these days?'

'Fairly strong on the wing, I fancy. How is the grey matter, Jeeves?' Surging about pretty freely?'

'Yes, sir.'

'Thank heaven for that,' said young Bingo, 'for I require your soundest counsel. Unless right-thinking people take strong steps through the proper channels, my name will be mud.'

'What's wrong, old thing?' I asked, sympathetically.

Bingo plucked at the coverlet.

'I will tell you,' he said. 'I will also now reveal why I am staying in this pest-house, tutoring a kid who requires not education in the Greek and Latin languages but a swift slosh on the base of the skull with a black-jack. I came here, Bertie, because it was the only thing I could do. At the last moment before she sailed to America, Rosie decided that I had better stay behind and look after the Peke. She left me a couple of hundred quid to see me through till her return. This sum, judiciously expended over the period of her absence, would have been enough to keep Peke and self in moderate affluence. But you know how it is.'

'How what is?'

'When someone comes slinking up to you in the club and tells you that some cripple of a horse can't help winning even if it develops lumbago and the botts ten yards from the starting-post. I tell you, I regarded the thing as a cautious and conservative investment.'

'You mean you planked the entire capital on a horse?'

Bingo laughed bitterly.

'If you could call the thing a horse. If it hadn't shown a flash of speed in the straight, it would have got mixed up with the next race. It came in last, putting me in a dashed delicate position. Somehow or other I had to find the funds to keep me going, so that I could win through till Rosie's return without her knowing what had occurred. Rosie is the dearest girl in the world; but if you were a married man, Bertie, you would be aware that the best of wives is apt to cut up rough if she finds that her husband has dropped six weeks' housekeeping money on a single race. Isn't that so, Jeeves?'

'Yes, sir. Women are odd in that respect.'

'It was a moment for swift thinking. There was enough left from the wreck to board the Peke out at a comfortable home. I signed him up for six weeks at the Kosy Komfort Kennels at Kingsbridge, Kent, and tottered out, a broken man, to get a tutoring job. I landed the kid Thomas. And here I am.'

It was a sad story, of course, but it seemed to me that, awful as it might be to be in constant association with my Aunt Agatha and young Thos, he had got rather well out of a tight place.

'All you have to do,' I said, 'is to carry on here for a few weeks more, and everything will be oojah-cum-spiff.'

Bingo barked bleakly.

'A few weeks more! I shall be lucky if I stay two days. You remember I told you that your aunt's faith in me as a guardian of her blighted son was shaken a few days ago by the fact that he was caught smoking. I now find that the person who caught him smoking was the man Filmer. And ten minutes ago young Thomas told me that he was proposing to inflict some hideous revenge on Filmer for having reported him to your aunt. I don't know what he is going to do, but if he does it, out I inevitably go on my left ear. Your aunt thinks the world of Filmer, and would sack me on the spot. And three weeks before Rosie gets back!'

I saw all.

'Jeeves,' I said.

'Sir?'

'I see all. Do you see all?'

'Yes, sir.'

'Then flock round.'

'I fear, sir —'

Bingo gave a low moan.

'Don't tell me, Jeeves,' he said, brokenly, 'that nothing suggests itself.'

'Nothing at the moment, I regret to say, sir.'

Bingo uttered a stricken woofle like a bulldog that has been refused cake.

'Well, then, the only thing I can do, I suppose,' he said sombrely, 'is not to let the pie-faced little thing out of my sight for a second.'

'Absolutely,' I said. 'Ceaseless vigilance, eh, Jeeves?'

'Precisely, sir.'

'But meanwhile, Jeeves,' said Bingo in a low, earnest voice, 'you will be devoting your best thought to the matter, won't you?'

'Most certainly, sir.'

'Thank you, Jeeves.'

'Not at all, sir.'

I will say for young Bingo that, once the need for action arrived, he behaved with an energy and determination which compelled respect. I suppose there was not a minute during the next two days when the kid Thos was able to say to himself, 'Alone at last!' But on the evening of the second day Aunt Agatha announced that some people were coming over on the morrow for a spot of tennis, and I feared that the worst must now befall.

Young Bingo, you see, is one of those fellows who, once their fingers close over the handle of a tennis racket, fall into a sort of trance in which nothing outside the radius of the lawn exists for them. If you came up to Bingo in the middle of a set and told him that panthers were devouring his best friend in the kitchen garden, he would look at you and say, 'Oh, ah?' or words to that effect. I knew that he would not give a thought to young Thomas and the Right Hon. till the last ball had bounced, and, as I dressed for dinner that night, I was conscious of an impending doom.

'Jeeves,' I said, 'have you ever pondered on Life?'

'From time to time, sir, in my leisure moments.'

'Grim, isn't it, what?'

'Grim, sir?'

'I mean to say, the difference between things as they look and things as they are.'

'The trousers perhaps a half-inch higher, sir. A very slight adjustment of the braces will effect the necessary alteration. You were saying, sir?'

'I mean, here at Woollam Chersey we have apparently a happy, care-free country-house party. But beneath the glittering surface, Jeeves, dark currents are running. One gazes at the Right Hon. wrapping himself round the salmon mayonnaise at lunch, and he seems a man without a care in the world. Yet all the while a dreadful fate is hanging over him, creeping nearer and nearer. What exact steps do you think the kid Thomas intends to take?'

'In the course of an informal conversation which I had with the young gentleman this afternoon, sir, he informed me that he had been reading a romance entitled *Treasure Island*, and had been much struck by the character and actions of a certain Captain Flint. I gathered that he was weighing the advisability of modelling his own conduct on that of the Captain.'

'But, good heavens, Jeeves! If I remember *Treasure Island*, Flint was the bird who went about hitting people with a cutlass. You don't think young Thomas would bean Mr Filmer with a cutlass?'

'Possibly he does not possess a cutlass, sir.'

'Well, with anything.'

'We can but wait and see, sir. The tie, if I might suggest it, sir, a shade more tightly knotted. One aims at the perfect butterfly effect. If you will permit me –'

'What do ties matter, Jeeves, at a time like this? Do you realise that Mr Little's domestic happiness is hanging in the scale?'

'There is no time, sir, at which ties do not matter.'

I could see the man was pained, but I did not try to heal the wound. What's the word I want? Preoccupied. I was too preoccupied, don't you know. And *distrait*. Not to say careworn. I was still careworn when, next day at half-past two, the revels commenced on the tennis lawn. It was one of those close, baking days, with thunder rumbling just round the corner; and it seemed to me that there was a brooding menace in the air.

'Bingo,' I said, as we pushed forth to do our bit in the first doubles, 'I wonder what young Thos will be up to this afternoon, with the eye of authority no longer on him?'

'Eh?' said Bingo, absently. Already the tennis look had come into his face, and his eye was glazed. He swung his racket and snorted a little.

'I don't see him anywhere,' I said.

'You don't what?'

'See him.'

'Who?'

'Young Thos.'

'What about him?'

I let it go.

The only consolation I had in the black period of the opening of the tourney was the fact that the Right Hon. had taken a seat among the spectators and was wedged in between a couple of females with parasols. Reason told me that even a kid so steeped in sin as young Thomas would hardly perpetrate any outrage on a man in such a strong strategic position. Considerably relieved, I gave myself up to the game, and was in the act of putting it across the local curate with a good deal of vim when there was a roll of thunder and the rain started to come down in buckets.

We all stampeded for the house, and had gathered in the drawing room for tea, when suddenly Aunt Agatha, looking up from a cucumber sandwich, said:

'Has anybody seen Mr Filmer?'

It was one of the nastiest jars I have ever experienced. What with my fast serve zipping sweetly over the net and the man of God utterly unable to cope with my slow bending return down the centre-line, I had for some little time been living, as it were, in another world. I now came down to earth with a bang: and my slice of cake, slipping from my nerveless fingers, fell to the ground and was wolfed by Aunt Agatha's spaniel, Robert. Once more I seemed to become conscious of an impending doom.

For this man Filmer, you must understand, was not one of those men who are lightly kept from the tea table. A hearty trencherman, and particularly fond of his five o'clock couple of cups and bite of muffin, he had until this afternoon always been well up among the leaders in the race for the food-trough. If one thing was certain, it was that only the machinations of some enemy could be keeping him from being in the drawing room now, complete with nose-bag.

'He must have got caught in the rain and be sheltering somewhere in the grounds,' said Aunt Agatha. 'Bertie, go out and find him. Take a raincoat to him.'

'Right-ho!' I said. My only desire in life now was to find the Right Hon. And I hoped it wouldn't be merely his body.

I put on a raincoat and tucked another under my arm, and was sallying forth, when in the hall I ran into Jeeves.

'Jeeves,' I said, 'I fear the worst. Mr Filmer is missing.'

'Yes, sir.'

'I am about to scour the grounds in search of him.'

'I can save you the trouble, sir. Mr Filmer is on the island in the middle of the lake.'

'In the rain? Why doesn't the chump row back!'

'He has no boat, sir.'

'Then how can he be on the island?'

'He rowed there, sir. But Master Thomas rowed after him and set his boat adrift. He was informing me of the circumstances a moment ago, sir. It appears that Captain Flint was in the habit of marooning people on islands, and Master Thomas felt that he could pursue no more judicious course than to follow his example.'

'But, good Lord, Jeeves! The man must be getting soaked.'

'Yes, sir. Master Thomas commented upon that aspect of the matter.'

It was a time for action.

'Come with me, Jeeves!'

'Very good, sir.'

I buzzed for the boathouse.

My Aunt Agatha's husband, Spenser Gregson, who is on the Stock Exchange, had recently cleaned up to an amazing extent in Sumatra Rubber; and Aunt Agatha, in selecting a country estate, had lashed out on an impressive scale. There were miles of what they call rolling parkland, trees in considerable profusion well provided with doves and what not cooing in no uncertain voice, gardens full of roses, and also stables, out-houses, and messuages, the whole forming a rather fruity *tout ensemble*. But the feature of the place was the lake.

It stood to the east of the house, beyond the rose garden, and covered several acres. In the middle of it was an island. In the middle of the island was a building known as the Octagon. And in the middle of the Octagon, seated on the roof and spouting water like a public fountain, was the Right Hon. A.B. Filmer. As we drew nearer, striking a fast clip with self at oars and Jeeves handling the tiller-ropes, we heard cries of gradually increasing volume, if that's the expression I want; and presently, up aloft, looking from a distance as if he were perched on top of the bushes, I located the Right Hon. It seemed to me that even a Cabinet Minister ought to have had more sense than to stay right out in the open like that when there were trees to shelter under.

'A little more to the right, Jeeves.'

'Very good, sir.'

I made a neat landing.

'Wait here, Jeeves.'

'Very good, sir. The head gardener was informing me this morning, sir, that one of the swans had recently nested on this island.'

'This is no time for natural history gossip, Jeeves,' I said, a little severely, for the rain was coming down harder than ever and the Wooster trouser-legs were already considerably moistened.

'Very good, sir.'

I pushed my way through the bushes. The going was sticky and took about eight and elevenpence off the value of my Sure-Grip tennis shoes in the first two yards: but I persevered, and presently came out in the open and found myself in a sort of clearing facing the Octagon.

This building was run up somewhere in the last century, I have been told, to enable the grandfather of the late owner to have some quiet place out of earshot of the house where he could practise the fiddle. From what

170

I know of fiddlers, I should imagine that he had produced some fairly frightful sounds there in his time, but they can have been nothing to the ones that were coming from the roof of the place now. The Right Hon., not having spotted the arrival of the rescue-party, was apparently trying to make his voice carry across the waste of waters to the house; and I'm not saying it was not a good sporting effort. He had one of those highish tenors, and his yowls seemed to screech over my head like shells.

I thought it about time to slip him the glad news that assistance had arrived, before he strained a vocal cord.

'Hi!' I shouted, waiting for a lull.

He poked his head over the edge.

'Hi!' he bellowed, looking in every direction but the right one, of course.

'Hi!'

'Hi!'

'Hi!'

'Hi!'

'Oh!' he said, spotting me at last.

'What-ho!' I replied, sort of clinching the thing.

I suppose the conversation can't be said to have touched a frightfully high level up to this moment; but probably we should have got a good deal brainier very shortly – only just then, at the very instant when I was getting ready to say something good, there was a hissing noise like a tyre bursting in a nest of cobras, and out of the bushes to my left there popped something so large and white and active that, thinking quicker than I have ever done in my puff, I rose like a rocketing pheasant, and, before I knew what I was doing, had begun to climb for life. Something slapped against the wall about an inch below my right ankle, and any doubts I may have had about remaining below vanished. The lad who bore 'mid snow and ice the banner with the strange device 'Excelsior!' was the model for Bertram.

'Be careful!' yipped the Right Hon.

I was.

Whoever built the Octagon might have constructed it especially for this sort of crisis. Its walls had grooves at regular intervals which were just right for the hands and feet, and it wasn't very long before I was parked up on the roof beside the Right Hon., gazing down at one of the largest and shortest-tempered swans I had ever seen. It was standing below,

171

stretching up a neck like a hosepipe, just where a bit of brick, judiciously bunged, would catch it amidships.

I bunged the brick and scored a bull's-eye.

The Right Hon. didn't seem any too well pleased.

'Don't tease it!' he said.

'It teased me,' I said.

The swan extended another eight feet of neck and gave an imitation of steam escaping from a leaky pipe. The rain continued to lash down with what you might call indescribable fury, and I was sorry that in the agitation inseparable from shinning up a stone wall at practically a second's notice I had dropped the raincoat which I had been bringing with me for my fellow-rooster. For a moment I thought of offering him mine, but wiser counsels prevailed.

'How near did it come to getting you?' I asked.

'Within an ace,' replied my companion, gazing down with a look of marked dislike. 'I had to make a very rapid spring.'

The Right Hon. was a tubby little chap who looked as if he had been poured into his clothes and had forgotten to say 'When!' and the picture he conjured up, if you know what I mean, was rather pleasing.

'It is no laughing matter,' he said, shifting the look of dislike to me.

'Sorry.'

'I might have been seriously injured.'

'Would you consider bunging another brick at the bird?'

'Do nothing of the sort. It will only annoy him.'

'Well, why not annoy him?' He hasn't shown such a dashed lot of consideration for our feelings.'

The Right Hon. now turned to another aspect of the matter.

'I cannot understand how my boat, which I fastened securely to the stump of a willow-tree, can have drifted away.'

'Dashed mysterious.'

'I begin to suspect that it was deliberately set loose by some mischievous person.'

'Oh, I say, no, hardly likely, that. You'd have seen them doing it.'

'No, Mr Wooster. For the bushes form an effective screen. Moreover, rendered drowsy by the unusual warmth of the afternoon, I dozed off for some little time almost immediately I reached the island.'

This wasn't the sort of thing I wanted his mind dwelling on, so I changed the subject.

'Wet, isn't it, what?' I said.

'I had already observed it,' said the Right Hon. in one of those nasty, bitter voices. 'I thank you, however, for drawing the matter to my attention.'

Chit-chat about the weather hadn't gone with much of a bang, I perceived. I had a shot at Bird Life in the Home Counties.

'Have you ever noticed,' I said, 'how a swan's eyebrows sort of meet in the middle?'

'I have had every opportunity of observing all that there is to observe about swans.'

'Gives them a sort of peevish look, what?'

'The look to which you allude has not escaped me.'

'Rummy,' I said, rather warming to my subject, 'how bad an effect family life has on a swan's disposition.'

'I wished you would select some other topic of conversation than swans.'

'No, but, really, it's rather interesting. I mean to say, our old pal down there is probably a perfect ray of sunshine in normal circumstances. Quite the domestic pet, don't you know. But purely and simply because the little woman happens to be nesting–'

I paused. You will scarcely believe me, but until this moment, what with all the recent bustle and activity, I had clean forgotten that, while we were treed up on the roof like this, there lurked all the time in the background one whose giant brain, if notified of the emergency and requested to flock round, would probably be able to think up half-a-dozen schemes for solving our little difficulties in a couple of minutes.

'Jeeves!' I shouted.

'Sir?' came a faint respectful voice from the great open spaces.

'My man,' I explained to the Right Hon. 'A fellow of infinite resource and sagacity. He'll have us out of this in a minute. Jeeves!'

'Sir?'

'I'm sitting on the roof.'

'Very good, sir.'

'Don't say "Very good". Come and help us. Mr Filmer and I are treed, Jeeves.'

'Very good, sir.'

'Don't keep saying "Very good". It's nothing of the kind. The place is alive with swans.'

'I will attend to the matter immediately, sir.'

I turned to the Right Hon. I even went so far as to pat him on the back. It was like slapping a wet sponge.

'All is well,' I said. 'Jeeves is coming.'

'What can he do?'

I frowned a trifle. The man's tone had been peevish, and I didn't like it.

'That,' I replied with a touch of stiffness, 'we cannot say until we see him in action. He may pursue one course, or he may pursue another. But on one thing you can rely with the utmost confidence – Jeeves will find a way. See, here he comes stealing through the undergrowth, his face shining with the light of pure intelligence. There are no limits to Jeeves's brain-power. He virtually lives on fish.'

I bent over the edge and peered into the abyss.

'Look out for the swan, Jeeves.'

'I have the bird under close observation, sir.'

The swan had been uncoiling a further supply of neck in our direction; but now he whipped round. The sound of a voice speaking in his rear seemed to affect him powerfully. He subjected Jeeves to a short, keen scrutiny; and then, taking in some breath for hissing purposes, gave a sort of jump and charged ahead.

'Look out, Jeeves!'

'Very good, sir.'

Well, I could have told that swan it was no use. As swans go, he may have been well up in the ranks of the intelligentsia; but, when it came to pitting his brains against Jeeves, he was simply wasting his time. He might just as well have gone home at once.

Every young man starting life ought to know how to cope with an angry swan, so I will briefly relate the proper procedure. You begin by picking up the raincoat which somebody has dropped; and then, judging the distance to a nicety, you simply shove the raincoat over the bird's head; and, taking the boat-hook which you have prudently brought with you, you insert it underneath the swan and heave. The swan goes into a bush and starts trying to unscramble itself; and you saunter back to your boat, taking with you any friends who may happen at the moment to be sitting on roofs in the vicinity. That was Jeeves's method, and I cannot see how it could have been improved upon.

The Right Hon. showing a turn of speed of which I would not have believed him capable, we were in the boat in considerably under two ticks.

'You behaved very intelligently, my man,' said the Right Hon. as we pushed away from the shore.

'I endeavour to give satisfaction, sir.'

The Right Hon. appeared to have said his say for the time being. From that moment he seemed to sort of huddle up and meditate. Dashed absorbed he was. Even when I caught a crab and shot about a pint of water down his neck he didn't seem to notice it.

It was only when we were landing that he came to life again.

'Mr Wooster.'

'Oh, ah?'

'I have been thinking of that matter of which I spoke to you some time back – the problem of how my boat can have got adrift.'

I didn't like this.

'The dickens of a problem.' I said. 'Better not bother about it any more. You'll never solve it.'

'On the contrary, I have arrived at a solution, and one which I think is the only feasible solution. I am convinced that my boat was set adrift by the boy Thomas, my hostess's son.

'Oh, I say, no! Why?'

'He had a grudge against me. And it is the sort of thing only a boy, or one who is practically an imbecile, would have thought of doing.'

He legged it for the house; and I turned to Jeeves, aghast. Yes, you might say aghast.

'You heard, Jeeves?'

'Yes, sir.'

'What's to be done?'

'Perhaps Mr Filmer, on thinking the matter over, will decide that his suspicions are unjust.'

'But they aren't unjust.'

'No, sir.'

'Then what's to be done?'

'I could not say, sir.'

I pushed off rather smartly to the house and reported to Aunt Agatha that the Right Hon. had been salved; and then I toddled upstairs to have a hot bath, being considerably soaked from stem to stern as the result of my rambles. While I was enjoying the grateful warmth, a knock came at the door.

It was Purvis, Aunt Agatha's butler.

'Mrs Gregson desires me to say, sir, that she would be glad to see you as soon as you are ready.'

'But she has seen me.'

'I gather that she wishes to see you again, sir.'

'Oh, right-ho.'

I lay beneath the surface for another few minutes; then, having dried the frame, went along the corridor to my room. Jeeves was there, fiddling about with underclothing.

'Oh, Jeeves,' I said, 'I've just been thinking. Oughtn't somebody to go and give Mr Filmer a spot of quinine or something? Errand of mercy, what?'

'I have already done so, sir.'

'Good, I wouldn't say I like the man frightfully, but I don't want him to get a cold in the head.' I shoved on a sock. 'Jeeves,' I said, 'I suppose you know that we've got to think of something pretty quick? I mean to say, you realise the position? Mr Filmer suspects young Thomas of doing exactly what he did do, and if he brings home the charge Aunt Agatha will undoubtedly fire Mr Little, and then Mrs Little will find out what Mr Little has been up to, and what will be the upshot and outcome, Jeeves?' I will tell you. It will mean that Mrs Little will get the goods on Mr Little to an extent to which, though only a bachelor myself, I should say that no wife ought to get the goods on her husband if the proper give and take of married life – what you might call the essential balance as it were – is to be preserved. Women bring these things up, Jeeves. They do not forget and forgive.'

'Very true, sir.'

'Then how about it?'

'I have already attended to the matter, sir.'

'You have?'

'Yes sir. I had scarcely left you when the solution of the affair presented itself to me. It was a remark of Mr Filmer's that gave me the idea.'

'Jeeves, you're a marvel!'

'Thank you very much, sir.'

'What was the solution?'

'I conceived the notion of going to Mr Filmer and saying that it was you who had stolen his boat, sir.'

The man flickered before me. I clutched a sock in a feverish grip.

'Saying – what?'

176

'At first Mr Filmer was reluctant to credit my statement. But I pointed out to him that you had certainly known that he was on the island – a fact which he agreed was highly significant. I pointed out, furthermore, that you were a light-hearted young gentleman, sir, who might well do such a thing as a practical joke. I left him quite convinced, and there is now no danger of his attributing the action to Master Thomas.'

I gazed at the blighter spellbound.

'And that's what you consider a neat solution?' I said.

'Yes, sir. Mr Little will now retain his position as desired.'

'And what about me?'

'You are also benefited, sir.'

'Oh, I am, am I?'

'Yes sir. I have ascertained that Mrs Gregson's motive in inviting you to this house was that she might present you to Mr Filmer with a view to your becoming his private secretary.'

'What!'

'Yes, sir. Purvis, the butler, chanced to overhear Mrs Gregson in conversation with Mr Filmer on the matter.'

'Secretary to that superfatted bore! Jeeves, I could never have survived it.'

'No, sir. I fancy you would not have found it agreeable. Mr Filmer is scarcely a congenial companion for you. Yet, had Mrs Gregson secured the position for you, you might have found it embarrassing to decline to accept it.'

'Embarrassing is right!'

'Yes, sir.'

'But I say, Jeeves, there's just one point which you seem to have overlooked. Where exactly do I get off?'

'Sir?'

'I mean to say, Aunt Agatha sent word by Purvis just now that she wanted to see me. Probably she's polishing up her hatchet at this very moment.'

'It might be the most judicious plan not to meet her, sir.'

'But how can I help it?'

'There is a good, stout water pipe running down the wall immediately outside this window, sir. And I could have the two-seater waiting outside the park gates in twenty minutes.'

I eyed him with reverence.

177

'Jeeves,' I said, 'you are always right. You couldn't make it five, could you?'

'Let us say ten, sir.'

'Ten it is. Lay out some raiment suitable for travel, and leave the rest to me. Where is this water pipe of which you speak so highly?'

* * * * *

Rose Tremain was one of the first graduates from the creative writing course at the University of East Anglia. She is now a best selling author with novels such as *Restoration* (1989), shortlisted for the Booker Prize, and the highly acclaimed *Sacred Country* (1992), both set in East Anglia. Several early short stories are also set in the region including *A Shooting Season* that appeared in her first collection *The Colonel's Daughter* (1984), winner of the Dylan Thomas Short Story Award, and *Wildtrack* (page 236), with its intimations of *Sacred Country*, that was included in *The Garden Of The Villa Mollini* (1987). Tremain lives near Norwich with the biographer Richard Holmes. Her latest novel *Music And Silence* won the 1999 Whitbread Novel Award.

A Shooting Season

ROSE TREMAIN

'You're writing a what?'

'A novel.'

Looking away from him, nervously, touching her hair, Anna remembered, the last time I saw him my hair wasn't grey.

'Why the hell are you writing a novel?'

Grey hairs had sprouted at forty-one. Now, at forty-five, she sometimes thought, my scalp is exhausted, that's all, like poor soil.

'I've wanted to write a novel ever since I was thirty. Long before, even . . .'

'You never told me.'

'No. Of course not.'

'Why "of course not"?'

'You would have laughed, as you're laughing now.'

Anna had always been enchanted by his laugh. It was a boy's giggle; (you climbed a cold dormitory stairway and heard it bubble and burst behind a drab door!) yet their son didn't have it: at sixteen, he had the laugh of a rowdy man.

'I don't approve.'

'No.'

'It's an act of postponed jealousy.'

Well, if so, then long postponed. Six years since their separation; four since the divorce and his remarriage to Susan, the pert blonde girl who typed his poems. And it wasn't jealousy, surely? In learning to live without him, she had taught herself to forget him utterly. If she heard him talk on the radio, she found herself thinking, his cadences are echoing Dylan Thomas these days; he's remembered how useful it is, if you happen to be a poet, also to be Welsh. Three years older than her, he had come to resemble a Welsh hillside – craggy outcrop of a man,

179

unbuttoned to weather and fortune, hair wiry as gorse. Marcus. Fame clung to his untidy look. No doubt, she thought, he's as unfaithful to Susan as he was to me.

'How did it start?'

The novel-writing, he meant, but he had a way, still, of sending fine ripples through the water of ordinary questions which invited her to admit: I was in love with him for such a long time that parting from him was like a drowning. When I was washed ashore, the sediment of him still clogged me.

'I found there were things I wanted to say.'

'Oh, there always were!'

'Yes, but stronger now. Before I get old and start forgetting.'

'But a novel?'

'Why not?'

'You were never ambitious.'

No. Not when she was his: Mrs Marcus Ridley, wife of the poet. Not while she bore his children and made rugs while he wrote and they slept.

'Do your pockets still have bits of sand in them?'

He laughed, took her strong wrist and held her hand to his face. 'I don't know. No one empties them for me.'

Anna had been at the rented cottage for three weeks. A sluggish river flowed a few yards from it: mallard and moorhen were the companions of her silence, the light of early morning was silver. In this temporary isolation, she had moved contentedly in her summer sandals, setting up a work table in the sunshine, another indoors by the open fire. Her novel crept to a beginning, then began to flow quietly like the river. She celebrated each day's work with two glasses, sometimes more, of the home-made wine she had remembered to bring with her. She slept well with the window wide open on the Norfolk sky. She dreamed of her book finished and bound. Then one morning Margaret, her partner in her craft business, telephoned. The sound of the telephone ringing was so unfamiliar that it frightened her. She remembered her children left on their own in London; she raced to answer the unforeseen but now obvious emergency. But no, said Margaret, no emergency, only Marcus.

'Marcus?'

'Yes. Drunk and full of his songs. Said he needed to see you.'

'And you told him where I was?'

'Yes. He said if I didn't, he'd pee on the pottery shelf.'

'Marcus.'

The rough feel of his face was very familiar; she might have touched it yesterday. She thought suddenly, for all his puerile needs, he's a man of absolute mystery; I never understood him. Yet they had been together for ten years. The Decade of the Poet she called it, wanting to bury him with formality and distance. And yet he surfaced in her: she seldom read a book without wondering, how would Marcus have judged that? And then feeling irritated by the question. On such occasions, she would always remind herself: he doesn't even bother to see the children, let alone me. He's got a new family (Evan 4, Lucy 3) and they, now, take all his love – the little there ever was in him to give.

'You look so healthy, Anna. Healthy and strong, I suppose you always were strong.'

'Big-boned, my mother called it.'

'How is your mother?'

'Dead.'

'You never let me know.'

'No. There was no point.'

'I could have come with you – to the funeral or whatever.'

'Oh, Marcus . . .'

'Funerals are ghastly. I could have helped you through.'

'Why don't you see the children?'

He let her hand drop. He turned to the window, wide open on the now familiar prospect of reed and river. Anna noticed that the faded corduroy jacket he was wearing was stretched tight over his back. He seemed to have outgrown it.

'Marcus . . .?'

He turned back to her, hands in his pockets.

'No accusations. No bloody accusations!'

Oh yes, she noticed, there's the pattern: I ask a question, Marcus says it's inadmissible, I feel guilty and ashamed . . .

'It's a perfectly reasonable question.'

'Reasonable? It's a guilt-inducing, jealous, mean-minded question. You know perfectly well why I don't see the children: because I have two newer, younger and infinitely more affectionate children, and these newer,

181

younger and infinitely more affectionate children are bitterly resented by the aforementioned older, infinitely less affectionate children. And because I am a coward.'

He should be hit, she thought, then noticed that she was smiling.

'I brought some of my home-made wine,' she said, 'it's a disgusting looking yellow, but it tastes rather good. Shall we have some?'

'Home-made wine?' I thought you were a business*person*. When the hell do you get time to make wine?'

'Oh Marcus, I have plenty of time.'

Anna went to the cold, pament-floored little room she had decided to think of as 'the pantry'. Its shelves were absolutely deserted except for five empty Nescafé jars, a dusty goldfish bowl (the debris of another family's Norfolk summer) and her own bottles of wine. It was thirty-five years since she had lived in a house large enough to have a pantry, but now, in this cupboard of a place, she could summon memories of Hodgson, her grandfather's butler, uncorking Stones ginger beer for her and her brother on timeless summer evenings – the most exquisite moments of all the summer holidays. Then, one summer, she found herself there alone. Hodgson had left. Her brother Charles had been killed at school by a cricket ball.

Anna opened a bottle of wine and took it and two glasses out to her table in the garden, where Marcus had installed himself. He was looking critically at her typewriter and at the unfinished pages of her book lying beside it.

'You don't mean to say you're typing it?'

She put the wine and the glasses on the table. She noticed that the heavy flint she used as a paperweight had been moved.

'Please don't let the pages blow away, Marcus.'

'I'm sure it's a mistake to type thoughts directly onto paper. Writing words by hand is part of the process.'

'Your process.'

'I don't know any writers who type directly.'

'You know me. Please put the stone back, Marcus.'

He replaced the pages he had taken up, put the flint down gently and spread his wide hand over it. He was looking at her face.

'Don't write about me, Anna, will you?'

She poured the wine. The sun touched her neck and she remembered its warmth with pleasure.

'Don't make me the villain.'

'There is no villain.'

She handed him his glass of wine. Out in the sunshine, he looked pale beside her. A miraculous three weeks of fine weather had tanned her face, neck and arms, whereas he . . . how did he spend his days now? She didn't know. He looked as if he'd been locked up. Yet he lived in the country with his new brood. She it was – and their children – who had stayed on in the London flat.

'How's Susan?'

No. She didn't want to ask. Shouldn't have asked. She'd only asked in order to get it over with: to sweep Susan and his domestic life to the back of her mind, so that she could let herself be nice to him, let herself enjoy him.

'Why ask?'

'To get it over with.'

He smiled. She thought she sensed his boyish laughter about to surface.

'Susan's got a lover.'

Oh damn him! Damn Marcus! Feeling hurt, feeling cheated, he thought I'd be easy consolation. No wonder the novel annoys him; he sees the ground shifting under him, sees a time when he's not the adored, successful granite he always thought he was.

'Damn the lover.'

'What?'

He'd looked up at her startled. What he remembered most vividly about her was her permanence. The splash of bright homespun colour that was Anna: he had only to turn his head, open a door, to find her there. No other wife or mistress had been like her; these had often been absent when he'd searched for them hardest. But Anna: Anna had always wanted to be there.

'I'm not very interested in Susan's lover.'

'No. He isn't interesting. He's a chartered surveyor.'

'Ah. Well, reliable probably.'

'D'you think so? Reliable, are they, as a breed? He looks pitiful enough to be it. Perhaps that's what she wants.

'And you?'

'Me?'

'What do you want. Marcus? Did you come here just to tell me your wife had a lover?'

'Accusations again. All the bloody little peeves!'

183

'I want to know why you came here.'

'So do I.'

'What?'

'So do I want to know. All I know is that I wanted to see you. If that's not good enough for you, I'll go away.'

Further along the river, she could hear the mallard quacking. Some evenings at sunset, she had walked through the reeds to find them (two pairs, one pair with young) and throw in scraps for them. Standing alone, the willows in front of her in perfect silhouette, she envied the ducks their sociability. No one comes near them, she thought, only me standing still. Yet they have everything – everyone – they need.

'I love it here.'

She had wanted to sit down opposite Marcus with her glass of wine, but he had taken the only chair. She squatted, lifting her face to the sun. She knew he was watching her.

'Do you want me to go away?'

She felt the intermittent river breeze on her face, heard the pages of her novel flap under the stone. She examined his question, knew that it confused her, and set it aside.

'The novel's going to be about Charlie.'

'Charlie?'

'My brother Charles. Who died at school. I'm imagining that he lived on, but not as him, as a girl.'

'Why as a girl?'

'I thought I would understand him better as a girl.'

'Will it work?'

'The novel?'

'Giving Charlie tits.'

'Yes, I think so. It also means she doesn't have to play cricket and risk being killed.'

'I'd forgotten Charlie.'

'You never knew him.'

'I knew him as a boy – through your memories. He of Hodgson's ginger beer larder!'

'Pantry.'

She's got stronger, Marcus decided. She's gone grey and it suits her. And she's still wearing her bright colours. Probably makes not just her own clothes now, but ponchos and smocks and bits of batik to sell in her shops. And of course her son's friends fall in love with her. She's perfect for a boy: bony, maternal and sexy. Probably her son's in love with her too.

'Can I stay for dinner?'

Anna put her glass to her lips and drained it. He always, she thought, made requests sound like offers.

Anna scrutinised the contents of the small fridge: milk, butter, a bunch of weary radishes, eggs. Alone, she would have made do with the radishes and an omelette, but Marcus had a lion's appetite. His most potent memory of a poetry-reading fortnight in America was ordering steak for breakfast. He had returned looking ruddy, like the meat.

Anna sighed. The novel had been going well that morning. Charlie, renamed Charlotte, was perched high now above her cloistered schooldays on the windswept catwalk of a new university. Little gusts of middle-class guilt had begun to pick at her well-made clothes and at her heart. She was ready for change.

'Charlotte can wait,' Marcus told Anna, after her one feeble attempt to send him away. 'She'll be there tomorrow and I'll be gone. And anyway, we owe it to each other – one dinner.'

I owe nothing, Anna thought. No one (especially not pretty Susan with her tumbling fair hair and her flirtatious eyes) could have given herself – her time, her energy, her love – more completely to one man than she to Marcus. For ten years he had been the landscape that held her whole existence – one scarlet poppy on the hills and crags of him, sharing his sky.

'One dinner!'

She took the car into Wroxham, bought good dark fillet, two bottles of Beaujolais, new potatoes, a salad and cheese.

While she was gone, he sat at the table in the sunshine, getting accustomed to the gently scented taste of her home-made wine and, despite a promise not to, reading her novel. Her writing bored him after a very few pages; he needed her presence, not her thoughts.

I've cried for you, he wanted to tell her. There have been times when – yes, several of them – times when I haven't felt comfortable with the finality of our separation, times when I've thought, there's more yet, I need more. And why couldn't you be part of my life again, on its edge? I would honestly feel troubled less – by Susan's chartered surveyor, by the

185

coming of my forty-ninth birthday – yes, much less, if you were there in your hessian or whatever it is you wear and I could touch you. Because ten years is, after all, a large chunk of our lives, and though I never admit it, I now believe that my best poems were written during those ten and what followed had been mainly repetition. And I wanted to ask you, where are those rugs you made while I worked? Did you chuck them out? Why was the silent making of your rugs so intimately connected to my perfect arrangements of words?'

'So here we are . . .'

The evening promised to be so warm that Anna had put a cloth on the table outside and laid it for supper. Marcus had helped her prepare the food and now they sat facing the sunset, watching the colour go first from the river, then from the willows and poplars behind it.

'Remember Yugoslavia?'

'Yes, Marcus.'

'Montenegro.'

'Yes.'

'Those blue thistles.'

'Umm.'

'Our picnic suppers!'

'Stale bread.'

'What?'

'The bread in Yugoslavia always tasted stale.'

'We used to make love in a sleeping bag.'

'Yes.'

Anna thought, it will soon be so dark, I won't be able to see him clearly, just as, in my mind, I have only the most indistinct perception of how he *is* in that hard skin, if I ever knew. For a moment she considered going indoors to get a candle, but decided it would be a waste of time; the breeze would blow it out. And the darkness suits us, suits this odd meeting, she thought. In it, we're insubstantial; we're each imagining the other one, that's all.

'I read the novel, as far as you've gone.'

Yes. I thought you probably would.'

'I never pictured you writing.'

'No. Well, I never pictured you arriving here. Margaret told me you said you "needed" me. What on earth did you mean.'

'I think about you – often.'

186

'Since Susan found her surveyor?'

'That's not fair.'

'Yes, it's fair. You could have come to see me – and the children – any time you wanted.'

'I wanted . . .'

'What?'

'Not the children. You.'

For a moment, Anna allowed herself to remember: 'You, in the valley of my arms,/ my quaint companion on the mountain./ How wisely did I gather you,/ my crimson bride . . .'

Then she took a sip of Beaujolais and began:

'I've tried.'

'What?'

'To love other people. Other men, I mean.'

'And?'

'The feelings don't seem to last: Or perhaps I've just been unlucky.'

'Yes. You deserve someone.'

'I don't want anyone, Marcus. This is what I've at last understood. I have the children and the craft shops and one or two men friends to go out with, and now I have the novel . . .'

'I miss you, Anna.'

She rested her chin on folded hands and looked at him. Mighty is a perfect word, she thought. To me, he has always seemed mighty. And when he left me, every room, every place I went to was full of empty space. Only recently had I got used to it, decided finally to stop trying to fill it up. And now there he is again, his enormous shadow, darker, nearer than the darkness.

'You see, I'm not a poet any more.'

'Yes, you are, Marcus. I read your new volume . . .'

'No I'm not. I won't write anything more of value.'

'Why?'

'Because I'm floundering, Anna. I don't know what I expect of myself any more, as a poet or as a man. Susan's destroying me.'

'Oh rot!' Susan was exactly the woman you dreamed of.'

'And now I have dreams of you.'

Anna sighed and let Marcus hear the sigh. She got up and walked the few yards to the river and watched it shine at her feet. For the first time that day, the breeze made her shiver.

Light came early. Anna woke astonished and afraid. Marcus lay on his stomach, head turned away from her, his right arm resting down the length of her body.

A noise had woken her, she knew, yet there was nothing: only the sleeper's breath next to her and the birds tuning up, like a tiny hidden orchestra, for their full-throated day. Then she heard them: two shots, then a third and a fourth. Marcus turned over, opened his eyes and looked at her. She was sitting up and staring blankly at the open window. The thin curtains moved on a sunless morning.

'Anna . . .'

The strong hand on her arm wanted to tug her gently down, but she resisted its pressure, stayed still, chin against her knees.

'Someone's shooting.'

'Come back to sleep.'

'No I can't. Why would someone be shooting?'

'The whole world's shooting!'

'I must go and see.'

Marcus lay still and watched Anna get up. As she pulled on a faded, familiar gown, both had the same thought: it was always like this, Anna getting up first, Marcus in bed half asleep, yet often watching Anna.

'What are you going to do?'

'I don't know. But I have to see.'

The morning air was chilly. It was sunless, Anna realised, only because the sun had not yet risen. A mist squatted above the river; the landscape was flattened and obscured in dull white. Anna stared. The dawn has extraordinary purpose, she thought, everything contained, everything shrouded by the light but emerging minute by minute into brightness and shape, so that while I stand still it all changes. She began to walk along the river. The ground under her sandals was damp and the leather soon became slippery. Nothing moved. The familiar breeze had almost died in the darkness, the willow leaves hung limp and wet. Anna stopped, rubbed her eyes.

'Where are you?'

She waited, peering into the mist. The mist was yellowing, sunlight slowly climbing. A dog barked, far off.

'Where *are* you?'

Senseless question. Where are you? Where are you? Anna walked on. The surface of the water, so near her slippery feet, was absolutely smooth.

The sun was climbing fast now and the mist was tumbling, separating, making way for colour and contour. Where are you! The three words came echoing down the years. Anna closed her eyes. They came and shot the ducks, she told herself calmly. That's all. Men came with guns and had a duck shoot and the mallard are gone. When I come down here with my scraps, I won't find them. But that's all. The river flows on. Everything else is just as it was yesterday and the day before and the day before that. I am still Anna. Birds don't matter. I have a book to write. And the sun's coming up . . .

She was weeping. Clutching her arms inside the sleeves of the faded gown, she walks from room to room in the empty flat. Where are you! London dawn at the grimed net curtains . . . fruit still in the bowl from which, as he finally went, he stole an orange . . . nothing changes and yet everything . . . his smell still on her body . . . And where am I? Snivelling round the debris of you in all the familiar rooms, touching surfaces you touched, taking an orange from the bowl . . . Where am I? Weeping. The ducks don't matter. Do they? Keeping hold on what is, on what exists after the shot has echoed and gone, this is all that's important, yes, keeping hold on what I have forced myself to become, with all the sanding and polishing of my heart's hardness, keeping hold of my life alone that nothing – surely not the wounds of one night's loving? – can destroy. So just let me wipe my face on the same washed-out corner of a sleeve. And forget. A stranger carries the dead mallard home, dead smeared heads, bound together with twine. But the sun comes up on the same stretch of river where, only yesterday, they had life . . .

Marcus held Anna. They stood by his car. It was still morning, yet they sensed the tiredness in each other, as if neither had slept at all.

'I'll be going then, old thing. Sorry I was such a miserable bugger. Selfish of me to disturb you with my little problems.'

'Oh, you weren't disturbing me.'

'Yes, I was. Typical of me: Marcus Ridley's Lament for Things as They Are.'

'I don't mind. And last night –'

'Lovely, Anna. Perhaps I'll stop dreaming about you now.'

'Yes.'

He kissed her cheek and got quickly into the car.

'Good luck with the novel.'

189

'Oh yes. Thank you, Marcus.'

'I'll picture you working by your river.'

'Come and see the children, Marcus. Please come and see the children.'

'Yes. Alright. No promises. Are you going to work on the book today?'

'No, I don't think I can. Not today.'

'Poor Anna. I've tired you. Never mind. There's always tomorrow.'

'Yes, Marcus,' and very gently she reached out and touched his face, 'there's always tomorrow.'

* * * * *

A M Wilson: The daughter of a Victorian clergyman, Agnes Wilson was brought up in the Queen Anne rectory in south Norfolk where, a century earlier, Dorothy Wordsworth had established the first village school while staying with her uncle, the rector of Forncett St Peter. *Alma* is taken from Wilson's delightful collection of tales *Friends of Yesterday* (1903) based upon reminiscences of rural characters in Forncett (her Sedgebrook) and the surrounding villages.

Alma

A M WILSON

The Primitive Methodist chapel and the windmill stood side by side in the middle of a gorse-covered common. The chapel was square and red, and shaded from the world by a row of sycamores; the windmill was round and white, its doors and small mysterious windows painted a pale green; and between the two young Mr. Beales the miller had his modest dwelling.

'The chapel that lie by the windmill,' or 'the windmill that stand right agin the chapel,' was the time-honoured direction given to the occasional stranger searching after food for the body or for the soul. Mr Beales might be said to present a combination of both. On week days he plied his floury trade with worldly assiduity; on Sunday, clad in garments of the palest grey, he presided over the musical portion of the services, and if the minister was (as he usually was) a wandering one, entertained him at the mid-day meal.

The miller was so thin and small and white, it seemed as if all the colour and courage must have been crushed out of him by his own mill-stones. It was perhaps the force of contrast that had led him to love Alma. Alma was as tall as a grenadier, cherry-cheeked and black-haired, possessing a deep contralto voice, which was the pride of the chapel members, and with a tendency to clothe herself in brilliant colours, which was their despair.

She was the daughter of a farmer who had married late in life, and the affection between her and Mr. Beales - 'Fred,' as he was more often called – dated from their school-days. Each was an only child, and neither of them was of sociable disposition. In those days Alma was a timorous girl with stiff black curls, and Fred a precise little boy with a starched frill and a blue ribbon bow. They climbed the rickety ladder of learning together, and wooed each other with slate pencils, bantams' eggs, green apples, and such-like youthful offerings. At times Alma would be invited to tea by old

191

Mrs. Beales, and afterwards Fred would escort her into delightful dusty corners of the mill, while the big sails outside went 'flip-flap' and the golden grain spun round and round in the great clean hopper. The children would fill their hands with it, letting it slip between their fingers; and the mill-cat – white too, like everything else – would come and rub her head against Alma's starched pinafore.

Later on, the boy was sent away to learn book-keeping, while Alma remained at home. At their occasional meetings they 'walked out' together after the approved fashion on Sundays, and spent long silent evenings at each other's homes; but she was large and shy while he was small and shy, and somehow their courtship was not a plant that flourished. Years passed by, and at his father's death Fred became sole master of the parental mill. As long as his mother was alive, there seemed a satisfactory reason for him to 'keep single'; but when that good lady had gone to join the old miller beneath the sycamores, the village was puzzled to know why the wedding should be further delayed.

'Possible Fred don't think I could leave you and father,' Alma said frankly to her mother on one of the frequent occasions when the subject was under discussion. And indeed Mr. Hamond's mental condition at this time might well give rise to anxiety. He was a masterful old man who had made his own way in the world, but the bad times of the last few years had so preyed upon his mind, that it was evident to all a very little push in the wrong direction might unhinge it altogether. When he took to driving the turkeys which were fattening for Christmas round and round the fifty-acre field with the aid of his old bob-tailed cattle-dog until the stoutest of them fell by the way and rose no more, and then sat brooding, supperless, in the kitchen till past midnight, it was not surprising that Alma and her mother trembled for the future.

'I can't think what make your pore father act so silly,' sighed Mrs. Hamond. 'That's not as if it run in the family. There's only his mother and your uncle Tom died in the 'sylum, but if your pore father carry on like this, I doubt that's where he'll have to go.'

But poor old Mr. Hamond escaped this dismal fate by catching a chill during one of his erratic rambles, and dying quite suddenly just when Alma and her mother, their heads tied up in dusters, were plucking the survivors of the harassed turkeys for the Christmas market.

The funeral took place at the parish church. Mrs. Hamond had a lively respect for the Rector: and felt moreover that for these great occasions of life and death the chapel was inadequate. With a distinct preference for

Dr. Watts's hymns, and the methods of the 'Primitives,' she tried, when circumstances permitted, to divide her favours equally. Thus, when afflicted with twins, she took the boy to be 'named' at the church, and the girl to be 'received' at the chapel; hoping thereby to serve, as it were, both God and Mammon. The church twin unfortunately died, whereas Alma grew up to be a prop to her own conventicle. Poor Alma! she laid aside her bright colours, and, draped from head to foot in crape, supported her mother through the sad ceremony, upheld by the thought that Fred, his pallor accentuated by the size of his hat-band and the blackness of his gloves, was 'following' with the relations.

'I have always reckoned you as good as a son,' said Mrs. Hamond to Fred in a burst of affection, when the party had returned to partake of the funeral baked meats.

Alma turned redder than ever, and the bugles gracing the erection upon her head shook suspiciously, but Fred still preserved a nervous silence.

'Thank you, Mrs. Hamond, I'm sure,' he said. 'I have always had a great respect for you, and Mr. Hamond – and Alma,' he added after a pause.

When Mr. Hamond's affairs were looked into, it transpired they were far from satisfactory. The farm was heavily rented, and the last few years had been unfortunate. In hopes of better days the old man had borrowed money at high interest, and when the drawers of his battered bureau were turned out, it was found he had left everything at sixes and sevens. The auction did but little to right matters, and, as soon as a new tenant was found for the farm, mother and daughter, with their most treasured household gods, moved into a tiny cottage on the outskirts of the common. And then one day Fred suddenly made an offer.

It was a September Sunday afternoon, when they were walking home from chapel. The gorse was blooming in patches all over the common, filling the air with a scent like ripe apricots, and among the short turf there was a constant gleam of mushrooms.

When they reached the sandy lane that led towards Alma's home, the young man stopped abruptly, and looking down at his shining Sunday boots found courage to begin.

'There's something I want to ask you, Alma!'

'Oh, Fred!' faltered Alma, opening and shutting her hymn-book nervously.

'I don't know how that may be with you and your mother, but they do say you haven't been left too comfortable. And so if you won't think me presuming, I wanted to ask you something.'

'Oh, Fred!' Alma faltered again, dropping the hymn-book in her agitation.

Fred picked it up, smoothed down the crumpled leaves, and then proceeded –

'Mrs. Dix, what have always made the tea at the chapel, told me yesterday she couldn't undertake it any longer, and I thought, possible, Alma, you'd take her place. There's always a good few stay to dinner, and though that don't bring in much, that's regular, and I always have thought you make such a wonderful good cup of tea.'

Alma's heart sank.

'Thank you, Fred,' she said very faintly. 'I'll ask mother.'

The duties of tea-maker at the chapel were not heavy. They consisted in slipping out into the vestry before the sermon, and causing the big kettle to boil by the time that the minister left the pulpit. A good many of the congregation 'came from far,' and as these generally stayed on for the afternoon service, they brought their dinner, and the chapel elders provided the tea at the moderate charge of one halfpenny a cup.

Alma took great pride in her new occupation. She scrubbed the deal table for an hour every Saturday till it looked like satin, and was so obliging in warming up dinners and drying wet garments, that her fame was soon spread abroad, and quite a number of extra cups and saucers had to be added to the original stock.

With Fred at the harmonium and Alma wielding the huge china tea-pot in the intervals of leading the choir, it seemed as if the finger of fate pointed more than ever before to a closer union between them. And then without warning the crash came.

In a circle where the same familiar faces in the same bonnets appear in the same seats Sunday after Sunday, the advent of a new-comer produces a sort of electric shock through the assembly. There was a good deal of whispering and nudging in the chapel one bright spring morning, when a young lady with an unmistakable 'city' air made a hesitating entrance during the first hymn. She looked about her for a minute, and then dived into a seat behind the harmonium, causing Fred to play several wrong notes, and the clarionet to catch his breath and choke. Instruments have now vanished from even the remotest of our country churches, but an orchestra may still be found in out-of-the-way chapels, where they accompany the old-fashioned psalm-tunes with an ardour which atones to some extent for their lack of musical ability.

Alma thought she detected symptoms of amusement in the new-comer as the hymn pursued its winding course with pauses and repetitions innumerable. The service dragged on till its prescribed limit, when at last the little sandy-haired minister – a stranger, too, with an accent of the 'shires' – mopping his forehead with a large coloured handkerchief, reached his peroration.

There was an immediate shuffling of feet, hats were taken down from the pegs on the walls, and a brisk conversation commenced. The new-comer returned the hymn-book to Fred at the harmonium, and in so doing inquired of him whether there was any house near by where she could get a glass of water.

'If you will just step into the vestry, Miss,' said Fred, considerably fluttered, 'you will find either water or tea, whichever you prefer.'

The girl looked distractingly pink and white, and as she spoke she disclosed a row of teeth as pretty as a kitten's.

'This way, if you please,' he continued, politely opening a small door beneath the gallery, which led into the room where stood Alma, her Sunday gown covered with a large apron, dispensing tea.

'A young lady to take tea, Alma,' said Fred.

'My name is Miss Finch, Miss Alice Finch,' said the girl glibly, addressing Alma, but glancing at Fred; 'and I am staying with my aunt and uncle at the Hempland Farm. Just down from London. Thank you, the tea will be very refreshing;' and then, seeing the milk jug, she added, 'I'll take some milk in it, please.'

'Run you into the chapel, Frank, and ask Mr. Stollery if he have brought any milk with him – say there's a lady come to tea' – said Alma to a big, light-whiskered man of blank expression and wearing a shepherd's-plaid scarf, who sat nursing an enormous bible and his dinner in a basket. Although so big, he was one of the 'little ones' of the earth. He loved the chapel, and Alma, and the Sunday meal, and saved all his ha'pence for this sublime treat of the week, his relations being only too pleased to be quit of him for the whole day. He now hurried back with a message from Mr. Stollery, who was practising the afternoon's music on the double-bass, 'that last night's tempest had turned the milk too faint to bring.'

Fred looked so perturbed, that Miss Finch hastened to explain that she did not really mind at all. 'Seems funny you shouldn't have milk in the country, though, don't it?' she said; and taking up her cup of tea, she smiled, and drank it off at a gulp.

This was however premature, and there was a look of pained surprise on the faces of the company.

'Won't you start the blessing, Alma?' said one old lady in a voice in which horror and reproof were about equally blended.

Alma, shutting her eyes, struck up the time-honoured grace which always heralded the mid-day meal; and at the signal, other stragglers poured in from the chapel, and took their places round the festive board.

Fred appeared pained at the incident, and pressed a fresh cup of tea upon Miss Finch, who inquired rather sternly if he thought she might venture to drink this one without offence, adding soon after – 'Well, I must be going home, or aunt will wonder where I am got to. She is so fidgety. Good-morning all – I suppose there is only one road over the common?'

Fred opened the door for the fair visitor, and, regardless of consequences, shut it behind them – and then found himself walking across the heath beside her, and talking with an ease which astonished himself. By the time the road to the village had been reached, he had learned amongst other things that Miss Finch was 'in the millinery,' that she had broken down in health, and was staying for a few weeks with her relations, her home being in London – and that, if he was anywhere near Hempland Farm, she would go so far as to say that her aunt would be delighted to see him. She rattled on in a style which, after his doleful love-making with Alma, was wholly novel and delightful, and Fred returned home having totally forgotten that the hungry little minister was waiting for his dinner in the mill-house.

Alma washed up the tea-cups sadly. Her crape had looked dingy in the bright April sunshine, compared with Miss Finch's elegant attire. She felt large and awkward and unhappy, and was even disposed to be grateful to 'Frank' when, with dog-like devotion, he followed her home in her solitary walk.

Next Sunday Fred arrived at the chapel in a bright blue neck-tie in company with Miss Finch, and boldly left it with her under the stony gaze of the entire congregation'

Some weeks later Alma received a letter in Fred's handwriting bearing a London postmark.

'DEAR ALMA,' it began,
'I hope this will find you as well as, thank God, it leave me at present. Dear Alma, I am afraid you will be surprised to hear that I am thinking of

selling the windmill and going into business in the town. Dear Alma, I am afraid you will be surprised to hear that I am going to marry Miss Finch. I hope you will send me your good wishes as we have been friendly so many years. With my best respects to your mother, I am.

Your constant well-wisher,'

'FRED BEALES.'

'Well, of all the sly ones –' exclaimed Mrs. Hamond, when Alma had finished reading the letter out loud.

'But it's go further and fare worse, and that's what I always say.'

'Pore Fred!' said Alma, the tears rolling down her crimson cheeks; and that was all her comment on the letter, which cut short the cherished hope of five-and-twenty years.

* * * * *

Missing

ELSPETH BARKER

'C'est un beau chien,' said the Frenchman. Mary and he stared at the black lurcher curvetting and galloping in and out and round about the vast cylindrical straw bales, zigzagging almost horizontal to the stubble.

'She's a bitch,' said Mary. 'Actually,' she added, so as not to seem rude, although she felt like being rude. Why was he here at all, when he was her daughter's friend? And why wasn't Ellen here?

'Chienne alors,' shrugged the Frenchman, *'même chose.'*

Rage mounted in Mary.

'It's not at all the same thing; perhaps it is in France. Here we look differently at dogs.'

Woodpigeons cooed and mourned in the heavy August trees, tarnished already with the ebbing days of summer. An exhaust backfired, scattering the pigeons out against the clouded sky. Ellen's car jolted up the drive, roaring and revving. A Cromer Carnival pennant clung to the wireless aerial and two huge grizzled dogs glowered from the windows. Thank God for that, thought Mary. Now perhaps he'll go. In the sharp shadow cast by the bales he looked like Louis Jourdan playing Dracula. Or the man on the old Gitanes packet. Or was it Gauloises? She was too old for all this. Now Ellen stood beside him in her dreadful paramilitary trousers, and they were beaming at her. Extraordinary behaviour. The low sun dazzled her eyes.

'We've something to tell you, Mother,' said Ellen. The Frenchman nodded vigorously.

'You say,' he urged.

'No you,' Ellen pushed him forward.

Mary's heart lurched. Surely they weren't planning to marry. Not *Ellen*. He cleared his throat.

'I have found the grave,' he pronounced, each word slow and careful. 'I have found at last the grave of your husband.'

Ellen's mother Mary had learned a few things in her time, as she sometimes told her unfriendly daughter. One of these was to live with grief, or rather to live without it, beyond it. She had been alone a long time now, existing, Ellen thought, not only beyond grief, but also beyond love. Mary's husband had died invisibly in the Normandy landings, missing, presumed dead, a couple of months before Ellen was born. These days Mary didn't think about him much. Sometimes, but not often. And she had never thought much about Ellen. She was old and dusty and almost immaterial, shrinking her way out of life. She tried to live in abeyance from mortality. She preferred the evanescent, brooding endlessly on wind and weather, hunched over her wireless. If she considered life or death she became weighed down, oppressed; there had been too much of both and she could not succumb to either. The passing moment exacted all the strength she had left. 'I'm tired of living and I'm tired of dying,' she sang to herself. That wasn't right and she couldn't remember any of the other lines and she didn't care. Words came uninvited and tangled in her brain and set themselves to music. They would hang about for weeks, until they were replaced by something else, a phrase or two of poetry, an advertising slogan, some old-time ribaldry.

Even on this strange evening, when Ellen and the Frenchman had gone, and dusk and owls had invaded her garden, her skull was buzzing with a sprightly jingle:

> It's a fine tanking day
> And as balmy as May
> And the crew to the tank parks have hurried . . .

She persuaded herself there was nothing she could do about it, and it was better than thinking, when there was time to pass before any hope of sleep. So, humming briskly, she moved her frail body about her house; her bones clicked and creaked like knitting needles. The air was cold now, so cold that she sipped it, rather than breathed it and chill presaging the bleak East Anglian winter. Draughts skittered through the window frames and lifted the edges of threadbare rugs. As darkness gathered through those unlit, unpeopled rooms, she could almost believe that she had attained the ghostly state of her aspiration. There but not there. Intimations of the past lay all about her and in her solitude she might choose to remember, to forget, or to rearrange. Only very rarely, as now, was she caught unawares, overwhelmed by a great, retching pang of agonized grief, which left her shaken and gasping, clutching at the walls for support, slithering to the floor.

She sat there very still and stared at the runnels on her finger-tips where dust and skin cells merged; ashes to ashes. An old familiar image lingered in her head, a heave of sea the colour of muddy milk, waves racing and breaking under a dingy sky, frameless, boundless, implacable. And with it a sense of absolute terror. Slowly it receded. She breathed more steadily and concentrated on her becalming method, a memory of a house from her Norfolk childhood, the home of her cousins. It was damp and half derelict, and when they had got round to making it habitable, after many years of habitation, a slab of rotten plaster had crumbled from the wall, revealing a staring, ecstatic eye, a web of golden hair. Soon a colonnade of saints and heavenly bodies gazed out in troubled piety from the dining-room walls.

'All the way round too,' grumbled Uncle Randal. 'What on earth are we to do?' The planned rewiring would cause grievous injuries. The mighty, smoking fire would discolour and desiccate. Worse was to come. In the upstairs corridors and largest bedroom an ancient hunting scene emerged, all swishing tails and stabbing fangs and spears. A boat at bay snarled and a crown rolled beneath the stamp of hooves, just where the socket for Aunt Ruth's electric fire should be.

'Wheesht,' said Randal. 'Aye, wheesht's the word,' agreed the workmen. Within days the figures were again immured, sealed in by thick layers of plaster and distemper. As a nervous small child, Mary had found the thought of those saints and horsemen, vigilant but invisible, wonderfully comforting. Now she imagined herself joining them, becoming part of that house, fading slowly into the plaster, into self-effacement, there and not there. Thus fortified she accomplished without effort the three hot-water bottle evening ritual and retired to bed.

But this night was different. Peter has been found. Or, more likely, bits of Peter. She thought again of that muddy sea, breaking forever on its forlorn strand. She had gone to that great curve of beach once, years ago, with her friend Josephine, trying to imagine what Peter had seen, last seen before he fell. Josephine had said it would be good for her, a laying of a ghost. Mary didn't find it good at all. Josephine had brought a picnic to enjoy at this maritime charnelhouse. Mary walked down to the sea; the tide was far out and the sands shone under a pallid, fitful sun.

She was remembering the first time she met Peter. He was dressed in cricket whites, waiting to bat. He leaned slightly forward on his bat and she saw a crusader leaning on his sheathed sword. A perfect, gentle knight in a world then crowded with possibility, a future in which the past would renew itself, complementing and deepening the present; no opportunity would ever be cancelled, no prospect rendered void. One would grow a little older, but not to any irretrievable degree. There had been a day in Oxford when they had wandered together through water meadows thronged with cowparsley and birdsong. Mary was intensely happy. So many years later, how well she recalled that day. It was warm and uncertain; spring sunlight glanced through rain-soaked leaves and the air was blurred and pungent with blossom and earth and damp, charged with an erotic excitement and poignancy which Mary had noticed then and since in ancient university cities. An exhalation compounded of hundreds of yearning springtimes, aspiration thwarted, unfocused desire, urgent joy and mild, pastoral melancholy. She felt a quiver of fear.

'You want to watch this place,' she said. 'It's an ambush, isn't it? Toils of enchantment. Toil and moil, warp and weft. Funny that; could you say it warps you?' She eyed Peter sidelong, hoping to provoke him. But he wasn't listening; or rather he was listening to the bells, clamorous as always, and the cuckoo calling over the high walls. Springstruck, he moved, tranced as a pilgrim through the scent of wallflowers and then of bluebells as they turned into woodland along the river. A path, freshly hacked through undergrowth, led them to a clearing, and in the centre of the clearing a scowling priapic statue squatted, one arm extended as if grudgingly to shake hands. As they drew closer they saw that in fact the arm was pointing them back towards the river. Beyond stretched an overgrown garden, starred pink with campion and bramble. The sun shone strongly now and insects hummed and buzzed through the tall flowering grasses, nettles and elder. The house at the top of the garden was smothered in creeper; vine and clematis clambered to the roof edge, felt their way under the tiles, still dark from the early rain, and curved luxuriantly down again. They had wrenched the balconies from the wall and suspended them in airy cages of leaf and tendril. Above the porch an odd rectangle of brickwork remained bare, shadowed randomly by the faintest of markings, like ancient drawings or a forgotten script.

'Look,' said Peter, 'just watch this.' The markings were gaining in definition; they resolved into imposing Roman capitals, they grouped, they formed a word: PARADISE, they proclaimed. Mary sat down abruptly in the sodden grass. She was frightened and hot and something had bitten her on the eyelid. Her heart thudded. Peter was smiling down at her.

'It's all right,' he said, 'don't look like that. It's meant to be a surprise. And I didn't know if it would really happen.'

'What on earth do you mean? How did you know? Have you been here before? What is it *doing*?'

201

Peter pulled her up and hugged her. 'It's lichens.'

Lichens. Mary had never heard this word pronounced. *Lichens.* She was overwhelmed with love for him.

'This place used to be a pub or an inn or something and it had metal letters on the wall. You get these lichens left underneath them and they develop just for a few minutes when it's hot after it's been raining. Then they fade away again. Wait and see.'

Mary could not bear to watch the fading.

'Let's go, quick, and then it'll always be there.'

It was too late; the space was blank again and an ancient, angry face glared down from an upstairs window. Squashed and distorted against the pane, its bulging cheeks resembled the gargoyle features in the clearing.

So it had been.

She became aware now of the chill of the sands; she was shivering. She glanced back at the picnicking Josephine and could only make out a huddled form, intent on its Tupperware boxes. The shore and the dunes and the further cliff line were blanked out by a low hanging thick white fog. Looming here and there near the waterline, the tractors which dragged speedboats down to the sea might have been the rusty skeletons of tanks, and occasional distant figures were visible only in parts, a head, a glimpse of torso, a flailing arm. The tide crept swiftly inshore, the colour of her imagining, muddy milk. Fear gathered, thudding, in her head and heart.

So on that cold August night, Mary lay awake; she thought of Peter and his grave and all the half life lived since he had gone, the surprising resolution of middle age into old age and her relief then that soon it would all be over. And her guilt now at so many years wasted, that others could have cherished. But if Peter had not been taken from her, how different it would have been. She might have loved Ellen, instead of finding her a dismal encumbrance. Ellen might have grown up to be pretty and loving and marriageable instead of going around in army surplus clothes and breeding weird curly-coated dogs with webbed feet.

'As mentioned in Shakespeare. *Water-rugs,*' she claimed.

Everything that had mattered was so long ago; she thought her feelings had all leached away and she had nothing left. Nothing but that intermittent pain of missing Peter, of missing being loved, of the abiding loss of her share of the world.

Missing

All that summer a comet had hung in the sky above Mary's garden. Ellen claimed that it was also suspended above the shanty town ensemble of wire-netting pens and corrugated iron huts which comprised her kennels, but Mary had certainly not seen it there. She enjoyed the comet's strangeness, its air of preoccupation, as if it were brooding upon its imminent departure into unreachable black voids for another four thousand years. She felt personally privileged by its coming and she treasured its unmatchable evanescence; it made her bold and dismissive and untruthful.

'What then is life?' she asked it. She was seized by an irrational fear that it would disappear while she and Ellen were in France at Peter's grave. The night before they left she stood out on her dewy lawn, hands clasped tight; staring up at it she recited silently a rhyme half forgotten from childhood:

> *Star light, star bright*
> *First star I see tonight*
> *I wish I may, I wish I might*
> *Have the wish I wish this night.*

But she didn't know what to wish. The comet dreamed on, impervious. Somewhere across the river a goose was laughing.

They drove to Portsmouth in Ellen's rackety, dog-smelling car. Tufts of fur eddied down shafts of sunlight and strewed themselves delicately over the padded shoulders of Mary's severe grey coat and skirt, still very serviceable after fifty years of wardrobe and mothballs. On the boat, out on deck and hanging on to the rail, she shut her eyes and tried to will herself to push through time and emerge on the far side, a forties sweetheart, a forces sweetheart, Peter's sweetheart. But her legs were too wobbly and her hands too gnarled. The bright breeze made her cheekbones ache; her eyes watered.

Ellen had rented a house near Caen. It was unnecessarily large, and gloomy; on the walls were tattered, blackened copies of ancient funeral notices and Ellen announced proudly that it was here that Charlotte Corday had stayed in the weeks before she murdered Marat.

'It's dead cheap because of that,' she said.

But it had a large and beautiful garden where apples hung red and gold from trees swagged with mistletoe. At night shooting stars plunged from the heavens, but Mary looked in vain for the comet.

On a brilliant blue day of Indian summer, Ellen took Mary to the graveyard. Slow and silent, they walked together up the long, green slope between the crowding multitude of white stones. Mary leaned heavily on Ellen's arm; she had no thoughts at all, no feelings, only a thudding heart and a great weariness. But as they turned down the avenue of Peter's grave her step quickened. She let go of Ellen's arm; she pushed her hair back and smoothed it, she shook out her skirt and moved forward, head high, serene and eager, a ghostly bride advancing to her lover.

In late afternoon they returned to the house. Ellen's friend François brought tea out to the garden. Mary took her cup and smiled at him, surprising him.

'Thank you, Peter darling,' she said, surprising him more. She studied her tea, its swaying disc of surface. It was reminding her of something, but she could not focus on it; she saw a pinpoint of sunlight reflected and she heard the roaring of the sea. She slipped sideways from her chair to the grass and lay there, staring unseeing up at François, her hands still clasping the delicate cup.

They cremated her in Caen and Ellen took the ashes, a rosebush and a trowel back to the war graves. She laid the ashes in Peter's oblong of turf and above she planted the rose. She walked away down the green slope to the gateway. Poppies trembled there in the long grass and she thought how strange it was that they should be the flowers of remembrance and of forgetfulness. She believed then, and not for the first time, that she had inherited her mother's cold, passionless nature, for she felt nothing but a powerful longing to be done with all this, and never to return. Several days later she found beneath a carpet in Mary's house a dusty brown paper bag. In it was a photograph of her parents as she had never seen them, he in his uniform, she in a flowered dress, but laughing and young and ardent, gazing at each other.

'Before my time,' Ellen thought. Out in the twilight sky, the comet was tilting away into renewed aeons of solitude. She was overwhelmed by desolation, a longing to arrest the moment, to declare that love is as strong as death; but this she could not do. Anyhow, it was time to feed her dogs.

* * * * *

Mary Mann achieved considerable success as the writer of romantic fiction but her many novels have long been out of print. During her years at Shropham in south Norfolk Mann was confronted by widespread deprivation. Conditions that brutalised the rural workforce inspired the remarkable collection of stories published in 1903 as *The Fields Of Dulditch*, tales of human endurance in a world of cruelty and superstition that stand alongside those of Thomas Hardy.

The Witch Of Dulditch

MARY MANN

The woman who is confidently accused by her neighbours of having formed a compact with the Evil One, and of having until the day of her death exercised her supernatural powers with the devilish malignity natural to her tribe, was far removed in appearance from the popular conception of a witch.

She was a quiet, inoffensive-looking person, with a pale, smooth skin, rather prominent eyes, and scant, fair hair, brushed plainly behind her ears, and twisted into a small but protuberant knot at the back of her large head. She was married in her fortieth year; and it was on the occasion of her wedding that she was first openly accredited with the evil reputation which stuck to her through the rest of her life.

For some twenty years before her marriage Queenie Mask lived in our parish in the capacity of housekeeper to Mr George Ganders, called among us 'Gentleman George' – the epithet not having been applied to him so much on account of the graces of his person or the refinement of his mind, as for the fact that he is the lucky possessor of property bringing him in twenty pounds a year; such annuity removing far from him the necessity of stooping to earn his daily bread.

Rose Cottage, in which Mr Ganders and his housekeeper lived alone, stands a dozen yards back from the line of cottages bordering the grass-edged road. In the heater-shaped front garden – wide as the cottage itself at the top, narrow as the gate which opens out from it at the base – a couple of large standard roses flourish: a giant of battle, crimson-hued, and the pink-petalled 'maiden's blush.' Up their stems convolvulus and sweet pea are always carefully trained, and the land around them is sweet with self-sown mignonette. Over the front of the cottage itself a small-flowering, dark red rose grows and blows luxuriantly.

Inside, in the perpetual twilight of the small 'keeping-room,' there is a constant smell of apples, crossed at certain times of the year by a stronger smell of onions, mingled with faint odours of lavender and dried rose-leaves, and blended with the pungent fragrance of herbs drying on the tea-tray in the window. The window, by the way, is never opened. Long ago, in the days of Gentleman George's comparative youth, it had been fastened with a couple of nails to cure it of rattling when the wind blew, and the nails have not been withdrawn. Strong smells Mr. Ganders does not object to, but a 'flap' of air is an abomination to him. His garden is as sheltered as a room – his room is as close as a box.

In the drawers of the large press entirely filling one side of the room separate species of apples are kept; the key of each drawer is in Gentleman George's pocket.

In Queenie's day it was as much as her place was worth to touch those keys, to finger the contents of those drawers. She was a woman, honest to the backbone, who would not have robbed her master of the value of a split pea, yet was she guarded from temptation and watched by him as if she had been a seven-times-convicted thief. It was he who weighed out the flour for the daily dumpling; who, with his own 'shut-knife,' pared and cored the apples, lest there should be undue waste; who counted the potatoes he put into the pot.

It was the interest of his life, this strict guard exercised over his household goods. The pride of his life was that on every day of the three hundred and sixty-five he was enabled to produce from the pocket of his coat (smelling like a cider-press) an apple for himself and one for Queenie.

A tiny orchard was at the back of Rose Cottage; the trees therein had been arranged with a view to apples all the year round, and nobly the intention was fulfilled. No hands but Gentleman George's own were allowed to touch the product of his trees. He kept a suspicious eye on Queenie in the autumn gales, and was always on the spot to catch the windfalls. He gathered the apples himself, stored them himself, was careful to turn each one as it lay in its nest of straw every day with his own fingers. His talk was ever of 'Norfolk biffens,' of 'Rollands,' of 'Ribstone pippins,' of 'Pearmains.' If two or three of the codlings went rotten, or a 'Dr Harvey' had to be thrown away, the fact afforded master and servant after-supper conversation for a month.

But there was no talk in Rose Cottage when once the shades of night came on, for Queenie would not talk in the dark, and Gentleman George did not 'hold with' the expense of candle or lamp when there was no work to be done. So by eight o'clock in the autumn evenings, and by seven in the winter, the doors were fastened, the remnant of the fire in the grate carefully damped, and the household retired to rest. Yet did Gentleman George, not a heavy sleeper himself, greatly grudge the hours wasted by his housekeeper in repose. On baking mornings – those momentous weekly events when seven loaves of bread were cooked and an apple-roll made - Queenie was up before the dawn. On the fortnightly occasion when Gentleman George's two shirts and the less important items of the family linen were washed, the poor soul was bending over her tub by four o'clock of the summer morning, the master sitting beside her and keeping a keen eye on the soap. Then there were the brewing days, when a gallon and a half of the liquor facetiously termed among us 'guide-ye-right' – because with any amount of it on board you are said to be able to pursue a straight path – was brewed, an occurrence which necessitated a rising in the small hours of the morning. In a word, at those times of the year when the sun rose early enough to save Mr. Ganders's candles, Queenie was rarely allowed to press her pillow after daybreak.

But she was a meek and exemplary woman, and never complained. For all those twenty years she had no holiday, as Gentleman George objected to gadding; for nearly all that time she had not set eyes on one of her own relations, as they lived in a neighbouring parish, and Gentleman George was averse from visitors. Such a life had made of the naturally quiet and retiring woman a very silent and timid one. Of the experiences of her past life, of those kin of hers, whom she had not forgotten, although the longing to see them had probably left her, she may have thought as she darned her master's grey woollen stockings, or put yet another patch in his much-mended flannel shirt, sitting on the doorstep, to catch the last light of day, or sitting on the fender, the blaze of the fire on her work. She was a faithful soul, not one easily to forget, and her thoughts of these things may have been long and deep, but she kept them to herself. Gentleman George was not a person inviting confidences from the most effusive; and other companion had she none.

The hospitalities of Rose Cottage never extended beyond the entertaining of a passer-by with a few minutes' gossip at the gate. The only refreshment the master of the establishment ever offered to his kind was an apple pulled from the coat pocket where a few of those delicacies always lurked. He prided himself on his reserve in these matters. He interfered in no one's business, he wanted 'no interfarin'' in his, he declared. Friends meant money, he was fond of saying. If you shook a hand, sooner or later it was in your pocket. If every man would keep his door shut, and his mouth shut, and his pocket shut, all the world might be as prosperous and as individually satisfactory as Gentleman George himself. Whereas now 'all the world' slouched past to the ale-house, where wages were spent and foolishness talked, or toiled home from labour in the fields to bare cupboards and overcrowded beds. And why? asked the astute bachelor from the safe security of his own position, his rose trees, his apple orchard, his twenty pounds a year at his back – looking out upon the world of fools beyond his gate. Because each man having in an evil moment opened his door to a woman, a crowd of children had come in. A rural philosopher is Mr George Ganders; somewhat blear-eyed in appearance, a fringe of white whisker, thick locks of iron-grey hair, surmounted by a very broken-down black felt hat, framing a florid, sheepish face; attired always in a manner befitting his title to gentility in a suit which once had been black – a suit honourably distinguished among those clay-hued garments worn by the neighbours he could afford to despise.

Queenie had a profound admiration of the worldly-wiseness of her master. She accepted his dicta on all such matters, not even conceiving the possibility of dissenting from them. But she looked rather wistfully at the prematurely aged women from the cottages on either side and over the way who came to their doors in the mornings to watch their children toddling off to school, or shaded their eyes from the rays of the setting sun, looking out for husbands and big sons coming home from work. Often she saved that apple, polished to shininess by her master's red pocket handkerchief, his daily offering to her merit, and bestowed it secretly on a neighbour's child.

Within sight of Rose Cottage, if you stand by the gate and look past the cottages to the left of you, past the ugly red-brick chapel of which our Dissenters are so proud – having at their own expense lately rebuilt it of glaring brick, with large shining windows, with all available crudity of material and architecture – past the small plantation of spruce and larch, where the nightingale is always first heard in Dulditch, is the small thirty-acre farm called Brummles. The name is a corruption, it is supposed, of 'Broomhills,' most of the land now under cultivation having been, within the memory of the oldest inhabitant, waste land, growing broom and heather. The reclaiming those thirty acres has been a mistake, the present tenant declares, and certainly they yield starvation crops.

'God A'mighty knowed best,' this gentleman is heard to say, shaking his head. 'Ef He went and planted fuzz bushes 'twer a sign th' sile wor'n't suited to corn. Ef He up and called a fiel' 'Good-for-nothin' fiel',' 'twor a goin' agin Prov'dence to look for good to come out on't.'

Here is he, he will continue, 'Benjymun Squorl' (only the rector, who prides himself on his nicety of pronunciation – 'his finneckin' talk,' his parishioners term it – persists in addressing Mr Squorl by his rightful patronymic of Squirrel), 'had been fule enough to run agin Prov'dence – which yer might as well bash yer hid agin a brick wall as done it – and hung these hare tree-and-thutty acres o' rubbage about 's neck!' As the 'refuge' (refuse) 'o' the 'arth,' he is wont to say he regards the farm which he rents. 'Ay – come to that – th' refugest o' th' refuge!'

Beside his unsatisfactory holding, poor Squorl was troubled with a helpless, good-for-nothing wife. Her one recommendation in sight of the child-ridden neighbours had been that she bore him no children; but perhaps Benjymun, who was of a tender and kindly nature, may have held a different opinion on this point. That she mismanaged his home, made the worst butter in the county, lost all her young chickens, and always had tainted pork in the pickling pot, was common talk. She ended by dying miserably of a cancer in the breast, having given poor Benjymun the miseries of a two years' illness, and left him with a doctor's bill likely to prove a drain upon his resources for the rest of his life.

The duties in attending on her being so disagreeable, and she herself so little of a favourite among them all, the neighbours deserted her in the last stage of her terrible illness, and no nurse could be found. Day and night her husband and herself dressed that ghastly sore, which she all along eagerly displayed with an entire absence of prudery to any stray visitor who could be prevailed on to set foot in her room. Dreadful stories (I have reason, I thank God, to believe exaggerated) of her suffering, said to be 'terrufic,' touching stories of Benjymun's fidelity and attentiveness were extant. How, in addition to his heavy work on the farm (for poor Squorl had a difficulty in finding the money for wages, and was always 'short-handed'), he now had to milk the cow, to make the butter, to clean the kitchen, to do the washing for the poor woman which no one else would undertake, to sit up with her as the end drew on 'o' nights.'

These tales, repeated over hedges as she was hanging out the linen,

209

called from neighbour to neighbour across her garden-gate as she sat on the doorstep sewing of summer evenings, Queenie heard. Her own mother had died of a 'sore' – (it was by that generic title that poor Mary Squorl's dread disease was known among us). She longed to concoct a remedy from the 'comfort' (comfrey) root, which grew in the back garden, but Gentleman George at once vetoed the design. He never had countenanced the establishment of friendly relations with his neighbours, he 'were not goin' to begin with no comfort rutes' to please Queenie.

But Queenie's interest was kept alive, and once or twice she ran out to the gate and stopped the poor husband, hurrying by to make his small purchases at the shop, to whisper timid inquiry about the sufferer.

Then there came a day when she, having been to the mill for her weekly stone of flour, found that she had a quarter of an hour to spare before her master would expect his tea. Screwing up her courage, she hurried on to Brummles, resolved at length to carry out her great desire to speak a kindly word to the poor unfriended creature who was dying as Queenie's own mother had died.

She had never before set foot in the little farmhouse – in worse repair and with no better accommodation than many of the cottages – but she stood on no ceremony now, for she had small time to spare. Finding the kitchen empty, untidy, desolate, the fire dead in the grate, the remains of the meals of which Benjymun had partaken for days past on the table, she mounted the dark staircase, and, emerging from that steep and tortuous way, found herself at once in the sick-room.

Benjymun was there, sitting on the side of the bed. No fire was in the room, although the biting winds of early spring blew up the open stair. But a coldness icier than that of east wind or of frost seemed to smite Queenie in the face as she entered.

'I come to see ef so be as I kin help yer, po'r sufferin' soul!' she said, hurriedly advancing toward the bed.

The woman was lying on her back, her waxen-hued face turned upward; but at the sound of the strange voice – as it seemed, for probably the ears were deaf then to all earthly sound – the skeleton head slowly turned, the hollow eyes fixed themselves with an awful stare upon Queenie's face, and in a minute Benjymun Squorl's wife was dead.

It was a great relief to the widower that in the supreme moment which he had superstitiously dreaded, when the last bodily pang came and the

210

soul of his wife took flight, he was not alone with her. He both thought and talked a great deal of the happy coincidence of Queenie's appearance at the moment of poor Mary's demise.

'She jus' twirled her eyes on her, giv' a gulp – and were gone,' he said many times, telling the tale, using always the same phrase, after the manner of his kind. 'She di'n't seems no matters worse than she'd ha' done for weeks; but she twirled her eyes on ter Queenie and were off.'

Gentleman George of course heard the tale. The woman had been so long a-dying, her sufferings were so great, her death such a relief, that even he could not upbraid Queenie for having made things easy to her.

'She'd ha' been a'lingerin' on Benjy's hands now, mayhap, ef it hadn't been for Queenie a droppin' in,' he said, with some natural pride in his retainer, as the neighbours stopped to talk at his gate. 'Queenie cou'n't du no less, po'r critter. She jes' twirled her eyes, and –'

Gentleman George, repeating the now popular phrase, would brush one hand over the other to illustrate the perfectly easy manner of Mrs Squorl's departure.

On the day of the funeral both he and Queenie stood at the gate to see the little procession pass, and Gentleman George nodded with friendly condescension to the chief mourner as the coffin was carried by. Yes, Queenie here, his housekeeper, this woman at his side, unostentatious as she seemed, and averse from taking any credit to herself, she had had a hand in that matter!

The poor woman was put into the ground on a Saturday, and the next day an event almost unprecedented in the annals of Rose Cottage occurred. Squorl o' Brummles, on his way home from afternoon church, stopping to speak to Mr Ganders, leaning on his garden gate, found that gate opened to him, and was bidden to enter.

The widower came into the stuffy front room, sacred to all the vegetable odours under heaven, and looked around him, marvelling at the combined luxury and comfort of the apartment. Every inch of the brick floor was covered with carpet; curtains shrouded the window. Sunday afternoon was always converted into a festival at Rose Cottage by the appearance of a red and blue checked cloth upon the round table, in the centre of which a dessert dish, green of hue and shaped like a leaf, was placed filled with apples. Two biffens, destined for the delectation of master and housekeeper, were roasting on small pieces of brown paper on the hob. Queenie, stiff and upright in her Sunday dress, occupied the

Windsor chair on one side of the hearth; to Mr Ganders himself evidently belonged the other.

The poor widower, sitting there in his brown velveteen coat, a crape band upon his arm and another on the billycock hat, two sizes too large for him, and coming well down over the long ringlets of his iron-grey hair as rusty as the hat, thought of the uneven, unscrubbed bricks of his own front kitchen, of the broken victuals upon the table, of the cold and lonely hearth. His kind are not generally open to impressions, but he felt the contrast like a revelation. He had heard the word 'comfort' without rightly understanding its meaning till now. There had been none in his life. Here, in this breathless little box of a room, was Comfort. And Queenie, sitting prim and upright in her Sunday dress of violet merino, with little stripes of black velvet running round the short skirt and round the tight sleeves from which her red, rough wrists emerged, was its presiding genius.

Benjymun is no more artistic than the rest of us in Dulditch. He does not understand the beauty of proportion, nor delight himself in grace, nor intoxicate his senses in colour. But the way that Queenie Mask's red-braided holland apron sat upon her meagre bust, half covered her full, short skirt, the fashion in which her scant, straight hair was brushed smoothly on either side her high, narrow head and passed behind her wide, white ears, appealed strongly to Benjymun's taste. Looking at her, he pushed the rusty hat a little off his brow as he breathed the warm and heavy air, and uttered a sigh that was partly for his lost wife and partly for Gentleman George's housekeeper.

He did not offer many observations during that visit. The warmth, and the scent of the apples, and the unusual experience of a new idea which had come to him were altogether rather overpowering to Squorl. He felt unusually heavy about the head and a little sick, if the truth must be told.

'Th' p'or soul!' said Queenie, talking him over afterwards with her master; ''tis trouble pas' speech wi' him. Did ye note how he sighed and sighed as ef 's very inside was a-comin' up; and never so much as ope'd 's mouth?'

But if the visitor was not talkative he was in no hurry to depart, and his host, having at length opened his door to his kind, felt a rarely experienced pleasure in showing off his possessions. The various drawers in the oak press were unlocked, and the different kinds of apples lying snugly in their straw exhibited, their several properties of growth, of eating, of keeping discoursed on. The body of the canary, which had hung in the window for a dozen years or more, filling the room with song, and whose death had been a great grief of Gentleman George's life and a real sorrow to Queenie, was shown. Queenie had interred its corpse in a moss-filled paper box with a glass lid, having first driven black beads into its head to take the place of eyes. She felt a little bashful pride in having this resourceful dodge pointed out to the widower. A little shelf full of books, which Mr Gander's father had bought for a song at an auction, was inspected.

'They ain't smart 'uns,' their present owner said, with a decent veiling of his natural pride in his possessions. 'They ain't a sight to look on, but them as know tell to me that theer's a won'erful wally set on this here antikity by the gentry.'

He flicked his red handkerchief softly at the volumes suspended by green cord on their little shelf.

'I don't read 'em myself,' the master said with the conscious air of one whose life-business allowed no space for trifling – 'I don't read 'em, but there they be.' He took down a work entitled *The Mariner's Guide: A Treatise on Navigation*, and opened it, showing the charts and hieroglyphics before Benjumun's uncomprehending eyes; shut it again beneath his visitor's nose, and restored the volume to its place between the Rev Samuel Clapham's *Sermons* and the second volume of Bulwer Lytton's *Rienzi*. The other works of which the library was composed were an odd volume of the *Quiver* and a dozen unbound numbers of *All the Year Round*.

Queenie stooped forward to turn the 'beefuns' on the hob.

'Tell Mr Squorl about the Cleopatrick; giv' um th' hist'ry, master,' she said.

''Tis another antikity,' Mr Ganders said, with an affectation of disparagement.' 'Tain't on'y th' gentry that keer for sech.'

He fetched from its accustomed nail a small black-framed print which had suffered serious damage from sun and damp before ever it was hung upon the Rose Cottage walls. It was covered with brown and yellow spots, its lines were blurred and faded.

'This here is a French party,' Gentleman George explained, his broad finger-tip on the principal figure. 'That theer little sarpent she've ketched hold on, she's about to swaller it for a merracle. This here young person aside on her she be a-washuppin o' Cleopatrick. 'Tis a Scripter subjec',

213

and bein' antikity is wallable. 'Twas th' postman, a-callin' to ax me for the faviour of an apple, come ten yare las' Janiwary, as giv' me th' hist'ry.'

Altogether, the bereaved Squorl must have spent a pleasant and an improving afternoon. It was his host himself who had to suggest his departure.

''Tis gittin' for our hour for tea,' the Gentleman said. 'I take my males reg'lar. Queenie, set the kittle bilin', wummun. I'll see Squorl ter th' gate.'

'Good arternune, and thenk ye,' Benjymun said.

It was to Queenie Mask that the departing visitor addressed his thanks, which might have struck his host – who, if he had not exactly stayed him with flagons, had at least comforted him with apples, and had shown him, out of his treasure-house, things new and old – as odd and ungracious in Benjymun.

By ten o'clock the next morning the widower was there again, thus showing greater appreciation of his entertainment than the master of Rose Cottage quite approved. He rattled the locked gate at the end of the heater-shaped garden, and Gentleman George, hearing his name called, went out to him there.

'Mr Ganders, bein' onaisy, I ha' come fur yer adwice,' he said with great gravity. 'Yer a man o' th' warld, wi' book-larnin', and knowin' th' wally o' things, and I'd thenk ye fur yer adwice. My p'or woman's dead; and, bor, I'm lost without her – lost; and tha's th' down fac'. Theer's bakin' day a-comin' on, and th' dairy, to say nothin' o' th' wash – and theer's a sight o' duds i' th' chamber-corner a-waitin' for th' tub – and I'm ter'ble upset i' my mind.'

'I heerd,' said Gentleman George, condescending to bring his mind to bear upon his neighbour's trouble, 'the neighbours was a-passin' the word as Meelyer Sprite were a-waitin' on yer.'

'Meelyer's charge is high – sixpence a day and her wittles. A man can't stan' agin it.'

'A wife's chaper and more ecomical,' Ganders said. 'Wheer theer's housekeepers theer's all mander of expenses – and theer's waste. Though I ha'n't tied myself up thus fur, I bain't a denyin' a wife's ecomical, Squorl.'

Benjymun's face lightened.

'I ha' tarned my thought in that theer d'rection, I don't gainsay,' he admitted with eagerness, 'and as yu – a man o' th' warld, and allust much thought on i' th' place, and wi' proputty – see northin' agin th' coorse o' my takin' a second wife, I may as well let on as I ha' tarned my eyes on

Queenie. I shall be obligated, Mr Ganders, ef yer'll contrive so's I can marry on her at oncet.'

The course of Benjymun's true love did not run smoothly, and his courting was carried on under difficulties; but it came to a speedy and triumphant conclusion for all that.

When once Queenie was aware of the man's intention – and, in spite of the locked gate and the unwinking watch kept upon her, she learnt it somehow very quickly – she contrived to let it be known that she favoured it.

'I ha' allust wished to try my hand at th' dairy wark,' was all she said when her master endeavoured by threats, by coaxings, by tears, by bribery to put her off the project.

She said the same thing to Benjymun on the occasion of the only interview between them.

She said the same on her wedding-day, walking soberly homeward in the violet dress, covered for the occasion by a brown ulster of a very cheap and thin description, white-gloved, a black straw hat with white ribbons on her pale smooth hair. At her side walked Mr Squorl, also white-gloved, in his old brown velveteen, still wearing the band of crape on his arm and on the hat which covered the whole of the back of his iron-grey head, and was, indeed, only prevented by a pair of serviceable ears from extinguishing him.

The wedding was not, in appearance, such a festive occasion as the funeral of a few weeks back. Queenie had invited two of her neighbours to support her through the ceremony, but these ladies had declined, giving no reason. As the new-made wife passed her old home on her husband's arm, these former acquaintances of hers laughed with a jeering note, standing in their doorways. A little farther on one of them caught up a white-haired toddler who had run out into the road and hurried indoors with it.

'Why, Meelyer,' Queenie said, who was fond of children, 'let th' little un be! We shorn't do um no harm!'

But Meelyer pressed the child's head upon her breast and looked back with a gaze at once frightened and vindictive at the bride.

'Likelies I'll lave my Wulfrid i' th' track o' one that ha' th' evil eye,' she muttered as she went.

Gentleman George, leaning upon his little gate, looked after the

215

wedded pair as they passed with an expression of the frankest ill-will.

'Ongrateful wretch!' he said, as his old servant looked up and nodded to him. 'Ongrateful, black-hearted wretch!'

Poor Queenie, walking with the strange man at her side, who was her husband, but with whom she had hardly interchanged a dozen words, could not feel very elated at such a reception by her old friends. She had to keep up her courage by the reflection that her ambition 'to try her hand at the dairy work' was to be satisfied at last.

And the dairy, under the new management, proved a success. 'Queenie weren't niver a mawther to go about things in a halflin' way,' her worst enemies admitted. A new complexion was put upon the uneven, broken bricks in the Brummles kitchen. Washing-day ceased to be a terror, whose misery (in the shape of wet linen flapping about Benjymun's ears and encumbering his dinner-table) no longer extended itself over the whole week. The weekly bake became a pleasurable as well as an eventful occasion. His expenses were cut down, but he had never tasted 'no sech a wittles' as Queenie now set before him, her husband gratefully declared. Queenie was shocked indeed when she learned from Squorl that her predecessor had 'ran him up' at Littleproud's for tinned lobster, tinned salmon, even tinned beef, and such-like 'fancical' articles with which certain weak-minded and idle housekeepers are apt to be tempted.

'Theer ain't no support in them theer ertifeecials,' Benjymun announced, squaring his elbows over his savoury meal of pig's fry, onions, and potatoes.

Queenie, who, in the atmosphere of her husband's approbation, expanded even to the extent of expressing ideas of her own, had advanced the proposition – become proverbial since in Dulditch – that no woman should hold herself fit for wife or housekeeper who could not ' go through a pig.' She was now enabled, four times a year, to prove her own efficiency for such post by this process. From the gouged-out eyes, which went into the swill for the animal's successor, to the tip of its curly tail, which formed an ingredient in the pork-cheese Benjy enjoyed so much for supper, there was not an ounce of waste material.

But, although his wife gave satisfaction to the good man who had so quickly made his choice, outside the doors of Brummles dark things were spoken of Queenie.

She had 'twirled' her eyes on poor Mary Squorl to some purpose! She had bewitched the poor husband! Why was it that everything began to prosper now at Brummles? Why did the pig fat twice as quick as other people's? How came it that the pork was never 'slammacky'? Why did the cow, that had always 'gone dry' half the year, now give a plentiful supply of milk nearly up to the time of calving? Why was the butter, that used to be pale and 'intmenty,' now of the colour of buttercups? Let Queenie explain these matters if she could.

And by-and-by there happened a more wonderful thing still. Brummles boasted no orchard, but in the garden behind the house were one or two very old apple trees, and growing close to the gable-end of the house was a pear tree that in the memory of man had never grown fruit. Behold these trees, in the first spring after Queenie's marriage, each blossoming like a bride!

This was a memorable circumstance in itself; not much short of a 'merracle,' indeed, if one omitted to take into consideration the fact that Queenie, in her spare hours, worked like a man in the back garden, digging there and pruning the old roots of the trees, which had spread themselves wide beneath the rarely troubled soil. But a more significant event was to follow. For the first time since the tenancy of Gentleman George the orchard of Rose Cottage was bare of blossoms!

What proof more conclusive of the power of the evil eye was wanted than this?

If it had been that more was needed, look at Gentleman George himself. Gentleman George, who, having tried and discharged three different housekeepers since Queenie's desertion of him, now chose to dispense with those expensive luxuries altogether, and lived alone, preparing his own meals, making his own bed, sweeping his floor, and weeding his garden in tragic solitude, interrupted only by weekly charing visits from Amelia Sprite!

Sad tales Meelyer had to tell of him. How he wept over the food he could not make to his taste; how he was fearful as a child to be left alone when the house was locked at night; how, by the hour at a time, he hung over his gate and looked towards Brummles, only to rush within doors and hide his head if Queenie appeared, dreading above all else that she should turn the evil eye upon him as she had turned it on his orchard.

Was not all this, coupled with the improvement in Queenie's own position, enough to rouse the wrath of the neighbours?

When the autumn came, and Mrs Squorl, mounted on a rickety ladder, gathered the plentiful crop of apples in her own garden, the women drew round the gate and flung stones at her, so that she had to desist. She said nothing of this to Benjymun, possessing in a really fine degree that '*grand héroisme muet des âmes fortes,*' which belongs by right to a certain order of woman; but she left the rest of the apples and the abundant produce of the *Bon Chrétien* (The 'Bun crick,' Squorl called it) for her husband to gather. He was a quiet, inoffensive man, but Queenie knew very well the women would not stone Benymun.

Later, Mr Ganders fell sick, and lay lonely and weeping in his bed. Then Queenie put a pork-cheese and a new-baked loaf and a little currant cake in a basket, and ventured within the precincts of her old home. She was not unobserved. A neighbour, wringing her hands free of soap-suds, called loudly on Meelyer Sprite, washing her own doorstep ('lickin' it over,' Queenie had said to herself contemptuously as she passed), and the pair, entering the house simultaneously with Queenie, dashed into Gentleman George's bedroom, and slammed the door of that apartment in her face.

Then from the bedroom sounds between a howl and a roar arose, in which Queenie easily recognised her old master's voice becoming articulate now and again in the bellowed forth entreaty, 'Kape 'er away from me. Tarn 'er out. T'row 'er into th' roadway. Don't let 'er twirl 'er eyes on me.'

Queenie listened, grown pale, then took her small basket on her arm again, and went back to Brummles.

When Benjymun came in to supper, the meal was ready, the hearth clean swept, the kettle singing pleasantly on the fire, and Queenie herself, very pale, with red-brown rims round her white-lashed eyes, sat sewing at a patch she was putting into his sleeve-waistcoat. Benjymun, happily unobservant, made a remark or two as to the bad state of the land, 'like a pit' from yesterday's rain, and in five minutes after bolting his last mouthful was asleep in his chair, loud snorts breaking the stillness, the aroma from his working clothes and his heavily steaming boots filling the atmosphere.

Mr Ganders having recovered from his illness, made a pilgrimage to Runwich and had an interview with Mrs Hubby – she who is so successful in the treatment of ringworm, of whooping-cough, of sores. Mrs Hubby is an exceedingly fat and red-faced woman, with an iron-grey moustache and a thick voice. She keeps a tiny shop behind a red curtain, ostensibly getting her living out of ointments and washes, and pills which have a great local celebrity, but carrying on at the same time a secret and lucrative occupation, not even guessed at by the clergyman of her parish and the better-class people of the place. Counselled by the resourceful ladies on either side of him, Gentleman George determined to engage the wise woman of Runwich to baffle the Dulditch witch.

He returned from the interview hopeful of the success of the undertaking, but naturally depressed over the parting with the five shillings which had been necessarily sacrificed to the preliminaries.

As the charm proceeded, Mrs Hubby proved herself a perfect horse-leech's daughter in the matter of asking for more. Again and again had Gentleman George to put that unwilling hand of his into his breeches' pocket in search of crown pieces. When the day, and the hour, and the minute of Queenie's birth had been given, after Mrs Hubby had on several occasions consulted the stars and concluded other occult ceremonies necessary to the end in view, she conveyed to her employer the intelligence that for the complete overthrow of the enemy a piece of gold, accompanied by three of the longest hairs out of Mrs Squorl's head, was necessary. The gold, in the enthusiasm of his pursuit, Mr Ganders might have contributed, but the scheme must fall through from the impossibility of procuring the necessary hairs out of the witch's shining, smooth locks.

'She be a sight too deep for th' wise wummun,' the neighbours who were in the secret said to each other. 'Tha's a masterpiece, that be, what can hamper old Mrs Hubby.'

Queenie's persecutions were doubled; the children, with whom she longed to make friends, ran from her, shrieking if they were small, howling and pelting her with stones when they were of larger growth. 'Down to Littleproud's' on Saturday evening, where happier women stood, basket on arm, to 'mardle' through the process of 'getting up' their parcels of sugar and cheese and candles, she was let severely alone. Did a death occur in the parish, of pig, of cow, of child, the disaster was laid at her door. The hunted look which her eyes had begun to wear grew more perceptible after each such fatality; her own prosperity, although she worked early and late to attain it, became a shame and a terror to her.

When the story of the consultation with the wise woman at Runwich reached her ears she set her face like a flint. Her old master, he whose home had been her home for twenty years, for whom she had spent the best days of her life, whose interests still – so much had she become in

219

that monotonous time a creature of habit – were to her above and beyond the interests even of Benjymun Squorl, he to have meant her that wrong! He should have his way.

With a trembling hand she unfastened the small protuberant knot of her hair and pulled out a lavish amount, considering the scarcity of the supply, of the shining strands. These she folded in a paper, and, scrawling in the untutored hand her name and his upon the envelope, despatched it to Rose Cottage.

Before nightfall the three long hairs and the necessary gold piece were in the hands of Mrs. Hubby of Runwich.

That was a night of bitter frost; the first sharp frost of the year. The unusual cold awoke Benjymun at an unduly early hour, and he found that the place beside him on the pillow was empty. He had a great pride in the energy and cleverness of his wife – or not so much in that perhaps as in the perspicacity which had led him to choose a woman of such parts.

'She's arter sum'at,' he said to himself now, chuckling with swelling satisfaction.

She had got up to inspect the cow who was expecting her calf; or she was getting the copper fire alight, that her washing might be out of the way before her neighbours were astir. He sighed with content as he pulled the patchwork 'twilt' up to his chin, and turned over again on his pillow. With a mate so filled with zeal, so given over to good work, a husband was entitled to a half-hour's extra snooze in such weather.

However, Benjumun himself was no laggard, and when the light of day was beginning to peep in cold streaks through the kitchen lattice he had descended, tallow candle in hand.

The place was tidied for the day, the floor swept, the fire laid ready for lighting, the kettle filled, the table set for breakfast.

Benjymun, in the time of the late Mrs Squorl, had been used to doing these offices after a fashion for himself. He stooped now and thrust the candle between the bars. When the straw, which was the groundwork of the fire, blazed up, suddenly illuminating the room, he saw what he had not observed before, that the breakfast table, graced with its slab of white bacon, its small section of cheese, its pat of butter, its basket of bread, was set for one person alone.

'She've forgot her and me make two,' he said with a slow chuckle. He thought this would be a matter to joke the 'wummun' about on future occasions: on summer evenings when he, lounging against the door-post, watched her weeding the onion-bed, digging up the first mess of potatoes, gathering the broad beans for tomorrow's supper; or on Sunday afternoons when, no stress of work being on their minds, light badinage was not out of place.

Having made sure that the crackling, spluttering fire had really 'caught,' he set the kettle thereon, and blowing out his candle, went forth into the biting coldness, the dark unpleasantness of the morning.

A fringe of icicles was hanging on the brown thatch of the house, on the roofs of the tumble-down farm buildings. Queenie was not in the wash-house; the copper fire was not even lit; she was not in the dairy. It was certain, then, that she must be in the cowshed.

But she was not there. The heifer – to whose purchase-money Queenie had contributed the seven pounds which represented the savings of twenty years in Gentleman George's service – had been milked, and was turned, together with the cow to whose confinement Brummles was anxiously looking forward, into the yard. The animals did not appear to appreciate their release, but stood against the door of the yard with lowered heads, their breath hanging visibly in the air, the grey chill dawn around them, the frost-fringed straw beneath their feet.

When the daylight was a half-hour older, struggling feebly in the chill air against the powers of darkness, Benjymun returned for his breakfast. He expected confidently to find his wife awaiting him. But no sign of her was there, and although he called her loudly, outside and in, there was no answer.

'What in tarnation be th' wummun at?' he said to himself, for the first time uneasy and irritated as well as puzzled. All at once that single cup and saucer on the breakfast table seemed to convey a message the reverse of jocose. Queenie had never deserted him in this fashion before. There was an element of discomfort in the new departure, if not of anxiety.

He poured the boiling water upon the tea in the earthen pot; and then his eyes, roving uncomfortably around, fell upon the old hat and ulster which, except on Sundays, Queenie always wore abroad, hanging from their accustomed nail upon the door.

Then Queenie was not out of the house after all!

He gazed in slow astonishment at the poor garments, seeming to retain, in their slim outline and the unobtrusiveness of their fashion and colouring, so much of the likeness of their owner. Presently his eyes, slowly travelling downward, fell upon two pairs of boots beneath the press, the only two pairs possessed by his wife, as he well knew.

Tarnation again! She could not have gone out on such a morning in the only other foot-covering she possessed – the old carpet slippers, patched and mended, and only assumed when, the day's work being done, she was at liberty to warm her toes upon the fender.

With a shaking hand Benjymun pushed his cup away from him and started upstairs to the one bed-chamber. The room was as empty as when he had left it. He pulled away the sheet, depending from tapes, which hung before Queenie's 'violet' frock and her best ulster; he opened the box containing, wrapped in layers of white paper, the hat she had worn upon her wedding morning. All were in their places. Benjymun turned cold with the mystery of the thing as he looked.

She was gone – and she was gone in her stocking-feet, bareheaded!

As he turned slowly – for a numbness seemed to have fallen upon brain and limb – to descend, his outer door was opened and his name called sharply.

'Hi, Squorl, Squorl!'

A small, white-headed boy who worked at Brummles was standing in the kitchen, the door in his hand; his usually florid face was pale, his round blue eyes were wide and unwinking; there had been the sound of disaster in the shrill, high voice.

'Theer's summut wrong at th' roun' pond, master,' he cried excitedly; 'I come that waay to wark and I hulled a stone to see ef 'twould beer – and – theer's summut wrong and I dussen't go alo-un.'

Without a word, but with a trembling in his legs and a dreadful feeling of constriction across his chest which turned him sick, Benjymun stumbled out of the little gate, so low that a man could pass his legs over it, across the by-road and the field where the rime frost, which

> *'Enchants the pool*
> *And makes the cart-ruts beautiful,'*

had whitened the grass.

Across the wide meadow, plain in the otherwise trackless expanse, were the marks of two pairs of feet: one those of little Johnie Lawrence in his hob-nailed boots, the other lighter, less distinct, such as might have been caused, Benjymun knew it, by a woman walking in her stocking-feet.

The farmer ran in such slow, stiff, stumbling fashion as was alone possible to him, the child keeping a little ahead, but ever looking fearfully

222

back to be sure that he was not alone. The small pioneer went on talking excitedly, but without conveying any meaning to Benjymun, whose senses also appeared to be frozen and who could not catch the words.

But when the pond, with its one pollard willow, its fringe of melancholy brown reeds, rattling in the deadly chill of the breeze which suddenly swept across the meadow, was but a few yards ahead, the boy stopped and, turning his face full upon the man who followed, pointed to what lay beneath the willow behind the loudly shivering reeds.

'Yar wummun's drownded,' he cried, shouting the words angrily in his nervous terror; 'be yu deaf that you can't hare me, mister? Queenie's drowned. I knowed 'twere har. I see'd th' colour o' har gownd.'

The child would not touch her. He put his knuckles in his eyes and began to cry dismally when Squorl called to him for help.

'I sholl drame on 'er,' he sobbed. 'I wush I ha'n't hulled the stun – that hit her flop i' th' face. She gi'en me tu eggs for my supper las' night. I wush I ha'n't sin her.'

The pond was but a few feet deep. Only a very determined suicide could have found death there. She (having accomplished the cold journey in her stocking-feet in order that her boots should not be destroyed) must have broken the ice, laid herself down, and deliberately suffocated herself.

Although with Queenie's death the ban was taken off his orchard, and his trees are pink and white as ever in the spring, weighed down with fruit as rosy and golden as of old in the autumn, Gentleman George has never recovered his old health and spirits. He has no relish for his daily apple. He takes no pleasure in his library of 'antikities,' nor in the Cleopatrick on the wall, now that Queenie is no longer there to call on him for the scriptural history of that 'French party.' Meelyer Sprite, who does his washing, rules him with an iron rod in the matter of soap, and refuses to give him an account of the candle-ends. He pities himself extremely.

'Things is all at Harrudge i' th' house,' he says to those passers-by who speak a sympathetic word at his gate, 'and I myself bain't no matters to spake on since that ongrateful wummun tuk and desarted on me.'

Mr Ganders has run down mentally through missing the hand that wound him up to effort. For lack of the accustomed prop he has come neck and heels together in moral and physical collapse; and he 'bain't a patch,' as we say in Dulditch, on the well-brushed, spruce and intellectual

Gentleman George of old.

Johnnie Lawrence makes a circuit of half a mile in coming to his work in the dark winter mornings, or returning in the half-lights of the winter afternoons. For Queenie's spirit haunts that shallow pool beneath the pollard willow; her voice can plainly be heard screeching above the sorrowful rattling of the brown reeds.

'Tis well she chuse th' shaller water,' Queenie's old neighbours say. 'The mawther knowed well enough that sech as har 'ud never sink. Har badness 'ud ha' kep' har afloat i' th' deepest ocean-sea.'

* * * * *

Sylvia Townsend Warner lived much of her life in Dorset but before moving to the country she had been working in London on the ten volume *Tudor Church Music* project. From this developed a love of music and long before her friendship with Peter Pears in the 1970s Warner was a great admirer of Britten's work. In the 1930s Warner and her lover Valentine Ackland had lived for several months in Norfolk close to where Ackland's mother had a house on the coast at Winterton. Warner became a prolific writer of short stories, many first appearing in *The New Yorker*, and it was the combination of her affection for East Anglia and her musical background that provided the context for *On Living For Others* that first appeared in the collection *A Spirit Rises* (1962).

On Living For Others

SYLVIA TOWNSEND WARNER

Explaining that he wished to walk home across the fields, Hugh Whiting left his suitcase at the station, to be picked up later in the day.

'Didn't think to see you back so soon,' said the booking office clerk, who four hours earlier had issued him a return ticket to London and watched him board a local train. 'Hope nothing's wrong, sir.'

'Nothing at all, Parker. I changed my mind. Silly to go to London on a day like this.'

The words made Parker more conscious of the warm air, the blue sky. He strolled to the doorway and watched Mr Whiting go down the road and turn off into a grassy track, walking with an easy rhythmical stride. The young porter came out to see what Parker was looking at.

'Pretty good for a man of his age,' said Parker, as if he took pride in it.

'Regular old bachelor, isn't he?'

'Bachelor in his way, may be. He was married when he came here first. But she died. He went away for a couple of years, then he came back to Badknocks, and there he's lived ever since.'

The track led to a group of farm buildings, where the footpath branched off through the fields. They were beanfields, and fields of standing hay. The beans had just come into bloom. The clusters of black-and-white flowers gave out a smell like that of lilies, but with a lighter sweetness. Oboe, Hugh thought, not clarinet. The distinction had occurred to him many years before, and every summer recurred. He was a composer – eminent rather than well known. The course of time that had made him eminent had also made him somewhat out of date. The reason he had packed the suitcase and taken the ticket for London was that on that same afternoon the Ferrabosco Society was performing a seventeenth-century masque he had orchestrated for them. A meeting of the Advisory Committee would follow, and afterwards he was to dine and

225

sleep at Adela Turpin's flat, where he would find Humphrey Dudgeon, whose opera on Hannibal was in rehearsal for the Aldeburgh Festival. If only he had not made that silly joke . . . One should never make jokes on the telephone; the acoustics aren't right for it. To his inquiry how a sufficiency of elephants could be got on to that small stage Adela had replied, 'But it's *opera da camera*, darling!' Thoughts of this, and of the Advisory Committee, where Hilda Carpentras would repeat that the 'cello is no real substitute for the viola da gamba and everyone would snub old Jones, assailed him even before his local train reached its first stop. By the time it had got him to the main-line junction, he had turned from stoicism to opportunism, telling himself, as he walked up and down the platform, that if he had stayed at home a sense of duty would have teased him into doing something about Mrs Pilkington's Mass, a commission he had spent the last six months in wishing he had never accepted. If the London train had not been late, presumably he would have got into it. But it was late. This was the last straw, and he clutched it. He sent off telegrams of apology, ate some buffet sandwiches, and when the local train came in, which it did with exact punctuality, he returned by it. Now he was walking through the smell of bean flowers, which would not have happened if he had not set out for London. And tonight he would lie down in his fourposter bed with the quickened appreciation of knowing how nearly it had been exchanged for a skimpy divan in Hampstead.

He reached the summit of a gentle rise and looked down, like a returning Ulysses, on the landscape that had been his for so many years. He could see his ilexes but not the house itself. A tune that came to him long ago and had associated itself with this first view of the ilexes resumed its easy hold on him. It wasn't much of a tune, and he had never made anything of it, but at this point of the walk it would come up and link arms with him, as though it had waited to meet him there, and for the rest of the way would accompany him, step for step. He was grateful for its company, for he was wearing his town shoes, and by the time the path brought him into the lane they were hurting his feet. The rope-soled shoes he gardened in lay in the porch and sitting down on his doorstep he changed into them. Then he tried the door. It was locked. Audrey, excellent creature, had finished her cleaning and gone home. He let himself in. Audrey had closed all the windows but left the inner doors open, so that air should circulate. He saw that everything was just as he'd left it, just as it should be. All he had to do was go round and open the windows. But first he must get rid of those shoes. He could not put them down on anything in the passage, for there was nothing to put them down on. Julia had said, 'Let us leave the passage just as it was, so that there will always be something to remind us of how we felt when we first walked in.' And the passage had remained just as it was, with the row of pegs, and the wallpaper of gaudy roses on the low ceiling, under which her coffin had been carried out. Holding his shoes he went upstairs and into the bedroom.

A man and a girl were lying asleep on the fourposter bed. The girl was Audrey. She lay on her back with her mouth half open. The man lay sprawled across her, with his head on her breast. Their lovemaking had cast them into so deep a sleep that neither of them stirred. Ugly, and dishevelled, and disquietingly life-size, they had nothing beautiful about them – only a nobility of being completely unaware.

Hugh was half-way down the stairs before he realised that the man's face was known to him. It was the face of the Rural District Council's rodent officer, a stocky young man who from time to time came to the door offering to put down rat poison, and whom he as often turned away. But as he had never before seen him half naked and asleep, the recognition had been delayed. Now his laggard fury exploded. It was the outrage committed against his bed that angered him. His bed, his honourable lonely bed, had been dishonoured, like a Shakespearian bed. And by a rodent officer! If it had been a plain ratcatcher he could have laughed it off, so much are we at the mercy of a word. But a rodent officer had usurped his bed, and he felt ready to roar like Othello.

The flare of rage, with no action to feed on, quivered out, and left him to grope between desolation and embarrassment. With the pleasure of return torn from him, and made an interloper in his own house, he stood there, still clasping the pair of shoes, and could have wept over his disappointment. But if you are an old man, and employ a young woman to scrub floors with her strong red arms and her willing nature, and go off on a summer's morning and return unlooked for, you have no one but yourself to blame if your return is not what you expected of it.

On his desk lay the *Canzona* for contralto and two bassoons, and in the kitchen was the coffee pot. But there was nothing for it; unfortunate righteous householder that he was, he must creep away like a criminal and leave an untroubled exit for the lovers. Since the shoes could not be left, mutely accusing, at the foot of the stairs, he stepped cautiously into the sitting room, where they could be concealed under the sofa; and at the same moment, as though he had provoked it, there was a vague languishing sound overhead, a yawn that shaped itself into an endearment – Audrey waking to her rodent officer.

He thrust the shoes under the valance and stole out of the house and down the path, glancing guiltily from side to side. But there was no one in sight, to betray him by bursting into conversation. Still undecided where to shelter himself, he turned down the lane, past the pond and Mr Duke's barn and the milestone, past all things he had noticed with temporary leave-taking when the taxi drove him to the station that morning. One thing had become quite certain. He would resign from the Ferrabosco Society. If it had not been for that inept organisation he would not now be wandering comfortless, and driven into the embraces of a bramble patch because an approaching car was too wide for the lane. As it passed him, it slowed down. It stopped. A voice said, 'Isn't that you, Mr Whiting?' A man and a woman got out and bore down on him, the woman saying, 'I knew it was you. I never forget a face. I'm Candida Pilkington, you remember, and this is my husband. We're touring Suffolk, and we thought we'd call in on you and ask how my Mass is getting along. How lucky to catch you like this.'

'Very lucky,' Hugh said. So it was, in a sense; very lucky for the pair slumbering in his fourposter bed. 'Particularly lucky for me,' he added. 'I'm on my way to the church, and now you will be able to give me a lift.'

He had not the slightest idea what was to be done with them, but at least he could show them the church. They were papists, but that was no reason why they should not conform with the decent customs of England, one of which is church-showing. He must also show them who was master.

So he watched them turning the car, without essaying helpfulness, and when they had finally done so he got in as though he were accustomed to bestowing these little favours.

'Are you having a music festival?' Mrs Pilkington's manner indicated a matching readiness to bestow little favours. 'I do think it's such a step forward, using your Anglican churches for festivals. Poor things!'

'Ours is a very small church. Turn to the right.'

'All over pews, too, I suppose. Those fatal pews! Now, in Portugal —'

'Take care of that dog! It's deaf. Personally, I'm in favour of pews. People must sit down somewhere.'

The dog was bearing this out. Mr Pilkington halted, sounded his horn, and then said to himself in a subdued way, 'Silly of me, of course.'

The money was his, as well as the wife, poor wretched man, thought Hugh. 'It's a very old dog,' he went on. 'And being old, it has not much to be interested in except its fleas. So I dare say we shall be here for some time. Tell me about Portugal.'

Portugal and the dog accounted for nearly ten minutes. Ten minutes would seem no time at all to Audrey and her lover. Allowing them, say, another hour for dalliance and fond farewells, and adding a quarter of an hour to that, to keep on the safe side, and subtracting Portugal and the dog, one hour and five minutes must somehow be disposed of before he could invite the Pilkingtons to his house . . . Stay! Audrey, warm-hearted and domesticated, would certainly give the rodent officer tea. Two hours and five minutes. The hour was now three-forty-five. By six he might call Badknocks his own again . . . But no, not at all! There was the six-o'clock news broadcast to be reckoned with; the rodent officer would scarcely leave before he had heard the cricket results. Cricket results and fond farewells . . . Better say six thirty.

'Harold! Why don't you get out and move that dog? I can see Mr Whiting is worrying about the time.'

If he had said he was going to the village he could have made something of this. But he had committed himself to the church, and so must do what he could with it. The church had much to offer. They might look through the burial register for Pilkingtons. Or a notice about swine fever in the porch might lead to a visit to Paigle Farm, where Mrs Duke would give them tea.

'Here we are. I don't suppose I shall be long. Perhaps you'd rather wait outside?'

This was mere hopeful foolishness, since he felt assured that nothing would prevent Mrs Pilkington from coming into the church in order to animadvert on its deficiencies. There was nothing about swine fever, so he showed them in.

'If I were to be taken into a church blindfolded,' she said, 'I should know from the moment I was inside what form of faith —'

'Nice little church,' interposed Mr Pilkington.

'So should I,' said Hugh, with blandness.

After a slight pause, Mrs Pilkington observed, 'I can't see why you shouldn't have a festival here, Mr Whiting. It's quite large enough. Too large for the congregation, I've no doubt.'

'We might talk about that. But first of all, I've got to measure some

229

organ pipes. Where would you like to sit?'

One should never go without a piece of string in one's pocket. Hugh never did, and now he furtively tied some knots in it. When he had measured a rank of visible pipes and scribbled on a piece of paper, he called out encouragingly that now he was going on to the diapasons. Secluding himself in the usual organist's den behind the organ case, he spent the next half hour reading *Thirty-Two Voluntaries by Caleb Simper*, a work that he found there. He read with professional attention, coming to the conclusion that Simper missed a lot of opportunities.

Another expedient suggested itself to him.

'Well, that's over,' he said as he emerged from behind the organ case. 'I'm sorry if I kept you waiting, but one can't hurry over these things. Now, since I've got you here, I'll take you up on the tower.'

'Mr Whiting, before you do that—'

The tower door was locked. 'I expect the key's in the vestry' he said. 'I won't keep you a moment.'

'— there are one or two little suggestions I'd like to make,' Mrs Pilkington went on.

She'd like to make suggestions, would she? Disregarding the woman, he hurried into the vestry. A bunch of keys was rather imperfectly concealed behind a fire extinguisher, and probably one or other of them would fit the tower door; but this was of less importance now, since a far fruitfuller and more congenial expedient had met his eye.

He returned, jingling the keys.

'One or two little suggestions, Mr Whiting.' Mrs Pilkington repeated.

He began trying the keys.

'About my Mass.'

Her mass indeed! The fourth key turned the lock. The opened door disclosed a narrow cascade of steps, with a dead rook lying on one of them.

'Harold has no head for heights,' Mrs Pilkington said.

Hugh had no stomach for dead rooks, and found he could temper justice with mercy. He locked the door and waved the Pilkingtons into a pew, and leant against a pillar, looking down on them – which he could do handsomely, since he was both long and lean.

'I am proposing to write this Mass strictly *a capella*, Mrs Pilkington. It will be for five voices.'

'Why, we've got more than that, I can assure you. Sneckheaton is a very musical neighbourhood and there isn't much our choir won't undertake.'

'Five vocal parts. The number of voices singing a part is more or less immaterial, provided there is a proper balance of tone. I hope your tenors are under control. North Country tenors are apt to be aggressive.'

This was a mistake, for by incensing Mrs Pilkington's racial loyalty he renewed her determination to make that Mass her own. A sort of solo for Jimmy Rawson, who could have sung in opera only he wouldn't leave his mother, was one of the suggestions she had at heart; another was places where the congregation could join in; another that *Hosannas* should be sung, *pianissimo*, by a small body of trebles in the loft, to bear out the sense of *in excelsis*. 'And what was the last thing? I know it was very important. Harold, what was the last thing? Oh yes, I remember. *Et in unam ecclesium*. Mr Whiting, I want that section to be all in unison, and thoroughly emphatic. I want it to stand out, with a real broad, compelling melody; for, as I see it, that's one of the vital spots in the creed, and we can't make too much of it.'

There was this to be said for her suggestions, Whiting thought: they helped to pass the time. By now Audrey might be thinking about tea. He was.

'Well,' he said briskly. 'If you'll come into the vestry I will give you an idea of the music I have in mind. – on the harmonium.'

'On a harmonium?'

'A harmonium.'

'But why can't you play it on the organ? Can't you play the organ?

'I prefer the harmonium for *a capella*.'

The vestry faced north. It smelt of mice, paraffin, and ink. When Hugh opened the harmonium, a cloud of dispirited dust rose slowly into the air, and when he tried the pedals, a smell of mouldy leather was exhaled. He eyed the stops. Diapason, reed, bourdon, dulciana. He pulled out dulciana, and the knob fell off in his hand. But it was a game old instrument, and came snoring and tottering back to life under the easy rhythmical tread that Mr Parker had admired earlier that afternoon.

'Are you comfortably settled? Good! Now we'll begin. *Kyrie eleison*.' For the next thirty minutes, he extemporised in the key of G, drawing freely on Caleb Simper for his material, but chastening it. At intervals, he cast them a guiding word, or drew their attention to a canon at the octave. His guiding cry at *Et expecto* was answered by a snore from Mr Pilkington, who from then on snored as methodically as a ground base. The harmonium also threw in some touches of its own, not so easily reconciled with strict *a capella* style as Mr Pilkington's snores; but in the

231

main it answered to the helm. As for Mrs Pilkington, she stayed mute as a mousetrap.

I wonder what she's hatching, Hugh thought. He also wondered how much longer his ankles would hold out, for the bellows demanded a discreetly adjusted supply of wind, and discretion is a much greater tax on the ankles than fervour.

Wondering about his ankles, and Mrs Pilkington, and how Audrey and the rodent officer were getting on, he allowed his attention to stray from Caleb Simper and engage itself with Hugh Whiting, whose demands presently became rather engrossing and led him into the mixolydian mode and a five-four measure. Here a passage seemed to him so interesting that he paused to memorise it.

'And is that the end?'

As she spoke, Mr Pilkington suspended his ground bass.

'That is the end.'

'Oh. You didn't say so.'

He replaced the knob on dulciana and closed the harmonium, giving it, since he couldn't treat it to a bran mash, a grateful pat.

'Well, Mr Whiting, I'm afraid I've got to be frank. I don't like it.'

No?'

'No. I feel it lacks sincerity.'

Just so, with the same uninspired acumen, she would have said to the fishmonger, 'That herring's not fresh.' He was on the brink of esteeming her, when she continued, 'Mind you, we'll pay for it.'

'Naturally. One does, when one has commissioned a thing. Shall we go out, and look at tombstones?'

For, after all, he could not esteem her, and he did not suppose that the hypothetical fishmonger would have esteemed her either. Fishmongers resent bad manners; they are not marble slabs. Discarding the thought that he would get Pilkington's cheque having done uncommonly little to earn it, he began to question him about the tour through Suffolk.

'One thing's disappointed me,' said Pilkington. 'I did hope to see a man-orchis.'

'A man-orchis? Well, if you take the lane that goes off behind the Wesleyan Chapel and follow along it till you come to the second signpost, and turn left, and left again just after a bridge, and on till you come to an old windmill, and get out there, and go through a white gate—'

He broke off. They were now in the churchyard, and beyond the churchyard wall was the rector, hurrying forward with welcoming looks

232

to greet a young man. 'Here you are! I had almost given up hopes of you. Don't apologise, don't apologise! better late than never.'

The young man he had almost given up hopes of was the rodent officer.

The warmth of the sun and the blue of the sky and the blackness of the rector and the smell of the churchyard yews and the ache in his ankles and all the outrages of that interminable afternoon, from his dishonoured bed to Mrs Pilkington's acumen, together with the residual surliness that accompanies the knowledge that one has been behaving rather disgracefully, all melted, for Hugh, into a harmonious and Amen-like realisation that he could now go home. And alone; for Mrs Pilkington was getting into the car.

'Hurry up, Harold! We really must be getting on.'

'Yes. We really must be getting on,' said Harold. He said it in an undertone, as though addressing only himself, and just as he had said 'Silly me, of course' after sounding the horn at the deaf dog. No doubt he often addressed himself, not having much expectation that remarks addressed to others would be attended to, except possibly in the confessional. 'Goodbye, Whiting. It's been a very interesting afternoon. Very interesting. I'm afraid we've taken up a great deal of your time.'

'Harold!'

Harold lingered, as though he were waiting for something he knew wouldn't happen, then turned and walked to the gate. How extraordinary, thought Hugh, that those two may have lain together as obliviously as Audrey and the ratcatcher.

'Goodbye, Mr Whiting.' Mrs Pilkington said.

'Stop! Stop, I'm coming with you', Hugh called.

Since Mr Pilkington was at the wheel, the car stopped. Hugh got in. He said to Mrs Pilkington, 'Your husband wants to see a man-orchis – *Aceras anthropophora* – and he won't find the place unless I go with him.'

Mr Pilkington made unerringly for the Wesleyan Chapel, followed the lane behind it, kept on past the first signpost and at the second turned left, and left again after crossing the bridge, and drew up beside the old windmill. There was no need to guide him; the directions were written on his heart. Mrs Pilkington stayed in the car, remarking that they didn't want her – her acumen again – and that she'd rather sit quietly with a book. They walked for a couple of miles over heathy pasture land, for the most part in silence. Mr Pilkington appeared to be in a species of trance, and Hugh was tired. When they neared the place where the man-orchises grew, he sat down and left Mr Pilkington to find them for himself. Mr Pilkington strayed and gazed and strayed and gazed, and watching him Hugh reflected on the pursuit – so arduous and so haphazard – of other people's pleasure, and how, in the course of that afternoon, quite without volition or design and totally against his preconceived notion of how he would spend it, he had been instrumental in the pleasure of three people, only one of whom it had ever occurred to him to wish to please, and that one with no more than a very moderate and unspecifying impulse to be pleasant, since the utmost he did by way of pleasing Audrey was to praise her for not disturbing his papers, give her presents at Christmas and Easter, and tip her when she had done something that pleased him. Yet she, and that fellow who was even now preparing an excruciating death for some harmless church mice, and Pilkington – where would their rounded pleasures be if chance had not impressed him to drudge and trudge and moil on their behalf? Chance, and weak-mindedness, since he could perfectly well have hidden in his own garden and never met the Pilkingtons at all. Not that his motives had been entirely pure. It was to spare his own feelings as well as to spare Audrey's that he had slunk from the house. It was as much to wipe Mrs Pilkington's eye as to gladden Mr Pilkington's heart that he set out for the man-orchises. But he was not interested in the nature of his motives. A pure motive is a barren theme; no speculation branches from it; it is incapable of contrapuntal development. Indeed, his motives, even though impure, had counted for very little. Fortuity and a resolute illusion of free will had shaped his course, wrenching him away from the rational intention of a quiet afternoon under his own roof and hurling him unprepared into a career of living for others. It was a very disorderly way to live. Yet there were people who made a practice of it; and though they were usually wan and fractious, they got on somehow; they brushed their hair and caught their trains and kept out of Bedlam. No doubt it was largely a matter of technique, of keeping in practice. It must be admitted that in the matter of living for others he was out of practice. He was a selfish dog – a quiet, cleanly, abstemious, and selfish dog. And his legs ached, and midges were biting him, and he wanted to creep back into his kennel.

Pilkington was beside him, saying rather sternly, 'I hope you don't take unreliable people to see them – people who might dig them up.'

'You're the only person I've taken.'

Pilkington flushed with pleasure. I've managed that quite well, thought Hugh – though in fact he had spoken defensively and with no intention to please.

Seeing the man-orchises had conjured up a new Pilkington. All the way back, he held forth about wild flowers – those that are regional, those that are true rarities, those that are escapes, those that are dying out through the actions of man. The war, he said, had done incalculable harm, turning the British flora upside down. He knew a great deal, and was rather boring. Fairies are said to live on nectar and the scent of flowers, and Pilkington was like a fairy who had just had a good meal. His eupepsia swept him over the reunion with Mrs Pilkington; he quelled her resentment by being so much more aware of his own satisfaction, and in the end she was forced in self-defence to say that she had been enjoying her book, and had seen a weasel.

'Mr Whiting looks tired,' she remarked.

'Oh dear, I hope not.'

'What he needs is some brandy.' She produced a flask and a cup, stating that one should always take brandy with one, and that she always did. Nothing could render her less unamiable, but it was admirable brandy. Hugh began to feel more like his usual self, and when they assured him that the least they could do was to drive him home, he said that it would be even better if they would first drive to the station, where he had a suitcase waiting to be picked up.

* * * * *

Wildtrack

ROSE TREMAIN

Micky Stone, wearing camouflage, crouches in a Suffolk field, shielding
his tape recorder from the first falling of snow. It's December. Micky
Stone, who is approaching his fiftieth birthday, perfectly remembers
touching his mother's fingers as she stood at the metal window of the
cottage kitchen, watching snow fall. She was saying something. 'Isn't it
quiet?' she was saying, but ten year-old Micky was deaf and couldn't hear.

Now, in the field, holding the microphone just above his head, he hears
the sounds it gathers: the cawing of rooks, the crackle of beech branches
as the birds circle and return. He hears everything perfectly. When he
looks down at the tape machine, he hears his head turning inside his
anorak hood.

Seven operations there were. Mrs Stone, widowed at thirty-five, sat in
the dark of the hospital nights and waited for her son to wake up and hear
her say, 'it's all right.' And after the seventh operation she said, 'it's all right
now, Micky,' and he heard. And sound entered his mind and astonished
him. At twelve, he asked his mother: 'who collects the sound of the trains
and the sea and the traffic and the birds for the plays on the wireless?' And
Mrs Stone, who loved the wireless plays and found in them a small solace
in her widowhood, answered truthfully: 'I've never thought about it,
Micky, but I expect someone goes out with a machine and collects them.
I expect a man does.' And Micky nodded. 'I think I'll become that man,'
he told her.

It was a job you travelled for. Your life was a scavenge-hunt. You had
lists: abattoir, abbey, accordion, balloon ascent, barcarole, beaver and on
and on through the alphabet of things living and wild and man-made that
breathed or thumped or yodelled or burned or sang. It was a beautiful life,
Micky thought. He pitied the millions who sat in rooms all their working
days and had never heard a redshank or a bullfrog. Some people said to

236

him, 'I bet it's a lonely life, just listening to things, Micky?' But he didn't agree and he thought it presumptuous of people to suggest this. The things he liked listening to least were words.

Yet Micky Stone had a kind of loneliness in him, a small one, growing bigger as he aged. It was connected to the feeling that there had been a better time than now, a short but perfect time, in fact, and that nothing in his life, not even his liking of his work, would ever match it. He remembers this now, as the sky above the field becomes heavy and dark with the snow yet to fall: the time of Harriet Cavanagh, he calls it, or in other words, the heyday.

Suffolk is a rich place for sound. Already, in four days, Micky Stone has collected half an hour of different winter birds. His scavenge list includes a working windmill, a small town market, a livestock auction and five minutes of sea. He's staying at a bed-and-breakfast in a small town not far from the cottage with the metal windows where he heard his first sounds. He's pleased to be near this place. Though the houses are smarter and the landscape emptier now, the familiar names on the signposts and the big openness of the sky give him a sense of things unaltered. It's not difficult, here, to remember the shy, secretive man he was at nineteen and to recreate in the narrow lanes the awesome sight of Harriet Cavanagh's ramrod back and neat beige bottom sitting on her pony. The thing he loved most about this girl was her deportment. He was a slouch, his mother often told him, a huddler. Harriet Cavanagh was as perfectly straight as a bamboo. And flying like a pennant from her head was her long, straight hair, the colour of cane. Micky Stone would crouch by the gate at the end of his mother's garden, close his eyes and wait for the first sound of the horse. It always trotted, never walked. Harriet Cavanagh was a person in a hurry, flying into her future. Then, as the clip-clop of the hooves told Micky that the vision was in sight, he'd open his eyes and lift his head and Harriet in her haste would hail him with her riding crop. 'Hi, Micky!' and pass on. She'd be out of sight very quickly, but Micky would stand and listen till the sound of the trotting pony had completely died away. When he told his mother that he was going to marry Harriet Cavanagh, she'd sniffed and said unkindly, 'oh yes? And Princess Margaret Rose too, I dare say?' imagining that with these words she'd closed the matter. But the matter of Harriet Cavanagh didn't close. Ever. At fifty, with the winter lying silently about him, Micky Stone knows that it never will. As he packs his microphone away, the snow is falling densely and he hears himself hope that it will smother the fields and block the lanes and wall him up in its whiteness with his fabulous memories.

The next morning, as he brushes the snow from the windscreen of his car, he notices that the driver's side window has already been cleared of it – deliberately cleared, he imagines – as if someone had been peering in. Unlocking the door, he looks around at the quiet street of red Edwardian houses with white-painted gables on which the sun is now shining. It's empty of people, but the pavement is patterned with their footprints. They've passed and gone and it seems that one of them stopped and looked into Micky Stone's car.

He loads his equipment and drives out of the town. The roads are treacherous. He's looking forward to hearing the windmill when, a few miles out of the town, it occurs to Micky that this is one of the stillest days he can remember. Not so much as a breath of wind to turn the sails. He slows the car and thinks. He slows it to a stop and winds down the window and listens. The fields and hedgerows are icy, silent, glittering. On a day like this, Harriet Cavanagh once exclaimed as she passed the cottage gate, 'Gosh, it's beautiful, isn't it, Micky?' and the bit in the pony's mouth jingled as he sneezed and Micky noticed that the animal's coat was long and wondered if the winter would be hard.

Now he wonders what has become of the exact place by the hawthorn hedge where he used to stand and wait for Harriet on her morning rides. His mother is long dead, but he suspects that the cottage will be there, the windows replaced, perhaps, the boring garden redesigned. So he decides, while waiting for an east wind, to drive to the cottage and ask its owners whether they would mind if he did a wildtrack of their lane.

It's not far. He remembers the way. Through the smart little village of Pensford Green where now, he notices, the line of brick cottages are painted loud, childish colours and only the snow on their roofs unifies them as a rural terrace, then past two fields of apple trees, and there's the lane. What he can't remember now as he approaches it is whether the lane belonged to the house. Certainly, in the time when he lived there no cars ever seemed to come up it, only the farmers sometimes and in autumn the apple pickers and Harriet Cavanagh of course, who seemed, from her lofty seat in the saddle, to own the whole county.

Micky Stone feels nervous as the lane unfolds. The little car slithers. The lane's much longer than he remembers and steeper. The car, lurching up hill, nudges the banks, slews round and stops. Micky restarts the engine, then hears the wheels spin, making deep grooves in the snow. He gets out, looking for something to put under the wheels. The snow's almost knee-deep and there are no tracks in it except those his car has made. Micky wonders if the present tenants of the cottage sense that they're marooned.

Then it occurs to him that he has the perfect excuse for visiting them: 'I took the wrong turning and my car's stuck. I wondered whether you could help me?' Then, while they fetch sacks and a shovel from the old black shed, he'll stand waiting by the gate, his feet planted on the exact spot which, thirty years ago, he thought of as hallowed ground.

So he puts on his boots and starts out on foot, deciding not to take his machine. The silence of the morning is astonishing. He passes a holly tree that he remembers. Its berries this year are abundant. His mother, tall above her slouch-back of a son, used to steal branches from this tree to lay along her Christmas mantelpiece.

The tree wasn't far from the cottage. As he rounds the next bend, Micky expects to see it: the gate, the hawthorn hedge, the graceless little house with its low door. Yet it isn't where he thought it would be. He stops and looks behind him, trying to remember how far they used to walk, carrying the holly boughs. Then he stands still and listens. Often the near presence of a house can be heard: a dog barking, the squeak of a child's swing. But there's nothing at all.

Micky walks on. On his right, soon, he sees a break in the hedge. He hurries the last paces to it and finds himself looking into an empty field. The field slopes away from the hedge, just as the garden used to slope away. Micky walks forward, sensing that there's grass, not plough under his feet and he knows that the house was here. It never belonged to them, of course. When his mother left, it returned to the farmer from whom she'd rented it for twelve years. She'd heard it was standing empty. It was before the time of the scramble for property. No one had thought of it as a thing of value.

Micky stands for a while where the gate used to be. On my mark, he thinks. Yet the altered landscape behind him robs it of familiarity. It's as if, in removing the house, someone has removed his younger self from the place where he used to stand.

No point in staying, he decides, so he walks slowly back past the holly tree to his car. He gets in, releases the handbrake and lets it slip gently backwards down its own tracks. At the bottom of the lane, he starts the engine, reverses out into the road and drives away.

In the afternoon, he goes down to the shingly beach. The sun's low and the wind coming off the sea strong enough to make the sleeves of his anorak flap. He crouches near a breakwater. He sets up his machine, tests for sound levels, then holds the microphone at the ocean. He remembers his instructions: 'With the sea recording, Micky, try to get gulls and any other seabirds. And do plenty of selection, strong breakers close up, smaller splashing waves without much wind, and so on. Use your judgment.'

The scene his microphone is gathering is very beautiful. He wishes, for once, that he was gathering pictures as well as sound. The snow still lying high up on the beach and along the sea wall is almost violet-coloured in the descending afternoon. A film maker might wait months to capture this extraordinary light. Micky closes his eyes, forcing himself to concentrate on the sound only. When he opens them again, he sees a man standing still about thirty yards from him and staring at him.

Micky stays motionless, closes his eyes again, hears to his satisfaction gulls calling far off. When he opens his eyes once more, he sees that the man has come nearer, but is standing in the same attitude, intently watching Micky.

So Micky's thoughts return to the morning, to his discovery that someone had been peering into his car, then to his visit to the house which had gone, and he feels, not fear exactly, nor even suspicion, but a kind of troubled excitement and all the questions his mind has been asking for years about this place and the person he loved in it suddenly clamour in him for answers. He looks up at the stranger. He's a tall, straight-standing person. His hands are in the pockets of a long coat. In his stern look and in his straightness, he reminds Micky of Harriet Cavanagh's father, in the presence of whom Micky Stone felt acutely his own lack of height and the rounded disposition of his shoulders. But he tells himself that the fierce Major Cavanagh must now be an old man and this stranger is no more than forty-five, about the age Harriet herself would be.

Micky looks at his watch. He decides he will record three more minutes of sea and that then he will go over to the man and say what he now believes he's come here to do: 'I'm looking for Harriet Cavanagh. This may sound stupid. Are you in a position to help me?'

Then Micky turns away and tries to concentrate on the waves and the birds. He dreads speaking to the man because he was never any good at expressing himself. When Harriet Cavanagh said of the shiny white morning, 'Gosh, it's beautiful!' Micky was struck by her phrase like a whip and was speechless. Harriet had chosen a language that suited her: it was straight and direct and loud. Micky, huddled by his gate, knew that the dumbness of his first ten years had somehow lingered in his brain.

The three minutes seem long. The gulls circle and fight. Micky forces himself not to move a muscle. The sea breaks and is pulled back, rattling the shingle like coins, and breaks again. When Micky at last turns round, the man has gone.

On the edge of sleep, Micky hears the wind get up. Tomorrow, he will go to the windmill. He thinks, tonight I can hear my own loneliness like something inside me, turning.

Micky climbs up a broad ladder into the lower section of the mill. Its owner is a narrow-shouldered, rather frail seeming man who seems excited and pleased to show Micky round.

'It's funny,' says the skinny man as he opens the trap door to the big working chamber, 'my Dad once thought of buying a windmill, but he wanted to chuck out all the machinery and turn the thing into a house. But I'd never do that. I think far too many of the old, useful things have vanished.'

Micky nods and they mount a shorter ladder and scramble through the trap into the ancient body of the mill. Light comes from a window below the ratchet wheel and from the pulley hatch, where the sacks of corn are wound up and the bags of milled flour lowered.

'We're only in use for part of the year,' says the owner, 'but we can lower the grinding wheel so that you can get the sound of it.'

Micky nods and walks to the window and looks down. Every few moments his view of the icy fields is slashed by the passing of one of the sails, but he likes the feeling of being high up for once, not crouching or hiding. And as he stares and the arms of the windmill pass and re-pass, he thinks, I must stand up tall now for what I want and what I have always wanted and still do not possess: the sound of Harriet Cavanagh's voice.

'All right, then?' asks the mill owner, disappointed by Micky's silence. 'I'll set the wheel, shall I?'

Micky turns, startled. 'Thank you,' he says. 'I'll set up in here. Then I'll do a few minutes outside.'

'Good,' says the mill owner, then adds, 'I like the radio plays. "The Theatre of the Mind" someone said it was called and I think that's a good description because the mind only needs sound to imagine entire places, entire situations. Isn't that right?'

'Well,' says Micky, 'yes, I think it is.'

It's dark by the time Micky gets back to his lodgings. As he goes in, he can smell the meal his landlady is preparing, but he doesn't feel hungry, he's too anxious about what he's going to do. He's going to telephone the big house where Harriet lived until she married and went to live in the West Country. Though Major Cavanagh and his wife will be old, Micky senses that people who live comfortably live long and he feels certain that when the receiver is picked up it will be one of them who answers. And he knows exactly what he will say, he's prepared it. 'You won't remember me, Major, but I'm an old friend of Harriet's and would very much like to get in touch . . .'

There's a payphone near the draughty front door of the guest house. Micky arranges 10p coins in a pile on top of it and searches in the local directory for the number. It's there as he expected. Cavanagh, Major C.N.H., High House, Matchford.

He takes a deep breath. His landlady has a television in her kitchen and music and laughter from a comedy show are blaring out. Micky presses the receiver tight to his ear and tries to shut out the noise. He dials the number. He hears it ring six times before it's picked up and a voice he remembers as Mrs Cavanagh's says graciously, 'Matchford two one five.'

'Mrs Cavanagh,' Micky begins, after pressing in the first of the coins, 'you won't remember me, but –'

'This isn't Mrs Cavanagh.' says the voice, 'Will you hold on and I'll get her.'

'Harriet?' says Micky.

There's a pause. Micky reaches out and holds on tightly to the top of the payphone box.

'Yes. Who is this?'

'Micky Stone.'

Another pause. The laughter from the landlady's TV is raucous.

'Sorry. Who?'

'Micky Stone. You probably won't remember me. I used to live with my mother in Slate Cottage.

'Oh yes. I remember you. Micky Stone. Gosh.'

'I didn't think you'd be here, Harriet. I was going to ask where you were so that I could ring you up and talk to you.'

'Were you? Heavens. What about?'

Another burst of laughter comes out of the kitchen. Micky covers his left ear with his hand. 'I hadn't planned what about. About the old days, or something. About your pony.'

'Golly yes. I remember. You used to stand at the gate . . .'

'Wait!' says Micky. 'Can you wait a moment? Can you hang on?'

'Yes. All right. Why?'

'Hang on, please, Harriet. I'll only be a minute.'

Micky feeds another 10p coin into the pay slot, then runs as fast as he can up the stairs to his room. He grabs the tape machine and the microphone and hurtles down again. His landlady opens her kitchen door and stares as he rushes past. He picks up the telephone. The recorder is on and turning, the little mike held against Micky's head.

'Harriet?' Are you still there?'

A pause. Micky hears the door of the kitchen close.

'Yes.'

'So you remember me at the gate?'

'Yes . . .'

'I once helped whitewash your stables and the dairy . . .'

'Yes. Lucky.'

'What?'

'Lucky. My little horse. He was called Lucky. My children have got ponies now, but they don't awfully care about them. Not like I cared about Lucky.'

'You rode so well.'

'Did I? Yes. I loved that, the early morning rides. Getting up in the dark. It was quite a long way to your lane. I think it'd usually be light, wouldn't it, by the time I came up there? And I'd be boiling by that time, even in snowy weather. Terribly hot, but awfully happy. And I remember, if you weren't there sometimes, if you were working or having breakfast or something, I used to think it was rather a bad omen. I was so superstitious, I used to think the day would go badly or Lucky would throw me, or Mummy would be cross or something, and quite often it went like that – things did go wrong if I hadn't seen you. Isn't that stupid? I'd forgotten all that till I spoke to you, but that's exactly how it was. I suppose you could say you were my good luck charm. And actually, I've often thought about you and wondered how you'd got on. I was rather sad when they demolished Slate Cottage. Did you know they had? I remember thinking every bit of one's life has kind of landmarks and Slate Cottage

243

was definitely a landmark for me and I don't like it that it's not there any more. But you knew it had gone, did you?'

'Not till today . . .'

'Oh, it went years ago. Like lots of things. Like Lucky and the morning rides. Horrid, I think. I hate it when things are over. My marriage is over. That's why I'm staying here. So sad and horrid it's all been. It just makes me think – jolly stupidly, because I know one can never bring time back – but it does make me see that those days when I was growing up and you were my lucky charm were important. What I mean is, they were good.'

Lying in bed, Micky waits till the house is quiet. Outside his window, the snow is falling again. When he switches on the recorder and listens to Harriet's voice, he realises for the first time that he forgot to put in a new tape and that most of his work at the windmill is now obliterated. About a minute of it remains, however. As Harriet Cavanagh fades to silence, her words are replaced by the sound of the big sails going round and round.

* * * * *

George Ewart Evans: On arriving in the remote east Suffolk hamlet of Blaxhall just after the war Evans was unaware that his new friendship with elderly neighbours would change the course of his writing and lay the foundations of what has become known as Oral History. *Ask The Fellows Who Cut The Hay* (1956), a celebrated tribute to the people of Blaxhall, was followed by a series of remarkable books that explore the traditional rural culture of East Anglia. In 1973 Evans returned briefly to fiction with the publication of *Acky*, an affectionate collection of gently subversive stories about a wiley old horseman living on the edge of a broad heath in the village of Fenhall that catches perfectly the language and humour of Suffolk. In *Acky And Justice* Evans has borrowed the butter cross in Bungay and relocated it further south in his fictional market town of Fordham.

Acky And Justice

GEORGE EWART EVANS

One fine evening Acky said to Sarah: 'I'll take you on thet trip to Ipsidge I promised you – if you're in a mind to come.' Sarah, however, was undecided, and Acky pressed her:

'You want to git out more, gel. When was it you were last abroad? You're allus a-setting indoors: I reckon if you were an owd hin you'd ha' brought off three lots o' chicks since Christmas. You don't want to worry about the weather. It won't change. The gnats are a-weaving, and the swallows climbing up high; and look! the sky is a red as a soldier's coat. We can cycle over to Fordham and catch a bus from there. We can then come back what time we like.'

Sarah was at last persuaded to fall in with Acky's plan; and early next morning they were standing on the pavement by the bus-stop in the market square at Fordham, after cycling the few miles from Fenhall and storing their bikes in Fred Partridge's house near by. Sarah was in a good humour and her best hat; and Acky had his horseman's suit on and a silk square or muffler tied round his neck with an expert knot at the side. His ear-rings caught the sun, and his face shone with good humour as he sniffed the fresh morning, and watched the small happenings of the street: the passers-by, the shopkeepers arranging some of their stock outside on the pavement, and the postman collecting the letters from a pillar-box. Then he chuckled and continued chuckling noisily until Sarah said sharply:

'What's got into you, bor? You'll have the whole street coming over to see what's up, if you don't give over.'

'It's the white lady up there,' Acky said, nodding towards the Butter Cross, the circular wooden structure that stood in the centre of what was once the town market. On its top was a splendid figure of Justice, with scales in one hand and a sword in the other.

'She allus was up there,' said Sarah. 'What's funny about her? I think she's very lovely.'

'Ah, you're right, gel. You're right. She's some fine. But you're wrong about one thing. She ain't allus been there. She were missing for some long while. That's the reason I was a-chuckling. She remind me of Bertie Russett.'

The bus came along just then; and after they had settled in their seats Sarah asked: 'But what has Bertie Russett to do with the statue of Justice on top o' Fordham Butter Cross?'

'All in God's good time, like the parson say. You want to take a hint or two from Job. But the marrow o' the matter is I take Bertie Russett out with me one night to see what we could git. There was a particular covey over there at Fordham that I used to visit with Fred Partridge. But Fred had been called up. This was the first year of the war, rightly the second; it were in June 1940 or early July. I forget the exact date. But I recollect the night as though it were yesterday – What were we a-doing on yesterday? – No, clearer than yesterday! I could ha' gone out that night alone, but I got a particular cause to have some'un with me that night – not because of the keepers. They weren't looking for poachers then: like everybody else they were a-sarchin for Garmans. It were a couple o' weeks after Dunkirk. And they reckoned the Garmans were a-going to arrive from all sides: from the air, along the roads, up the rivers from the coast, from under the ground a'most. The Home Guard, Home Defence or whatever they used to call theirselves were out in their droves night and day, all with their fingers on the triggers o' their breech-loaders, their 303s, their 4.10s, their 12-bores – anything they got under their stairs. Pikes out o' the museum some on 'em had! Now I could manage the birds and the keepers; but I didn't want to be mistook for a Garman and have my backside peppered by a 12-bore, or ma' skull stove in with a pike by some Home Defence billy who were a-rearing to do his duty. So I take Bertie Russett along with me to keep us both out o' trouble.

'Bertie he were some keen. He were like a boy a-going on a Sunday school treat as we set out that night. He wanted to try out his owd man's gun, the kind you take down and hide in your pocket; but I say to him: "There are a rare lot too many guns about tonight, Bertie. We'll leave that at hoom, and we'll just use our wits; atween us, I doubt, we got enough o' them to win ourselves our breakfast. And leave that pipe o' yourn in the drawer, Bertie. We'll keep a total blackout, like they say." You recollect at that time o' day, you could get a good price for a rabbit. Folk weren't too particular; anything would do if you could put it into the pot.

'It were some quiet as we made our way out toward Fordham. There were no raids, no anti-aircraft guns a-barking and a-shattering the night – that come later in the year. But the searchlights were a-flitting across the sky like the spokes of a big wheel; and chance times two would stay right still and make a kinda big pyramid o' light – a tent big enough to put two counties in.

'These Guards were everywhere: at the bridges, the crossroads, the electric pylons, the charch – anywhere they think the Garmans might take a fancy to. Me and Bertie know we had to go some careful. But we got round them half-tidy; and we got over to this covey, about half past eleven it were. We'd already got a bagful o' rabbits. For you ma' depend, once you got away from the road and the houses you could go on as you like. They were a-letting the game to look arter itself: there was bigger game afoot; everybody were after Garmans! So Bertie and me had it all to ourselves; and we were doing right well and really couldn't carry much more, and were thinking of making our tracks towards hoom. But then of a sudden Bertie put up his hand, warning like, dropped his bag and hared off out in front somewhere, moving as silent as Sunday. And I'd been out with Bertie afore, and I knew his gait, so I stay right still where I were. He come back in half a minute breathing hard:

' "It's the Garmans, Acky," he say "Four on 'em. I see 'em as plain as you!"

' "Where?" I say.

'It weren't pitch dark, and once you'd got used to it you could see middling tidy.

' "Just to the other side o' that hedge. They come across that meadow. Four on 'em; and they carried suthen with 'em. They stop right there," he whisper, "near that spinney in the corner o' the meadow."

' "C'mon," I say to Bertie, "we'll have a peek at 'em. But don't say nawthen. Keep dumb till I give you the down."

'So we move forward quickly and got to the hedge, another twenty yards and I see 'em! Bertie was right: there were four on 'em with a big black thing on the ground beside 'em. And now they were a-digging as though they were on piece-work. Me and Bertie laid under the hedge a-waiting on 'em. There they were a-digging down and down, taking turn – two and two about – till they were nigh out o' sight. Then one on 'em say, quiet-like: "Thet will do, lads!" and the two who were in the hole threw up their shovels and they come out. Then they lowered this big, black

247

thing into the hole and started a-filling in the hole like they were a-covering up a murder. Afore they finish I put my hand on Bertie's shoulder and give him the *go-back*; and we make for the place where we left our bags. Bertie picked up his and was away in front; and after we been walking for some while he stop and he say: "Them weren't Garmans, Acky!" He were a bit annoyed as though someone had tricked him. "Him that spoke, I know 'un right well." So I stopped and I say:

' "You're right, Bertie. They ain't Garmans; not one on 'em have ever been across the water. But see here, Bertie: you and me ain't seen nawthen tonight! Nawthen! Do you git the drift o' that, Bertie?"

'His head were down as though he were a-weighing this up some hard; and then he look up sly-like:

' "No, Acky," he say, grinning. "We ain't seen a thing." '

Acky stopped and looked out of the window of the bus and pointed to a field of corn they were passing. 'He got a rare field o' barley there, Sarah. It'll make Burton barley, I doubt.'

Sarah looked at him with annoyance: 'But what happened? What was it they were a-burying? Or is it you're going to keep the second part o' your serial till the next time we go to Ipsidge?'

Acky chuckled.

'That's a rare idea, gel. That would stop your puttering; jus' tell you a serial-story and not give you a chance! I mun think about that right hard. But I thought you could put the ends of the story togither now that I started you off; without me having to spell out every word of it for you.'

'Get on with it,' said Sarah.

'Well, I didn't see Bertie for a few days after that jaunt; and on the Saturday I take my owd bike to Fordham to get some parmit or other (it were all parmits at that time o' day: parmits for meat, parmit for butter, parmit for this and parmit for that, parmits for pigs, a parmit to breathe a'most!). And I meet Bertie a-cycling along with his head down. He look a bit down-in-the-mouth, too; and when I say, "Hi, Bertie!" he say:

' "I got my calling-up papers, Acky."

'You see, he come off the land and got himself a job up at the aerodrome, because there was more money in it. And that were it! With a month they nab him and he were in the army afore he knew one side o' the runway from the other. So when I see how it was with Bertie I took him to Fordham *Lion* to cheer him up; and after a pint or two he were holding his head much higher. Then we come out and stand on the pavement, right there where we were now a-waiting for the bus. And two o' the Fordham folk come along, two women; and one on 'em look up and say:

' "My goodness! She's gawn!"

' "What?"

' "She's gawn. Her with the scales and the sword: Justice! Whativer's happened to her?"

'And afore the other could open her mouth, owd Bertie he turn to har and he say:

' "She's been called up, ma'am. Most o' the J's ha' gone some weeks since. But seemingly they're not so quick a-gitting them into the A.T.S. or the W.A.A.F.; or maybe they've made a sailor of her and put her in the W.R.E.N.S."

'And Bertie look at me some cunning. He knew. He knew! He spotted it afore I did. And they say that Bertie were only fifteen ounces!'

'You mean,' asked Sarah, 'this Bertie had guessed what you saw that night when you were out poaching?'

' 'Course he did! Four on 'em; and I knew every man jack of 'em. All from Fordham. They put her away for fear of the Garmans. A rare night's work: a-burying Justice! And it didn't need a passon to git a moral out o' thet. In the war they say she is one of the first to git the warm end o' the stick; and there she were right out o' sight, with her mouthful o' dirt; she couldn't speak up or nawthen – buried for the duration.'

Sarah snorted: 'You should ha' been a passon yourself! But they must ha' got her back! We now see her. It's the same one as before the war, ain't it?'

'Yeh,' said Acky, with one of his knowing high-pitched laughs. 'They got her back safe, and she were none the worse; but it were a rare lot o' trouble.'

'Well, you better tell me the rest of the story. We got four or five miles yet to reach Ipsidge.'

'Right, gel,' Acky said, after a mischievous pause of a minute or two, just to keep Sarah on the hook. 'Well, it were like this. After that day at Fordham I clean forgot about Justice. Bertie Russett went to the war; and all thet business went clean out o' ma hid. And you mun know there were plenty o' things to fill it up: the horses, the pigs, and the Home Guard which they got me into myself later on; and then there were the children, and all manner o' what-not: parmits, licence-papers! And as you well recollect it went on for years after the war finished. But four or five year after the war is over owd Fred come over here from Fordham – suthen about his pigs, most likely – and I say to him, not meaning much, jus' giving him the sele o' the day like:

' "How are things in Fordham, Fred?"

'And he laugh, and he say: "Oh, they're in a rare muddle over there. They're all a-calling one another names; and the Town Reeve he's nearly out o' his mind. They reckon they're going to make a case out of it!"

' "Glass or boards?" I say. But owd Fred, without paying any regard, say:

' "Naw! They say they're a-going to pull the Council!"

' "Pull the Council!"

' "Yeh, they threaten to have the whole bunch of 'em up in court. They reckon that some'un has nobbled Justice – that statue that used to be on the Butter Cross. Some say they hide har at the start o' the war because of the Garmans. Some say, Yeh! That's right. But they can't find her! And most on 'em say – or *think*, leastways, even if they don't say – that some'un up and sold her. She were made o' lead, you recollect; and you ma' know how much lead is a-fetching. She were a rare thing, Acky. I doubt you remember har. She were a right strappin' wench. She were the fust thing I miss in Fordham when I come out o' the army."

' "I recollect har right well," I say. "But what does the Town Reeve say in the matter?"

' "He say he knows nawthen about it. And he's loike to be right."

' "O'course he's right. This 'un sartinly knows nawthen. He weren't in Fordham at that time o' day. John Bailey were the Reeve; and he got himself killed with that flying-bomb. He were the one that buried her."

' "Buried her!" Owd Fred looks at me as though he were a-seeing me for the first time. "What you know about this here, Acky?"

' "I reckon I better come over to Fordham and sort things out," I say, "afore you togither will shoot the Town Reeve; or dew suthen clever like that!"

'Yeh, I figure I knew exactly what had happened; and I were right. John Bailey were the only one o' those Bertie and me see that night – the only one who know exactly what they are about. The other three that were with him didn't know their ass from their appetite. They were jus' there to do the carrying and the digging, to kinda make the spade handles longer. When John Bailey went hoom, o'course no one knew. They couldn't find har. Justice, she ha' gone astray.'

'So you went over to Fordham and told them where to find her?'

Acky looked at Sarah for a moment or two before replying:

'It weren't as easy as that, gel. We had to hev a confabulation first – a bit o' talk. I knew where she were; and they wanted to find her. So we had to come to an arrangement first.'

'What arrangement?'

'Well, there was . . . well, the Town Reeve he call it by some long owd word – suthen. Yeh, I got it: a honorarium! That's it! But I didn't pay regard to what he called it, as long as I got it.'

'Honorarium! Acky Flatt, you got the nerve o' the Devil. You mean you asked them for money? How much was it?'

'Never you mind how much! How do you think I bought that rare hog I got from Ipsidge market?'

'Yes, I recall it now,' Sarah said grimly. 'You went to Fordham and you didn't come home that night!'

Acky grinned: 'That were the night I laid on owd Mother Greenfield's pillow, under the hedge about half-way to Fenhall. We were bound to have a celebration after I showed 'em where she were. But when they dug her up, I were whoolly stammed to see how John Bailey had put her away. He done the job parfect: wrappings and tilts and tarpaulins, she were done up better than an Egyptian mummy. She'd been a-lying by that spinney for close on five year; and she took no harm at all. And in less than a week after they's got her above ground again, there she was a-queening it over the Butter Cross – as spruce and as pure as a maid.'

Sarah was silent for some minutes after Acky had finished his story; and he spent them looking idly at the blue, cloud-scudding sky pretending that he wasn't really interested in any comments she would like to make. But at last she asked him:

'You weren't the only one who knew where Justice was to be found. How about Bertie Russett; did he get anything?'

It was now Acky's turn to rake his own thoughts:

'Oh, Bertie knew,' he said after a pause, 'he knew right well. But Bertie got nawthen. Bertie never come back! You didn't know that, gel? Fred Partridge, he once told me how it happen. He were out there at the time. It were some big battle out in Africa – El Alamein, I reckon. The tanks were a-moving forard, and Bertie and some others were a-following one of 'em right close. Then the tank got a direct hit. Well, they couldn't find a hair o' Bertie's head. Nawthen, of him or the others.'

They were both silent for a while as the bus travelled through suburban streets. Then Acky chuckled again.

'What's it this time?' asked Sarah. 'What's funny about that?'

'That Bertie was a rare bo'; and I allus laugh when I think o' that night's poaching we had togither. A rare bo' was Bertie. But here we are at Ipsidge, gel. I reckon you should ha' paid ma' fare for giving you all thet entertainment.'

* * * * *

Terence Blacker is the author of four novels including *Revenance* (1996), a contemporary ghost story set in the countryside around Diss where Blacker lives in an old farmhouse. The story was inspired by the author's interest in John Skelton, a former rector of Diss and the first poet laureate. *The Vendor*, which occupies the same territory was commissioned for 'Tales From East Anglia', a series of short stories first broadcast on BBC Radio 3 last year.

The Vendor

TERENCE BLACKER

'Poplar Farm – a period residence in a desirable rural location within easy reach of shopping and multi-leisure facilities, nestling in Suffolk's famous Waveney valley. The house, Grade II listed, is in need of some renovation.' Reading yet another brochure in yet another estate agent's office, Mark Wheeler sighed. 'In need of some renovation. That sounds like code for a total wreck.'

'You are so cynical, Mark.' Tina Wheeler smiled apologetically at Mr Bryce, the estate agent. 'Personally, I like the idea of somewhere that nestles.'

Behind his desk, Mr Bryce stirred. 'For some people, "needs renovation" is another way of saying it's authentic – it hasn't been messed around. All the original, traditional features are in place. Properties as unspoilt as Poplar Farm rarely come on the market and, when they do, they tend to get snapped up pretty sharpish.'

'Authentic, traditional.' Mark glanced at his wife. 'That is what we're looking for.'

'It's what I call organic,' said Mr Bryce. 'An organic part of that rather special East Anglian landscape. And very commutable of course.'

'Our plan is to downsize, work from home,' said Mark. 'Set up a computer terminal, ISDN line, car port, *en suite* office.'

'Our own little cottage industry, basically,' said Tina.

For the first time, the Wheeler's eight-year-old son Sam, who had been sitting between them, looked up from the screen of his mobile phone. 'Is there a swimming pool?' he asked. Mr Bryce glanced at his notes as if momentarily uncertain as to whether Poplar Farm offered swimming pool facilities. 'There's just the pond at the moment,' he said.

'We can build one, darling,' said his mother quickly. 'And a tennis court. You'd like that, wouldn't you?'

253

'Maybe,' said Sam.

From behind his desk, Mr Bryce looked at the Wheeler family. He had been selling property in the area for almost forty years and had recently experienced a weariness, a sort of deal fatigue, that was quite new. He found himself mildly depressed by the commuters, downsizers and rural fantasists who now swarmed up the M11 in their people-carriers and their jeeps with blacked-out windows like some invading army on the move. This part of the country was regularly being 'discovered'– the last influx had been the great hippy migration of the 1960s – but what was happening now was edgy and competitive – as if Suffolk and Norfolk were an undervalued company ripe for a quick takeover at a good market price.

'Shall I tell the vendor to expect you this afternoon? His name's Mr Hubbard.'

It occurred to Roy Hubbard that it had been unwise to leave last night's dishes in the sink. Bryce would not have approved. 'You have the location, you have the property – but presentation skills are of the essence,' the estate agent had said when he had first visited Poplar Farm, going on to lecture Roy about tidying away clutter, cleaning the windows, drawing the curtains, brushing at least some of the dog hair off the bedspreads. 'The aroma of freshly-ground coffee is always reassuring to a buyer.'

But Roy was a farmer. He had no time for presentation skills. Clutter was part of his life. As for aroma, there had been a few of those wafting through the house over the years but freshly-ground coffee had not been among them.

'Would you like some tea or something?' As the Wheeler family stood uneasily in the kitchen, Roy nodded in the direction of a blackened kettle on the Rayburn.

'We won't, thanks,' said Mark.

'Juice for the young man?'

Sam was looking around the low-ceilinged room, taking in the Fison's calendar and frayed bird prints on the walls.

'No, thanks,' he said.

'Mr Bryce said you're a farmer,' said Mark.

'Was,' said Roy. My father farmed arable but there wasn't enough land to make that pay. After he died, I went into pigs and – that didn't work out either.'

'Pigs are lovely aren't they?' Tina said quickly. 'I collect china ones. It's a sort of hobby.'

Roy looked away. 'Now there's a coincidence,' he said. 'So . . . this is the kitchen.' He waved an arm feebly, then quoted the words of a previous would-be buyer. 'The walls may need a lick of paint.'

'Interesting yellow,' said Tina.

'White,' said Roy. 'The yellow's staining from the stove.'

'Oh. I see.'

As he led them up the stairs, Roy sensed that once again, his sales pitch was going wrong. Farming friends had told him that now was a good time to sell – Londoners would buy almost anything that was a bit secluded in East Anglia – but something about Poplar Farm seemed to put people off.

Yet the more he saw the house in which he had lived all his life through the eyes of strangers, the more powerful became the certainty that he would never feel at home anywhere else. Where his visitors saw problems and defects, he saw what he loved best about the place – a slanting ceiling, a head-cracking beam, the ancient pump which sprung noisily into life, topping up the water tank from the well outside. Perhaps that was because this house was like him – awkward, cussed, creaky, set in its ways, in need of some renovation.

Roy said little as the Wheeler family made their way through the bedrooms. 'Lots of space,' said Mark at one point. 'Bags of potential,' said Tina. When they reached the bathroom, there was a moment of uneasiness, caused not so much by its general dirt-fringed state as for the intimate glimpse it offered of his daily life.

'Needs a bit of clean-up,' Roy muttered. 'It's a bachelor pad at the moment.' He gazed at the bath, remembering a scene from 15 years ago –

Jane, his wife, the sleeves of her shirt rolled up, kneeling, washing their two young children, who were in the bath. The evening sun was shining in and, outside the windows, house-martins were visiting the nests they had built under the eaves.

'What was that scrabbling we heard in one of the bedrooms?' Tina laughed nervously. 'Not rats, I hope.'

'Shouldn't be,' said Roy. 'We get rats in the autumn when the sugarbeet comes in but a dose of poison soon sorts them out. No, you'll have heard the swifts nesting. We've got swifts in the loft, swallows in the woodshed, house-martins under the guttering.'

'That doesn't sound entirely sensible, structure-wise,' said Mark. 'If we converted the loft, the swifts might just have to find somewhere else.'

'You'd have a problem getting permission.' Roy spoke without turning around as he led the party down the stairs. 'There's a colony of bats in the roof. They're protected.'

'No!' Tina stood on the stairs, her hands clasping her head. 'Bats in your hair – don't!'

Roy looked genuinely surprised. 'Never heard that. They're company, part of life here – just like the birds that wake you up now and then by falling down the big chimney into the bedroom. Wood pigeons, crows, a swallow – had a tawny owl once.'

'An owl? Cool,' said Sam.

'It's not the slightest bit cool,' said his mother. 'Rats, bats, owls – they said this was a rural location, not a jungle.'

'I'm sure there are pest officers who can deal with that sort of thing,' said Mark.

They looked around downstairs. Although Tina continued to be slightly on edge, as if at any moment an owl or a bat might fly out from a chimney and tangle in her dark curls, the family seemed to like the farm in spite of the dust, the unpaid bills covering the dining-room table, the yellowing back issues of *Farmers Weekly* in the corner of the sitting-room.

'Lastly . . .' Roy opened a door adjoining the kitchen. 'The music room.'

Mark, Tina and Sam stood in a small, bright room. There was a piano against the back wall and a music stand nearby. 'We had musical evenings.' Roy said.

'Really?' Tina looked at him with more interest, as if a farmer who liked music was something of an oddity. 'Where are the family now?'

'They . . . popped out.' He turned for the door, then hesitated. Somehow the sight of Sam standing there made the lie that he had been telling for the past few weeks seem like a small but unforgivable domestic betrayal. 'Popped out permanently, as it happens. They're all staying with my wife's family in Ipswich.'

'Why?' It was Sam who asked the question.

'Sam,' said Tina. 'Don't be so –'

'We went under last winter,' said Roy. 'It had been tough for some time making a living from pigs – loads of new government regulations, cheap imports, the supermarkets taking every penny they could – but we were just about breaking even. Then the Classical Swine Fever epidemic broke out last year. I couldn't sell or move the stock – we had a thousand weaners where there should have been 250 – a lot of them died from the overcrowding.'

'Oh dear,' said Tina.

'Cleaned me out. There was no money coming in and . . . it got difficult. My wife decided to move to Ipswich until . . . things improved. I've just got a job selling agricultural machinery. It's time to move on, as they say.'

An awkward silence descended on the room.

'Funny name *Classical* Swine Fever,' Tina laughed, rather too loudly. 'It makes it sound like some kind of advertising slogan - not any old swine fever but classic.'

Mark seated himself on a chair and had opened the french windows. Beyond the orchard, a combine was harvesting the barley field which had once belonged to Roy's father.

'Would it be all right if I checked that we're getting a signal?' he asked.

'Signal?'

'I've got a new palm-top,' said Mark. 'State of the art jobby. Works off the mobile connection. Important for my work.' Lovingly, he laid the appliance on a table by the window. 'I'll leave it here and check, after we've had a look outside.'

Roy showed them around the garden, the orchard, the outbuildings and the paddock. As they wandered back, Mark went ahead to check whether his computer could receive its signal.

'Maybe you'd like to check out the cess-pit,' Roy said to Tina. 'It's the usual soakaway system – the waste matter provides excellent fertiliser for the orchard.'

'I think we'll take that on trust,' said Tina.

'Can I look at the pond again?' Sam asked.

'Yes, but be careful,' said his mother.

'I don't believe this.' Mark appeared at the front door, the palm-top in his hand. 'I've got a signal but I also seem to have something crawling across the screen. I just can't delete it.'

Roy walked over to Mark and peered over his shoulder. 'You won't delete that,' he said. 'It's a thunderfly. They get into everything at this time of the year.'

'But this is state of the art. It's won design prizes. It shouldn't let in . . . flies.'

'Maybe it wasn't designed for places like Poplar farm,' said Roy.

'Well, we did say we wanted organic,' Tina murmured.

'That's not organic.' Mark switched off the palm-top. 'That's unnatural.'

'Tell you what,' said Roy. 'You take a look around the place on your own. I'll fetch that son of yours.'

Sam was sitting beside the pond. 'I saw a rat, swimming,' he whispered as Roy approached.

'Water voles.' Roy pointed to the far bank where several dark burrows could be seen. 'That's where they live. You know Ratty in *The Wind in the Willows*?

Sam nodded.

'He was a water vole.'

A pair of swallows skimmed over the dark water of the pond, chattering as they went.

'This place is just so wicked,' said Sam.

Roy looked around him and smiled. 'Yes,' he said. 'It's wicked all right. Let's get back to your mum and dad.'

In Mr Bryce's experience, the more you knew about the property business, the less you understood about why precisely people chose the houses they did.

He would, for example, have laid serious money on the Wheeler family from London buying some decorous, tidy family home on the outskirts of somewhere like Woodbridge. Instead, they had just put in an offer for that wild and woolly property, Poplar Farm. Equally surprising, the vendor, Mr Hubbard, had seemed pleased that it would be the Wheelers who would be buying. He had said something about Ratty having done the trick.

'Ratty?' thought Mr Bryce. 'What on earth was all that about?'

* * * * *

Ruth Rendell came to Suffolk in 1970 and several novels as well as a number of short stories draw on her knowledge of East Anglia. Although the coast is more readily associated with the detective thrillers of P D James, Rendell once lived in Aldeburgh and in *Front Seat* (1983) (page 97) she lays claim to a stretch of this murderous terrain. Most of her time has been spent at the other end of the county in the village of Polstead, notorious for the Victorian murder of Maria Marten in the Red Barn. Polstead was also in the heart of a cherry-growing district and the tradition of placing scarecrows in the fruit trees gave her the idea for *The Orchard Walls* (1982).

The Orchard Walls

RUTH RENDELL

I have never told anyone about this before.

The worst was long over, of course. Intense shame had faded and the knowledge of having made the greatest possible fool of myself. Forty years and more had done their work there. The feeling I had been left with, that I was precocious in a foul and dirty way, that I was unclean, was washed away. I had done my best never to think about it, to blot it all out, never to permit to ring on my inward ear Mrs Thorn's words:

'How dare you say such a thing! How dare you be so disgusting! At your age, a child, you must be sick in your mind.'

Things would bring it back, the scent of honeysuckle, a brace of bloodied pigeons hanging in a butcher's window, the first cherries of the season. I winced at these things, I grew hot with a shadow of that blush that had set me on fire with shame under the tree, Daniel's hard hand gripping my shoulder, Mrs Thorn trembling with indignant rage. The memory, never completely exorcised, still had the power to punish the adult for the child's mistake.

Until today.

Having one's childhood trauma cured by an analyst must be like this, only a newspaper cured mine. The newspaper came through the door and told me I hadn't been disgusting or sick in my mind, I had been right. In the broad facts at least I had been right. All day I have been asking myself what I should do, what action, if any, I should take. At last I have been able to think about it all quite calmly, in tranquillity, to think of Ella and Dennis Clifton without growing hot and ashamed, of Mrs Thorn with pity and of that lovely lost place with something like nostalgia.

It was a long time ago. I was fourteen. Is that to be a child? They thought so, I thought so myself at the time. But the truth was I was a child and not a child, at one and the same time a paddler in streams, a climber of trees, an expert at cartwheels – and with an imagination full of romantic love. I was in a stage of transition, a pupa, a chrysalis, I was fourteen.

Bombs were falling on London. I had already once been evacuated with my school and come back again to the suburb we lived in that sometimes seemed safe and sometimes not. My parents were afraid for me and that was why they sent me to Inchfield, to the Thorns. I could see the fear in my mother's eyes and it made me uncomfortable.

'Just till the end of August,' she said, pleading with me. 'It's beautiful there. You could think of it as an extra long summer holiday.'

I remembered Hereford and my previous 'billet', the strange people, the alien food.

'This will be different. Ella is your own aunt.'

She was my mother's sister, her junior by twelve years. There were a brother and sister in between, both living in the north. Ella's husband was a farmer in Suffolk, or had been. He was in the army and his elder brother ran the farm. Later, when Ella was dead and Philip Thorn married again and all I kept of them was that shameful thing I did my best to forget, I discovered that Ella had married Philip when she was seventeen because she was pregnant and in the thirties any alternative to marriage in those circumstances was unthinkable. She had married him and six months later given birth to a dead child. When I went to Inchfield she was still only twenty-five, still childless, living with a brother-in-law and a mother-in-law in the depths of the country, her husband away fighting in North Africa.

I didn't want to go. At fourteen one isn't afraid, one knows one is immortal. After an air raid we used to go about the streets collecting pieces of shrapnel, fragments of shell. The worst thing to me was having to sleep under a Morrison shelter instead of in my bedroom. Having a room of my own again, a place to be private in, was an inducement. I yielded. To this day I don't know if I was invited or if my mother had simply written to say I was coming, that I must come, that they must give me refuge.

It was the second week of June when I went. Daniel Thorn met me at the station at Ipswich. I was wildly romantic, far too romantic, my head full of fantasies and dreams. Knowing I should be met, I expected a pony carriage or even a man on a black stallion leading a chestnut mare for me, though I had never in my life been on a horse. He came in an old Ford van.

We drove to Inchfield through deep green silent lanes – silent, that is, but for the occasional sound of a shot. I thought it must be something to do with the war, without specifying to myself what.

'The war?' said Daniel as if this were something happening ten thousand miles away. He laughed the age-old laugh of the countryman scoring off the townie. 'You'll find no war here. That's some chap out after rabbits.'

Rabbit was what we were to live on, stewed, roasted, in pies, relieved by wood pigeon. It was a change from London sausages but I have never eaten rabbit since, not once. The characteristic smell of it cooking, experienced once in a friend's kitchen, brought me violent nausea. What a devil's menu that would have been for me, stewed rabbit and cherry pie!

The first sight of the farm enchanted me. The place where I lived in Hereford had been a late-Victorian brick cottage, red and raw and ugly as poverty. I had scarcely seen a house like Cherry Tree Farm except on a calendar. It was long and low and thatched and its two great barns were thatched too. The low green hills and the dark clustering woods hung behind it. And scattered all over the wide slopes of grass were the cherry trees, one so close up to the house as to rub its branches against a window pane.

They came out of the front door to meet us, Ella and Mrs Thorn, and Ella gave me a white, rather cold, cheek to kiss. She didn't smile. She looked bored. It was better therefore than I expected and worse. Ella was worse and Mrs Thorn was better. The place was ten times better, tea was like something I hadn't had since before the war, my bedroom was not only nicer than the Morrison shelter, it was nicer than my bedroom at home. Mrs Thorn took me up there when we had eaten the scones and currant bread and walnut cake.

It was low-ceilinged with the stone-coloured studs showing through the plaster. A patchwork quilt was on the bed and the walls were hung with a paper patterned all over with bunches of cherries. I looked out of the window.

'You can't see the cherry trees from here,' I said. 'Is that why they put cherries on the walls?'

The idea seemed to puzzle her. She was a simple conservative woman. 'I don't know about that. That would be rather whimsical.'

I was at the back of the house. My window overlooked a trim dull garden of rosebeds cut out in segments of a circle. Mrs Thorn's own garden, I was later to learn, and tended by herself.

'Who sleeps in the room with the cherry tree?' I said.

261

'Your auntie.' Mrs Thorn was always to refer to Ella in this way. She was a stickler for respect. 'That has always been my son Philip's room.'

Always . . . I envied the absent soldier. A tree with branches against one's bedroom window represented to me something down which one could climb and make one's escape, perhaps even without the aid of knotted sheets. I said as much, toning it down for my companion who I guessed would see it in a different light.

'I'm sure he did no such thing,' said Mrs Thorn. 'He wasn't that kind of boy.'

Those words stamped Philip for me as dull. I wondered why Ella had married him. What had she seen in this unromantic chap, five years her senior, who hadn't been the kind of boy to climb down trees out of his bedroom window? Or climb up them, come to that . . .

She was beautiful. For the first Christmas of the war I had been given *Picturegoer Annual* in which was a full-page photograph of Hedy Lamarr. Ella looked just like her. She had the same perfect features, dark hair, other-worldly eyes fixed on far horizons. I can see her now – I can *permit* myself to see her – as she was then, thin, long-legged, in the floral cotton dress with collar and cuffs and narrow belt that would be fashionable again today. Her hair was pinned up in a roll off her forehead, the rest left hanging to her shoulders in loose curls, mouth painted like raspberry jam, eyes as nature made them, large, dark, alight with some emotion I was years from analysing. I think now it was compounded of rebellion and longing and desire.

Sometimes in the early evenings she would disappear upstairs and then Mrs Thorn would say in a respectful voice that she had gone to write to Philip. We used to listen to the wireless. Of course no one knew exactly where Philip was but we all had a good idea he was somehow involved in the attempts to relieve Tobruk. At news times Mrs Thorn became very tense. Once, to my embarrassment, she made a choking sound and left the room, covering her eyes with her hand. Ella switched off the set.

'You ought to go to bed,' she said to me. 'When I was your age I was always in bed by eight.'

I envied and admired her, even though she was never particularly nice to me and seldom spoke except to say I 'ought' to be doing something or other. Did she look at this niece, not much more than ten years younger than herself, and see what she herself had thrown away, a future of hope, a chance of living?

I spent very little time with her. It was Mrs Thorn who took me shopping with her to Ipswich, who talked to me while she did the baking, who knitted and taught me to knit. There was no wool to be had so we unpicked old jumpers and washed the wool and carded it and started again. I was with her most of the time. It was either that or being on my own. No doubt there were children of my own age in the village I might have got to know but the village was two miles away. I was allowed to go out for walks but not to ride the only bicycle they had.

'It's too large for you, it's a twenty-eight inch.' Mrs Thorn said. 'Besides, it's got a crossbar.'

I said I could easily swing my leg behind the saddle like a man.

'Not while you're staying with me.'

I didn't understand. 'I wouldn't hurt myself.' I said what I said to my mother. 'I wouldn't come to any harm.'

'It isn't ladylike,' said Mrs Thorn, and that was that.

Those things mattered a lot to her. She stopped me turning cartwheels on the lawn when Daniel was about, even though I wore shorts. Then she made me wear a skirt. But she was kind, she paid me a lot of attention. If I had had to depend on Ella or the occasional word from Daniel I might have looked forward more eagerly to my parent's fortnightly visits than I did.

After I had been there two or three weeks the cherries began to turn colour. Daniel, coming upon me looking at them, said they were an old variety called Inchfield White Heart.

'There used to be a cherry festival here,' he said. 'The first Sunday after July the twelfth it was. There'd be dancing and a supper, you'd have enjoyed yourself. Still, we never had one last year and we're not this and somehow I don't reckon there'll ever be a cherry festival again what with this old war.'

He was a yellow-haired, red-complexioned Suffolk man, big and thickset. His wide mouth, sickle-shaped, had its corners permanently turned upwards. It wasn't a smile though and he was seldom cheerful. I never heard him laugh. He used to watch people in a rather disconcerting way, Ella especially. And when guests came to the house, Dennis Clifton or Mrs Leithman or some of the farming people they knew, he would sit and watch them, seldom contributing a word.

One evening when I was coming back from a walk, I saw Ella and Dennis Clifton kissing in the wood.

Dennis Clifton wasn't a farmer. He had been in the R.A.F., had been a fighter pilot in the Battle of Britain but had received some sort of head injury, been in hospital and was now on leave at home recuperating. He must have been very young, no more than twenty-two or three. While he was ill his mother, with whom he had lived and who had been a friend of Mrs Thorn's, had died and left him her pretty little Georgian house in Inchfield. He was often at the farm, ostensibly to see his mother's old friend.

After these visits Daniel used to say, 'He'll soon be back in the thick of it,' or 'It won't be long before he's up there in his Spitfire. He can't wait.'

This made me watch him too, looking for signs of impatience to return to the R.A.F. His hands shook sometimes, they trembled like an old man's. He too was fair-haired and blue-eyed, yet there was all the difference in the world between his appearance and Daniel's. Film stars set my standard of beauty and I thought he looked like Leslie Howard playing Ashley Wilkes. He was tall and thin and sensitive and his eyes were sad. Daniel watched him and Ella sat silent and I read my book while he talked very kindly and encouragingly to Mrs Thorn about her son Philip, about how confident he was Philip would be all right, would survive, and while he talked his eyes grew sadder and more veiled.

No, I have imagined that, not remembered it. It is in the light of what I came to know that I have imagined it. He was simply considerate and kind like the well-brought-up young man he was.

I had been in the river. There was a place about a mile upstream they called the weir where for a few yards the banks were built up with concrete before a shallow fall. A pool about four feet deep had formed there and on hot days I went bathing in it. Mrs Thorn would have stopped me if she had known but she didn't know. She didn't even know I had a bathing costume with me.

The shortest way back was through the wood. I heard a shot and then another from up in the meadows. Daniel was out after pigeons. The wood was dim and cool, full of soft twitterings, feathers rustling against dry leaves. The bluebells were long past but dog's mercury was in flower, a white powdering, and the air was scented with honeysuckle. Another shot came, further off but enough to shatter peace, and there was a rush of wings as pigeons took flight. Through the black trunks of trees and the lacework of their branches I could see the yellow sky and the sun burning in it, still an hour off setting.

Ella was leaning against the trunk of a chestnut, looking up into Dennis Clifton's face. He had his hands pressed against the trunk, on either side of her head. If she had ever been nice to me, if he had ever said more than hallo, I think I might have called out to them. I didn't call and in a moment I realised the last thing they would want was to be seen.

I stayed where I was. I watched them. Oh, I was in no way a voyeur. There was nothing lubricious in it, nothing of curiosity, still less a wish to catch them out. I was overwhelmed rather by the romance of it, ravished by the wonder. I watched him kiss her. He took his hands down and put his arms round her and kissed her so that their faces were no longer visible, only his fair head and her dark hair and their locked straining shoulders. I caught my breath and shivered in the warm half-light, in the honeysuckle air.

They left the place before I did, walking slowly away in the direction of the road, arms about each other's waists. In the room at Cherry Tree Farm they still called the parlour Mrs Thorn and Daniel were sitting, listening to the wireless, drinking tea. No more than five minutes afterwards Ella came in. I had seen what I had seen but if I hadn't, wouldn't I still have thought her looks extraordinary, her shining eyes and the flush on her white cheeks, the willow leaf in her hair and the bramble clinging to her skirt?

Daniel looked at her. There was blood in his fingernails, though he had scrubbed his hands. It brought me a flicker of nausea. Ella put her fingers through her hair, plucked out the leaf and went upstairs.

'She is going to write to Philip,' said Mrs Thorn.

Why wasn't I shocked? Why wasn't I horrified? I was only fourteen and I came from a conventional background. Adultery was something committed by people in the Bible. I suppose I could say I had seen no more than a kiss and adultery didn't enter into it. Yet I knew it did. With no experience, with only the scantiest knowledge, I sensed that this love had its full consummation. I knew Ella was married to a soldier who was away fighting for his country. I even knew that my parents would think behaviour such as hers despicable if not downright wicked. But I cared for none of that. To me it was romance, it was Lancelot and Guinevere, it was a splendid and beautiful adventure that was happening to two handsome young people – as one day it might happen to me.

I was no go-between. For them I scarcely existed. I received no words or smiles, still less messages to be carried. They had the phone, anyway, they had cars. But though I took no part in their love affair and wasn't even with accuracy able to calculate the times when it was conducted, it filled my thoughts. Outwardly I followed the routine of days I had arranged for myself and Mrs Thorn had arranged for me, but my mind was occupied with Dennis and Ella, assessing what meeting places they would use, imagining their conversations – their vows of undying love – and re-creating with cinematic variations that kiss.

My greatest enjoyment, my finest hours of empathy, were when he called. I watched the two of them as intently then as Daniel did. Sometimes I fancied I caught between them a glance of longing and once I actually witnessed something more, an encounter between them in the passage when Ella came from the kitchen with the tea tray and Dennis had gone to fetch something from his car for Mrs Thorn. Unseen by them, I stood in the shadow between the grandfather clock and the foot of the stairs. I heard him whisper:

'Tonight? Same place?'

She nodded, her eyes wide. I saw him put his hand on her shoulder in a slow caress as he went past her.

I slept badly those nights. It had become very hot. Mrs Thorn made sure I was in bed by nine and there was no escaping the house after that without being seen by her. I envied Ella with a tree outside her window down which it would be easy to climb and escape. I imagined going down to the river in the moonlight, walking in the wood, perhaps seeing my lovers in some trysting place. My lovers, whose breathy words and laden glances exalted me and rarefied the overheated air . . .

The cherries were turning pale yellow with a blush coming to their cheeks. It was the first week of July, the week the war came to Inchfield and a German bomber, lost and off course, unloaded a stick of bombs in one of the Thorns' fields.

No one was hurt, though a cow got killed. We went to look at the mess in the meadow, the crater and the uprooted tree. Daniel shook his fist at the sky. The explosions had made a tremendous noise and we were all sensitive after that to any sudden sound. Even the crack of Daniel's shotgun made his mother jump.

The heat had turned sultry and clouds obscured out blue skies, though no rain fell. Mrs Leithman, coming to tea as she usually did once in the week, told us she fancied each roll of thunder was another bomb. We hardly saw Ella, she was always up in her room or out somewhere – out with Dennis, of course. I speculated about them, wove fantasies around them, imagined Philip Thorn killed in battle and thereby setting them free. So innocent was I, living in more innocent or at least more puritanical times, that the possibility of this childless couple being divorced never struck me. Nor did I envisage Dennis and Ella married to each other but only continuing for ever their perilous enchanting idyll. I even found Juliet's lines for them – Juliet who was my own age – and whispered to myself that the orchard walls are high and hard to climb and the place death, considering who thou art . . . Once late at night when I couldn't sleep and sat in my window, I saw the shadowy figure of Dennis Clifton emerge from the deep darkness at the side of the house and leave by the gate out of the rose garden.

But the destruction of it all and my humiliation were drawing nearer. I had settled down there, I had begun to be happy. The truth is, I suppose, that I identified with Ella and in my complex fantasies it was I, compounded with Juliet, that Dennis met and embraced and touched and loved. My involvement was much deeper than that of an observer.

When it came the shot sounded very near. It woke me up as such a sound might not have done before the bombs. I wondered what prey Daniel could go in search of at this hour, for the darkness was deep, velvety and still. The crack which had split the night and jarred the silence wasn't repeated. I went back to sleep and slept till past dawn.

I got up early as I did most mornings, came downstairs in the quiet of the house, the hush of a fine summer morning, and went outdoors. Mrs Thorn was in the kitchen frying fat bacon and duck eggs for the men. I didn't know if it was all right for me to do this or if all the cherries were reserved for some mysterious purpose, but as I went towards the gate I reached up and picked a ripe one from a dipping branch. It was the crispest sweetest cherry I have ever tasted, though I must admit I have eaten few since then. I pushed the stone into the earth just inside the gates. Perhaps it germinated and grew. Perhaps quite an old tree that has borne many summer loads of fruit now stands at the entrance to Cherry Tree Farm.

As it happened, of all their big harvest, that was the only cherry I was ever to eat there. Coming back half an hour later, I pushed open the gate and stood for a moment looking at the farmhouse over whose sunny walls and roof the shadows of the trees lay in a slanted leafy pattern. I looked at the big tree, laden with red-gold fruit, that rubbed its branches against Ella's window. In its boughs, halfway up, in a fork a yard or two from the glass, hung the body of a man.

In the hot sunshine I felt icy cold. I remember the feeling to this day, the sensation of being frozen by a cold that came from within while outside me the sun shone and a thrush sang and the swallows dipped in and out under the eaves. My eyes seemed fixed, staring in the hypnosis of shock and fear at the fair-haired dangling man, his head thrown back in the agony of death there outside Ella's bedroom window.

At least I wasn't hysterical. I resolved I must be calm and adult. My teeth were chattering. I walked stiffly into the kitchen and there they all were, round the table, Daniel and the two men and Ella and, at the head of it, Mrs Thorn pouring tea.

I meant to go quietly up to her and whisper it. I couldn't. To get myself there without running, stumbling, shouting, had used up all the control I had. The words rushed out in a loud ragged bray and I remember holding up my hands, my fists clenched.

'Mr Clifton's been shot. He's been shot, he's dead. His body's in the cherry tree outside Ella's window!'

There was silence. But first a clatter as of knives and forks dropped, of cups rattled into saucers, of chairs scraped. Then this utter stricken silence. I have never – not in all the years since then – seen anyone go as white as Ella went. She was as white as paper and her eyes were black holes. A brick colour suffused Daniel's face. He swore. He used words that made me shrink and draw back and shiver and stare from one to the other of the horrible, horrified faces.

Mrs Thorn was the first to speak, her voice cold with anger.

'How dare you say such a thing! How dare you be so disgusting! At your age – you must be sick in your mind.'

Daniel jumped up. He took me roughly by the arm. But his grasp wasn't firm, the hand was shaking the way Dennis's shook. He manhandled me out there, his mother scuttling behind us. We were still five or six yards from the tree when I saw. The hot blood came into my face and throbbed under my skin. I looked at the cloth face, the yellow wool hair – our own unpicked carded wool – the stuffed sacking body, the cracked boots . . .

Icy with indignation, Mrs Thorn said, 'Haven't you ever seen a scarecrow before?'

I cried out desperately as if, even in the face of this evidence, I could still prove them wrong, 'But scarecrows are in fields!'

'Not in this part of the world.' Daniel's voice was thin and hoarse. He couldn't have looked more gaunt, more shocked, if it had really been Dennis Clifton in that tree. 'In this part of the world we put them in cherry trees. I put it there last night. I put *them* there.' And he pointed at what I

268

had passed but never seen, the man in the tree by the wall, the man in the tree in the middle of the green lawn.

I went back to the house and up to my room and lay on the bed, prone and silent with shame. The next day was Saturday and my parents were coming. They would tell them and I would be taken home in disgrace. In the middle of the day Mrs Thorn came to the door and said to come down to lunch. She was a changed woman, hard and dour. I had never heard the expression 'to draw aside one's skirts' but later on when I did I recognised that this was what she had done to me. Her attitude to me was as if I were some sort of psychopath.

We had lunch alone, only I didn't really have any, I couldn't eat. Just as we were finishing, I pushing aside my laden plate, Daniel came in and sat down and said they had all talked about it and they thought it would be best if I went home with my parents on the following day.

'Of course I shall tell them exactly what you said and what you inferred,' said Mrs Thorn. 'I shall tell them how you insulted your auntie.'

Daniel, who wasn't trembling any more or any redder in the face than usual, considered this for a moment in silence. Then he said unexpectedly, – or unexpectedly to me, 'No, we won't, Mother, we won't do that. No point in that. The fewer know the better. You've got to think of Ella's reputation.'

'I won't have her here,' his mother said.

'No, I agree with that. She can tell them she's homesick or I'll say it's too much for you, having her here.'

Ella hid herself away all day.

'She has her letter to write to Philip,' said Mrs Thorn.

In the morning she was at the table with the others. Daniel made an announcement. He had been down to the village and heard that Dennis Clifton was back in the Air Force, he had rejoined his squadron.

'He'll soon be back in the thick of it,' he said.

Ella sat with bowed head, working with restless fingers a slice of bread into a heap of crumbs. Her face was colourless, lacking her usual make-up. I don't remember ever hearing another word from her.

I packed my things. My parents made no demur about taking me back with them. Starved of love, sickened by the love of others, I clung to my father. The scarecrows grinned at us as we got into the van behind Daniel. I can see them now – I can permit myself to see them now – spreadeagled in the trees, protecting the reddening fruit, so lifelike that even the swallows swooped in wider arcs around them.

In the following spring Ella died giving birth to another dead child. My mother cried, for Ella had been her little sister. But she was shy about giving open expression to her grief. She and my father were anxious to keep from me, or for that matter anyone else, that it was a good fifteen months since Philip Thorn had been home on leave. What became of Daniel and his mother I never knew, I didn't want to know. I couldn't avoid hearing that Philip had married again and his new wife was a niece of Mrs Leithman's.

Only a meticulous reader of newspapers would have spotted the paragraph. I am in the habit of reading every line, with the exception of the sports news, and I spotted this item tucked away between an account of sharp practice in local government and the suicide of a financier. I read it. The years fell away and the facts exonerated me. I knew I must do something, I wondered what, I have been thinking of it all day, but now I know I must tell this story to the coroner. My story, my mistake, Daniel's rage.

An agricultural worker had come upon an unexploded bomb on farm land near Inchfield in Suffolk. It was thought to be one of a stick of bombs dropped there in 1941. Excavations in the area had brought to light a skeleton thought to be that of a young man who had met his death at about the same time. A curious fact was that shotgun pellets had been found in the cavity of the skull.

The orchard walls are high and hard to climb. And the place death considering who thou art, if any of my kinsmen find thee here . . .

* * * * *

Ronald Blythe was born in Suffolk and is best known for *Akenfield* (1969), his remarkable study of change in the English village. His output ranges through poetry, fiction and essays including *From The Headland* (1982) and the highly acclaimed *Word From Wormingford* (1997), the village in the Stour valley where he lives in an old farmhouse once the home of the painter John Nash. In his early years Blythe was intrigued by the cultural life of the region and its provincial dramas are the subject of *And The Green Grass Grew All Around* (page 62) published in *The Stories Of Ronald Blythe* (1985) and *The Catch* published in *Immediate Possession* (1961) where the redoubtable Miss Foxfellowe makes her first appearance.

The Catch

RONALD BLYTHE

Divided by no great distance from the spiritual autonomy of Canon Retort, but by an Asian vastness of belief, lived Dr Crow the Rector of Pannington. The Canon was encumbered with a permanent expression of displeasure in most things and possessed features which were a well-turned expression in egotism but Dr Crow had been rewarded by heaven with a presence of the utmost splendour. He was very tall and supported on the haughty column of his neck an aquiline countenance clouded with silvery hair. He might be said to be of the enviable but limited company who are blessed for merely waiting. Time alone separated him from diocesan small-clothes and an elegant finale in the Close. There are heads that are made for mitres as are mitres made for heads. Whereas, still physiologically speaking, Canon Retort would get nowhere, which, to be just, is what he desired. 'Never rush into print, my boy,' he advised me on more than one occasion. Cultivate a decent atrophy, he might have added, then stand back and admire your own stony dignity!

The characters of my two friends were further exposed by the interiors of their respective churches. Canon Retort had the shiniest church imaginable. Not a day went by but some member of the ladies' guild could be seen rubbing up the d'Jumberville brass or brightening the terrible ceramics in the chancel with Johnson's Wax. The imperial bird beneath the sacred book glowered goldenly. The finials of the sidesmen's wands flickered like stars. One fancied that the very banners had been through the mangle and that only the inaccessible clerestory was freed from frequent smirches by the duster, an unreachableness which permitted the Canon to share in some degree the frustrations of the iconoclasts. In this comfortable place he preached adequately upon the necessity to discredit all thought after Inge and never to trust the Government.

271

Some way from this parish, but sufficiently near to threaten it, loomed Pannington. And here one did not need to begin with interiors. The churchyard was enough. Frequently I have seen Dr Crow's small, yet charming flock straggle from the porch to its transport, bobbing like a field-studies school in a veritable sea of burdock and vetches. Inside, hassocks burst and revealed the pale chaff of ancient harvests and if urbanity chose to desert the Doctor for a moment and he beat his fist upon the pulpit, dust and fragments would sift softly down from its bedraggled hangings. Dr Crow preached amidst the distraction of the Breen tombs. Around him marble viscounts sustained in near-nude superlatives the doubtful glory of their days. Their ladies attitudinised like county Dianas and their short-lived children enjoyed a roundness in stone so tragically denied them in the flesh. The Breens, from the modest crusader in the sanctuary to the immodest Augustans in the family chapel, took up every bit of space in the church other than what was strictly required for windows. Their torsos and thighs disturbed the devout and their boastful epitaphs left me gasping.

These monuments were the cause of much contention in the archaeological neighbourhood. The early ones were moralities. 'As we are, so shall ye be.' The later ones, with a frank approach to pomp, stood buskined before the villagers, staring at them with sightless arrogance and if not putting the fear of God into them, at least exacting a wholesome respect for the Breens. That they were ever viewed in a different way must be attributed to a monograph, *The Breen Memorials at Pannington*, by Adelaide Foxfellowe, F.R.S.A. Since this publication and a digest of its more salient points in a score of county guides, never a week passed without some sightseeing group or other troubling Dr Crow by its presence among his rickety pews. Sometimes they were vulgar, and would write him stiff letters about the state of the hassocks or the mouse-dirts round the organ. So in time he got to dislike his church all cramped with gesturing peers, seeing all too clearly in each marble lord the genealogical source of his chief anathema, the current Viscount Breen. He would stalk by their sandalled toes and fulsome inscriptions with great splendour in his grubby cassock and even audibly sniff, inflecting his beautiful nostrils at their stony-nosed supercility.

Although Lord Breen attended church regularly, he never spoke to Dr Crowe unless the occasion absolutely demanded it. He came in late and left as soon as he could and all the time Dr Crow preached – which was a

The Catch

long time, because he enjoyed doing it – his Lordship would study the heroic limbs of his forbears and try not to listen.

Sometimes Canon Retort would bicycle over from Hulge to commiserate with his reverend colleague on the vicissitudes of the religious life. Dr Crow never looked forward to this and would sit about in a rather privileged way as he listened to the Canon's troubles, interjecting into their flow a great many of his own. His pride on these occasions would not let him be discreet. 'What have *I* to hide?' he would shout at the Canon, slanting his beautiful head, and this candour allowed his confidant to carry some very odd facts to Breen Hall. All of which did not assist amity in the Pannington-Hulge Archdeaconry.

Matters came to a head in their usual precipitous way and through the usual agency – the archaeological society. Or more correctly, the archaeological socie*ties*, for had there not been two of them, this and so much other trouble might have been avoided. Enough at this point to say that Canon Retort was the leader of one and Miss Foxfellowe the arbiter of the other. Once it had all been one but now there was so great a rift that all who did not wish to be personal and acrimonious in their social approach to the past, had to make a polite choice and stick to it. Through no little tact I managed to receive notices of both groups and spent many a happy hour in the wake of Canon Retort and Miss Foxfellowe as they stumbled over barrows or down from belfries.

So it was that I heard of that large fish, Dr Crow, who had escaped the net of either group, choosing, it would seem, to be a solitary when it came to investigating antiquities. Every conceivable bait had been dangled before the Doctor by both parties but he was yet uncaught.

On a lengthening spring day, the trees bright in early leaf, I accompanied Canon Retort upon a final attempt to get Dr Crow to join *his* Archaeological Society. Rumours of the Doctor's translation were rife and the Canon, looking ahead, could not be blind to the enormous advantages that a bishop or even a dean would bring to his group. Miss Foxfellowe, who had no need for such advantages, being born to the bench, as it were, was equally determined to win Dr Crow – if only to spite the Canon. Remembering this, I smiled as I pedalled behind the Canon as we manoeuvred Pannington's mazy laurels.

We had scarcely sat down to tea when Canon Retort treacherously led the Doctor on to the thorny subject of rectories.

'This house is an anachronism, Retort. Seventeen bedrooms. Think of it!'

273

'Other days, other ways,' replied the Canon, adding, 'Mr Nugent's union was fruitfully blessed.'

'How many were there?' enquired Doctor Crow hesitantly, who could never bring himself to believe in either prodigiousness or his predecessor.

'Eleven,' said the Canon, 'and heaps of housemaids.'

Dr Crow repressed a shudder and extracted Thucydides from a near bookcase.

'Well now there is only Miss Crow and myself and Mrs Meadowsweet and I think it is disgraceful that we should be saddled with a barracks. *Not* that I should want anything that was not a *residence*, you understand. Hulge Rectory, for instance, would neither suit our temperament nor contain our furniture.' He turned his head, and smiled. 'But I do think Lord Breen should *act*.'

'I suppose it is a large place to run?' enquired the Canon inflammably.

'Huge? It's monstrous! *And* impossible to heat. Fortunately a number of rooms in that rubbishy wing are empty for not a breath of heat would percolate through to them. Why, if I had to think of this house in any way other than a temporary shelter on life's path I really don't know what I should do! And certainly poor Miss Crow could scarcely be sanguine over such a prospect. I say it is a disgrace – and would say so to his face.' He meant Lord Breen's face.

Canon Retort, who hadn't realised how passionately the Doctor felt about his enormous rectory, fumbled for his trump-card.

'I could approach the Faculty,' he said with diffident concern. 'I am always in contact with the Faculty, you know. I could recommend their views to his Lordship . . . There could be little difficulty . . .'

The Doctor, who saw the ramshackle Victorian accretions at last in progress of being swept away from the noble heart of his eighteenth-century home, showed true gratitude. With no small effort he acknowledged that he would be much in the Canon's debt if such a relief came to pass. 'There is nothing that I would not do in return,' he added rashly.

We parted amicably, Dr Crow hoping that I 'wouldn't leave it so long before I came again.'

I visited Pannington again about a fortnight later. It was grey and cold, one of those wintry days which wither summer with a sudden January breath. I wondered if the Doctor could have forgotten how eagerly he had asked me to come, so like the day was his welcome. Hardly were we seated before the fire than the doorbell announced another visitor. 'My dear Miss Foxfellowe!' I heard him cry, hardly suppressing the astonishment in his voice.

'I had to come,' she was explaining, each slow syllable accorded an organ splendour, 'the matter is most important.'

'You have waited too long, dear lady,' said Dr Crowe. 'We would like to see you more often.'

I heard her ill-fitting old shoes slapping the linoleum in the hall and soon sat between them, the exquisite Doctor on my left and on my right, perched upon a crippling chair, Miss Adelaide Foxfellowe, her great hat skewered to her hair, her face a fierce homily on the vanities of the flesh. For some time we all played a conversational game. The Doctor had been at the point of showing me a document which now reposed in his pocket when the doorbell rang and although a certain tautness in his attitude acknowledged that the matter still occupied his thoughts, he did not mention it. Miss Foxfellowe, too, seemed inhibited by my presence and when she did speak it was about little in particular, although she made any trifle an axiom by the mere utterance of it. I was about to offer my excuses and depart when the Doctor dropped the elaborate charade he was making of rectory tea and no longer attempting to conceal his anger, pulled a letter from his pocket and said in a strangled voice:

'*This* came this morning!'

Miss Foxfellowe changed her spectacles and selected an ancient lorgnette from an armoury of such aids which swung from her neck. She then read out in a voice like Deuteronomy Lord Breen's letter.

' "My dear Doctor Crow,

You have no doubt heard of the society for the Sustenance of Aged Nannies – the S.S.A.N. – but as your scholastic inclinations keep you detached from many practical employments, you may not have heard of a recent nation-wide call to improve the lot of these worthy women.

At a working-party presided over recently by Lady Breen it was decided that a central repository for the collection of second-hand furniture should be inaugurated from which gifts can be made to Aged Nannies *within the county*.

Naturally the location of the repository was discussed and being aware of the changed circumstances at the Rectory and the charity which must of necessity have a large place in the heart of a clergyman, I recommended that no better place than the unused rooms of Pannington Rectory could possibly be found.

Your views on the matter will be welcome by me. I need hardly tell you of the urgency of the matter.

Yours sincerely,
Breen." '

'But,' I protested, 'he said that he would approach the Faculty to have the empty wing demolished. I was here, with him,' I added to explain my interruption.

'Do you dine out?' enquired Miss Foxfellowe of Dr Crow, ignoring my presumption.

'Rarely,' answered the Doctor, who found the question obscure.

'Things are clearer for those who do,' she said.

'I don't understand, forgive me.'

'If I tell you that I have it upon incontestable authority that Lord Breen has concurred with an absurd suggestion made to Canon Retort that the tombs should be painted, would you understand?'

I shared to the full Dr Crow's perplexity at this strange statement.

'*The tombs painted*?' repeated the Doctor like one entranced.

'Painted!' reiterated Miss Foxfellowe in a tone more suitable for Jezebel than a minor Plantagenet effigy. 'You remember, of course, when new, the earlier Breen monuments gleamed with heraldic colours and now that only suspicions of that old glory remain – there is a snippet of crimson on the left thigh of Sir Percinade where it burgeons out from the greave . . . Think, Dr Crow, of all that brilliance caressed away by the wondering hands of time.'

'More likely scrubbed off by Oliver Cromwell,' muttered the Doctor whose mind now seethed with terrible confusions of old wash-stands, Aged Nannies and Sir Percinade's legs.

Miss Foxfellowe, who only heard what she wanted to, didn't hear this.

'Now some hardly-informed person,' she continued, 'is to come along with a tin of paint and Mompson's "Little Ways With Old Knights" and make the finest monuments in all Suffolk look like – like a letter-box!'

She shook with anger and the felt lobelias in her hat waggled wryly. 'You must stop it,' she said.

'My dear lady,' said Dr Crow urbanely, 'you may be sure that when the proposal comes to me I will not countenance anything which might offend the finest taste in these matters.' He bowed a little in her direction. 'And there is, of course, always the permission of the Faculty to be obtained. Even *I* could not add a bar to the Breen bannerings without *that*.' He smiled, enjoying his wit.

Miss Foxfellowe, who had made a slow journey in an old bus, at a great age, on a cold day, found levity unacceptable.

With malice she answered, 'The Faculty's permission was given last night in exchange for – a good dinner . . .'

This took some time to sink in. When it did Dr Crow breathed, 'How *dare* he?'

Miss Foxfellowe, enjoying her visit, suddenly said:

'The Canon was asked to dinner to meet Melisande Shutter.'

'Melisande Shutter . . .?'

'Miss Shutter of Mediaeval Restorations, Ltd. She wants to paint the tombs.'

'Who else was there?' enquired the Doctor weakly.

'Canon Retort,' replied Miss Foxfellowe irritably, as though to a child.

Still looking perplexed the Doctor said, 'But *he* isn't the Faculty.'

'Oh, is he not?' she answered, as though this was news.

When one has been left in the dark for longer than one cares to remember, the smallest chink lets in a startling light. Dr Crow, who up to this moment had prided himself on the rarity of the occasions when he could be induced to dine at Lord Breen's awoke to the painful fact that he was not usually asked. Other people were invited, it would seem. And often. Other people, but not he, the Rector of Pannington. Even when matters affecting his church and house were at stake. Who were these people who directed pantechnicons across his lawns eloquent with job-lots for old women? Whose those natures which would revive the deserved obscurities of the Breens! Canon Retort! Miss *Shutter*! With awful clarity he saw himself reduced to a pawn in the Retort-Breen game, all his magnificence gone. For a moment only and then, as if to recompense him for their brief failure, they saw more plainly than ever. There before him was Miss Foxfellowe! Adelaide Foxfellowe, F.R.S.A., who although eighty if a day, had only recently excavated a particularly charming Celtic prince whose beads were at the moment being rethreaded at the V. & A. Miss Foxfellowe, who although in possession of a face on which the years could find no space to wreak further vengeance, still retained a voice which, against the bat-squeak conservation of the day, was like Handel to a whistle. Miss Foxfellowe, whose uncle was a bishop in great Lightfoot's time! Miss Foxfellowe, who knew more than all of them put together!

'What's to be done?' he asked, renewed equality returning grace-notes to his voice.

Miss Foxfellowe answered slowly, sharing her portentousness with the demands of a scone which Miss Crow had just brought in.

'*I* have not,' she said, 'held with the Faculty these thirty years. As long as it was content to restrict itself to the minor details of pew-arrangement and Tortoise-heaters I felt that the present administration might remain. But now that it is to concern itself with graver matters' (here she was obviously thinking of her own great authority on sepulchral affairs), 'I find it my duty to reveal what time might have fitly hidden.'

'You mean,' I said, hurriedly breaking into the conversation, 'that the Faculty exists, but has no actual power?'

Miss Foxfellowe, who did not care to have short cuts taken across the demesne of her success, did not answer but began to extract a thick old notebook from the gloomy depths of her coat.

'Here,' she cried triumphantly, 'are the Minutes of the first meeting of the Faculty which, as the then Secretary, are, of course, in my own hand!'

'But the Faculty was founded *years* ago!' I said.

'It was founded in 1889,' replied Miss Foxfellowe with dignity. 'Hardly an age in the chronicles of the righteous. However, my dear Doctor, as I was saying, it is quite evident that the rules of the Faculty, which insist that all decisions should receive the vote of a quorum of six, have long been disregarded. Yet it would, I think, be a mistake to produce this book now, for the manner of doing so would smack of uncharity.'

'What then?' asked Dr Crow.

'We must make an act of representation to the Bishop requesting him to instate a faculty of six proper persons to advise on the fabrics of our ancient buildings, because the other body exists only in name.'

'Does it?' replied the Doctor, looking a little worried. 'And what of the Canon? Misguided as I suspect him to be, yet I would not care to make moves against him in my own name. I could not do *that*, you understand.'

Miss Foxfellowe fixed Dr Crow with a glaucous eye before replying.

'Moves against him?' She sounded shocked. She may even have been shocked. 'Believe me, dear Doctor, the matter will be a purely diocesan affair. No individual voice will be heard.'

And as Miss Foxfellowe explained her plan to deprive her ancient enemy, Canon Retort, of yet one more aspect of his historic powers, I fancied the scene at Breen Hall at the fateful dinner-party. The Canon, well-intentioned but too far advanced now in the intoxicating cup of genealogy to see beyond its brim, had gone, as he had ever gone, to Breen Hall – with a flutter in the breast. After the cheese he would bring up the little matter of the Rectory. It was all to have been so simple. Lord Breen would say that he quite agreed and that the old place must be made more habitable. Dr Crow would at last be in his debt and it would only need a word then to induce his stubborn, but now grateful, colleague to join the Canon's Archaeological Society. *That* would show the Foxfellowe faction where true authority lay! They would have dined in the small dining-room where the Turners chivvied the Stubbs and distant lamps sent out smoky messages to each other across the gloomy spaces. Lord Breen would have been seated in an old studded chair, so very mediaeval that it might be one of Bancroft's props. On his right would have been Miss Shutter, imperfectly Plantagenet, and with the appetite, no doubt, which always seems to accompany a flair for archaeology. Then, Canon Retort, snuffling, avid, foxed yet oddly guileless. At the far end would have sat Lady Breen in the worn velvet and rhinestones which she reserved for small occasions. It was so easy to see what had happened. Lord Breen had been persuaded by Miss Shutter to have his ancestral monuments re-coloured. Her suggestion had been warmly received, as indeed any suggestion would have been which might add to the glory, posthumous or not, of the Breens. So, of course, the Canon, who was also the Faculty, must come to dinner and give the scheme his blessing. Lady Breen had said that the plan would look less ostentatious if accompanied by a charitable act and so won a point for which she had laboured some time. The Rectory must give up its empty spaces for the belongings of Aged Nannies. It would be a good deed in a naughty world. So when the poor Canon left Breen Hall he did so without having a single opportunity to mention the only plan which might, by its felicity, have lured the Doctor into the Canon's Archaeological Society.

From this dreamy reconstruction I was abruptly brought to earth by the solid satisfaction of Miss Foxfellowe's concluding remarks.

'More parochially,' she was saying, 'a letter from the New Suffolk Archaeological Society could not fail to carry great weight with the trustees of the Faculty.'

Here she paused, letting her meaning sink in. The probability of what would happen if power remained vested in the Canon were all too clear to Dr Crow.

'I shall be pleased to support you in any way that I can,' he said, almost humbly.

Like a wizard Miss Foxfellowe conjured a crumpled membership form from an ancient recess about her person. Fastidiously, his hand beautifully white above the grey paper, the Doctor committed himself to the Foxfellowe following.

'Painted,' I heard her sniff as he did so. And then, '*Painted!*'

* * * * *